http://www.fast-print.r

DAHAB

ISBN 978-178456-392-9

Dedicated to my late father, Alan Bean, for the great inspiration he provided to me throughout his life

THE AUTHOR

Chris Bean is a well-known Cornish fisherman participating daily in catching, marketing and industry issues for more than four decades. His passions are oil painting, geology and fitness. He has had the good fortune to serve as a fisheries consultant in many countries of the developing world. The fictional work of *Dahab* draws on his rich and varied experiences while working overseas with grass-roots people combined with the knowledge retained from his original profession as a mine geologist. Friends have described him as a hopeless romantic.

DAHAB

By CHRISTOPHER BEAN

DAHAB

We saw them come and go
I wondered secretly if anyone ever noticed,
If their arrival or departure got recorded.
Funny thing, the desert, and Dahab,
Funny place,
So many people there that take a camel,
Or a pick-up truck,
Into that blue and silver enchanting land.
And leave into the desert or the mountains,
Funny people Bedouin,
Span half a dozen countries,
Yet seem unaffected by them, or time.
Look at their camels, their beat-up Land Cruisers
Watch them walk. So straight, so white,
No fat ones, no young ones,
Just tough remnants of ageless tradition,
Proud and polite,
Pita bread and white cheese,
Hi-Fi players and video cassette recorders.

Funny place Dahab,
Full of Planet Children,
Finding out much about themselves,
Yet no more of the planet than the sand on the
beach.
'Planet Child', sings the wind in the palms,
'Come. Come to my bosom,
Come lay down in my arms,
Under my branches, under the spell of Moses,
On the coral sand,
Come Planet Children, come.'

ONE

Travellers and lovers sprawled among the rugs and cushions of Dahab's cafeterias and bars as they waited for love's inevitable call to soothe their sun-soaked bodies.

Jack Polglaise felt particularly alone among the young Western backpackers and the weekend student revellers from Tel Aviv University. He was part of the scene, yet apart from it. He was there to work. His mission was to allocate outboard engines to the area's small co-operatives of fishermen as part of an aid programme. The negotiations had been protracted and long, the site visits remote and difficult and the searing heat of Sinai's August sun continually slowed his progress.

He was acutely aware of the gap between his situation as a consultant for an international organisation and those who each evening thronged the narrow dirt strip separating the shanty bars from the beach. Nonetheless, with no guesthouses or hotels on the east coast of Sinai, he had done like everyone else and at night had rolled out his sleeping bag in one of the many travellers' camps. This evening, in further hopes of better blending in, he had shed his work gear in favour of more casual clothes.

He ducked under the low entrance of the Crazy

House bar and paused on the threshold while he assessed the situation inside. He noted a vacant space at the end of a low table in the darker part of the room and strolled casually towards it.

Two fair-skinned women and a young Arabic-looking man were sprawled on cushions near the other end of the table. Jack guessed the women to be German or Scandinavian, possibly aged about thirty or even closer to his own forty years, unlike that of the average Dahab 'planet child' – a reassuring thought in a venue where he had become depressingly conscious of his age.

Whether the young man was Egyptian or Bedouin Jack could not tell in the dim light. He was perhaps no more than eighteen, dressed in the Western classical cut-off jeans and T-shirt, he was probably a punter, a guide, or more probably a hanger-on trying his chances with a white girl. If so, Jack reckoned, his own presence at the table might be a welcome diversion. With a bit of luck, one of the women might even be un-partnered and offer the female company he badly needed after all his dealings solely with male Arab society for the duration of his current trip. He ordered a Stella beer and relaxed among the cushions, tuning into the conversation.

The women were speaking German with an occasional snippet of English for the benefit of their Arab companion who clearly did not understand their language Jack interpreted the further of the two women as telling the youth how she was a teacher and that she hated it. She hated the ingratitude of the children and was taking a year out to consider what to do and financing her travels with the occasional waitressing job.

Jack could not recollect children ever being grateful to their teacher. It was not their way. He decided her logic was somewhat flawed, or maybe it had been an error in translation on his part. He tuned out and reflected on his earlier days as a geologist and how that training had stayed with him and given him such extra pleasure while travelling. It was so rewarding to be able to look at the desert's arid landscape and understand something of its makings, how the mountains formed, and to speculate on the ore bodies such remote places might be hiding. There had been many things to catch his eye in Sinai's stark naked beauty as he drove along the mountain tracks to the fish landing sites.

Among the west coast's young rocks, he had seen the vivid lilac and black layers of manganese minerals. In other crumbling rocks he had stopped to examine, heaps of glassy slabs that had turned out to be merely gypsum but here in the high mountains of eastern Sinai he had seen mostly the ancient granites of the continent's basement. This cradle of three religions was built on a terrain both rugged and foreboding, majestic yet mystical. To Jack, it was an area for which it was impossible to have anything other than respect. Sinai.

Every turn in the road held his interest; every

change in colour had its intrigue. Only two days ago he had noticed a speck of turquoise at the side of the road and wondered about its origin. It was in a recently blasted road cutting through high mountains behind Dahab on the main road leading south. He resolved next time he drove through the cutting to stop and take a closer look

He knew only one copper stain in a million indicated a copper ore body, nevertheless it had aroused his curiosity which had today been heightened by learning the meaning of Dahab, the village where he was now lodged.

The words of the nearer of the women suddenly jolted his thoughts back to the present. He heard her say she had abandoned her career as a *geologist.* She was telling the Arab boy that after three years in the field, and despite her qualifications, the male dominated industry had never given her responsibility beyond working with a theodolite to measure angles and distances.

'A surveyor's job,' she added with disdain. Most of her work, she said, had been transposing other people's fieldwork to the drawing board. 'Men's work. Inside the office,' she scoffed. 'The rightful place for women, I suppose.'

Jack took a closer look. His first impression was of someone neither beautiful nor plain. Blonde shoulder length hair almost covered her face as she leaned forward but what he could see looked pleasant enough. Her smooth skin had a bright complexion and there was girlishness about her turned up nose. A slightly pouted mouth hinted that she could be stubborn.

Her hair formed ringlets around her cheeks and neck giving her a cherubic appearance. He guessed she lost little love on men and already had a distinct chip on her shoulder from earlier experiences in this part of her life.

Jack found himself interested in her. Maybe it was the fight she exhibited that intrigued him. He hoped she would glance his way and continued studying her. A blue one-piece printed sleeveless dress did nothing for her youth. He was pondering on this when she reached forward to pick up her glass and an ample portion of a very full mature breast presented itself inside the arm hole.

This was no limpet breast like those he often saw on the Israeli models parading up and down Dahab's beach, but the breast of an adult woman who had more on her mind than being a slave to a sun paradise. He felt an unbidden surge of adrenaline in his veins.

'So when the boss had added to my duties as a mathematician and draughtsman the chore of making coffee and tea for the other five geologists in the office, I quit.' She paused before adding a contemptuous 'Men!'

She sipped her drink and continued, 'Was it two sugars or one? Why must you have coffee only in the mornings? And so on. Those guys can't be serious. I left work nine months ago, took a winter job in Basel as a waitress, earned enough for a month's skiing at the end of it and then worked in a kibbutz for six weeks. Israel is an experience. History in the making and at the same time all those names you remember from Sunday school as a child, Jericho, Bethlehem and the Sea of Galilee; very exhilarating.' Another pause, then, 'But the Israelis, they are hard to take at times.'

The Arab boy laughed, though as a Bedouin he had probably enjoyed more good times sharing the fruits of Israeli occupation than any of his forefathers in their relative freedom. That he was able to comfortably sit together with these two attractive and intelligent women symbolised that.

'I wonder about this place,' she said, staring into the night and addressing the remark to nobody in particular. 'I wonder about Dahab,' she added softly, almost mystically

Her words hung in the air like a pall of smoke. They lured Jack towards her. Impulsively he moved slightly closer. 'Maybe it is those copper showings in the road cutting,' he said, his voice almost a whisper.

In any normal circumstance his remark would probably have been regarded as bizarre, something not even requiring an acknowledgement. But Jack's earlier musing had helped him judge the situation more accurately than he had imagined. It was as if a fire cracker had gone off beside her, ripping away any mystique and personal thoughts all in a matter of seconds. She wheeled round on Jack as if to strike him for shattering her secret.

Surprised at her reaction and unable to account for the effect his words had caused, Jack drew back and looked her in the eye with an apologetic smile.

Her reactions moved in a split second from anger to dismay and finally into composure as she returned a faltering smile, 'You saw them then?'

Jack nodded and added, 'In the road cutting about fifteen ks to the south, on the top of the rise; in the breccia.'

It was enough for her. He had pinpointed what she had seen and which had so far believed no one else could possibly have noticed. She was no longer the only owner of geologically trained eyes in Dahab. Gone in a flash were her secret hopes that she alone might trace those copper stains to something more exciting, something that would gain her fame and recognition as a woman geologist.

Jack surmised what the look in her eyes was revealing and opted for a conciliatory tone and a friendly smile, 'They weren't very big were they? What I saw were the size of a matchbox.'

'You were sharp to see them. Two triangles each about four centimetres long and a thin line going up the hanging wall,' she said.

'Ah! You checked them out?'

'No,' she said. 'I was passing by in a car.'

'I didn't see the line along the hanging wall,' he confessed. 'I was driving.'

'Pig,' she thought, 'typical male to have an

excuse for his oversight.'

She relented and smacked the palm of his hand Egyptian style and laughed, '*Taban*! Of course.'

During these exchanges she had eased herself along the bench away from the other two who had lapsed into their own conversation, sensing that whatever she had been saying wasn't meant for their ears.

'Jack,' he said, putting his hand forward again more formally.

'Anke,' she said shaking his hand lightly and in response to his raised eyebrows added, 'That's what my friends call me when they don't call me 'Ozone' for always wearing blue,' she laughed. My real name is Katarina which I don't like so much. Just call me Anke because it is simple.'

She dismissed the name issue and continued in a lowered voice,

'How did you know that I would recognise these copper signs?'

Her words became confused with the subtleties of the English language and she gave a slightly embarrassed giggle, and then they laughed together.

'The answer's simple,' he said. 'I overheard you say you were a geologist. However, I didn't know you had seen the showings. I tossed the idea at you to answer your wonderings about Dahab.'

'Hmm' she sighed, satisfied, but deciding not to give away any more of the thoughts that had haunted her for a week.

She pondered on research she had made into the heavy gold bracelets and rings worn by the Bedouin women, the information she had painstakingly put together from repeated difficult gatherings with Bedouin womenfolk as she tried to discover where they had bought their heavy, crudely worked jewellery. The answers had always been the same.

'Not bought – *abu, abu.*'

And when asked 'where did father buy?' the same repetitive answer, 'Not bought. *Abu Kabeer, Abu Kabeer.*' Grandfather. Then she had concluded if grandfather didn't buy it or great-grandfather didn't buy it, then he *got it.*

'From where did he get it?' she had asked.

'*Gabel,*'– mountains, they had replied, waving vaguely over their shoulders to the stark wilderness of Sinai.

'*Gobblie, khalas, bayeed.*' A long time ago. Finished. Far away.

Thus her line of investigation had ended but not without heightening her interest.

She knew that in this geological environment, quartz veins were the only passages through which hydrothermal mineralisation may have taken place, faults with deep-seated origins coming from the fluid magma itself shortly after the emplacement of the great granite batholiths of Sinai.

She knew quartz was one of the last minerals to come out of solution from the hydrothermal liquids along with the last of the copper minerals and, more importantly, *the noble metals.* It was this last fact that had preoccupied her since sighting the copper stains; the association of copper traces with the deposition of noble metals.

A sudden gentle wind made the candles flicker and they turned from their respective thoughts to look outside where the moon created a ribbon of spangles on the calm sea as the evening breeze stirred off the land.

Jack's thoughts had revolved around the same ideas and that week he had asked his Egyptian colleagues in a roundabout way whether they knew of any old or existing mines in the area. They had told him there were none there now but old Bedouin tradition was that their forefathers mined riches from the mountains but nobody knew where today. It was through these conversations he had learned about the meaning of the name Dahab.

He threw another questing shot at her.

'Do you know what the name Dahab means?'

He saw her struggling for an answer, seeking a suitable response to this person who seemed to be reading all her innermost thoughts. She faltered.

'No,' she spluttered.

Jack was unconvinced. He paused, waiting for her eyes to lock on to his. Eventually he held her gaze. 'It's an old Bedouin word,' he said. 'It means gold.'

TWO

Anke sat quietly picking through the debris of her own schemes and dreams while Jack was up at the bar getting in more drinks – three beers, and a lemonade for the Arab youth.

During his brief absence she swallowed her pride and decided there could be benefits in befriending this older man; at least find out which oil company or geological survey team he was working with. Perhaps it would open some new doors. Clearly he was there to work rather than as a tourist like most other non-Arabs in the area. For a start, he was probably fifteen years or so older than the average Dahab person. And whereas most people arrived in Dahab by foot, shared taxi or bus, he had said that he was driving through the road cutting. She had also noted the pen clipped in the breast pocket of his bush shirt. This certainly was not customary dress for a Dahab tourist.

'Cheers,' she said, accepting the beer, 'you work here with *petrole*?' she enquired using the Arabic word.

'No.' He paused, initiating a cat and mouse game, 'the US Government.'

'Oh,' she said, somewhat surprised. 'Are the United States doing a geological survey in Sinai?'

He considered what she had said and wondered about the grammar, whether the 'are' should be an 'is'.

She stared at him awaiting a reply.

'Er ... no,' he said, shaking himself from his side-track. 'At least I don't think so.'

She felt relief at his response. At least her plans would not be overrun by a massive geological team with four-wheel drive vehicles, helicopters and all the hi-tech gear available to the American government. But what was this man doing here? She was well aware a war was brewing in the area just across the water with Iraq occupying Kuwait and a build-up of armed forces every day in Saudi Arabia. Even the Gulf of Eilat – and she looked out of the door, yes, that bit of water outside – was being blockaded by American warships. She suddenly shivered and felt she was already caught up in a war.

She lowered her head towards him. Her voice became very serious 'You are part of that operation?' She pointed a finger at Saudi Arabia without moving her hand so as not to raise attention to them. The intrigue she had been living on all week had become infectious and she could easily imagine she was sitting alongside an undercover agent and should not expose him. The other woman and the Arab youth had moved outside at the beginning of this *tete a tete* and her new isolation only heightened Anke's growing belief that some mysterious organisation that had been watching her was now coercing her into some dangerous task force.

Jack pondered her intense expression, uncertain how much further he could carry on this game. As he lowered his eyes briefly to reach for his drink he found himself looking directly down the open front of her dress at two beautiful round swaying bosoms. Within their blue sleeve, they looked like halves of mystical fruit; their tips just nestled into the fabric. He felt a tingling among the hairs on the back of his neck. The glance was just micro seconds long but the impression stayed with him far longer.

Jack's emotions skipped around his brain in the same disorganised fashion that he had become all too familiar with in recent years. Each similar surge of adrenaline through his veins he had found to be both exciting and motivating, even though it be out of control. This emotional turmoil often fired the creation of his best paintings or inspired his poetry. He allowed himself to drift with it for a few seconds before steadying himself and, with a definite softening towards the woman, he clutched her wrist gently in a manner characteristic of the local culture, and said laughing,

'Shit, no, I'm a fisherman.'

'A fisherman?' she echoed and then repeated herself, half in disbelief, using the German, 'Ein fisher?'

Before she could throw up her arms in complete rejection of his story he quickly told her what he did. He backed up his account by producing a photograph of himself standing knee deep in fish on an Arab dhow surrounded by smiling Yemeni fishermen. Behind him could be seen the net hauler bringing on board what seemed like an endless string of rose-coloured snappers.

'You really are a professional,' she said with a new confidence.

'It's easy to do the job one has spent the last twenty years doing,' he said, 'especially if you have luck as well.'

'Luck? Are you always lucky then?'

He remembered those mystical fruits of a few moments ago, and again studied her sharp intense eyes, noting her thick unplucked blonde eyebrows. He laughingly considered her question,

'I guess I am.'

'I thought you were a geologist, I don't know any fishers that look at rocks,' she said.

Jack remembered the reason she had related to the Arab boy for quitting her geologist job it and he felt an immediate rapport.

'I graduated as a mine geologist, spent two years in the high Arctic, found an ore body for a company, got no thanks for it, so I quit the industry, bought a fishing boat and went fishing. Since then I've always worked for myself, even when I work with organisations it is more or less on my terms and I design the programmes. I don't like empire building senior professionals.'

Anke stared at him. She had not met anyone who could handle two professions. She felt very drawn to this man for the way that he had found a solution to the same situation she was in. She felt an urge to engage him to help her, or at least discuss her problems.

'That's incredible, I wish I could become a fisher; it would solve a lot of things for me.'

She'd said enough. She was at a loss for a way to introduce these problems and had no wish to make a fool of herself. She lowered her eyes to make a pretence of studying the label on the beer bottle.

Jack looked at her for a long time. Her upturned nose had attracted the desert sunshine and had a distinctive glow about its end. The cherub-like pout of her mouth fascinated him and the more he contemplated it, the more sensuous it became. A chain of freckles traced itself about her cheeks and over her nose and he noticed her finger nails, as her hands rested alongside her face, were short like a man's. He began to like this no-nonsense person very much.

'How do you mean?' he asked gently. 'To me it seems that you've already got ideas about solving the problem.'

'Tell me,' she exclaimed, quickly looking up from her study of the beer label somewhat surprised.

'What about the copper showings?'

She started. Her previous week's enquiries among the Bedouin womenfolk again flashed before her mingled with the excitement of her dreams, of getting into the mountains and finding something, of proving herself and defying those creeps back at her old job in Germany. The images flashed past her in what seemed an insane ribbon of fantasy.

'Ah,' she sighed at length, 'I suppose they are nothing.' She paused and looked into his eyes as if searching for help. 'It's just that I thought ...' She broke off, not sure whether to descend to the level of childhood dreams.

Jack came to her rescue.

'Shit,' he exclaimed. 'Come on, let's check the bloody thing out. You have a packsack?'

'Yes,' her eyes wide open.

'OK, *bad bukerah*, the day after tomorrow, is Friday; a day off for me, Saturday is a standard weekend day off also with my project though I normally work it. *Malesh*, never mind, I won't this week, and Sunday is an *eid*, an Egyptian holiday. That makes three clear days. We should sort something out in that time. What do you reckon?'

'I er...er ... 'she hesitated, weighing up the immensity of his proposal, her face lighting up all the time. Finally, she stamped a foot lightly, gave a big grin, wrinkled her nose and exclaimed,

'*Sheise*!' She used the Germanic version of his own exclamation. 'Why not?'

Instinctively they shook hands to seal the deal and put their heads together to work out a plan.

'Three days, that means eighteen bottles of water at three each a day,' she said. 'That's twenty-seven kilos, thirteen each.' Her mind was running on excitedly. 'That leaves seven kilos for food and then a bed roll. Hope the fisher is feeling strong,' she laughed.

Jack added his own thoughts. 'We must leave very early to get clear of the road before anyone is around, and then we should see no one. The Egyptians sleep late.'

'Is it not allowed?' she asked cautiously.

'You know this country,' he said, 'Everything is allowed until you try to do it and then it needs twenty permissions and signatures from this and that authority. Everybody likes to feel important and get in on the act. I'm sure that if we made a five-hundred-dollar donation to the Geology Faculty in Cairo for research, it would arrange the permissions in a few days and send some expensive students with us. Alternatively, we could apply directly to the government seeking to investigate possible mineral deposits in Sinai and after six months would be told that a joint venture had been arranged for us and everything would be settled once we had put half a million dollars up front for salaries and equipment.'

'But surely we can just look?' she said anxiously.

'Sure, we just look. We try not to be seen and if any awkward questions get asked we say we are just looking at stones for beads. Everybody in Dahab wears beads, *mish quidda?*' Isn't it so?

Relieved that the mission would not be burdened by others and exhilarated by its air of intrigue, she dwelt on the practical aspects, happy to have her convictions reinforced by the strange fisher.

'We should take the breccia vein at the east side of the road,' she said. Her mind raced on, 'I remember that side of the ridge is not so high to climb over and then you don't see the road anymore.' Her German accent became more pronounced as her excitement increased.

Jack admired her perception and immediately decided he could rely on her not to screw up regarding the peculiarities of the local security services. He started to voice his thoughts about them both being crazy, 'Anke,' he began, conscious of using her strange name for the first time; then caught a determined look in her eyes enough to defy an army and quickly changed tack 'Er ... I think we could do with a couple more beers.'

They exchanged knowing smiles and he went to the bar.

*

Next morning, Jack met up with his counterparts and drove to Sharm El Sheik at the southern tip of Sinai to check out two boats belonging to fishermen. They had asked his organisation for new engines and he had to see that the modifications were being carried out.

The wind had already freshened as he left Dahab and swirls of dust swept across the narrow desert plain that skirted the mountains. The sun had popped a red tongue through the mountains across the water in Saudi, creating a sombre silhouette of an American warship as it crept up the gulf towards Eilat.

The realities of the day made nonsense of his dreams of the past night. Then there had been visions of scrambling through the mountains of Sinai with a geological whiz-kid; of finding riches, unravelling history and the warm comforting thought of perhaps another sighting of the beautiful mystical fruits lurking beneath her dress.

Had he imagined the whole conversation of the previous evening? There was an unusual silence in the car as he entered the mountains, preoccupied with his thoughts, and took the south fork to follow the wadi up to the pass. The road led past a kilometre- long massif of tertiary sediments tilted on a granite ridge, nose-diving towards the wadi bottom, sliding, geologically speaking, into the Rift Valley. Jack knew it to be called the Sleeping Camel thanks to the last hundred-metre block resembling a camel's head resting on the sand. The huge vertical sided rock towered a three hundred metres above the flat wadi floor, giving it a commanding position over the south and north forks of the road.

With the early sun picking out the profile of the camel, the mystique of Sinai surged back to his brain and renewed excitement invaded his body. He began to think he must be a captive of Sinai in the same way Moses was for forty years. Even as he considered the question, his car swept round a curve and climbed towards the cutting he and Anke had spoken eagerly about the previous night. Here in the mountains it was windless. The low sun had coloured the distant peaks a lilac hue and the nearer ranges mustard; royal and appropriate he thought. There were no signs of man's disturbance in the area apart from the narrow ribbon of asphalt, not a trace of vegetation; it could have been the moon, he thought. There was a still coolness in the shade that made him want to run along the wadi bottom skipping and singing in childish delight in the manner of an infant that had discovered the echo for the first time.

He slowed the engine, making an exaggerated climb to the cutting. The rock faces were in the shade as he cruised slowly through, scrutinising them on each side. Anke had been correct, he noted with satisfaction: the breccia vein on the south side climbed close to a hundred metres up a rough rocky slope and disappeared over the ridge, whereas on the northern side it was less distinguishable. There it had become mixed up with screes formed from a crumbling dyke higher up. To understand it, a great deal of searching would be required in full view of the road. No, he thought, Anke was right. As he passed the vein, he could see no copper stains as he had previously. Then, thinking back, he remembered them as facing the opposite way to the direction he was driving now. He checked his mirror but could see nothing in its diminished image so slid the engine

into top gear, put his foot down and sped on to
Sharm El Sheik.

*

Anke was also up early in another camp in
Dahab. She had been unable to go back to sleep
after the first light had pierced her small room and
the wind started banging the shutter. She had
crept out to the bathroom and showered before
anyone was up, washing the clothes from her kit
bag. Afterwards she had retreated to her room and
completed her diary for the previous day. She
ended the entry with the words, *'Made
arrangements to go into the mountains for three
days with an English fisher and search for gold.'*

She stared at the words, at their improbability,
and wondered too if she was living in a fantasy
world. She pondered the point for a long time
before abruptly shutting the book, pulling a blue
T-shirt over her bikini, grabbing her shoulder bag
and striding out to the *suq* before her conviction
waned.

She bought six round packs of cheese, two kilos
of dates, half a dozen wrapped sugary sesame seed
bars, some green peppers and onions and a kilo of
under ripe tomatoes, and finally, after a great deal
of thought and considering the weight, a small
bottle of orange cordial. Satisfied that this
represented an energy sustaining diet and would
not spoil in transit she went back and deposited
the loot in her room. She then slipped out again
and bought a carton of bottled water. A boy

insisted in carrying the eighteen kilos back for her and stood his ground on the threshold until she had parted with a quarter of a guinea.

She closed the door and sat on the carton and grinned,

'Ach so,' she said, 'the little expedition commences.'

She idly turned on her pocket radio while she gathered her thoughts. The announcer was saying, *'The American State Department spokesman said today that they had not ruled out the possibility of a surgical nuclear strike on Iraq's chemical and biological warfare installations.'*

She turned it off with a sigh. It would be just her luck if a biological and nuclear war broke out all around her as she was about to begin her new career as an exploration geologist. She wondered if she would hear the bangs or feel the dust if she was deep in the heart of the Sinai mountains. Could war pass her by without her even knowing? Would the first sign be a choking cloud of poison gas? What could she do anyway? She put the radio on the pile of stuff she was leaving behind. She decided the State Department was not going to issue any more statements enough to force her to abandon her search for gold.

*

Jack phoned his Cairo office from Sharm el Sheik and told them he might be diving for the long weekend and then go to earth for a couple of days to get his final report finished. As far as his organisation was concerned, he would be out of the action for the next few days. He was suitably vague with his local colleagues as to his whereabouts, telling them he may spend the long weekend with a friend in Cairo or go to Suez where he wanted to look up other old friends. He completed the confusion by nodding at the pearl blue sea there at Sharm el Sheik with its inviting reefs and saying, 'What I should really do is come back here and do some diving.'

The others agreed and said they would be having family reunions and be celebrating the *eid* back in Dahab with lots of relatives coming over from Alexandria.

Jack nodded. He could imagine.

It all made him reasonably happy. His vague plans were convincing and he decided to give a week's rent to the camp attendant. He would tell him he might go with a friend to Sharm for the weekend, but was keeping his things in the room and *baksheesh* would be available if he kept an eye on them.

His work in Sharm failed to go to plan. One of the fishermen's boats had been inadequate and had been persuaded by the dejected owner to look at another one, with assurances that it would certainly qualify for a new outboard. The other one was located only after three landing sites had been visited. Finally, the son who was operating the *felucca* insisted on barbecuing fresh fish for their late afternoon meal. Out of respect Jack had agreed and the afternoon had slipped away. The son had given a long explanation about the special fishing spots only he knew about, claiming that to be invaluable. Indeed, it was the only credential required for anyone applying for a new engine, Jack had philosophically agreed, and approved his application.

The sun was setting as the pickup climbed into the mountains leaving the simmering coastal plain behind. As the last tangerine segment kissed good night to the rim of Moses' cradle, Jack eased the vehicle to the side of the road, allowing his colleagues to kneel for a while among the hot stones and make their evening prayers. Soon afterwards he put the lights on and it was a further hour before they climbed the rise to the cutting. With the lights fully on and straining his eyes, he could see no stains in the breccia vein. He shrugged his shoulders and drove on.

An evening calm descended on the sea as he cruised back into camp after dropping off his colleagues. The full moon peeped over the Saudi mountains as the sun had done in the morning as he left. He marvelled at the symmetry and thought there was little wonder that the people of the desert and the fishermen gave it such importance in their folklore. Its rhythm and predictability were so much more evident to them in their lands of no cloud cover, much more so than it was in the northern latitudes where sun and moon were often both obscured for days.

The night was as still and romantic as on previous days. The lovers and travellers of Dahab continued to throng the track along the seafront while the enticing smell of barbecued fish and lobster hung in the air.

THREE

Touch me, touch me, I want to feel your body, your heartbeat next to mine, Samantha Fox shouted invitingly into the clear night air. Tables outside the Crazy House bar and Toba Restaurant were laden with all the delightful produce of the Red Sea. Hungry Planet children clustered round settings that resembled artwork created from colourful fish framed by ragged lines of rock lobsters set head to tail.

Saving all my love for you, Whitney Houston cried out from the next bar, drawing deep breaths from those gathered around as they tried to join in her powerful top note with varying degrees of success.

Jack laughed, oh to be young and crazy.

Ten metres down the track the familiar sounds of Pink Floyd vibrated round the palm branches greeting him as he entered the bar. *Just another brick in the wall* pounded out from the loudspeakers.

Jack felt at home. I was there, he thought, recalling Berlin and once again warmness swept through his mind as he went inside into the semi darkness letting the disciplines and hassles of the day slip away.

He saw Anke sitting on a rug beside the same table as the night before and went over to her.

'Hi.'

'*Salem elay coum*,' she smiled.

'Have you eaten? I got held up.'

'No, I thought I'd wait for you,' she said.

He was touched. She had not revealed such friendship before and he felt bad about being late for their first appointment.

'Fish? Pizza?' he asked before sitting down.

'Pizza. Champignons,' she replied, dismissing the mundane matter of food in one quick sentence.

Jack went to the bar and ordered the food. He returned with a tray and two glasses of steaming sweet Egyptian tea. He beamed at her. 'Well? What's the situation?'

'Packed,' she said with a finality that defied further explanation. 'Only bread to get but I thought to get it tonight to be the freshest.'

Well done, he thought. He had seen a pick-up going round the area most evenings.

'Have you checked out from your camp?'

'No. I've left half my things in the room and told the owner that I might go to Sharm for the weekend with friends, so he must keep the room for me until I get back. I paid for four days anyway.'

'Brilliant,' Jack replied and told her of his own similar arrangements.

The pizza arrived and they ate it hungrily and unceremoniously, preoccupied with thoughts of the coming days. The air was electric, full of anticipation, and Jack found himself looking at her without really meaning to. Anke caught his gaze and raised her eyebrows as if to ask what he was thinking.

She had caught him off guard. He faltered and said almost the first thing that came to mind, although the answer was obvious. 'Are you fit?'

'Yes. I think so,' she said cautiously, clearly seeking a reason for his question.

He explained. 'I ask because I would like to leave my vehicle here so as not to arouse suspicion and that means an early two-hour hike to the cutting. What do you reckon?'

'I had already assumed so,' she said with a smile. 'We cannot leave a car in such a place. The walk would be very good in the early morning.'

Jack sat back in the cushions delighted with her response.

'We'd better say three-thirty,' he grinned. 'I don't think we'll see anybody at that time.'

They heard the 'peep-peep' of the pick-up outside as it did the evening bread round.

'You get it,' he suggested, 'I'll pay for the pizza and catch up with you outside.'

They shared out twenty flat plate-sized pita breads and walked back among the Planet children to where Jack must enter his camp. It was the first time they had walked together and Jack felt very conspicuous being shoulder to shoulder with the tall, big framed, fair German, who was so unlike the petite dark-skinned partners he had spent earlier parts of his life with.

He reflected on the comparison and felt a little uncomfortable.

Who was leading who into this, he wondered, never previously having been anything but a leader. She looked vaguely Amazonian in her blue tube printed cotton dress with her wide well-tanned shoulders, long elegant neck and straw coloured hair falling about her face in ringlets. He felt he had definitely met his match this time. But there still remained that inner driving force that set him aside from most of his fellow men, the fire that allowed him to tackle a job and succeed where most would have long since cried off. It also gave him the confidence to seize her wrist in the local fashion as they were about to part company. He squeezed it lightly in a sense of bonding before releasing and agreeing to meet her on the highway at the appointed hour.

After taking the bread to his room Jack went back out and rounded up some food plus a carton of water. Finally, after some thought, he took a towel over to his car and surreptitiously took a hammer and cold chisel from the tool box. He returned to his room with them wrapped inside the towel and closed the door.

Nine bottles of water were stuffed into the bottom of his pack in two layers followed by the hammer and cold chisel. He tested its weight and groaned, prayed for a heavy thirst the first day, and packed the food on the top. Reaching for the bed roll he surveyed what was left in the room, grabbed up clean underwear, socks and toilet bag, then, after some reflection, the whole of his first aid kit.

*

Twenty-four hours Greenwich Mean Time, the radio beeped out., *This is the World Service of the BBC. Here is the news.*

He sat up with a start and rubbed his eyes, mentally adding three hours. It was 3 am in Dahab and he was going searching for gold. He shook himself. Could this be true?

The crisis in the Gulf deepened late last night the radio continued. *Iraq's President Saddam Hussein announced in a state television program that his country would not hesitate to use every means at its disposal to deter Imperialist and Zionist aggression including weapons of mass destruction...*

Jack switched the radio off and put it away in its case. Better off not to know, he reflected.

He finished his packing and folded up the camp's foam bed roll that he had decided to 'borrow' for a couple of days. He tied it into a tight bundle with the neatly spliced ropes that he had prepared the night before.

All was quiet with a light breeze as he let himself out of the camp. Somewhere a dog stirred and barked before going back to rest. The full moon, now with a chip off the top comer, was well on its way to setting in Sinai's mountains.

There was just enough light for him to see a figure making its way to the highway three or four hundred metres away. 'On cue,' he remarked to himself, glad he had avoided any suggestion she might need an alarm clock.

She met him on the asphalt.

'*Salaam alay coum*,' she said in a low voice.

'*Elay coum salaam*,' and God be with you too, he responded with a grin as they stepped out in the direction of the mountains.

Within minutes the moon had set and it became quite dark and cool. As Jack had predicted, everyone was asleep at this hour. Within forty-five minutes they had cleared the last structures in Dahab without seeing a soul. They were now at the gap in the mountains where the road followed the wadi into the interior.

They had only spoken once. As they passed the gloomy outlines of tiny man made caves at the side of the wadi, Jack informed Anke that his colleagues had told him that the caves were ancient food stores and secure places. The rest of their walk was in silence.

The sleeping camel loomed ahead of them, looking all the more grotesque in the faint light of the stars. Under its head they turned off to the south and started up the long incline to the cutting some six or seven kilometres away.

Five minutes up the road they heard the sound of a car approaching from behind them. They wheeled around, wondering what their best tactic should be if they were questioned. The watched the car's lights in the valley below as it rounded the Camel's Head coming from the direction of Taba in the north and felt a great sense of relief as it swung away and they saw its red taillights as it went on down to Dahab.

The incident was sufficient to alert them that they would be regarded as an oddity, plodding along out there at 4 o'clock in the morning. It would be better not to be seen at all.

They decided that if another vehicle came along they would bolt off the road and lie flat among the stones to avoid detection. Jack secretly doubted how effective that would be in practice and was thankful that it never had to be put to the test. He was sure the sight, of two heavily laden foreigners stumbling across rough ground and plunging themselves to the earth as if fleeing an approaching enemy in a war zone was somewhat bizarre and would only work if the driver had poor lights and was half asleep.

Anke sensed the need to be off the road. She lengthened her stride and continued at a brisk march. 'Jesus Christ,' muttered Jack to himself, 'what's this, bionic woman?'

He adjusted his modified kit bag and followed a few metres behind. The quiet pit pat pit pat of her feet drew his attention and he noticed she was wearing ankle socks and rubber-soled, cushioned walking boots. He guessed they didn't come from any Woolworth's of this world. Her grey pack-sack was robust and frameless. It showed no sign of sag even with the weight of water. The criss-cross interlocking straps were obviously intended to support hardware, probably crampons. Even in the poor early light he could see it was not one of the Mickey Mouse affairs he had seen accompanying many of the train and taxi travellers in Dahab.

The stars were fading and dawn was creeping into the sky as they reached the rise and the much talked about breccia vein. Anke went straight to the place where she had seen the copper stains. Despite the dim light they were able to pick them out and follow the thin line of secretion up the hanging wall of the vein. Her index finger traced it for a metre or more as a thin line of turquoise and red. Small as it was it was certainly significant and both marvelled at it.

From the level ground at the top of the rise they could see down neither side so after checking the rest of the vein in the gathering light, they back-tracked fifty metres to the beginning of the cutting and scrambled up to the ridge to ensure they would be out of sight.

Jack took the lead. With the agility of a goat he picked a route that zigzagged up to the ridge with the minimum of hand climbing. His steady leg pushes were like a machine. He felt at home. Free. Open countryside was his domain. An eye cast over his shoulder showed Anke was close behind. No worries there, he comforted himself. Smiling, he sucked in a deep breath of Sinai's cool early morning air and prepared for adventure.

He had mentally marked the point in the vein where it cut the ridge and in less than ten minutes he swung off his kit bag within a metre of the spot. Now safely behind the horizon as it would appear from the road, he lay down on the soft spalls of decaying granite.

Anke's head and shoulders appeared over the ridge moments later. Her cherub mouth gave a pout smile as she heaved herself over and flopped down beside him.

After regaining her breath, she rolled out her packsack, unzipped the bottom compartment and hauled out a water bottle. They both took a long drink.

'You're just trying to lighten your load,' Jack teased.

'*Taban*,' of course, she laughed. She cocked her head, 'I hear a car.'

They moved gingerly towards the lip of the ridge and peered down. They watched as a black and white Peugeot taxi snaked its way up the pass before easing through the cutting and rolling away towards Dahab. There were no more vehicles in view for the two or three kilometres they could see in either direction. They lay at their vantage point and surveyed the country.

'It is incredibly beautiful,' Jack acknowledged.

'It's a paradise,' Anke added.

Strange, he thought, that she should say that. It was such a departure from her normal clinical descriptions. Maybe she was not bionic but human after all.

The sun must have peeped over the Saudi mountains somewhere behind them because its first rays were stealing their way up through the passes to light up the high mountain tops of the interior. The only colour to describe them was lilac. The wilderness, the aridity and loneliness invested the panorama with a primeval majesty.

The lilac merged into blue as the sun rose higher and the blue turned into mustard as Sinai climbed out of the night. It was a timeless, ageless expanse of mountain after mountain scattered without reason, without order. Black basic dykes ran northwest-southeast. They were a fairly recent introduction in the geological time scale, running across the terrain regardless of wadi or mountain for mile upon mile. Being generally harder than the other rocks, they had formed walls running up one mountainside and down the next, dominating the landscape.

Some of the black basalt dykes were much thicker than others, Jack noted, as much as fifty metres in some cases, and their progress through the wilderness could be easily tracked from their vantage point.

'What age is this lot?' he asked, nodding generally in front of him.

'Phew.' She drew in a long breath.' These basement granites are generally reckoned to be Precambrian, six hundred million years or more. The opening up of the Rift Valley becoming the Gulf of Eilat and the Red Sea is very recent. That Sleeping Camel and those other sediments sitting at the top of those mountains to the north must be Tertiary.'

'Man, this area has had some rough treatment over the years' said Jack. 'Those rocks resting on the tops of the mountains over there are sitting on a wave platform, flat as a table top.'

'Ja, and those tertiary sediments themselves were laid down at the bottom of an ocean, which means that these rocks have been pushed up at least five thousand metres and maybe much more.' She paused to look again in awe at the land around them, 'As the Rift formed and Africa floated away from Asia the whole thing probably split and split again along lines parallel with the rift. That's what all these black dykes are; basaltic fluid from deep in the crust which rushed up to fill the fractures.'

'Fractures fifty kilometres long and fifty metres wide,' said Jack. 'I'm glad I wasn't around at the time.'

'That breccia vein is different,' Anke continued. 'It must be very old, not much later than the granite itself. I've not seen any others like it in this region. Have you?'

'No.' Jack looked at the nearby rocks. 'It would be good to have seen plenty of quartz; would have made it easier to track the vein. This area is really deficient in quartz. I wonder why?'

'Don't know,' she replied. 'Anyway, too much quartz is always barren. We need just enough of the fine white rock to follow the trail.'

Anke rolled over and idly picked up a piece of the 'white rock' lying beside her. She regarded it thoughtfully before balancing it in the palm of her hand and striking it hard against a similar but larger fragment nearby.

The blow rang out like a gunshot. She picked up a piece of the disintegrated stone and scrutinising it closely through a fold-up magnifying glass she extracted from her shorts pocket.

Jack was impressed but said nothing. He took up another fragment and checked it out thoroughly but saw nothing but milky white quartz. He selected a fragment broken off the rock she had used as an anvil and found it much more interesting. It had fractured to reveal a cavity. Perfect pinhead size clear quartz crystals were all over the fracture plane. At the edge, before it again forming a homogeneous quartz mass, were some little flat bladed yellow-green crystals about five millimetres long lying down in a row like fallen dominos.

'Hmm,' he said confidently. 'This vein is mineralised all right.'

She looked up from her magnifying glass, wondering what he had found.

'Marcasite,' he said with an element of pride, well aware he needed all the brownie points he could get if he was to keep up with this woman.

She looked at him quickly. She was astonished that the fisherman knew this mineral. She studied it through her magnifying glass. 'You're right,' she acknowledged, not taking her eye away from the glass. 'The low temperature form of iron pyrites. It's quite rare.' She gave him a teasing but reassuring smile, 'Jack Fisher, you're right and you know what that means?'

Jack chorused the reply as if reading from a text book, cocking one eyebrow, 'The right environment for the low temperature deposition of noble metals?'

She gave an affirmative nod and reached for the water bottle. She drained it to the last quarter before passing it over to Jack to finish off.

He pointed to the southeast. 'It looks as if we have to make it over that second ridge before we do any serious banging and scratching around.'

Anke looked to where he had pointed. It was a narrow strip of broken white fragments climbing in steps up the next ridge. Twice it was cut by small black dykes but the marbled trail of quartz continued unabated on the other side before going over the horizon.

She was puzzled. 'Don't you think it's strange that there has been no investigation of this before?

I thought the Israelis were pretty smart and would have checked it out but I don't see signs of any disturbances.'

Jack considered her question for a moment before replying. 'The Israelis were an occupying force. I don't think they had much time for digging in road cuttings and in any case I imagine this one was blasted through by the military and their main objective was to get tanks and personnel to Sharm el Sheik. Also, wasn't it evening, sunset, when you spotted those copper stains?'

'Yes.'

'I thought so. I've passed there several times in the day but you can only see the stains in the evening when the sun is low enough to strike directly into the cavity. They are not as obvious as you might think, maybe only visible for half an hour a day and even then only to a keen geological eye.'

Satisfied, she wriggled into the straps of her pack and started off down to the little wadi a hundred metres away.

Jack's gaze followed her, as she pushed out her chest to gain comfort within the straps of her pack. Today she was wearing a bra under a sky blue T-shirt that had a little black and white swimmer on the front. The frayed hem of her denim shorts ended about two inches below the crotch, out of which came long powerful legs that could belong only to a German woman. She was tall and big-framed but her bottom curved in beautifully under her shorts to a small waist. She certainly was a one helluva lovely woman, he decided.

Anke was scampering down the scree filling the valley with a sound not unlike running water, and strangely incongruous in the desert. He took a firmer route around a headland of rock and caught up with her at the far side of the wadi. Here the vein emerged from the rubble and continued steeply up the rocky slope for a hundred metres or so to the second ridge.

Standing shoulder to shoulder in the shade at the bottom of the climb, they examined in detail the structures in front of them. The vein was barely half a metre wide but contained an extravaganza of colours and shapes, with white quartz dominating the borders and irregular bits of coarse and fine grained granite embedded in it. Anke remarked that if nothing else the vein should be sliced up and polished to make ornamental table tops.

Here and there they found slight but encouraging red and green stains of iron and copper minerals confined to the upper contact. They then climbed up the steep rocky face to the next ridge, stopping occasionally to examine what they could see but without yielding to the temptation to hammer away at every loose piece of vein.

When they gained the top they were greeted by a blaze of morning sun. They put down their packs and rested on the eastern sunny side of the ridge.

They felt they could relax now they were far enough into the wilderness to be unseen and able to tackle the job they had set out to do without being disturbed.

'Breakfast time,' Jack sang out, pulling pita bread and feta cheese out of his pack along with a bunch of travel-weary grapes.

Anke laughed. 'I thought you fishers would have at least something from the sea.'

He dived back into his pack, flinging aside two pairs of pants and socks and tugging out a half-metre length of dried shark meat, as stiff as a board and with the texture of fibre-glass matting.

'A la carte,' he taunted her.

'*Sheise! Was ist das?*

'Das ist your actual sustaining seafood protein mien geologist,' he laughed. He tore off a ten centimetre strip and offered it to her.

She scrutinised it as suspiciously as if it had been a piece of white wire wool. Then she made the most magnificent pout Jack had seen in his life and he doubled up. While he was laughing she popped it in her mouth and chewed for a few seconds, rested, and then chewed for a full minute, wincing at the salt content.

'*Sheise*. How much water did you bring?' She continued chewing. 'Does 'sustaining' in English mean long time?'

They both laughed.

FOUR

Anke contributed her dates, green peppers and orange cordial to the mountain top breakfast and silently meditated while they ate. She was aware of a glowing happiness gradually spreading through her whole system. Perhaps her life had been on hold for all the years since she had graduated and now the button had been released. In front of her was the expanse of Sinai, the expanse of nothing, no development, only the pristine beauty of an untouched geological paradise. She felt a queen in a land where no rivals could interrupt her reign. There had been no persons before her she thought, no one to understand the epochs of dramatic tectonic creations and upheavals that had taken place there. Here she could map, sample, postulate theories and maybe make discoveries that no other person had made. It may have been Moses' wilderness, she thought, but it was her Eden.

She caught the aromatic scent of the dried shark and turned her thoughts to her companion. She felt warmly towards him. He minded his own business in all their contacts and not played the role of the dominating professional male. Yet he was clever, she thought, and she enjoyed that. She stole a quick glance at him, his thoughts clearly far away and perhaps engaged like hers in the mysteries of Sinai. She studied his face, profiled against the horizon; the beard had a hint of grey in it and his eyebrows were shelves of bushy hair. He must have passed forty, she thought, yet his eyes were sparkling blue and sensitive and she couldn't help noticing earlier the way he had sprung up the mountainside, tanned, nimble and muscular, not a bit of fat on his seventy kilo frame unlike most of his contemporaries. Anke liked the way he assumed she was his equal, never patronisingly asking if she was all right or if he was going too fast. He did nothing to give her an inferiority complex for being female and at the same time she felt that he recognised her need to come out from under a cloud.

Impulsively, as if in a gesture to acknowledge the friendship and equality, she moved only a few metres away and squatted down for a pee. The sound she made intentionally signalled her declaration of peace, at least with this one male.

She wondered what Jack might be thinking about as she went back to their packs and started rearranging her things. He was still focussed apparently on the mysteries of Sinai but his eyes were no longer suspended in idle thoughts but fixed on something in the distance. Perhaps she had embarrassed him, she thought in a moment of anxiety, and he felt he had to pretend to be occupied elsewhere. Or maybe the signal had been wasted on him and he hadn't even noticed. She was unsure which was worse. But that was silly thinking; he had noticed all right for she had seen his head turn briefly in her direction. She felt ashamed and thought he must be shocked and was avoiding her eye.

Jack spoke quietly, defusing the situation, 'You know something? I think someone has been here before. If that is the vein over there,' he pointed to a spot on a hill about two kilometres away, 'and it appears to be in the right direction, then they are old workings. That maybe something to do with Dahab.'

She dropped her previous thoughts with relief and followed his finger.

'Ja, I see what you mean, but I cannot see the vein clearly. We must be looking at another structure. It is too puzzling I cannot understand anything from here. We must go slowly mapping and sampling before we get to that area to understand it all.'

'Aye aye captain,' he said, quite happy to fall in with a well-organised approach. She took it that her leadership was inferred and that he was assuming the role of a subordinate. This made her feel odd. She began to regret the incident of her signal and wanted to re-establish the former equality.

The sun was warm by now and the distant mountains were beginning to take on their day-time chocolate and tan colours, melting the subtler lilacs and mustards of the dawn and leaving the expanse of a simmering desert for the next eight hours.

Jack took off his shirt and tucked it into his belt. Anke watched the muscles ripple across his back and down his arms and marvelled at his tight teak coloured skin and clear bone structures highlighted by his glistening perspiration. This was a man who was slim but not skinny; wiry and fit with the hair of his chest just meeting the lowest point of his beard.

'Luckily you do not to have to worry about the sun.' She lightly touched her nose to confirm it wasn't already getting burnt.

'I can burn,' he said, 'but 1 am fairly well protected now after many days at sea this summer.'

'You like your life on the sea?'

'I guess I do. It's clean and free from dust, mosquitos and flies, which is something, and yes I do like it regardless. It's active and very challenging, trying to put everything you know together to persuade old Mother Nature to give up her riches. It is very similar to being a geologist but, like I said before, I have a lot of luck as well.'

'Have you brought your luck along with you now?' She sounded anxious.

'Maybe.'

He smiled to himself, thinking back to the delightfully erotic feelings he had while Anke was performing her morning toilet a few minutes earlier. What a good job she could not read his mind, he thought.

Do you have a lucky charm, a gene or something?' she asked. 'Do you get visions from the signs in the sky? Is there something you can predict like a fortune teller that makes you smile so?'

'No I'm afraid not,' he sighed. 'But we are both lucky just to be here, in the majesty of this wilderness and full in our own minds with so much knowledge that we can begin to unwrap its secrets. All that must be lucky.'

'Ach so,' she said philosophically, still not understanding his smile. She heaved her pack on and pointed to the rising ground a hundred metres away.

'Let's check that first good outcrop over there. I can see the quartz and the vein coming away from the rubble of this flat ground.'

They took the slight downward slope to where she had pointed. It was mostly flakes of granite and black dyke fragments. They were now on a saddle leading across to the next ridge. On their northern side was a disarray of minor ridges and irregular outcrops that lacked any pattern. The buttress of a mountain ridge two kilometres away was the only dominant feature. On their southern side the ground fell away with increasing depth to the southeast. With its progress blocked by the mountain range ahead the young valley had formed a deep wadi and appeared to change direction at right angles, disappearing round to the southwest and out of sight.

There was no sign of life, not even the tiniest bit of vegetation to be seen anywhere. However, there were what looked like animal tracks in the sand of the distant wadi. This was to be expected as there was surely no part of Sinai not trodden by generations of Bedouin and their goats as they searched for feed or merely tracked between one spot and another. The absence of rain ensured the tracks remained for years.

Initially, the next outcrop looked to contain nothing of interest. The quartz was milky white and the fragments of breccia much smaller. The only feature of note was that the vein itself was much wider. Anke remarked on this and unzipped one of the many pockets on her pack and took out a hard-backed field notebook with attached pen. She dug deeper and produced a fold-up protractor and a tailor's cloth tape measure.

'Wow you came prepared,' said Jack. 'Now you are embarrassing me. All I have is shark meat.'

She felt warmly towards him, 'I still have to find something,' she said softly, 'and in any case it is my profession and I feel lost without some things.' She reached into another side pocket and produced a small compass.

'Now that I recognise,' he laughed, 'but 1 prefer mine to have gimbals, a big light in it, and a hundred horse power not so very far away.'

'There's no light,' she said, 'but 1 have one horse power just two metres away,' she teased, mimicking his biceps.

'That makes two horses then,' he countered, indicating her long and powerful legs.

'Ach so,' she laughed.

She sat on the top of the small outcrop, measured the width of the vein and opened her protractor. She placed it on the edge against the footwall where a piece of quartz had flaked away leaving the clean surface of the host granite rock. She adjusted it for level and took an apparent dip reading followed by a true dip reading. She recorded the figures in her notebook before eyeing in the vein on the ridge behind them and taking a compass bearing.

As he watched, Jack recalling his days as a geologist in the field and how attention to detail and examination of all the facts had led him to find an ore body where others had failed. He admired Anke's approach for here was nothing, no history of mining, nothing to go on other than a single copper stain in a wilderness of probably hundreds more. Almost certainly a nothing vein and yet she was mapping in every detail. He knew somewhere, someday her persistence and determination would be rewarded and it made him feel good to be working with her.

She sketched in the black dykes as far as she could make out on either side of the vein and then set out to measure the nearest one. Although Jack thought this was overkill he volunteered to do the measuring, pacing the distances and measuring the dykes with the tape measure. Anke had him traipsing off up to a kilometre to bring back news of distance and thickness of all the dykes she had sketched in.

'You know,' he said thoughtfully after numerous measurements, 'these dykes are relatively new. They are all virtually parallel, they cut the vein at the same angle, at what ... sixty degrees? But then the vein carries on the other side as if nothing has happened. Right?'

Jack paused for a moment, concentrating on the small dyke in front of him, then measuring the veins on either side. The one on the far side was a few centimetres wider. 'There's a difference, which means these are not only fissures filled with basalt but also block faults.'

She looked at him seriously.

He continued. 'The Rift valley is only ten kilometres away at the most and all this land between here and the coast, and behind us as well maybe, has slipped down in blocks like giant steps towards the rift. *Mish quidda*? Isn't it so?'

Anke measured the widths of the vein again and looked at the fragments in it on either side.

'There is no correspondence,' she said at last. 'Everything is smaller in the far side.'

'That figures,' Jack said. 'The far side would represent a cooler zone higher up the vein, further away from the hydrothermal source. That explains the increasing quartz and the smaller fragments. It also means that the further we follow the vein in this direction the more likely we are to reach the very coolest zones of its hydrothermal deposition where noble metals may have been deposited. The same thing happened in the Kenyan Rift valley where block faults took the high ground and the most recent sediments went to the bottom of the valley. The geology then becomes the very opposite to what you would expect. As you go down into the valley the rocks get younger.'

He waved his arm to include the area around them. 'In this case the block faulting has been purely vertical but if we come across a dyke with any horizontal component in the faulting ...' he paused and lightly probed her shoulder with his outstretched index finger, 'and so, mein geologist, we are going to have to look hard for our vein.'

She pouted. He laughed, and the balance between them began to be restored. Jack strolled half a dozen metres away and relieved himself even more unconcernedly than Anke had done. With his back turned he was unable to see the smile or hear her sigh of gratitude.

They went on over the loose rubble of the flat ground to the next good outcrop where a dyke crossed the vein at the foot of a small ridge. They made their measurements with Anke writing down every little detail and then turned their attention back to the vein, examining small fragments and breaking off pieces here and there to scrutinise the fresh faces. After an hour of having seen no copper or iron stains they began to despair of finding further mineralisation.

Jack peered into a depression in the vein on the far side of the outcrop. With the sun streaming straight into the deepest recesses, he could clearly see that there was only milky white quartz that looked quite barren.

'No more currents in the cake,' he said.

Anke, who had been peering over his shoulder, stood back and stared at the vein again.

'Something is wrong,' she said.

Jack turned round sharply. By now he was beginning to understand that what she really meant was, something is right.

'This hollow is unnatural. Isn't it so? Why should it be *in* when the rest of the vein is *out*?'

There was something in the way her grammar changed to a more direct translation of the German that made him smile but he also sensed her excitement.

Jack stood up and regarded the recess. She could be right, he thought. He glanced over his shoulder to what in the distance he had earlier thought to be old workings. They were hidden by a ridge in the foreground but even there on that next shallow ridge he could now see other small recesses in the vein. There alongside the holes were quite clearly the tell-tale screes left by man's disturbance of the natural processes of rock degeneration.

Jack looked at Anke. A slight breeze was whipping the fine ends of blonde hair about her cheeks like little golden watch springs and a glow had returned to her face as she had followed his glance to the next outcrop. It reminded him of his youth when he used to go hunting with beagles. In the first few moments of suddenly coming across a scent the little dogs simply stood still and allowed their senses to absorb and tune into the new challenge. Then the adrenalin surged through their veins and they sped after their quarry like mad things, yelping and bounding, charging through thickets with complete disregard for their self-preservation. So it was with Anke, he mused; the glow was certainly caused by adrenalin.

She steadied her pack and strode off at a brisk march to the next ridge, leaving a dust trail behind her as she crossed the shallow basin. Jack followed in her wake keeping his eyes addressed to the little workings that appeared in several places up the side of the ridge.

The trials were no more than a metre deep and the debris from these earlier excavations had been strewn either side and rested among other naturally weathering fragments of granite and dykes; only the fresher whiteness gave them away. The milky quartz from the natural erosion of the vein was not so very different and a casual observer could have easily missed the old workings.

As they headed southeast the steeper parts of the ridge were still in the shade. Anke was half way up to the first pit before Jack had picked his way through the rubble on the scree at the bottom.

He looked up and watched the soles of her green and black walking boots and a metre of powerful Teutonic leg muscle pushing her generous female backside over a ledge and out of sight. He wondered how many other women combined the power, the femininity, the intelligence and the dedication of this one, and decided there were precious few.

He gave his thoughts a sudden jolt. *If I am not going to let that woman take over this whole trip and control my mind, I'm going to have to snap out of this day-dreaming and put some fight into it.* Never before had he recognised his leadership as being under challenge; and it wasn't going to be this time, he told himself.

Anke unclipped her pack and laid it down next to the half-metre wide trench that had been excavated in the breccia vein in front of her. As she searched for signs of mineralisation she reckoned no more than a ton of rock had been taken out. She noticed small brown stains here and there as she turned over the rock piles on either side, looking for a suitable fragment to crack open. She crashed a fist sized piece down on the hard vein surface and a quarter of it broke off.

Please, let there be something, she prayed, although it was not her usual solution to problems but Jack coming along behind her and she wanted so much to show him something.

Bright glints of brassy crystals twinkled at her, each no bigger than a pinhead. One tiny crystal right on the edge of the fracture showed brown on the outside face.

'Pyrites,' she said quietly to herself, 'At least we are back into mineralisation again.'

She turned and saw Jack's head and tanned shoulders appear over the ledge. He looked fresh and relaxed, with just a faint sheen of perspiration on his skin. She wiped a trickle of sweat away from her brow with the back of her hand and noticed dark blue arcs of sweat had stained her T-shirt under the arms, despite the early hour. She began to realise how hot it was going to get in the Sinai interior.

Jack put his pack down and for a moment stood up straight with his back to her while he surveyed the panorama below and behind them. The sun caught the muscled layers of his back and shoulders, making Anke think of the discus throwers of classical art, the sinewy stamp of the older male in Greek mythology, the tough maturity that improves on the gentler curves of youth. If man was still part of in the animal kingdom, she thought, this one would be the leader of the pack, not so much for his qualities of strength but because of his wily tenacity and adaptability.

'I've found gold,' she said softly.

He turned, cocked an eyebrow and grinned. 'Fool's gold?'

'Hmm,' she said and they both laughed. She showed him the fragment in her hand and continued to check other pieces nearby.

She was now sure that fine-grained pyrites crystals were widespread throughout the vein as she could see minute brown iron oxide stains everywhere she looked.

Anke turned her thoughts to the time and purpose of these diggings. Whoever it was failed to find what they were looking for because they had soon given up, she decided. Casting her mind back to the old mining sites she had visited in Europe, she judged these old workings were generations old rather than mere years. With so little moisture in Sinai, oxidation to the brown material must be a very slow process and so it could not have been the occupying Israelis. The logical conclusion was that the only persons to have worked here were the Bedouin.

She thought Jack, as a mining engineer, would confirm her reasoning, and she was suddenly pleased with their partnership.

'*Mahandes,*' she used the respectful Arabic way of addressing an engineer, 'What is the age of the work?'

'I was wondering that myself,' said Jack. 'There are no crushing marks or drill holes, nothing has been blasted. Whoever dug this lot out did it with a hammer and moil. It is probably a lot older than we are ... than you are,' he corrected with a laugh.

She nodded and made some measurements. While she wrote the details in her notebook, he grabbed his pack and humped it up the forty or fifty metres of rising ground to the next pit.

After cracking open a few more rocks to check for other minerals and finding none, Anke sat down with her magnifying glass and examined the pyrites to see if there were traces of something else. In several places she noticed the crystals were in the form of small cubes and that some of the cubic cavities were void of any filling. She knew this meant the pyrites had only filled up spaces left by another mineral that had leached out over eons of geological time. The commonest of the cubic minerals was galena, lead sulphide, and that would make sense as Jack had said they were moving all the time towards the cooler zones of the vein.

Her studies were interrupted by a shout from Jack. She scrambled up to where he was basking in the full sunshine, sitting on a rock pile and resting his elbows on his knees. He had a big smile on his face. He tossed her a stone the size of a tennis ball. It fell into her hands with the weight of a cannon ball.

She didn't bother looking at it. 'Galena?'

'Galena and siderite,' he said.

Anke spent time inspecting the rock she held in her hands. Only a small portion was quartz; the rest was a sandy brown crystalline matrix with cubes of silvery galena scattered through it.

Judging by its sheer weight, she thought it must contain at least twenty per cent lead and would represent high grade ore if part of a large deposit. Even in this little vein there was possibly sufficient amount.

She was unable to conceal her elation. The subtle lines of her mouth broke from their normal tight pout to a beautiful Cupid's bow that lit up all her face.

'Brilliant *mein fisher*. We are not wasting our time after all. This is heavy mineralisation. See how little quartz there is now and this siderite is a low temperature iron mineral. We are in a new zone.' Her enthusiasm was palpable. 'Where did you find it? 'Come on, show me where you found it.'

In her excitement she momentarily lost grip of her formal disciplines. Jack couldn't resist exploiting this chink in her armour if only to enjoy the Cupid's bow a little longer.

'Can't,' he teased.

'Why?'

'I brought it with me.'

'No you bloody didn't,' she retorted, her eyes sparkling as she put her response into overdrive, her intelligence and femininity combining at full throttle. 'I saw the galena pseudo morphs in the pit below. You don't fool me. Where did you find it?'

Her eyes darted round the area before turning back to Jack.

'Ah, shit,' he sighed, pretending to be disappointed but with a twinkle in his eyes, 'You're too clever for me.' He pointed to the rock pile below indicating the location of his find.

'Come on sit down; let's have a drink and a bite to eat.' He stretched a hand out towards her You're overheating.'

Anke obeyed reluctantly. To her mind she was being amazingly self-restrained. For the first time in her life she had the real possibility of balancing her personal account as a geologist and here she was obediently sitting down and taking a mid-morning snack as if killing time at a railway station.

For Jack, these were moments he was to savour for a long time after the actual occasion. Their brief exchange had brought out all the fight, brilliance and seductive charm of his companion and he was enjoying it to the full. Although he remained sceptical that the trip would ever find anything with commercial possibilities, he would never hint at such feelings to Anke for fear of poisoning her intense enthusiasm. And anyway, he was thoroughly enjoying being swept along in the Sherlock Holmes–like world of Anke's exploration geology.

Maybe that's all we are going to find, he mused, a narrow veined lead deposit; in the middle of the mountains, in the middle of the undeveloped world. As much use as a hole in the head with refined lead selling at, what, three hundred pounds a ton.

Anke had put down her pack but was unable to resist the temptation to examine a few of the rock fragments cast aside from the pit and lying around her feet. They were strongly 'tanned' by the desert sun and dust but she could see that much of the quartz had been replaced by the buff crystalline siderite; even without cracking pieces open she could see plenty of small grey patches of galena.

Curiosity eventually got the better of her. She cracked a heavy sample open on another rock and studied it while making herself comfortable for the enforced rest imposed by Jack.

'Well you've found yourself a lead mine if nothing else,' he said.

'*Sheise*,' she responded irritably, 'you know as well as I do how much good that is out here.'

Jack nodded and decided to improve her mood by suggesting that perhaps there was some silver locked up with the lead, as quite often was the case.

'At sixty centimetres wide there would have to be a hell of a percentage of silver 'vapped up with the lead to make it worthwhile,' she said. But you're right, we must take some samples back with us and one day I'll get them assayed.'

Jack inwardly groaned at the thought of filling his packsack with lead and began to regret having mentioned the silver possibility. Maybe it was time to be less academic and more practical. 'The guys who hacked out these pits, breaking knuckle skin, sweating buckets pounding primitive tools into quartz veins in the midday sun; they were not looking for lead mines nor silver. Look what they have thrown away.' He waved at the rock piles. 'They were looking for the real McCoy.'

'The McCoy?' she asked, frowning.

'Dahab. Anke,' he laughed apologetically. 'I think McCoy is a whisky.'

'Aah,' she groaned, thinking the English talked too much in riddles. 'Yes we must take some samples. I vill at least have enough information to write a paper.'

So stubborn, thought Jack. *The good old German trait for precision and correctness emerges once more.* It put the brake on his intention to skip through these procedures. Better instead to move on to the much bigger workings he thought he had seen in the distance earlier.

They drank a bottle of his water, surprised at how easily it went down. Anke dug out some flat bread and a handful of dates for them to share along with a little bundle of plastic bags and said she wanted to detail the workings. She smiled at Jack's raised eyebrows and explained, 'I talked nicely to the man at the peanut stall yesterday and he gave me a long strip of these.' She slid the elastic band off the bags. 'They are for my shells I told him.'

Jack marvelled at her organisation. 'Very nice. What a wonderful idea, we get rid of all the water and replace it with lead.' He flexed his aching shoulder muscles as if to test their ability to respond to the challenge.

She was amused by his actions. 'Jack Fisher you are a strong man,' she said and mimicked Charles Atlas by putting her shoulders back, sticking her chest out and demonstrating her biceps.

'I bloody well need to be,' thought Jack, taking in the full roundness of her breasts as they darkened her T-shirt and perspiration helped define the aureoles around the nipples through the fabric. He soon became painfully aware of an uncomfortable stirring in his loins and looked away.

He wiped his brow and met her eyes again 'Okay, let's do what has to be done.' He took some of her sample bags and thumped his chest. 'How many kilos Mme?'

'What I really want to do is take a channel sample right across the vein,' she said and dived into another side pocket of her packsack.

This woman has no limits to her resourcefulness, thought Jack. He as he watched her take out a piece of angle iron about six inches long cut off square at one end and tapering to a point at the other. She proceeded to use it to niggle and tease small chips of rock off the vein, catching them in her hand.

She stuck the pointed iron into a fracture and prised off a small piece. 'I saw these in the Bedouin *suq*,' she explained. 'They started off as fencing posts for barbed wire during the Israeli conflict and the Bedouin got the idea that they would make good scrapers for the hides of their goats and sheep and so they cut them up into twenty centimetre lengths and sold them in the market. I took an end piece with the point still on because I thought it would be useful on this trip.'

The handful of chips went into the first bag. She repeated the exercise a metre away, taking care to get little chips all the way across the vein. She sat back on her haunches and rummaged around in yet another pocket of her packsack and finally produced a card of women's hair grips. Using a centre page torn out of her notebook she made small labels to identify each bag with its own number and placed a hair grip over the rolled down top, sealing the contents and label securely inside.

Jack marvelled at this show of efficiency and contented himself with looking on and considering the wider implications of their findings. He checked several other pieces on the rock pile, cracking some open and scrutinising their fresh surfaces. 'There is plenty of lead all right,' he thought, 'but not a trace or hint of anything else. I guess that's what the old Bedouin reckoned as well.'

His gaze ran up the rock pile over the forty or fifty metres to the ridge, a large black dyke running off in each direction like the backbone of the hill, the black basaltic rock being so much harder than the weathering granite. It was a notably large and dominant feature of the surrounding landscape. He was on the point of scrambling up to it when Anke asked, 'How far do you think we are from the road?'

Her voice was quiet with a childlike ring in it, like a student addressing her teacher in order to capture maximum notice.

It had the intended effect for Jack gave her all his attention and after due consideration said, 'Two and a half. maybe three kays ... no more.'

She nodded and told him that her calculations of all the segments of paced distances added up to two thousand five hundred and thirty-seven metres. 'It seems much more. Isn't it so?' she remarked.

'In Cornwall, there are hydrothermal veins up to five miles long,' he commented. 'I remember reading about the Great St Day Mining Company that had an unbroken stope three miles long. It was the county's richest copper mine for decades and then had a second life as a rich tin mine as they mined deeper down. So a mile and a half on this vein is probably about average, but now we have reached the lead zone anything could happen. Maybe the cooler zone won't exist or maybe it's worn away.'

'Ach-so. What are you looking at up at the top?'

Anke was anxious to be on the move again. The heat in the hollow was intense and there was probably a breeze up on the ridge. The sweat trickled down her face, over her reddening nose, rivulets down her cheeks and under her chin. She looked up at Jack, pushed her matted hair back and licked her top lip to savour the salt and then glanced about them, seeking shade.

There was none.

High up on the ridge there may perhaps have been the promise of a breeze but on those bare rocks leading upwards, Sinai's midday sun had no mercy. She knew there was little to do but drink water and battle on. She stood up, wiped her face on the sleeve of her shirt and waited a second until the light headedness cleared. Then she pushed on up the slope to the next collection of pits five minutes away.

Jack too was hot. He was tired from pacing out the kilometres to facilitate Anke's mapping requirements. For a brief instant he wished he was out at sea on a boat where there was always cool water and a breeze. Even so, he was not suffering as much as Anke. It was as if he was able to shut down his outer boundaries and allow his body to function normally within. His metabolism coped with the desert's furnace-like heat in the same way it coped with Arctic cold. He had pulled his hat down over his eyes and tied his shirt round his neck so it lay loosely over his shoulders to protect them. He sweated only lightly.

His eyes followed the progress of Anke's backside up the slope and the animal in him suddenly was glad he was not after all out at sea with a bunch of fishermen. There was no power in the world, he decided, that was stronger than the attraction of man to woman. Controlling it was the very art of living itself, he reasoned, and guiding that control to the very edge, a fraction back from the limit, provided the high that gave the impetus and fuelled the driving force of most of his activities.

The detail of Anke's, long powerful Teutonic thighs gradually diminished as she advanced up the rocky slope and left Jack pondering the whole bizarre escapade. He wondered if in this sizzling heat he could be exactly sure of his own reason for being here in the desert with a woman he hardly knew.

Watching her innocently addressing the work in hand and knowing that her every upwards step required intense effort made him uncomfortable. It shamed him to realise he was guilty of contemplating her as an extraordinarily sexually attractive being. He had no right to enfold her in a shroud of sensual mystique. Yet how could he be expected to separate the vibrant and aggressive field geologist from the Nordic goddess with golden ringlets who oozed attraction in her every movement and, worse, appeared unaware of it?

Of one thing he was certain: Anke herself and Anke alone was in control of this being, and he, like others before him, would have little influence on her. She would remain a fantasy in his mind for this trip and probably a long time afterwards.

He adjusted his pack and made his way up towards his companion. As he picked his way through the strewn fragments of the vein, the slabs of granite and blocks of black basaltic dyke he was again drawn back to the other side of his motivation; the sheer miracle of nature that had produced the vein they were following. He wondered how nature could contrive against all the odds of chaos, to arrange in perfect order, the minerals they had encountered; the textbook sequence of copper, iron and now lead sulphides. If only the vein could stretch further into this wilderness before Mother Nature chopped its top off or it simply petered out. It would surely offer more. *The deposition of noble metals, the deposition of noble metals*, he kept repeating to himself in rhythm with his stride each time he heaved up to another ledge. His strength and enthusiasm were regenerated.

Anke was seated on the edge of a shallow pit poking around at the sides with her scraper. It was obviously the site of an earlier primitive investigation but the return of the vein material to mostly hard white quartz had not impressed the early prospectors. They had not taken away any material and given up after only a small pit had been made.

She looked depressed.

The pack had come off and the sample bags had come out again.

There's absolutely no stopping this woman, Jack thought. She was incredibly wet, her T-shirt rested heavily on her shoulders and breasts, her blonde hair was stuck to her neck and there was a trickle of blood coming from a scraped knuckle. Yet still her resolve continued. She would not give in to the harshness of the desert. Having already completed one cross section of sampling she was chipping her way across the second without saying a word. It was as if sampling offered an escape route when any faltering in her courage threatened to stop her.

Without a word, Jack bent over to take the scraper from her so she could note down the details and rest a little.

In that brief action there came a pause he was unprepared for and which took him a long time to sort out. Anke hesitated for a second or two before allowing the scraper to leave her grip. In that immeasurably small space of time, faster than the conscious brain could rationalise, Jack felt a shockwave of several intense messages; barriers started to come down and others went up.

Her reaction was a fluctuation of emotions; whether to allow herself to be organised by a man, fighting the desire to be relieved of an exhausting chore which in turn was overridden by an unexplainable surrender to the touch of friendship. This was more than she had conceded to anyone in a long time on any one of these issues, never mind all three at one time.

For Jack it had seemed the most natural thing in the world to take over when someone was struggling, whether it was woman or man. Anke's instant of hesitation had thrown him off balance and all his defence mechanisms had come into play. Had his action been interpreted as domination or interference? Her reaction had put him automatically on his guard. He was unable to imagine any plausible reason for her being so stubborn. Feminism to that extent was irrational; it had no part in a joint activity. It offended him and he felt as if stabbed in the back, a betrayal of friendship. If that was the way she wanted to play, he argued, their friendship was going to be difficult to maintain for he would not allow his more sensitive side to be exposed and vulnerable to her attack. She would be the nett loser. All his actions would have to be trimmed back if he had to consider whether he was stepping on feminist toes in everything he did.

Anke offered no explanation and the atmosphere refused to defuse itself. Jack went on building his own buffer zone to protect his position unaware Anke was wrestling with the concessions she had made to her defences. No more would he allow himself to be open to feminist attack. The more he thought about it the more he resented the mistrust. How could she doubt him when he had been as open and considerate as possible? Perhaps she was warning him off, he reasoned, giving her the benefit of the doubt. But that was still unfair as he had never treated her as anything other than an equal.

Anke also felt wretched and was struggling with her thoughts. She kept her eyes averted. She realised she had been trapped by her own obsession; her capitulation had been too late and Jack had surely registered it and resented it.

Anke let out a long sigh. Her watershed had been reached and she was unsure how to handle things from now on. How could she just go with the flow when she had been paddling her own canoe upstream for so long? She no longer needed this man as a companion but wanted him, she conceded with another long intake of air, as a friend.

Jack heard the sigh but thought better than to enquire its reason. He sensed something of her dilemma and decided not to brush the raw nerve.

They finished the sampling in silence. After she had clipped up the tiny bags with their labels she started to undo her pack. Until then Jack had carried the sample bags in his bigger packsack and would have done so now had he not been on the defensive. He watched her hesitantly, his whole nature being to offer help. As they reached the point of loading up he threw caution to the wind and asked her for the bags.

She made no attempt to conceal her relief, but looked up at him and with sheepish grin and tossed him half the samples.

'*Shukran Mahandes*,' thank-you engineer, she said and wiped the sweat off her face with her upper arm. Jack found her a plaster from his first aid kit, wrapped it round her knuckle without saying anything and they continued up the hill in silence.

'The black dyke there,' he pointed out, 'is much bigger than the rest. We had better check it carefully. Maybe it changes the pattern.' They scrambled up the rest of the slope to the ridge.

'It is changing our pattern anyway,' exclaimed Anke, reaching the top first and peering over. 'We cannot go down any more here.'

Jack lay beside her on his stomach at the edge of the dyke. There was an overhang for several hundred metres in each direction. Below them screes made the vein indiscernible. Scattered fragments of quartz off to their right were strewn randomly in the direction of the next ridge, indicating the vein was still there. There were also obvious workings on the flank of the next ridge a kilometre away and several suggestions of more small excavations on the flat saddle ground in between. The land to the south dropped off sharply nearly five hundred metres to a narrow flat sandy *wadi* that curved away to the south where it was deflected by the range of mountains ahead. The next ridge contained what appeared to be possible old mine workings.

The breeze that Anke had hoped for dried their perspiration and lifting their hair as they lay on their bellies taking in the cooling and the absolute magic of the undisturbed beauty of the terrain ahead. There was still not a single trace of life, not a bird, an insect or the merest vestige of vegetation. The *wadi* bottom still gave no clues to any recent life form passing by and, as Jack had suggested, the view probably had looked the same for tens of thousands of years and could even be that of another planet.

It was Anke who spoke first after a long silence. 'There seems to be a way down over there.' She pointed to a low spot in the ridge about half a kilometre away. 'We can climb along the top okay I think.'

Jack agreed with a grunt but his thoughts were elsewhere. He kept throwing a glance over his shoulder then returning to the vein in front again.

'You know something,' he said at length, 'I think the vein is faulted off to the right here by twenty metres maybe; look below at that line of quartz pebbles. It has to be offset from the vein behind us. I think the faulting will increase laterally as we approach the Rift Valley and that may be a big challenge for us if we are to find anything new. Hold my feet a minute. I'm going to see if there are any scratches in the footwall of this dyke to indicate lateral movement.'

Jack wriggled out over the edge while Anke clamped his ankles. He felt her warm hands shackle his feet to the ground and realised that it was the first time they had actually touched other than to shake hands. He felt vaguely turned on. The wind started to play orchestral music in his ears and with the compression of his chest on the ledge he could wildly imagine that she was lying on top of him. He dallied longer in this dream than he needed with his head under the overhang so that when he eventually wriggled back to the top again, he was quite light-headed and perspiring heavily.

She laughed at his red face and let go of his ankles.

'I thought you ver staying there forever. Did you find a cave painting or something?'

He laughed, covering up his little self-indulgences. 'No. But there are striations and they are diagonal not vertical so that means there is horizontal movement. We have to watch this or we will lose the vein.'

She moved towards the edge. 'Can I have a look?'

'You trust me not to let go?' he grinned. 'I wouldn't have to share the gold with you.'

'You need me to help you find it first, *mein fischer* so I don't think you let go so soon.' She gave him a warm smile there was again a twinkle in her eyes.

He knelt gently across her ankles and also held them with his hands as her head and shoulders disappeared over the lip. Jack allowed himself an unashamed, undisturbed visual exploration of her legs and buttocks, enjoying every moment. He savoured every contour, letting his mind float his physical person from one bronzed curve to another, from one thigh to another. He looked at the back of her knees; they were strangely pale and delicate in contrast to the rest of her powerful legs. They were dimpled and pink and looked so sensitive that he longed to stroke them.

He noticed her legs and ankles were covered in a delicate blonde down. This made her somehow animal and earthy in the nicest possible way as if newly presented to man from the Garden of Eden without the manipulations of the modern cosmetic industry. She lacked the bristles or sheen of English leg-shaving girls that left them slaves to their own unnatural devices. Jack much preferred this natural attitude towards female body hair and thought that he even might have an affinity to women with downy arms and ankles. As far as he was concerned, under-arm hair was a definite turn-on and led him to erotic speculation as to the luxuriant bush that there might be elsewhere.

His eyes played on the backs of her knees again, so soft and sensual. He recalled how some women could be very sensitive there, and the urge to stroke them returned. If only to see what would happen... but fought off the temptation.

He marvelled at the generous upward curve of her bottom, the frayed denim shorts giving it the appearance of a mushroom growing in the grass; the width of the hips narrowing so gracefully into the waist leaving him full of gratitude for the creation of the female form. His heart filled with admiration for the sculptor that made it.

Anke tried her best to judge the angle of the striations on the under face of the overhang. Her hair hung down and danced in the wind and she felt the discomfort of her breasts squashing on the lip of the ridge. She was also aware that her bottom posed a less than ladylike view to the eyes of her companion but in her light-headed state she reckoned he could either accept it and enjoy it or turn his head the other way. In any case, only moments earlier she had shocked herself by allowing her eyes to stray up the back of Jack's legs to where his shorts gaped and his red briefs didn't quite cover all the delicate parts that hung there. She had even let her eyes linger until she had felt a flush of heat emanate from low in her own body.

She struggled beneath the overhang to measure angles, using her fingers as measuring sticks. Then, with a final wriggle and stretch, she managed to flake off a loose piece of rock with fault scratches on it. She knew she was at balance point and grateful for Jack's increased pressure on her ankles. She had felt the sensitive tissue and tendons in the backs of her knees tighten with the extra effort and wondered in a brief moment of light-headedness if he had contemplated stroking them.

Grasping the stone in her hand she struggled to get up but Jack responded by hauling her gently back by her feet. She sat up even more red in the face than she had been before.

'You must have found those cave paintings,' he ribbed her. 'What have you got there?'

She laughed back at him. 'I stretched and strained and bruised my chest for that. I thought the marks would tell us the direction of the faulting of the vein but now I've lost the orientation. I think you have to be a Fledermaus to get it right.' She kissed the fragment lightly and hurled it in the direction of the old workings. 'Come on, let's get over there and see what's happening.'

She humped her pack on to her back and set off along the ridge for a place some way off that offered a route down.

Three hours later, in the heat of the afternoon sun, they were within a couple of hundred metres of the foot of the big ridge where the main excavations appeared to be. Suddenly Anke gave a shriek as she cracked open a piece of quartz thrown aside from a small pit. Jack sped back to where she was kneeling in a shallow pit, fearing she had hurt herself and again thankful he had packed his first aid kit.

There were freshly broken rocks all round her and the red scarf wrapped around her blonde hair for sun protection and made a convenient landmark. She beckoned Jack as he approached and handed him a piece of quartz.

'*Was ist das?*' she demanded excitedly in German.

He looked at the grey fern-like material running along the open fractures of the quartz rock.

'Phew! Looks like silver to me ... gotta be native silver, mein geologist. We're getting there.'

Caught up in her excitement, he started jumping up and down, the sweat running off him in little rivulets even though he was not normally a sweaty person. Anke's clothes were already wringing wet after sweating profusely for the last two hours.

They looked at each other and suddenly realised they should not be out there, exposed to the full blast of Sinai's August sun at two in the afternoon.

Jack wiped the sweat from his brow and glanced up at the old workings. 'Come on let's get in one of those caves for an hour or two and rest in the shade before we frizzle up. We can come back and make further checks when the sun is down a bit and not frying us alive.'

Anke looked at him with a hint of relief in her eyes. It was what she had longed to do but had refrained from saying it. She thought the heat was beyond imagination. At least in her wanderings in Dahab there had been a fresh breeze coming off the sea. Here there was nothing except right on the ridges. She had never experienced heat like this and was uncertain how much of it her body could endure without succumbing to its effects.

As they made their way up the bottom of the slope Jack pointed to the *wadi* floor some three kilometres away where a scattering of Bedouin black and white goats was disappearing round the curve to the south and out of sight.

'Signs of life,' he exclaimed. 'They are running loose but even their owner is asleep somewhere in the shade at this hour. How are you feeling ... hungry?'

'I don't know about hunger but my head tells me I need a drink and some shelter from the sun, said Anke. 'The workings here are quite extensive but shallow. We have to go to the highest one, which looks deeper, if we are to find any shade.' She pointed up to the trench leading into the mountain and ending under a huge black dyke that formed the highest part of the ridge. 'There is plenty of work for us here later on,' she said, casting her eye about the activities of the ancient miners.

They climbed three hundred metres up the steep slope until they arrived at the biggest of the ancient workings they had seen so far. Here the trench along the vein was up to two metres deep and ended in a cave with enough overhang where it met the black dyke to give afternoon shade. The bottom of the trench was also deep enough to escape the angled rays of the August sun. It looked like heaven on earth, Anke thought.

They sat propped against the southern wall and relaxed silently for a long time.

FIVE

'There is something is really practical about the Arab three o'clock lunch,' remarked Jack, breaking the silence. 'You can't work in the heat on a full stomach and so the working day is almost without food until two or three o'clock, creating an incentive to keep going until then at which time hunger and heat stop all work and everybody eats and rests. The Egyptians I work with take this heavy late lunch after which it is impossible to find them until dusk. I'm not suggesting that we go to sleep but I'm all for the big lunch right now. Come on, let's order the soup.'

Anke drained a litre of water down her throat without coming up for air but finally gasped just short of the full bottle. 'Aah ... now I can eat. Even the old bread will be a luxury. Isn't it so?' She smiled; she had regained her sparkle.

Jack was not prepared to debate the merits of the meal. His appetite had always been that of a wolf and he had already started wading into anything within reach, dry bread, cheese, tomatoes, shark meat and Anke's grapes. She quickly followed suit and they eventually restored their equilibrium. Time to get back to business, Jack decided.

'Let's have a look at your silver specimen again,' he said.

Anke passed over the piece of broken quartz with the little grey ferns on it. There was no thickness to the fine dendrites spreading along the fractures except in one place where two converged into a tiny blob the size of a match head. Jack folded a leather strap from his bag into a point and rubbed away at the blob. After a minute or so he inspected his work. His eyes lit up and he passed it over to Anke. The blob had been transformed from dull grey to a sheen like that found on a much polished silver teapot. There was no doubt what the grey material was.

'Native silver,' she confirmed, 'I never thought I would actually find some myself. I've only ever seen it inside the glass cases of mineral museums.'

'Me also,' admitted Jack. 'But these old workings still puzzle me. Silver mines? Maybe ... I guess the Bedouin do wear a lot of silver.'

'Some,' she agreed. 'But most of the silvery-grey jewellery and ornaments they wear every day are recently made from aluminium. The bangles and metals woven into their dress patterns are aluminium, only their heirlooms and celebration costumes have real silver in them.'

'Is that so?' said Jack. 'But surely no self-respecting miner who has gone to the trouble of hacking out these trenches in extremely hard rock, would then throw away what he was looking for up on to these rock piles.'

'If they were really looking for gold,' she said, 'it must have been pretty much high-grade for them to have discarded native silver.'

'I don't know about that,' Jack reflected. 'I don't suppose the old men, the metallurgists, would have done the digging. No, they would have sent young sons or labourers with little geological knowledge to graft out here. These guys would only be able to recognise the golden bright shiny stuff itself, and if you look at these little dendrites they don't look like minerals but more like fungus or grey secretions, not a valuable metal. I reckon they just didn't notice the silver metal on its own. Probably what silver they got they obtained from the concentrate when they crushed the gold ores.'

Anke agreed that was feasible. She took the metal scraper from where it had been tucked into her shorts and picked away at anything loose around her. It seemed to be all quartz. There were no more traces of lead or iron. That zone had obviously been left behind. If there was to be any gold it had to be here for the vein would surely soon decline into barren quartz as it was now so far from its source.

Her back rested against the black dyke which had cut off the old workings like a knife. The old miners had dug deepest and most extensively in that area and what she and Jack were sitting on were broken stones and so there was no way of telling how deep into the hard rock the trench extended. The only bit of the original vein remaining was the little canopy overhead against the black dyke, obviously left to give some afternoon shade. Anke stretching to her full height to reach the overhang and prise little chips from the fractures but was unable to dislodge any sizeable pieces.

Jack, still stirring from his lunch break, looked on incredulously as the tall blonde German woman levered and banged at the roof of the cave like the best of the male miners he had worked with back in the sixties. She had the longest reach he could recall on any woman.

Times had certainly changed, he reflected. The last time he had been barring down loose from the back of a stope to make it safe for an inspection, had been with an uncouth, garlic smelling, cursing Czech miner who had a hangover every time he came on shift at the small gold mine in the Northwest Territory. Now he was watching a fine blonde, T-shirted woman whose eyes sparkled and breath smelt fresh and whose full bosoms strained against the fabric as she stretched upwards, her nipples protruding like missiles angled skywards from their bunkers.

The tendons in her long neck shone like the polished bronze of some sculptured Greek goddess. The sight made him wonder if now, in the '90s, woman's equality was finally on the map. When the topic had been discussed in the past, he had always joked that the myth was exposed for what it was when it came to having woman miners.

Now, in front of his eyes, he could see the possibility of that myth becoming a reality.

It called his whole philosophy into question yet also excited him. As he watched her struggle to dislodge a sample that was proving too much for her scraper he decided that by offering to help he could also regain male domination. A simple demonstration of male know-how was needed to regain what he saw as the traditional upper hand.

He reached in his bag and unravelled the towel wrapped around the fifteen-inch cold chisel and three-pound hammer about which he had so far kept quiet.

'That looks like a man-sized job,' he said, pushing out his chest and flexing his biceps, unable to conceal a large grin.

'That's not fair,' she groaned. 'I suppose you have an air leg machine and a compressor inside your bag as well.'

'No. Thank God, these have been heavy enough. Now, let's see what riches can be uncovered with my tools.'

He tapped the cold chisel into the crack beside Anke's scraper so it fell to the floor like a child's discarded toy.

She picked it up in disgust and tucked it back into her shorts sulkily while miner Polglaise did his thing with his 'super tools'.

With two sharp blows of the hammer, a creak and a grind and a two-hundred-pound slab crashed to the ground almost before Jack could dive for cover. It resounded on the floor of the cave like a drum, narrowly missing Anke's pack.

'Holy fuck,' exclaimed Jack with echoes of his Czechoslovakian miner still in his brain. His astonishment was twofold, partly from the size of the slab and partly from the sound of its contact with the ground.

Anke pounced on the slab a few seconds later. 'Holy Jesus,' she shouted. 'Christ! Look there is vee-gee all over! Vee-gee! Vee-gee! Vee-gee!'

She jumped up and down, pointing all over the slab then threw her arms up and leapt at Jack, locking her legs round his waist. He staggered momentarily, braced himself and held his balance to take her weight.

'Jack,' her excited eyes met his, 'there is vee-gee all over, visible gold Fisher, vee-gee. Gold! We have found a gold mine.'

She drew in a badly needed deep breath and kissed him tightly on the lips for several seconds before they disengaged and knelt down to examine the slab.

'Phew,' breathed Jack almost in a whisper, 'that is certainly good stuff.'

'Stuff?' She was on the defensive. His words puzzled her.

'Good stuff? I mean it's high grade, maybe four or five hundred ounces a ton.' He lowered his voice still further and said slowly, 'I've never seen anything like it in my life. It is unbelievable. You would not need much of this to be a millionaire.

There's no doubt that's what the old guys were after. Who would worry about silver when a couple of hundred metres away there is stuff like this?'

The slab was criss-crossed by dozens of small fracture planes that had been too dusty to see on the exposed side. Most of these fractures showed specks of gold, sometimes running into lines an inch or so long. At that moment Jack understood why the lure of gold had been such an integral part of man's development, and of countries' histories, throughout the ages. No other element had played the role of instigator of wars, rebellions, conquests, settlements and migrations. Seeing it now in its raw beauty made him understand its uncompromising power that sucked at a person's very roots and reason.

It's irresistible, he thought and could already feel it affecting his own senses. He looked at Anke. With the inexperience of youth, she was even now being sucked into the trap that gold represented. Over the years he had learned to equate highs with lows and come out on a stable course, but Anke was in danger of being engulfed as thoughts of fame and fortune surged over her.

Jack's hands trembled. Anke was far more out of control, dancing up and down the small trench, in and out of the sunshine, her mind running wild, shooting incessant questions into the air without waiting for answers. 'A hundred and fifty thousand dollars a ton ...isn't it so? What was ore like that doing there? Why are the Bedouin not involved with it now? What happens to the vein the other side of the black dyke? How deep did the old men dig before they grew tired?'

Her last question was the one she thought Jack was turning his attention to as she watched him roll the slab to one side and begin removing the small pieces of broken rock that formed their floor, throwing them back down the trench.

'I thought so,' he cried after removing half a dozen chunks. 'There is staging here.' He indicated woodwork. He used his fingers to scraped away at it. 'There must be a stope under here shored up with this capping of wood. It's a wonder that the slab didn't break through it and send us down to God knows where. The hollow sound that came with the thud of that slab falling gave it away. I've heard that sound so many times before while working in shrinkage stopes.'

'Does that mean the vein has been mined quite deeply?' Anke asked.

Jack was suddenly on familiar territory and much of his old self-assurance had returned. He could speak with authority, even adopt a new role as teacher, 'If this staging is still good, and it seems to be solid, then the stope underneath will probably be open and we will be able to see the extent of the mining. Let's throw a few more rocks back and get a better look, maybe there is a ...'

His words faded as he scrutinised the yellow pine woodwork. He blew away the dust to reveal the painted sign of a black spread eagle, the symbol of the Egyptian government. Beneath the bird was some Arab writing daubed on with a paint brush. Jack removed a couple more rocks and blew away the dust. Embossed red lettering ... IVE AMMUN ... appeared.

'There is something wrong here,' said Jack, a tremor in his voice. 'I don't think this is old staging at all. The wood is too new and this looks like a box.'

He threw a few more stones aside, revealing a section of ten-gauge galvanised wire and the end of the woodwork. He blew at the dust. The letters read. 'IVE AMMUNITION,' read the lettering.

'Holy Jesus,' he gasped. 'I really wish I had not dropped that two-hundred-pound slab on this.'

Anke studied the box. '*Sheise*. You could have blown us up Mein Fischer. *Was ist das* anyway, bullets or 'vhot? It must be hidden here a short time only, all is new, even the vire.'

Her excitement had made her careless with her English. She was as excited as a child unveiling the mysteries of her Christmas stocking. Everything was happening far too quickly. She felt her brain was being carried along on a tidal wave. First the exhilaration of the hunt and discovering silver and on to actually finding gold of such high-grade that if quantities existed in depth and beyond the dyke, a fabulous fortune existed. And now all seemed to be confused: the old Bedouin and caches of modem arms did not mix. She did not like the thought that modern man was using their Aladdin's cave as a secret arsenal. This confused the issue. It cluttered her mind with factors she would rather choose to ignore.

Also playing on Anke's mind was the incredible 'high' of knowing that she was proving herself in the field of practical geology. It was a high she did not want to lose or suffer any interference.

She wanted to ignore the stupid ammunition box and see it go away. The thought of it sickened her and threatened her imaginary reign as queen over this pristine unexplored land.

Jack's thoughts were more practical. He was not going to rest until he had inspected the box thoroughly. He had already uncovered the top entirely. It was the size of a door mat and obviously no more than a year or two old, but the two straps of ten-gauge wire struck him as odd. They did not look to be the work of an arms factory but, as he pointed out to Anke, they rather had 'the Egyptian compromise' look about them.

He untwisted one wire to free one end of the lid. The other was too tight so he tried to unravel it with his cold chisel. When it still didn't budge he inserted the chisel underneath the wire and twisted it round, tightening the wire with each turn. The box gave out alarming creaking noises as the pressure increased. Jack hesitated and then, with a final twist, the wire parted with a sharp snap.

An intense smell filled the cave's confined space. Jack's eyes shot up in a knowing and concerned look, almost as if he wanted to protect Anke from seeing the contents of the box.

She quickly sensed his reaction and his concern. '*Sheise*, Jack,' she blurted out, 'you sixties children don't have a fucking monopoly. San Francisco is not the only place in the world you find hashish.'

Jack opened the box and the pungent aroma was almost enough to send their heads reeling. Neither said a word. The tremble returned to Jack's hands as he pulled back the cover inside the box to reveal two rows of seven neatly wrapped brick shaped packages. He took one out, uncovering another layer beneath. He unfolded the cotton sheet around the brick until the kilo and a half block of brown slightly sticky resin nestled in the palm of his hand.

'Holy Jesus,' he gasped. 'Lebanese Gold.'

Only once had he seen hashish larger peanut size piece and that had been in Egypt in the early eighties when smuggling and trading in the commodity were rampant. A mafiosi-style Italian tour operator had shown him a piece weighing a few ounces to demonstrate his machismo. He had referred to it as Lebanese Gold and claimed it to be the best in the market.

Anke was bewildered by their find.

'All is gold in this place,' Anke sobbed. 'How much is that box worth?'

'I don't know. My friends would pay ten dollars for a few grams back in the sixties. This box must be about fifty kilos, which makes it worth what …

a quarter of a million dollars I suppose, something like that, and maybe there are more boxes.'

'What are we going to do with it?'

After a long pause Jack said, 'As I see it there are four choices; we sell it, smoke it, report it or forget it.'

'They all seem like good ideas to me,' Anke laughed, briefly intoxicated by events before turning serious. 'What the hell are we going to do?' she wailed, desperation now showing in her voice

Jack replaced the lid with all the contents back in the box. His fingers continued to shake nervously as he put the wires back into position. 'One thing is for sure, we are getting the hell out of here before the owners come and find us with it or we will never live to even think about the gold.'

Anke shed tears as she helped him replace the stones and cover up the box. She felt cheated and also somewhat frightened. Her female equality had suddenly melted away to be absorbed in a black male cloud, darkened by an unknown mafia over which she knew she was powerless to do anything.

Jack could not remember when he was last so emotionally disturbed. What had started as a jaunt in the mountains with a lovely lady had turned into a crazy nightmare of possible fortunes and intense danger. He had never been involved in any sort of criminal activity and, while he might enjoy a quiet joint with friends, there was an appalling sense of obscenity in seeing the drug in such a massive quantity. He remembered having the same feeling when he had peered down into a vat of beer the size of a swimming pool at the Guinness factory in Dublin. It had nearly put him off drinking beer for days.

There was no logic in such thinking, he realised, no more than abattoirs should be taboo topics of conversation with the nation's meat eaters. But that's the way it was and the great heap of hashish could only mean trouble.

'Surely the owners don't intend leaving this box here for all that long,' he said. '1 can't wait to get away from here. It feels unhealthy, as if the spectre and keeper of the golden cave is chasing us away, standing guard over its treasures.'

Anke gave a sudden shudder. Casting a glance at the sky, she was thankful for the sun's low angle. Only about two hours until dusk. She gathered a scoop of desert dust in her hands and threw it up at the fresh face on the roof of the cave. Partly satisfied that the evidence of their digging was fading, she pulled her pack away from the raining dust and repeated the exercise. They then moved some stones away a distance up the trench and rolled the stone slab into the depression, keeping its tarnished side up and then roughly burying it. Finally, they scattered more desert dust on the floor of the trench until they thought it looked undisturbed.

An hour and a half later they were lying down together on the ridge high above the old workings, savouring the evening breeze and soothed by the changing colours of Sinai's heartland. The tans were fading into mustard and the sky was changing from blue to aquamarine and then to violet.

The massive black dyke that had cut the vein in their Aladdin's cave down below had dominated the climb to the ridge with a series of difficult screes and lengthy diversions. Their arrival point at the top was nearly a kilometre from the vein and they had to clamber back along the ridge to realign themselves with the old workings.

Here, on their eagle's perch high above the rest of the ragged terrain, they were at last able to collect their thoughts.

The vein was nowhere to be seen over the other side of the ridge as they studied the patchwork of criss-crossed ranges and dykes before them. They were at the highest point in the area and the ridge where they perched was like a flat, black, stony road, with its wide central section out of sight from any part of Sinai. Up here. they both felt secure.

Anke said, 'On the banks of the Rhine we build castles in such places and the British also, I think, in Scotland and Wales. Do you think we can throw rocks down when the drug barons come back? Or do we need some catapult or something?'

She laughed as she felt the tension of the last couple of hours start to melt away.

SIX

They walked along the ridge for another half hour hoping to find corresponding geology on the eastern side but eventually the fading light made them stop. Their black 'stony' road was undulating all the way but still remained higher than adjacent ridges. The sun set as an orange flame of sending wild sprays of fire into the low level dust bands of the Sinai sky as it kissed the ragged horizon of the interior mountains.

The dyke had created step-like structures along the ridge where the basalt had cleaved into perfect oblong steps and troughs. Jack put his pack down in a clean oblong trough and helped Anke off with hers.

'This will do,' he said, 'Some nice backrests, tables, chairs and bunks.'

'Ja perfect.' she grinned and began loosening her boot laces. 'I'll have a martini and lemonade ... and while you're there put some UB40 on the juke box.'

'We are getting a little low on martini but I can offer L'eau de Nile and may be a bit of Dylan.'

His fantasy was suddenly ripped apart by a sudden screaming roar overhead that sent them diving into the corners of their hollow. Three Tornado jets streaked over the mountains at low level and disappeared into the gloom of the east as quickly as they had appeared.

'Holy Jesus, Jack gasped as he slowly raised his head. 'I forgot there could be a war over there at any time. There's certainly not much warning with these guys. Do you think we will know if there has been an attack?'

'Aww,' Anke growled, 'I thought for a moment that they attack us.' She rubbed a shoulder bruised by her dive for cover. 'May be we only know when the air smells wrong and we get skin sores and streaming eyes.'

Jack laid his bedroll on a flat slab that provided a view to the west and invited her to put hers nearby. The breeze had gone with the last of the sun; the wilderness was perfectly still and totally silent as they lay on their stomachs, heads propped up on their hands. In the cool calm they let their thoughts unravel their long day.

'This place is full of paradoxes,' said Jack quietly. 'The cradle of humanity. Moses was supposed to have come down from a mountain over there with the Ten Commandments and when we look all we see are three Tornado jets. We think we are alone in a gold mine and have found some of the Earth's greatest riches and discover *there were others* there before us, probably ignorant of their surroundings, who turn it into a no-go storage area for their clandestine modern day riches.'

'I think you are right,' said Anke. 'This is like a maze, like a board game. At first you imagine you fight only the puzzle of geology then after the first throw there is the ogre of Egyptian security to get around. So after a while you throw a six and move on only to battle with blast furnace heat and the tortures of the desert. Isn't it so?'

Anke paused, 'Then when you think you've found the treasure, the rules are changed and someone throws in the vild card of drug barons. One false move and you don't even get the chance to start again, and all along the journey round the board you risk being vaporised by some other board operator five hundred kilometres away in the form of Saddam Hussein. Huh, it would be a fun game if it ver not a reality.'

Jack laughed at her assessment of their day and wished he had a dice.

They fell silent again and watched the sky fade until the ragged mountains on the horizon melted into the gloom. Anke pulled her boots up to make head rests and rolled lazily over on to her back. She cupped her head in her hands and stared up into the night sky.

'I used to dream of gazing at such skies when I was in Germany,' she said, 'but there it was either too cold or too cloudy to enjoy it for very long. I suppose you fishers know all the constellations.'

'You must be joking,' Jack retorted. 'We just punch buttons on satellite navigators these days to give us lat and long positions down to the accuracy of a tennis court. I might recognise the Plough and Orion but that's about my limit.'

'How then would we find our way out of this desert place if I had not brought my compass and we lost the vein?' she teased.

'My sixth sense, would get me out of any place,' boasted Jack. 'You take me to any location in a strange city and I will take you back to your starting point by the most direct route. I guess I'm lucky. I was born like that.'

'Aah,' she groaned. 'Your luck! I forgot you have always the luck with you. Maybe you should lose some of it because it is too strong. Most people would be satisfied to find gold worth thousands of marks each ton but, *nein, mein* fisher has to discover a million marks of hashish under it, all ready to market, without a crusher, without a concentrator, without smelter, already wrapped in a nice little box. Vhy don't you find the gold like this, in nice little bars, and then all we have to do is deposit them in our nice little Swiss bank accounts. Then we don't have to bother about money, only to write cheques for evermore against its value.'

'And what would we tell Egyptian customs as we were leaving Cairo on the way to Geneva? "Gold bars? Oh yes, just melted down grandma's earrings. No problem *Effendi,* put them on as cargo, there's a good fellow. Here's ten guineas baksheesh." Hmm! I'm sure they would go for that one."She gave him a sudden dig in the ribs, 'Hey, you just reminded me. That's what happened at the foot of Mount Sinai.'

She leapt up and felt in her packsack's pockets and came back with a pencil torch and a pocket edition of the Old Testament.

'Got this from Carlos, the young Brazilian guy who lives at your camp back in Dahab,' she said. "He's on some sort of pilgrimage and gave it to me when I was asking him about Moses. He said he could not understand the old English language. I have had to read it several times because the old English is difficult for me also but now I understand the story quite well. Listen to this ...'

While quickly thumbing the pages near the beginning of the book to find the exact text she gave the setting for the extract.

'After Moses had led the children of Israel out of Egypt across the Red Sea, which conveniently parted for them and closed behind them, engulfing the Egyptians who gave chase, they entered the wilderness, which is where we are, and finally camped at the foot of Mount Sinai. God is then supposed to have called Moses up into the clouds of Mount Sinai where he was given numerous instructions, including the Ten Commandments. There are pages of these instructions.'

Anke turned to Exodus chapter thirty-three verse two and began reading:

And Aaron said unto them, break off the golden earrings which are in the ears of your wives, of your sons and of your daughters and bring them to me. And all the people broke off the golden earrings that were on their ears and brought them to Aaron.

And he received them at their hand and fashioned it with a graving tool, after he had made it a golden calf: and they said, these be thy gods of Israel, which brought thee up out of the land of Egypt"'

As he sat listening to Anke reading, Jack decided there was something rather poignant about hearing the story of Moses as he lay there under the stars on a mountain top in the middle of Sinai. He felt his heart warm towards her and he knew that he was not only enraptured by the land about him but also that he had fallen in love. She had paused, waiting for a response.

'So you think if we change the gold into a calf and take it through Customs saying we melted down grandma's earrings they would let us through then?'

She had a ready answer. 'These guys, maybe crazy but Egyptians, Coptic or Muslim, share the Old Testament with the Jews and they know better than you or I what happened to the calf. The Israeli's drunk it.'

'Drunk it?'

'Yes. Moses went crazy when he came down and found them worshipping an idol. Listen, verse twenty,' and she resumed reading:

And he took the calf which they had made and burnt it in the fire and ground it to a powder and strewed it upon the water and made the children of Israel drink it.

'Powerful stuff,' said Jack. 'Only one thing wrong. You can't burn gold or grind it, come to that. Gold is the most malleable of all metals. Also it's not soluble in water. Imagine the uproar there would be if every time hands got washed, wedding rings dissolved away - disappearing down plug holes.'

She laughed. 'Must have been very impure ... stuff?' She added the last word with conjecture, looking at Jack for approval.

He grinned, 'Yes ... stuff.'

'It's a good story anyway,' said Anke. 'Even three thousand years ago people were obsessed by gold. And what about the items the children of Israel were instructed to bring as offerings to God? It seems the gold earrings were looted from the Egyptians because it says earlier that they *borrowed gold and silver* and that they *did spoil the Egyptians*, which I take means to steal it'

'Old animosities certainly die hard,' said Jack. 'Nothing much has changed, has it?'

'It's easy to be cynical,' said Anke, 'but really most of the troubles of this region stem from these early chapters of Exodus. I was amazed when I read them. At school we only had the nice stories told to us and none of the political implications. Listen to this when God is speaking to the Children of Israel through Moses:

*I will set thy bounds from the Red Sea even
unto the sea of the Philistines, and from the desert
unto the river: for I will deliver the inhabitants of
the land into your hand; and thou shalt drive them
out before thee.*

'Sounds like the Royal Command as we say in
English,' Jack said. 'The Sea of Philistines is the
Mediterranean. It's no wonder those guys on the
West Bank and Gaza Strip are pretty pissed off
and very determined to get their land back. I
suppose in nineteen forty-seven the Allies thought
they were on pretty safe ground having the
backing of the scriptures, when they carved out
the state of Israel in what had been Arab land for
hundreds if not thousands of years.'

Anke waited as he held a long pause before
voicing his thoughts. 'It may sound blasphemous
but what if that old man Moses who came down
from the clouds, the same guy who had previously
murdered an Egyptian landowner because he was
hard on his Israeli workers, what if this old guy
just simply made all this up?'

Anke gasped. 'Mama Mia! Well excuse me a
minute while I move away so as not to get burnt
by the thunderbolt. Made it up,' she echoed. 'You
mean all these laws of the Old Testament, the
fundamentals of the Jewish faith, Islamic faith
and the Christian faith, could all be based on one
old man's fantasies? That's quite a what if.'

'Yes,' agreed Jack, 'but if Moses had not been
believed it would mean the whole of history would

have taken a different course. Arafat would not be running round looking for a place for the Palestinians to live and probably Saddam Hussein would not have to threaten every infidel in the world with a holy war. The Jews and the Muslims did not believe Christ when he came along, at least not when he said he was the son of God, so what if people had not believed Moses? After all he was having a power base crisis and told Aaron and the priests not to come near the mountain when he went up Mount Sinai. He said he must be alone with God and maybe figured he would have to come down with a good story to convince the restless Children of Israel of his leadership. It's an old ploy when you have trouble within your own ranks to divert attention by launching an attack elsewhere. Look at Saddam Hussein.'

Jack took the torch and bible from Anke and cast his eye down the text to where Moses destroys the golden calf and begins to reassert his leadership.

Then Moses stood in the gate of the camp, and said, who is on the Lord's side? Let him come unto me. And all the sons of Levi gathered themselves together unto him.

'The sons of Levi were Moses' immediate family, his own clan,' interposed Jack.

And he said unto them, Thus saith the Lord God of Israel, Put every man his sword by his side, and go in and out from gate to gate throughout the camp, and slay every man his brother and every man his companion and every man his neighbour.

And the children of Levi did according to the word of Moses: and there fell of the people that day about three thousand men.

'If that's not putting down an attempted coup I don't know what is,' said Jack. 'Maybe the Kurds in northern Iraq would agree that there are alarming similarities today.'

Anke felt his interpretations beginning to annoy her. 'Fisher,' she almost exploded. 'They did believe him and that is that. It's no good you speculating three thousand years and a billion believers later that these were only fantasies of Moses because you are not going to change history now.'

Anke took the torch and bible from him and put them down carefully out of reach. Suddenly she turned and in a flash jumped on his unsuspecting body, sitting astride his stomach, pinning his arms down with her hands. He was helpless. His mind raced, trying to decide whether she was hugely upset and or simply playing, relieving the tension. Whatever the reason, this Amazonian, Aryan woman, was sitting on top of his stomach with her long warm thighs resting either side of his body. His mind floated, he knew his erection was only seconds away and there would be no way to hide it. It would rise up under her shorts and try to escape up her back.

In the nick of time, her knees poked into his ribs and he let go in a convulsion of hopeless tickled laughter. He bucked and rocked even with her weight on him until he was breathlessly pleading for mercy.

Anke enjoyed every moment of his discomfort. As he gasped for air she leant forward until her nose was only centimetres from his. She hissed at him through her teeth, 'Fisher, they did believe him and that is that.'

She relaxed her mouth into its natural pout and lowered it slowly on to his. He imagined from behind his closed lids that her eyes closed as well.

The world of Jack Polglaise spun off into another orbit, lost in a celestial haze that took him higher than the clouds. When he opened his eyes Anke was back on her sleeping bag, crouching down with her torch and bible and thumbing through the pages.

He propped himself up on his elbows and the light from her torch caught enough of the wet sparkle in his eyes and the smiling flash of his teeth and to tell her of his orbital mental flight into the clouds. Enough, also, for her to know that her impulsive action had raised more than her own heartbeat. She felt a warm drop of perspiration roll slowly down between her breasts and creep across her belly until it lodged in the waist band of her shorts as she fought to concentrate on the texts in front of her.

'I am not really religious,' she said, not daring to look in his direction while still off balance, 'but I'm not tempting fate while we're here. It's too close to heaven.'

'But I only said "What if ..."'

'Don't. Don't even think about it,' she commanded. 'Let's talk about gold and the Israelites. I've found the verses here.' She indicated her bible. 'The children of Israel were crazy about gold and this illustrates it. While Moses was up Mount Sinai he was instructed by God to order the Israelites to make for him so many things. They're all here in Exodus chapter twenty-five.' She began reading:

And this is the offering which ye shall take of them; gold and silver and brass.
And blue, and purple, and scarlet, and fine linen, and goats' hair,
And rams' skins dyed red, and badgers' skins, and shittim wood.
Oil for the lamp, spices for anointing oil,
And for sweet incense, Onyx stones, and stones to be set in the Ephod, and in the breastplate.

'Can you imagine,' she said, 'all these riches piled up? Masses of colour; sparkling metals; lovely smells of incense and anointing oils and animal furs. This God certainly knew what was nice to have in those days.'

She continued quoting – about the ark being overlaid with pure gold *within and without* and how it should have *a crown of gold round about* and *four rings of gold* with *staves of shittim wood*, to be overlaid with gold.

She read also of *a mercy seat of pure gold* and *two cherubims of gold.*

Anke sighed. 'And it goes on and on; candlesticks, dishes, bowls and tongs all of pure gold. Garments for the priests with rings of pure gold, chains of pure gold, and altar boards overlain in gold. The list spans five chapters. I asked myself many times where they got all this gold from.'

'I know where you are thinking Anke,' said Jack, partly recovered from his trance. He pointed into the darkness towards the area of the old workings. 'Down there. Well, maybe. It's a nice thought. I'll dream about it tonight and see if I come up with any conclusions.'

Secretly, however, he hoped his dreams would be a replay of Anke's attack. Anke's Germanic rendering of the old English verses had enchanted him. Briefly he felt as if he were a monk on some spiritual mission high in the mountains.

'Shalt I set thy table that we might eat and be satisfied afore going hence to our beds *mein* geologist?'

She laughed. 'I'm still waiting for my martini.'

SEVEN

Helped by the light from her pencil torch, Anke laid out their food supplies on a towel and sat in an oblong trough in the middle of the ridge facing Jack. Her back rested firmly against a smooth face of basalt. The rocks emitted warmth like hearth stones in the still night air

A peace descended on them as if they were sharing their supper table with the Gods. Shooting stars fell from the sky from time to time and seemed to disappear below them to the east and to the west. The sky was as intensely black as she could ever remember and no part of it was without countless tiny stars. Whole masses of the Milky Way shimmered in a haze of light; distant galaxies sparkled in every quarter of the sky. Some of the brighter stars seemed so intense and near that Anke had to readjust her eyes to bring them into focus after looking at those in the more distant backdrop. The whole sky had assumed a three-dimensional appearance that descended beneath them on either side.

Her thoughts strayed to Moses and what Jack had said. She inwardly acknowledged he could be right; however, the concept of God remained intact as a creator and guide of life, a supernatural force with the ultimate power to define, control and manage anything past and future. That concept could never change in her mind. How could it? she reasoned as she ran the palm of her hand along the warm basaltic rock and let her eyes follow a shooting star in an arc a third of the way across the sky. How could there be any doubt about the existence of an ultimate creator?

She considered the forces that had led to the creation of these ragged red granite mountains and the carving of the great rift valley a few kilometres away. It would be hard to ignore that or the vein they had explored. Wasn't it true that gold represented only a billionth of the Earth's crust and yet she and Jack had witnessed a site where, through an unbelievable chemical process of nature, gold had concentrated tens of millions of times over to represent a percentage rather than parts per billion? In such a place it was hard not to imagine God was talking to you.

Jack stretched towards her to pick up a piece of bread but diverted his fingers for them to gently squeeze one of her ankles. Then he delicately ran his knuckles up and down her lower shin bone rather like the way one might idly rub a cat or a dog behind the ear to assert friendship.

He gathered a disc of unleavened bread and returned to his back-rest. 'What a day,' he said softly. 'I'm sorry I raised all that argument about Moses. Now I feel ... I don't know ... selfish perhaps. I guess there was no need to verbally pollute this place with philosophies contrary to its tradition. Those arguments can wait until we are safely out of here. From now on I will render my soul to the land of Moses and not raise any dust.'

'Ach so,' said Anke. She felt relieved. *Perhaps I am beginning to understand this Englishman better now. It is his nature to present a radical standpoint to draw out the other person.* She liked that but resolved to be wary of rising to his bait in future.

She reflected how twice in the one day she had allowed her self-discipline to break down. Leaping up on to Fisher and kissing him on finding the gold was one thing, but lowering her lips slowly on to his and closing her eyes, even in a game, was quite another. What was happening to her? Had she taken leave of her senses? Why had she not looked away when the man's testicles showed under his shorts?

She shifted her position uneasily and put her legs on a new piece of ground. It strangely comforted her with its warmth and smoothness. Her calves and thighs enjoyed the warmth she found there as the first hint of the cool night air had brushed her cheeks.

The smooth warm rock took her mind back to when she had been hanging over the ledge with the sun playing on her legs and how she had felt the vulnerability of the backs of her knees and had half wished and half dared Fisher to stroke them in that moment of light-headedness.

The recollection excited her and she straightened her legs so that the soft delicate skin behind her knees came into contact with the blood warm rock. She closed her eyes, indulging her body with a few seductive moments of half mental half physical petting.

Remembering how Jack's salty lips had moistened and rendered to her own she wondered if he had enjoyed being the victim of her attack. She conceded there was a moment when she had sensed his powerful sensuality. While sitting astride his tight stomach she had felt a tingle in the air and his body smell had played chemical tricks with her secretion organs. Her suspicions were confirmed with a defiant squeeze of the muscles of her vagina to reveal the sweet tackiness still lurking there.

*

Jack tidied away after their meal and laid out his bed roll. He arranged a pillow, took off his shoes, slackened off his shorts and pulled up a light sheet to cover himself. Now he could submit totally to the enchantment of the heavens.

He fixed his gaze on the mass of stars above and let his mind drift back through the amazing day. He felt uneasy. He could not convince himself that it was possible to take a day's hike off the road and stumble across a millions of dollars' worth of riches without either trespassing or being followed. The owners of the hashish could obviously return to collect it at any time, but the old workings were surely only a short-term storage area until onward distribution was arranged. With any luck, he and Anke would soon be clear of the area and their involvement would never be known; but what of the old mine?

He could never imagine ore containing so much gold. Copper or lead-zinc, yes, that would be acceptable, but gold in those proportions was too incredible to think about. Every ton of that grade ore contained more value than he could earn in a lifetime. There seemed no logic, no reason to life itself anymore. He suddenly realised all values would change if he found himself with thousands of dollars in his pockets for the effort of less than a day's work. The driving force to maintain a lifestyle would be absent and he wasn't sure that would ultimately be good for him.

It was then that he made a conscientious decision.

There was no saying that there was any more high-value ore beyond the ton or so that formed the overhang against the dyke. What was available beneath the box and the broken floor was anybody's guess. One thing was certain, he was not going to hang around there the entire weekend finding out. One aspect of their find was still nagging at him and that was the location of the eastern extension of the vein beyond the dyke. They had travelled a kilometre either side of the old workings but there was no sign of anything on the eastern side at all, no similar geological structures, nothing,

The thought suddenly struck him that there was not a single *wadi* or area of low land on the eastern side. The maze of jumbled ridges and outcrops appeared to be boxed in by two substantial ranges at either end of their immediate view, both butting up against their own high basalt dyke.

He had noted another massive dyke some four or five kilometres away and parallel to their own. This completed the square and hemmed in an area of virtually inaccessible wilderness except to those hardy enough to climb into it on foot like themselves. This being so, he imagined they could have the sanctuary they needed for a couple more days of exploration without having to think about Bedouin or the military.

If we can find the faulted extension of the vein, we might have a virgin mine uncomplicated by drug barons and a sound basis for setting up an operating company with an Egyptian partner. However, it would be a huge challenge to make any sense of the new geology as all they had to go on were Anke's diagrams and measurements of the structures adjacent to the vein on the western side.

As he considered these geological issues Jack became aware of a gradual change in the environment. He turned towards the east as the moon struck its first rays of light over the horizon and immediately started to dim the intensity of the stars. He touched Anke with his foot and nodded to the moon rise. She had been scribbling in her notebook but seeing the curtain rise on the blue wilderness around them she was so spiritually moved that she put her torch and book away and wriggled into her sleeping bag, resting her head on her boots so as to get a ringside seat.

Words of a Robert Service poem came floating into Jack's head as he lay there. He recited them softly:

There's gold and it's haunting and haunting,
It's luring me on as old;
Yet it isn't the gold that I'm wanting,
So much as just finding the gold

'That's lovely,' said Anke, 'and so fitting. What is it?'

'It's from *The Spell of the Yukon* by Robert Service, a poet who was caught up in the Klondike gold rush at the turn of the century. He wrote many poems about the people who made the gold rush, and the wild beauty of the Yukon. His work has been described as poetry with hairs on its chest.'

'The Yukon,' she sighed, 'Even the name has a mystical sound to it ... still, no more than the mountains of Sinai,' she consoled herself. 'Like King Solomon's Mines, it mixes myth with reality. Isn't it so?'

The question needed no answer as they watched the moon climb out of the Rift Valley, bringing with it the familiar faint offshore breeze from the west. Jack pulled his sheet tighter around him. He looked at Anke in her lovely all-weather sleeping bag and he felt his body warm immediately.

She was all women, he reflected, and cast his mind back to when she had leapt on him in the old workings and then to when she had sat on him, taking her weight on her knees and hands. For all her size and height, she was as agile and subtle as a pre-pubescent twelve-year-old.

However, there had been nothing pre-pubescent, about the way she had held her lips against his. He heaved in a great breath and let out a long sigh. *Women,* he said silently, *will ultimately drive me to distraction.* He shut his eyes and fell into a deep sleep.

Anke hugged the sleeping bag closer to her body and idly watched the moon climb into the night sky. Her thoughts went over and over the geological sequences that had led them to discover the old gold mine. There was enough classical order to their finds for her to write a lengthy paper and enough evidence for her to attract or form a mining company with herself as spearhead. That is what she wanted, what she needed to balance the accounts of those frustrating negative years working in Germany.

The box of hashish continually interrupted her dreams, turning them into nightmares. Surely, she reasoned, once an organised team returned with surveying gear, organised camps for field operations, brought in four-wheel drive vehicles and so on, the owners of the dope would discretely take it away to find another hiding place and nothing further would be out of the ordinary.

Suddenly, she knew what she had to do. She would clear the way ahead by alerting the owners with a note saying it was no longer a secret hiding place and if they knew what was good for them they would take their box and never be seen in the area again. Her widened attitude towards cannabis couldn't allow an outright condemnation of their smuggling operation while seeing nothing wrong with smoking a joint in her own western society.

She thought she had detected the same conflicts going on in Jack's mind and his solution had been to run away from it. *That's fair enough in his case but he is not on an expedition to achieve an ambition.* She remembered the poetry Jack had recited earlier:

Yet it isn't the gold I'm wanting
So much as just finding the gold

Was that true? she wondered, and turned over uneasily in the sleeping bag. Didn't all women have a weakness for gold? Hadn't the Bedouin and Egyptian women looked exciting with their glinting gold earrings, neck chains, rings and bangles? Wasn't it a woman's prerogative to be lured by gold? Since the planet began women had been decked out in gold.

Anke's fingers went up to her bare ears, naked and unadorned. The piercings that existed there had only ever been filled with light impulsively bought pieces of art deco or costume jewellery, and worn briefly. She traced her neckline down to where a chain might have lain; her fingers touched the tight lacy confines of the upper hem of her bra and imagined a golden cross nestling there. She could surely be forgiven for wanting the merest tokens of womankind from her own gold mine. Why should she not look feminine once she had proven her equality? It was a hypocritical attitude, she recognised to spend her adult life striving to prove she was equal to any man only to ultimately demonstrate her female weakness.

She shifted uneasily in her sleeping bag as the different sides of her subconscious played tug of war with each other. She reached a hand behind her to undo the clasp in the middle of her back. With a quick wriggle and a dip of an arm she slid out of her bra. Smiling inwardly, she cupped her breasts in her hands and squeezed them gently upwards. At the same, time drew her knees up into the foetal position and pulled her head inside the bag.

Wickedly she squeezed her nipples, promising herself that men were going to have to gaze helplessly at those two lobes with a chunky gold cross sitting there while she instructed them to get back to their drafting tables and carry out her orders. Yes, and then she would lean forward across the table of the most lustful of all those men and when her breasts overshadowed his work and he was thinking that he was going to get special treatment she would whisper into his ear, 'Make us a cup of coffee, there's a good chap. Oh, and remember it's after one so add my normal afternoon one spoonful of sugar please.'

She grinned at the thought. Perhaps she could hire some of the guys from her old office; she knew they were threatened with redundancies and she could surely find them jobs with theodolites, especially if it was August and forty degrees.

She smiled at the thought of balancing the account. She brought a heel up to push her loosened shorts to the foot of the sleeping bag. Her fingers slid under the elastic of her pants and down through the mass of tawny curls to the welcoming warm stickiness she had felt earlier. Here another account had waited to be settled since the fisherman's erection had prodded her in the back only a few hours ago.

EIGHT

When Jack finally gave up trying to get back to sleep he reckoned from the moon's position well down to the west that it must be around four a.m. His limbs were stiff from the intense cold and there were no more towels and spare clothes to wrap around his freezing body. He decided the only solution was to get up and take a brisk walk along the ridge swinging his arms in exaggerated arcs to regain circulation and warmth.

During the night he had moved his bed roll into the hollow close to Anke's sleeping bag to escape the breeze and take advantage of any warmth that might escape from her cocooned bundle, but still he been unable to get warm again. There was a startling difference between sleeping up here on the ridge and on the beach in Dahab. He vowed to be more choosey about his next night's camp site.

For an hour he paced up and down the basalt pavement, slowly loosening his stiffened bones as he waited for the sunrise. Long before the moon set the eastern sky lightened and the first colour crept on to the mountain tops to the west. He noticed Anke moving about attending to her personal needs and left her to it while he caught the first of the sun's rays on his face as it slashed the eastern horizon in tangerine fire.

A few minutes later he joined her and they ate some of her sesame seed bars and some dates.

They agreed their first priority was to find a way down off the ridge and then systematically search for the continuation of the vein.

The day had become warming and beautifully fresh and clear by the time they trekked back along the ridge, making sure to stay most of the time on the eastern side of the black dyke so that their silhouettes were not visible against the skyline. By the time they had retraced their steps to a point above the old workings the new geology on the eastern side had become more familiar to them, thanks to having now viewed it for a second time. Anke shook her head in despair at the realisation there were no structures here to match those on the western side of the dyke.

Jack took a large slab of basalt and rolled it to the edge of the ridge on the eastern side. He propped it up so that it was clearly visible from down below. It was a marker that they would need later on, he said.

It took another two hours and three kilometres of several tough climbs before they found a way down on the eastern side where a large section of the overhang had broken off to form long steep screes below. The sun blazed down on them and the rocks began to feel warm and comfortable again.

Jack scrambled down to the lowest point of the dyke but there was still a five-metre drop to the top of the scree below. He looked up at Anke and cocked his eyebrows in an unspoken gesture that meant 'shit or bust'. He flexed his knees and dropped as lightly as possible on to the head of the scree, leaning back into the mountainside as he landed. Loose stones scattered alongside as he came to a stop twenty metres down the slope.

'Just pretend it is a piste at Innsbruck,' he shouted up to Anke. But she was in no need of coaxing to make the leap; she was already skimming towards him like a water skier. A bow wave of small stones and gravel buried Jack up past his ankles as he grabbed her as she came abreast of him.

'Jesus, I should have brought abseiling gear.' She looked back at the overhang and followed it along several kilometres in both directions. 'There's no other route down.'

'Nor up,' replied Jack with a pretence of alarm.

'*Sheise,* Jack. You will have to look for manna in a few days so you had better start reconsidering your interpretations of Exodus. Let's get back up the scree and look at the underneath of the dyke for indications of movement. We can always climb out of this wilderness by going up the far range butting up against this ridge. At least, it looked possible from our camp this morning.'

'You mean I won't have to spend forty years here with only a crazy German geologist for company?'

'Climb Fisher,' she commanded, 'or you will never see the Promised Land either.' She gave him a friendly dig in the ribs and set him wondering about her last remark.

At the top of the scree they found a high point to the fine material that ran back at an angle beneath the overhang to form a shady hollow and perfect sanctuary from the afternoon sun.

While Jack put down his pack and pulled off his shoes to tip out the gravel gathered during their descent, Anke moved forward to check the underside of the dyke.

Suddenly, she let out a piercing shriek and froze to the spot. Jack saw the quick movement of a brown and yellow snake sliding away between the stones in front of her. She cautiously retraced her steps to the security of his side. She shuddered. 'Ugh.'

'Ugh indeed,' echoed Jack. 'I guess this is more than a sanctuary for humans. I'm not so keen on walking along this parapet now.'

Anke shuddered again, 'I'm going to walk down there in the open desert and sunshine. The serpents can have their sanctuary.'

'You're not going to offer me an apple then?'

'The next time I think this is the Garden of Eden I'll let you know. Meanwhile I'm returning to the wilderness.'

'What about this fault?'

She hesitated and cast her eyes suspiciously in both directions before focussing on the blank face of the dyke. Then in less than twenty seconds she pulled her dip metre out of a side pocket, stuck it on the footwall of the dyke and rattled off her findings. 'Seventy-five degrees' true dip to west, no scratches, no ridges, no signs. That's it, I'm off, I'll write it up out there ...' and she set off down the scree.

Jack laughed and followed smartly on her heels, careful not to fill his shoes again. Once clear of the stones, they were back on hard ground with its carpet of red granite flakes and sun-beaten outcrops of hard pre-Cambrian basement rocks. There were several small black dykes about but none appeared to run into 'the great dyke' as they had come to call it. The little black dykes that ran parallel with the rift valley and provided no information.

Anke suggested that they walk back in the direction of the old workings, keeping an eye open for quartz fragments and mapping any structures that ran in towards the great dyke. This way would help them build up a picture to compare with the west side of the ridge.

The great rampart of the ridge towered high beside them to the west. Boxing them on all other sides were the near mountain ranges to the north, south and east. To Jack it was like being in a crater or a lost world. There was no hint of any wind. Only their footsteps and voices broke the silence, echoing back crisply off the underside of the ridge. He felt it to be a breath-taking environment, a place more suited to gods and mystical beings. It was a privilege simply being there.

'Ever since we jumped off the rim and down on to the scree I've felt that we were in another place, another world,' he said. 'It's so different from the open country we were in before. This basin has its own spirit and identity. Dahab and fishing projects, Europe and people, all seem a million miles away. It's as if we're walking on a virgin planet, free to unravel its mysteries. The serpent did not rise up against us ... it went on its way. This place is at peace with itself. I want to run and shout; I want to sing; I want to skip along the valleys; I want to dance in its dust and cry out "Look, I'm here, the human of your planet. I love you. I throw my arms out to you. Look after me for I am your servant and you are mine. We are brothers. Your serenity is greater than any other place in the universe; I respect, cherish and love you. Sing to me great wilderness of time. Sing to me for I am listening".'

Anke stopped and turned and stared at him. He grinned and looked away sheepishly, 'Got a bit carried away there,' he said.

She unleashed a smile he found both devastating and understanding. 'It's a good job I didn't let you loose on that hashish,' she said. 'But don't worry, I feel it too,' she said over her shoulder, unable to meet his eyes any longer.

They continued picking their way among chunks of dyke and red granite boulders until they were able to focus on a place where hard rock went right up to the great dyke. Jack bobbed along singing quietly to himself while Anke meandered on a roughly parallel course, checking an outcrop here and there. The singing and meandering quickly ceased and the sweating resumed when they had to climb for several minutes to regain the big dyke.

'Phew,' breathed Anke. 'It starts already to get hot.' Suddenly she perked up, 'Hey, look here.'

She dug out purple fragments of clay and gravel from between the dyke and the granite of the basin. The granite face had been torn and ground several centimetres deep into its normal matrix. Anke pushed out a section of this fault zone and for them both to examine. Enough slip planes, oriented particles and graphitic looking streaks lined up in the same direction. When orientated with the dyke they seemed close to horizontal, dipping perhaps five degrees to the south.

'There's no way to tell whether the movement has been to the north or south,' Jack said. 'But presuming it is still a block fault, the vein must lie to the south, the way we are going, judging by the slight dip in that direction. I never expected to see a horizontal fault here when all the others have been vertical. If this is right, we are in with a chance.'

Anke agreed that such a large horizontal displacement would explain why they hadn't found any similar structures here. 'I reckon we are a couple of hundred metres lower here than we were the other side of the ridge. To get similar surface structures we would have to be at least a couple of kilometres the other side of your marker on the ridge.'

Jack shook his head. 'That's impossible. All the other displacements where dykes have cut the vein have been centimetres not miles.'

'Not all,' she countered. 'Remember the ridge where you held my ankles?' He raised his eyebrows, how could he forget? 'We thought there was a displacement of many metres but we couldn't measure it.'

'True,' he conceded, 'but the gold vein was nearly vertical so it makes no difference whether we are two metres or two hundred metres lower on this side. That means we can search for quartz pieces as soon as we pass the marker on the ridge, *mish quidda*? Isn't it so?'

She nodded in agreement and they clambered down to more even ground and headed south. By ten o'clock they relocated the marker Jack had set up on the ridge. In most places along the way they saw only screes leading up to the great basaltic dyke. There was thus little point in staying close to the dyke and so they started mapping and measuring only when they were half a kilometre away from it.

When they came across some larger outcrops offered a bit of shade they sat down for a late breakfast. Anke downed a complete bottle of water without stopping. She claimed the air was as hot now as it had been at two o'clock the previous day. The great wall of the dyke deflected the sun's rays back into the basin like a parabolic mirror. The basin trapped the heat and there was no discernible air circulation. Anke's blue T-shirt showed dark wet patches all over the back where it rested between her skin and the packsack. Her hair stuck to her forehead and neck.

Jack called her attention to a bird of prey soaring in the thermal currents high over the ridge before swooping down to a nest on a ledge part the way down the overhang of the dyke. White guano stains running down the smooth rock face clearly marked the nesting site.

'Not a lot of threat to that nest,' said Jack.

'Whatever do they find to live on?'

'Rodents, small birds and maybe fish as we can't be more than a few kilometres from the sea. Just over that next range I guess. I thought at first it was an osprey; they live on fish but they usually nest in low scrub or marshes close to the sea. They are very rare. I once went really close to an osprey nest in southern Sudan to take a look but the adults became very aggressive and I came away without seeing inside. Can't even do that in Scotland. The nesting site in Loch Garten has a twenty-four-hour guard on it, the birds are considered so rare.'

'I should think they are pretty safe here,' said Anke. 'Two life forms from the animal and plant kingdom seen in two days hardly represents overcrowding.'

They moved on slowly, conscious of the heat and following even ground when possible. They carried water bottles, sipping mouthfuls every quarter of an hour. By noon they had mapped about ten small dykes coming from under the scree and heading out towards the centre of the basin. They detected no quartz or even any other form of mineralisation.

'It's gone,' declared Anke after another hour. 'We must be two kilometres plus now from the marker.' She looked frustrated but was not yet resigned to being beaten. 'Let's rest for a few minutes. There is no shade but 1 can't think in such heat when I'm moving along.'

They sat on a big granite slab in a flat exposed area of weathered bed rock. After a long weary silence Jack spoke.

'We passed last night's camp way back so all this geology is new to us from above and at ground level. The southern boundary to our Garden of Eden is less than an hour away so we will see if you are right about a route up.'

She pointed to the south east. 'There is some sort of drainage pattern away from the ridge so maybe there is an escape *wadi* or dried lake bed in the distance towards the sea. But it's not going to help us with the geology because it looks as if the outcrop is buried in sand further on.'

He followed her gaze and relaxed in the shimmering heat. His eyes briefly closed and his head went light. Waking with a jolt only moment later, he felt for an instant more awake than he had been for some while and his tunnel vision fell on an anomaly in the bed rock some fifty metres away. He shook off his weariness and strolled over to have a look.

It was the merest fracture in the granite, a hairline of black- tourmaline with secretions of red ochre that feathered out from it for two centimetres. He could see the fracture line disappearing under stones in the distance. Turning round he detected it running in towards the great dyke in more or less a straight line before becoming indistinguishable among the debris at the bottom of the scree.

He delved back into his memory, to when they first started mapping the day before and Anke had him pacing off lengthy distances. He called out to her: 'I seem to remember telling you I saw a stringer and you wrote something down. Can you check it?'

She thumbed through her notes and diagrams. After a few moments she gave him an apologetic look. 'Sorry, nothing. I couldn't have written it down.'

'You did. I saw you ... wait ... you didn't like stringer and called it something else ... fracture? Parallel fracture? I told you stringers are what we call structures parallel to or leading to an existing ore body in Cornwall. It was the only structure I saw all day older than the black dykes.'

'Got it,' she interrupted. 'Parallel fracture, twelve hundred metres north side of vein. But it was about two kilometres away from this big fault.'

'*Malesh*. Never mind. The vein went straight enough until it got cut in half. This little fellow is straight enough, it's parallel and the only thing the right age.' He wiped his brow. 'Twelve hundred metres, that's to the edge of the theatre Babe; to the wall of the Garden of Eden.'

He set his sights and started marching. At ten paces he stopped. 'My mind is so cooked I don't think I can count that much.'

She came and stood shoulder to shoulder. She prodded him lightly in the back. 'Count, Fisher,' she commanded with a laugh. I will cross off every hundred when you shout and if we stop I will write down the number you tell me.'

'There is nothing much to stop on unless we collapse,' he said miserably. 'We are going to lose the outcrop shortly and then it's only sand. Let's go for it; straight to the corner of the Garden.'

The white sand shimmered in the two o'clock sun and the mirages cut off the mountains' feet with blue lakes. We must be mad, both of us, mad, thought Jack; *Ninety-eight, ninety-nine, hundred. One, two, three, was that six hundred or seven hundred? Nine ... ten ... eleven ... must be half way to the mountain range. Nineteen ... twenty ...* He plodded on in a state of near delirium. They were nearing the comer and the breathless air was becoming more and more unbearable.

'Stop,' commanded Anke. He could only remember counting ninety. 'That's one thousand. At least there's some outcrop again now. Let's head straight up into the corner where the range is cut by the great dyke.'

They moved forward slowly. 'One hundred and seventy,' Jack murmured, looking up at the screes ahead and to his right. 'There's no point in counting any more. I've run out of Eden.'

Both were convinced that their Garden of Eden would bestow a perfect gold vein on them to complete its mystical image and neither was prepared to accept failure. There was no wall of quartz running across the desert like on the other side, only loose rubble of granite and black dyke from two intersecting screes. No pot at the end of the rainbow.

It was all so discouraging Jack was sweating heavily and his lids felt heavy. He could see Anke was suffering badly. Her face was bright red and her nose and cheeks looked cruelly sunburned, her T-shirt was soaked in sweat and perspiration was making her body shine like burnished brass.

Jack noticed a narrow wedge of shade up in under the dyke's overhang. They had to get in there, snakes or no snakes. To stay out in the heat much longer was far too dangerous.

Anke stopped and shuddered as they neared the shady little hollow.

'Serpents,' she wailed bitterly. 'Wait!'

She picked up a stone and lobbed it into the hollow and waited to see if she could hear anything. There was silence. She picked up another stone and was about to throw it after the first when her arm froze in mid-flight.

'Not another snake?' said Jack.

Anke was not listening. She was staring at what she held in her hand. It was a very dusty well-disguised piece of long-awaited quartz.

*

They rested briefly under the overhang of the Great Dyke and had something to eat. Even Jack's salted shark meat was attacked with surprising enthusiasm. He had extracted two packs of dehydration salts from his first aid box and they downed these a bottle of water each. Gradually their equilibrium was restored. Anke spread some soothing cream over her face. She was secretly thankful for Jack's enforced lunch break but still was unable to restrain herself from searching out another half dozen of small heavily disguised fragments of quartz from the dusty debris nearby.

The moment Jack declared lunch was over they ceremoniously lined up the fragments ready for cracking with his hammer. Using a large rock as an anvil each stone was split, with the fragments then passed to Anke for inspection under her magnifying glass.

One by one the broken pieces were lined up on the bank after undergoing her inspection. She remained tight lipped throughout. Even after inspecting the shattered pieces of the last stone she continued to ponder over them, examining every face. Eventually she gathered them in one hand and hurled them into the desert with all her force.

'Fisher,' she screamed. 'You will have to do better than that.'

Then she cracked. Eight years of exasperation, a hundred thousand pieces of data copied and processed. Now she knew it was all over.

Jack stared at her.

The pout collapsed at the corners of her mouth, her lips trembled. This was an Anke he did not know. Tears welled over her lids and rolled down her cheeks, making tracks through the protective cream. She staggered over to him and buried her face in his shirt. Great sobs shook her body as she began to cry like a child Jack put an arm around her shoulder and sat her down on the bank. He patted her gently on the back and twirled a finger tenderly in the golden hair at the base of her neck. He tried telling her not to worry, not to get upset about the silly old gold. That they had found the old mine was success enough.

These last remarks made her wail all the more. There seemed no comforting her. Jack worried that he had allowed her to push herself too far in the heat.

'You must rest,' he told her. 'It's not a disaster; we have done brilliantly. We don't have to find any more. We will rest here and tomorrow go home. Come on, don't cry.'

He held her tightly and rocked her gently to and fro as he remembered having done so many years before with small children. As he stroked her hair he brushed it carefully away from her face to give her some air. Gradually her crying subsided and she managed to squeeze out some words amid the sobs.

'You don't understand. Only in the last stone was there nothing. All is gold, Jack, all is gold like before.' She turned her face up to look into his. 'We are sitting on a gold mine.' The tears came again accompanied by a great long howl.

*

For a long extended moment Jack remained speechless. Looking over her head he could see the broken stones lined up on the bank and, sure enough, even from where he was he could make out traces of visible gold in one or two pieces.

'I'm so mean,' she sobbed. 'I don't deserve to have all these finds. I'm so mean to you ...'

'Mean? Come on, you're not mean to me. Don't be silly. You are ....'

'I'm horrible,' she interrupted.

She suddenly broke from his embrace and sat up, addressing him directly for the first time, no longer blubbing into his shirt. Her eyes were red and inflamed and her cheeks puffed up and streaked where the tears had run through the cream.

'You know what I was going to make you do?'

'No.' he said unconcernedly.

'Work with a theodolite in forty degrees,' she sobbed, and wiped her eyes with the back of her hand, 'and make the coffee,' she added, choking and collapsing into his shirt again.

'Really,' he said with a grin. 'Such an easy life! And you were going to pay me for all that?'

'No, no, not you personally,' she cried, grasping his arm. 'You will be an executive director with me. No, it is men! Those bloody men out there who put me down.' She started crying again and hung her head over his shoulder. 'I had such cruel ideas for them. It can't be right for me to think like that. It is just as if this is the Garden of Eden ... and I'm just like Eve, I can feel the evil in me. I hate myself.'

He hugged her tighter. 'Come on, it's a commercial world and you must do as you wish concerning this lot. You are holding most of the cards so you can control the game. As for me ... I'm going to finish my contract and go back to working in my fishing boat.'

'You're not! I need you. You'll be a partner.'

'No,' he said firmly. 'My reward is working with you, working with one hell of an incredible woman.' He squeezed her, 'That's enough for me. Send me a Christmas card each year. It's your show, Babe ... I just came along for the ride.'

'But Jack, this could be the richest gold find of modern times. It's an El Dorado; you can't go back fishing. I wouldn't have found it if you had not been here. Somewhere under our feet is an untouched ore body worth tens of thousands of marks each ton; it's not an old mine that may be worked out and one that is full of hashish and a home for the mafia. We have to make our plans together. Jack, you know about these things. I don't!'

Her passionate pleas failed to shift his resolve. He found himself speaking to her as instructing a thirteen-year-old who had thrown a tantrum over her homework. 'Anke, you're a big girl now. You have all the cards in your hand so you don't deal any until you know who is interested to play. Check all the big boys out. Drive the bargain you want before you breathe a dickie-bird about where you have been the last three weeks or so. RTZ, RST, Anglo American, Cominco .... There are dozens of international companies that would be able to do all the necessary things with the Egyptian government to set up operations. Don't get caught out with some crazy local entrepreneur who will talk to you nicely and then take you for a ride. Go to the top but don't show your hand until you have what you want stitched up in a legally binding agreement. If anybody can do it Anke, you can!'

He wiped her face with his neckerchief. 'Come on, dry your eyes. Don't even think about those miserable buggers from your old office in Germany. Just send them a director's report once in a while with a few pictures of the world's richest gold mine. Hey, come on, we haven't exactly found it yet!'

He offered her a drink of water. She thanked him in a very subdued voice but felt unable to look at him.

How odd, he thought, that his imagined role as a lover had for the moment turned into a real–time role of father. He looked at her for a long time, her head still hung down. *She really is lovely.* He walked away, shaking his head from side to side.
*

'Bring me another big stone,' Jack commanded as he blocked the running scree with one arm and held a series of big stones in place with the other. 'Put it here when my arm comes up ... right, now get another one for there.' He nodded to indicate the space above the forty kilo slab Anke had just put in place.

With a solid "thump" another chunk of rock blocked off the last of the gravel and stones running from the scree. Jack relaxed for the first time in twenty minutes and stood back with Anke.

They had created a stone wall a few metres long to block off the scree and prevent it running down the hillside into the overhang under the dyke. From behind this barrier they were able to remove stones and debris down to bedrock without more gravel and stones running down on to them and burying their excavations.

For an hour they used feet and hands to clean a small area down to the bedrock. They took some of the larger stones to reinforce the barricade and guard against further avalanches into their working area.

As they laboured through the rest of the afternoon the hard wall of the quartz vein was gradually revealed from under the dust and sand. Their working area looked more like a fortified cave dwelling by the time the long purple shadows of the great dyke stole across the Garden of Eden towards day's end. The debris they had cleared off the bedrock was piled behind them. With the smooth overhang of the dyke at their backs and the stone wall running up the hillside, only the raised lip of the hollow was open to the world.

Grimy and tired, they filled peanut sample bags with chips and carefully labelled them before lining them up at the back of the hollow to await their hair grip fasteners. Jack used his tools to cut three separate channels across the vein and chipped out several large pieces of quartz for them to examine. He and Anke stared at them incredulously for several minutes. Scattered throughout were fine gold flecks or fracture planes in little golden lines.

Both were momentarily overcome by this uncovering of the regal metal, defiant and beautiful in its pristine purity as it shone out at them from its virgin vein.

Anke entered all her measurements for the dip and direction of the vein and closed her notebook before she spoke, now feeling confident for the first time since her earlier outburst.

'The gold vein is perfectly hidden from both land and air exploration,' she said. 'The line of it takes it under the scree and out across the sandy plain. There is no way anybody could know it is here unless they had the measurements we have. The old Bedouin were opportunists not geologists.'

'Maybe they ran out of luck after they made the golden calf,' Jack suggested.

'Ach-so. The luck Fisher. Do you think some of your luck has rubbed off on to me by now? In the Garden of Eden the serpent tempted Eve to take the apple who then gave it to Adam and then they knew that they had sinned. In our case it is a Garden of Eden in reverse. The serpent has given me the chance to clean myself of the sin that I had inside me and now Adam must give Eve something to complete the image. I hope it is some of your luck because you have so much it can't be healthy!'

He grinned, relieved to see her happy and sharp again. 'I'll have to think about that,' he teased, 'but I think we could come to an agreement, maybe a cocktail of things. Luck on its own is pretty hard to transfer. You would have to have it wrapped in something to make it digestible. In its raw state it would probably slide off you and do you no good.

Right now you could open up negotiations by offering me some of that orange cordial you've not opened yet. I'm gasping.'

*

They sat on the rim of their hollowed out cave house in the cool of the evening and relaxed, their mood dominated by the spirituality of their surroundings. It was as near to paradise as Jack felt he could ever be; unimaginable riches uncovered by his own hands lay at his back and at his side was an Aryan treasure house of unfathomable depths that randomly erupted in unexpected waves of supreme pleasure. In front of him was the wilderness basin they now called Eden, hidden from humanity and unmatched in its beauty.

The last of the day's sun rested on the distant mountains colouring them tawny, gold and lilac. Gaunt rocks of ancient red granite stood like sentinels protecting the cradle of humanity. The savage heat of the day had subsided to become a soothing caress on the landscape. It was the land of God, thought Jack, if ever such a being existed.

He suddenly felt a desire to have his companion beside him to share this paradise. The unwritten formalities and treaties came melting down from his head and left him in a hot sweat as he rocked gently to and fro absorbing waves of music he heard singing across the desert. His ears filled with the imagined sounds of choirs humming undulating melodies that made his heartbeat speed up to synchronise and harmonise. His eyes became hot with tears brought on by the sheer ecstasy soaring through a heart so big and brimming with love for all things that it had to spill over.

The musicians rose up from the orchestra pit to envelop his body. The sound of drums crashed round his head as the choir, its humming now at a frantic pitch, bore him along like a leaf in a whirlwind into the very Bastille of her presence.

Anke, meanwhile, languid beneath her brown, red, white and black woven blanket, was gazing out from her sheepskin carpeted tent, when she saw Moses descend from the mountainside and Aaron run to meet him.

The scattered outcrops of rock had become the tribes of Israel and gatherings of elders at the foot of the mountain. She could see flocks of sheep and goats strewn around the plain attended by shepherd children. Curly-haired toddlers played between the tents and mothers squatted in front of camp fires, many nursing infants while others prepared food. She saw one group of older women twisting raw wool from a bundle into skeins of yarn. Elsewhere donkeys were being tended by groups of women with large clay pots hung over their backs, wet round their rims from water drawn from some distant well.

In front of her was a young woman whose long, raven black, wavy hair had been released from the confines of her head dress and was being attended to by another. Her hair shone in the sunlight and crackled with electricity as it was being brushed. A second woman was applying henna to the girl's feet in delicate sweeping black patterns. Anke imagined the sensual aroma of the wood and resin smoke steeping the prospective bride's young body. She sensed the comfort of the wooden comb as it caressed the woman's hair and the tenderness of the henna brush strokes on her feet.

She saw a small girl take a tumble in the dust and felt her own eyelids growing heavy but she just remembered seeing the child pick herself up and run over to her sitting mother and nuzzle into her breasts for love and reassurance. Her eyes then fell shut and was almost unaware of her companion moving closer to while she turned slightly and accepted his offered shoulder to rest her head.

The young bride-to-be let her cotton gown slide off her delicate shoulders while the other woman put a golden chain around her neck and gently lifted her hair through it. Anke watched her adjust a bright blue pendant to rest elegantly between the bride's perfectly rounded breasts. She moved her hands delicately down the girl's sides and then slowly raised them until her fingers slid up and over the young woman's breasts, leaving her dark nipples standing high and pointing to heaven. It was an act of the purest beauty and female awareness Anke had ever seen. It sent her own heart racing as if it would burst ... and then she woke.

When she opened her eyes she found her head tucked into Jack's neck and the palms of her hands caressing her knees. She did not want to move. Her dreams had brought a sense of order and peace; if she kept still perhaps her heart would stop pounding and Jack would not question her. Only the sound of his breath broke the silence. She would remain as still as she had been in her sleep but also savour the closeness of his maleness.

Was it only three days ago that my resolve to remain outside man's zone of influence began to crumble? How can it be possible that I resting here, my head on a man's shoulder like a roosting dove pretending to be asleep? Oh God, I can't believe this. I just can't believe this.

Jack did not know how long Anke slept on his shoulder but it was quite dark and starlit when she stiffly raised her head and detached herself.

'Thanks,' she said meekly, 'you are too good to me. 1 was dreaming. Did you dream also?'

Without waiting for an answer she told him about the wilderness and Moses coming down from the mountain and the activities of the camped tribes. She related all the pastoral scenes of her sleep but carefully skirted round the details of the wedding preparation.

'I thought it was you who was getting married in your dreams,' said Jack. 'At least that's what I reckoned when your heart started pounding. You were so hot I thought you were going to have a fever or explode.'

'Hmm,' she said. 'Maybe it's a fever. Be careful you don't catch it off me.'

They both laughed – and felt the same nervous electricity. She seized the moment.

'Jack, how much water have you left? We are both so dirty from all that digging it would be really nice to have some sort of wash.'

'Seven,' he said. 'How about you?'

'Six.'

'Thirteen in all. That's unlucky so we have to reduce it to twelve even if we pour one away, so we might as well wash use it for washing.'

'You fishers are too superstitious,' she laughed and took off into the darkness with a towel and a water bottle under her arm.

While his hands were still dirty Jack scattered some fine sandy material from the scree around their 'house' and kicked the floor about until it was level and soft. After the cold of the previous night he was thankful for their new sheltered camping spot and prayed the dark hours would be as beautiful as the evening had been. The sound of choirs and a distant orchestra still hummed in his head.

He heard water splashing nearby and the sound of cleaning of flesh. He smiled. *That's one hell of a body to cover with such a small quantity of water*

... then wondered how he would ration their supply over either of their bodies.

He was jolted out of his daydreaming by the aroma of perfume; a quite primeval reaction. He was aware of the power of pleasure and seduction created by the unsuspecting whiff of such an age-old potion.

Anke emerged bare-footed from the dark wrapped in a towel and smelling like a rose. Her face looked radiant and wild. Her eyes twinkled as she pleaded not to be chastised for using nearly a whole bottle of water.

'I'll promise not to wash again until we are back,' she said, putting on a little voice and standing close so that her scent filled the space around them. At that moment Jack would have seen no reason to stop her if she had asked to bath in the whole of their remaining water.

He gave an exaggerated sniff into the air.

'Wow. Are you going to a party tonight?'

'No, I'm taking you out to dinner,' she said confidently. 'A celebration dinner, so I thought I ought to dress up. We can't let this day go by. If this had been the Yukon I'm sure the guys would have got good raving drunk and gone gambling, not to mention whoreing.'

'That's a point,' he said, 'but what does a woman do? You are probably the first female to have found a bonanza. You are creating history so what are you going to do? You can't crawl back into town and get raving drunk in a bar. This is a

Moslem country. And it's pretty hard to get a poker game going. However, finding a squaw in the form of one of these slim young handsome Bedouin boys might not be so much of a problem. Anyway, you're forgiven for taking a whole bottle of water.'

'What about you, Jack? Don't forget you are a partner in this. Don't you feel the urge to celebrate? Will you accept my offer to take you out for dinner?'

He was astounded and at the upturn of her spirits. 'Dinner?' he laughed. 'Why not? I'll dig out my tuxedo and bow tie. Where are you going to take me?'

'What about Bait el Dahab?'

'The House of Gold. Sounds good. I'll prepare myself.'

After rummaging round in his bag for clean clothes Jack took off into the darkness with toilet bag, towel and water bottle. He stripped off in the starlight and was amazed how warm it was, like the hottest part of a summer's day in England. The rocks were warm and the heat was reflecting of the great dyke like a giant radiator. He stood naked on the open ground lightened by the weight of his sweat-ridden clothes and caressed by the music still running through his head. He thought of their dinner date and suddenly felt wild again. Like he had done in the middle of the day when he had said he wanted to dance, to sing, and to shout cries of exultation in the Garden of Eden.

High on life, he thought as he swayed from side to side while splashing water over his body. He poured water on his face, shut his eyes, threw his head back and sung into the night air ... *It's a Rainy Night in Georgia*

In that moment Jack felt at peace with his world. His muscles gleamed against the stars and his body swayed with the vibrations of Randy Crawford's voice. As water streamed over his genitals he cupped them gently to wash and pulled them up on to his abdomen. *It's raining all over the world*, he sung as the L'eau de Nile dissolved the muskiness from the arousals earlier that evening. He allowed a hand to linger a little too long in self-seduction and a surge of blood flooded through his loins stiffened all his manly parts.

Stop! In the name of love'... He changed his song just in time and swivelled round on one foot to complete his wash in dramatic martial movements.

His jubilation increased when he anointed his body with dashes of Eau de Cologne. That must have happened to Anke, he thought, as she perfumed herself. So many powerful spirits surging through his brain but at that moment. He thought of the Garden of Eden; of Adam. He could align himself so easily with Adam. He remembered lines from a poem called *Adam* he had written when his spirits were on a high that defied anything to alter them. The lines seemed so appropriate at that moment that he recited them aloud into the Garden of Eden's night:

Now in solid muscle form,
Running free into hollow, onto mound and sea
Of Savannah pasture, of washing waves,
Caressing thighs, sweet freedom finding.
Ears of wild bread corn, put arms around,
Their new dancing partner,
Their welcome party for his coming of age.

He donned clean pants, combed his hair and climbed up the slope to Bait El Dahab. A faint yellow light and a long shadow were cast up on to the smooth wall of the dyke. The shadow was moving about but on hearing his approach it stopped and settled into a single profile position. Jack stopped and took stock.

Her perfume hung in the still air but another smell blended with it. His mind did somersaults. He identified the other aroma: incense. He saw wispy smoke rising in the pale light and ... Christ! Her profile ... *Surely she can't be.* Adrenalin shot through his body. He started singing to let her know he was there: *It's a rainy night in Georgia.*

*

Jack climbed the last few steps and entered Bait El Dahab. He blinked in disbelief as he took in the sight before him.

Red glows marked where two joss sticks burned at each end of their shelter. Anke's sleeping bag lay open and spread out over the floor. On a white cloth in its centre she had placed a glistening piece of gold ore broken out from the vein that afternoon. Set on top was a candle, its yellow flame forming a perfect plume in the still air. Arranged in a ring around the candle were pita breads, dates, cheeses, tomatoes, shreds of shark meat, sweet bars of sesame seeds and nuts plus a full bottle of prepared orange cordial. Facing him, illuminated in candlelight, sitting cross-legged, calm and radiant was a bare-breasted Anke, delicately brushing the ends of her blonde hair where it rested down the front of her shoulder.

She offered him a formal welcome. '*Salem elay cum. Et fudal,* Mr Polglaise,'. Her voice was soft and tranquil as she bid him sit down. '*Elay cum salam Madam Katarina,*' Jack replied. '*Entee kwiese*? Are you well?'

'*Tamam Alf-shukran*. Fine thanks.'

'*Hamdurilla*. Thanks God.'

Jack met her eyes for the first time. They were fires of sparkling jewels enhancing her alluring smile. The lengthy Egyptian greetings had given him time to override his initial shock and restore confidence to continue as if everything were quite normal.

Taking his place formally opposite her, he sat cross-legged and studiously focussed on the array of food and the gold ore beneath the candle rather than fixing his eyes on those unbelievably magnificent breasts facing him like two beautiful grapefruits, pendulous, smooth and breath-taking.

'I'm not the only one around here that does not need to take the hashish,' he said. He now raised his eyes, confident that speaking gave him a legitimate reason to look also on her breasts.

She smiled, seductively, her pout melting into a Cupid's bow.

'You like my outfit then?' she said.

He put his head to one side, appraising the delicate lines of her body, curving down from the middle of her chest, framing in the two beautiful lobes like Botticelli's Venus on her scallop shell. Delicate pink nipples floated on brown aureoles, standing firm and high to confront the world. As he marvelled at her goddess-like body he became aware of a rapid unfolding inside his pants and knew there was nothing he could do about it.

He joked that he liked the buttons on the new outfit. She giggled and her chest shook in unison, which made her giggle even more. Jack sensed it was the first time she had ever behaved in this manner.

His eyes travelled from her shoulders down to her wasp like waist and on to the curves from her buttocks and that generous German bottom. She had knotted two blue head scarfs together to form a loin cloth – her only clothing. Jack wondered how much courage she had had to muster in order to put on this show, certain it was a stage debut, beautiful and surreal and lifting him to the very gates of heaven.

'1t feels as if I dine with the Pharaohs, with a queen of some ancient dynasty, maybe even Cleopatra.' he said softly.

No stopping me now, thought Anke. Her pulse felt a steady twenty beats above normal. *This is so intoxicating*. She stopped brushing her hair, crossed her hands in her lap and smiled across the candlelight at her sinewy, overtly masculine guest.

I do indeed feel like a queen, powerful and serene, untouchable in my own land, sitting high among my priestesses on my golden throne accepting this visitor from the pages of mythology, the son of a great patriarch of legends past. She was lost in her imagination. Her guest came from the north, she divined, for his eyes were blue and the sun had scorched his tawny hair red and gold. He probably came in some longboat to carry her off as a hostage queen. But he had fallen victim to her power and was now hopelessly in her clutches of love. *I will follow the directions of the gods. My royal line has to be established and this visiting prince might well be of the blood my children demand.*

She regarded the curve of his thighs, the hair-covered sharpness of the muscles, the boldness of his knees, his taut belly, the strong chest and the manliness of his reproductive organs straining under their blue cloth. She felt a heaving in her breasts and a dawning of desire.

She had earlier cut off two empty plastic water bottles to form cups that she now filled with cordial as delicately as if they were goblets being loaded with mead.

Jack accepted the offered drink. They reached through the candlelight and slowly put their glasses together in a toast. Anke held his eyes for a long time.

'To a breath from heaven,' she said.

'A breath from heaven,' he echoed.

As she sipped her drink with her elbows on her knees she felt her bosoms brush the inside of her arms and was aware of their fullness and her own stunning femininity and the sense of the celebration of life filling her body. The bitter shards of contempt that cocooned her past had fallen away. She felt soft, delicate and metamorphosed like a moth emerging from its chrysalis, all powerful and ready to fly for the first time.

The shallow indifference shown to suitors who had passed through her life before had vanished. Now she was in command with no fear of retribution; no danger of exploitation. She ran her tongue round the curves of her lips, let the backs of her knuckles gently track up and down the soft skin of her inner thighs, totally in control of her sensuality.

Hunger came only in small nibbles. The repast was played out as a fully fed cat might toy with a mouse. Anke covered the food and pushed it to one side then moved the candle off the sleeping bag. This night was for music, for dancing, for holding the chalice of love and bathing in the nectar that ran from its lips.

She stretched out, face downwards, propping her head up close to Jack's legs. His rock hard muscular thighs were only centimetres from her nose. She had watched his tendons draw those muscles together like steel bars when he had sprung up the hillside in front of her or lying on over-hanging the lip of the ridge and when he had hauled her up the rock faces. They drew her to them in an unconditional surrender that she did not understand. *This must be the path set for me by the Gods*. The sun had burned her cheeks but the heat she felt now, the fire running through her skin where it rested on his leg, was not sunburn. It came from inside. The rest of her body tingled for the same contact; she sensed her outstretched legs begging for his gentle fingers, the backs of her knees itching for his attention.

Anke felt Jack stroking her hair, turning the locks over in his fingers and guiding the strands away from her ears to create a pool of freshness around them. She thrilled to the thought of having even that tiny part of herself undressed by him. His hands, rough and strong, massaged her shoulders and then his fingers stretched down her spine to her waist sending shockwaves to the very heart of her being. Her eyes remained shut and her breathing smooth as she exhaled with a soft sound like the purr of a tigress.

She lost track time and drifted off on many imagined journeys, always in her blue loin cloth and with her bare breasts held high. She drove swinging chariots over cobbled streets, rode white stallions bare back, stood commanding oarsmen from the bow of her war canoe, caressed dark breasted brides with wedding perfumes, and lay prostrate on white coral sand while winged princes attended her with anointing oils.

When Anke next opened her eyes the candle was flickering in the evening breeze and the urge was on her to organise the final stage of the evening – the celebration of life itself, a journey into the heart of her subconscious and the ultimate limits of her desires.

She sat up and allowed Jack an unashamed visual caress of her body. Her prince was in no state to resist her now.

She leaned forward until she could brush her cheek against his beard. 'The queen has to arrange her palace,' she whispered.

Slowly she pulled back one side of the sleeping bag to reveal Jack's white sheet neatly placed on top of his bedroll. surplus clothes formed a pillow. She beckoned him into this boudoir; an invitation to initiate her ultimate surrender.

He offered her his hand and she raised long slender fingers at arm's length as God did in Michelangelo's *Creation of Adam*, only this time it was Eve and she was blonde and had tawny curls under her arms and she was not creating, but seducing, her Adam. He accepted her hand and she pulled him in beside her under the sleeping bag.

The shadows of their arms projected on to the great dyke at the back of Bait El Dahab and danced around crazily, making incredible shapes. They lay on their backs and manipulated the shadows into the Sphinx, into camels, and into the chariots of Tutankhamen; for the length of the candle they laughed and giggled together like children at a school camp; they told each other childhood stories; they talked of music, of loves and of dreams.

The candle flickered and died; the moon climbed into Bait El Dahab and as she turned on to her side towards him a nipple brushed his cheeks and he stopped it with his lips. He pulled the breast into his face and ran fingers up her back; he unfolded her legs and stroked her knees.

Her rose perfume laced the air with a mystical vibrancy like a dewy morning of a late Spring, when all life submits to the intoxication of singing, of growing, of nest building, of home making, fired with the potent power of the mating instinct, of procreation itself. She allowed his head to rest on her silky blue loin cloth while she ran her hands over his thick beard and down his steel hard chest, ploughing furrows with her fingers in circles round each little nipple through the sea of curly hairs. In her head. distant drums played a relentless accompaniment to each movement, growing louder with each circling motion.

His hands had taken up the same rhythm at the back of her knees. She knew her defences were at last breached. The prince's troops were marching over the drawbridge, through her abandoned portcullis. Her own people were standing at the sidelines waving flags and singing. The throng marched on and on into her fortress: all were shouting, waving banners and throwing garlands into the air. The drums were joined with violins, the violins with choirs and the ever-circling fingers stroked on and on over the ever yielding backs of her legs. The queen had no more attendants; she dismissed them in a single wave of abandonment. They withdrew from her bedroom singing and casting rose petals into the air and pouring their anointing oils about the bodies of their royal commanders, launching the couple off into their journey through paradise.

Anke threw her head back and let the golden ringlets dance on her shoulder blades. The pounding in her chest drew her eyelids together and brought her breath in long deep gasps. Hands advanced in slow circling arcs from the backs of her knees up her inner thighs caressing the soft skin with the tendermost touches. Her skin was alight. Burning desire surged through every tissue rising to her groin. No feeling had ever seized her as this one. Her whole body was melting to ever-encircling rhythm that now extended over her stomach and around her waist. She felt his lips smoothing her abdomen and his tongue tracing the top line of her loin cloth. The drums shook the fortress, the singing built to a crescendo throughout her palace, his tongue was moving up, consuming her, tantalising the aureoles of her breasts and then his head nestled there in her womanhood.

In that other world, cherubs flew in through the casement and joined hands around the lovers' satin-covered cradle and floated it out into the sunshine high above the crowds. The cheering and singing rose up to them as one pulsating giant chant, gradually becoming faster and faster. She threw her head from side to side and brought her teeth together. The soft caressing had gone beyond the limits of her sanity, beyond the boundaries of the blue loincloth into the very depths of her garden and to the sides of the holy fountain itself.

He was gently polishing the very orb of her life's blood. Life had no existence for her beyond this point and she felt her brain disintegrating. His finger circled; six circles, seven circles, every blood vessel in her body began to boil, the people below were screaming at the top of their voices in final exaltation, eight circles, the queen felt her spine arch into a bow, nine and ...

She never felt the circle completed. Her body exploded in uncontrollable spasms while a deep gurgle uttering emerged from her throat. Smoke filled the air and harps replaced the drums while cherubs bore her on a golden throne, melted as one with her prince, high above the Garden of Eden, even above the nest of the osprey.

NINE

For most of the morning five metres of smooth rock wall barred their progress to the top of the range on the southern edge of the basin. Eventually Jack had left the bags with Anke and found a vertical gully some distance off that he managed to chimney up by using his back and feet. He then scrambled back to the position above her.

'Pass the bags up to me then I'll give you a pull up,' Jack called down.

She had gathered flat rocks together and piled them up against the sheer rock face to give her a metre start. The bags came up safely and then he reached down and locked her wrists in his hands and hauled her up enough that she could swing a foot up on to the top edge. He leaned back and rolled her unceremoniously on to the ledge.

From there on it was a steady scramble to the top of the ridge without further rock climbing and then along the top until they finally helped each other on to the great dyke again. At the intersection of the ranges they rested. It was almost noon and had been getting hotter by the minute but here on the ridge they found a cooling breeze.

Looking back down on to the Garden of Eden they saw the basin of the sandy dried out lake stretching away towards the next rift valley range and further over to the north the jumble of small ridges and outcrops that made up the back of the 'Garden'.

Before their early morning start they destroyed Bait El Dahab by pulling out the lower stones in the barricade and letting the scree run in to cover the ore body knee deep in gravel and stones. From high on the dyke they agreed there was now no trace of the vein. It had been returned to its hiding place under the earth of Eden.

Anke felt the wind in her hair and smiled at her companion. She patted her packsack. 'I feel as if I need a Securicor escort,' she said. All the samples had been stored in her pack and the remaining ten bottles of water in his. 'How do you think we should get back to Dahab ... walk in the night like before?'

'I don't think that will be necessary because we are not being dropped off in the middle of nowhere this time. We can just pretend we are out walking for the day and hitch a ride back. It is not the same as getting off a vehicle at a point in the desert and then disappearing for three days.'

'Look, over there.' She pointed to a dip in the range where a tiny triangle of blue from the Gulf of Aqaba peeped through the peaks.

'Aah, the sea,' said Jack. She detected a hint of reverence in his words. A moment later they exchanged anxious glances as the grey hulk of an aircraft carrier moved southwards across the space blotting out the blue for a few seconds. To both, it

was an ominous sign that the Garden of Eden and
Bait El Dahab were only oases of peace in a real
world of threats bombs and minefields.

Anke let out a long sigh of despair. Were they
still walking on a knife edge? Was all this still to
be taken away from her? She pulled the straps of
her pack tighter to her body; nothing would be
taken without a fight, she resolved.

To avoid a lengthy detour along the ridge, they
decided to make a descent where they were and
then skirt along the shoulder. Within an hour they
arrived at a terrace they estimated was at an
altitude similar to the old workings. They put their
packs down among the boulders to provide seats
while they rested. From here they had a view into
the *wadi* bottom a hundred metres below and a
short distance up the valley before it curved round
blocking any sight of their outward route.

Suddenly they heard a noise from the *wadi*
floor. A sandy coloured military jeep had rounded
the corner of the *wadi* and rapidly approaching
them, a cloud of dust trailing at its rear.

'Military,' cried Jack. He looked for a hiding
place but there was nowhere to go. They were as
conspicuous as goal posts on a soccer field. There
was only one thing to do. 'Just sit still and hope
they won't look up.'

Anke felt sick. The jeep swung round the curve
and bore down on them. She saw two men in the
front seat. One was pointing up at them.

'Keep calm,' Jack said. 'I'll go and sort them out; tell them we're campers from Dahab making our way back there after a hike.'

The jeep slammed to a halt. A tall man in olive green uniform leapt out of the passenger side, carrying a gun. He shouted in their direction but his words were lost in echoes from the *wadi* walls and drowned in the throaty exhaust of the jeep. He shouted again but didn't wait for an answer and raised the weapon to his shoulder.

'Down,' shouted Jack

As they threw themselves to the stony ground a burst of automatic gunfire ricocheted off the side of the mountain above and below them.

Anke jumped up and cried out, clutching her leg. 'Stop them; stop them. My God they want to kill us.'

The army man shouted again, waving his free arm beckoning them down.

Jack slid his hands under the straps of his pack and slowly raised his arms above his head. He stood up and called out in Arabic. 'Wait, wait, we come down directly, no problem.'

He turned to Anke, said 'Forget your bag. It's behind a rock. Put your arms up before that crazy bastard shoots again. Can you stand?'

He saw a trickle of blood coming from a wound in her left calf muscle. She got shakily to her feet, pleased she could stand without too much pain. Jack looped an arm under her shoulder and they made their way slowly off the flank of the hill and on to the scree leading down to the jeep.

Anke whimpered. 'What are you going to tell them?'

'They will have to take you to hospital to remove that bullet. They should be pretty worried when they find out they have actually shot a tourist. Are you okay? The bone isn't broken is it? Poor darling I'm sorry; I'll make these bastards pay for this. Wait 'til they find out who my employers are.'

'My foot seems okay. I'm surprised it isn't worse. I'm frightened. Maybe this is top security area or something. If they get difficult we have to ask our embassies to help, isn't it so?'

'Don't worry. we will sort it out. Don't mention your bag, it's safe where it is.'

The driver, a fat man in camouflage uniform, leaned against the jeep door. On his head was the traditional black and white checked head dress worn by the desert people and typified by Yasser Arafat. A pistol stuck out of his wide green belt. Both men sweated heavily and were caked in dust. They oozed aggression, relieved only briefly when they glanced at Anke's bleeding leg.

Jack's attempt at a polite greeting was abruptly halted by the tall man with the automatic rifle who indicated them into the back of the jeep with haste. He took a pistol from its holster and waved them under the plastic back flap at the rear of the vehicle. As Jack helped Anke up he saw her whole ankle was a red mass of congealed blood and dust.

The jeep moved off down the *wadi* with the tall soldier occasionally turning round from the front seat to brandish his pistol at them. The lack of an exhaust pipe and the clanking of stones against the underside of the vehicle made it impossible to talk. Red dust clouded into the back through holes in the undercarriage. Jack and Anke clung to the wheel arches for balance and lessen the spine shattering jolts from the bumps.

The back of the jeep was laden with a couple of shovels and strips of perforated steel used under wheels when crossing soft sand. Anke kicked Jack's foot to draw his attention to a wooden box sticking out from under the pile. The writing was layered in dust but there was one broken ten-gauge wire strap and both knew where they had seen it before, and shuddered.

TEN

The jeep slowed to a halt a few minutes later. Through the windscreen they saw black and white goats scampering along a wadi. The fat man leaned out of the window and gave a whistle and a shout.

A few moments later a Bedouin youth of maybe twelve years appeared at the side window. The soldier reached inside his jacket and took out a bundle of notes, peeling off ten and handing them to the youth.

'*Shaukran*,' the boy said. Thanks. He grinned as he noticed Anke and Jack in the back.

'*Masalama*.'

'*Masalama*.'

The jeep roared off down the wadi to where the valley opened out and the sea appeared ahead. Anke and Jack saw the signs of a simple military coastguard outpost at the edge of the water. White painted stones defined the borders of an open area containing a brown tent and a concrete box-like building. Above the roof of the building were the typical two droopy masts with a radio aerial slung between them. The jeep slowed to pass between two barrels at the entrance to the site. A sleepy half-dressed figure who emerged from the tent was immediately dismissed by the driver, making it clear who was in command of the post.

The jeep slewed to a halt at the rear of the building Jack and Anke were immediately ordered out of the vehicle and through the side door into the hut. The place stank of stale smoke and sweaty clothes. The only chair consisting of a steel frame and a gory mixture of yellow and blue electric wire sleeving woven to make the seat. The back was broken in several places and the plastic sleeving was coming unravelled. The fat man flopped down on to it causing its legs to splay under the strain.

'Pass.er.ports,' he wheezed.

Jack explained that Anke had left hers with the campsite reception in Dahab and that his was in their pack.

The tall man prodded the pack with the barrel of his pistol.

'Open,' he said in English with great difficulty.

Jack searched for his papers.

'*Koula-hagga*,' the fat man barked, so Jack took everything out and laid it on the floor. There were ten bottles of water, a few clothes that could have been men's or women's, the hammer and cold chisel, first aid box, various food stuffs, and an envelope containing his passport.

The soldiers sniffed as the hammer and cold chisel came out but showed no other reaction. The tall man held the bag upside down and checked the pockets before tossing it into a comer. Jack handed him his pale blue passport but the fat man intercepted it and took it with a pained expression, his five-day stubble screwed up and a grimace on his face.

He held the passport at arm's length to focus right then he spat out his words, 'UN?'

'*Eyewa. Mashura esmak.*' Yes, fisheries project, explained Jack.

Clearly they did not like the fact they were detaining a United Nations passport holder and Jack hoped it would have enough sway to get them released and Anke hospitalised. He doubted they would notice the documents had expired at the end of his last UN contract or would ask for his current passport, which was in Cairo with his US employers.

They asked Jack for Anke's name and which camp she was registered at in Dahab. When they made him write the details down in their entirety it became clear that they intended collecting her passport.

Throughout this questioning Anke sat on the floor looking petrified and nursing her ankle. When Jack pushed the first aid box towards her with his foot, the tall soldier intercepted it and booted it away. He followed this with a hard kick in the shins that caused Jack to let out a yell. He felt their situation was getting worse by the minute. The fat man picked up the Red Cross box and opened it. A number of bandages and dressings fell out on to the dirty floor before he snapped it shut and tossed it into Anke's lap. After wiping away all the congealed blood and dirt antiseptic swabs she turned her attention to the wound itself.

With neither soldier prepared to address her personally, the dialogue being conducted in Arabic and all questions coming through Jack, she was eventually left alone to clean up her leg and dress the wound herself.

She considered the effects of being shot and was surprised how relatively painless it was. She had control of all the movements in her ankle and toes, although her darker moments had her imagining would fade and gangrene set in unless she could get to a hospital. With pain shooting up her leg every time she touched the area and she turned her face to the wall so the men could not see the agony in her face. The bullet must be removed, even if it meant cutting it out. She found a small scalpel in the kit and she hid it in her hand as she drew it towards her leg. Holding her breath and biting her cheek hard she made an exploratory dig. She shuddered as she felt a grating of knife on bone, perhaps her bone was shattered. She instantly withdrew the blade even though it had hardly entered the wound. Something heavy fell on the floor and fresh blood seeped from her leg.

Anke thought she ought to be sick but was surprised to realise she was not in much pain. She pushed cotton wool into the hole and counted to ten and took a big breath. She removed the bloodied wad and pushed in more cotton wool, holding it tight. The pain had almost gone. When she pulled out the cotton wool this time the bleeding had stopped. She found a tube of antiseptic cream in the box and squeezed a large dollop into the wound, put more cotton wool on top, added a plaster and finally held the lot in place with a bandage.

Among all the discarded dressing wrappers beneath her leg she found a centimetre-long sliver of granite coated in blood and felt disgusted with herself.

Nothing Jack said satisfied the soldiers. They raised their voices more aggressively at each demand. The tall man pushed and prodded him several times as if spoiling for a showdown. Even with the little Arabic in her vocabulary, Anke knew the word hashish was used several times and feared an accusation was being directed at them connected with the discovery of the box.

The fat man looked to be growing tired of the arguments. He saw no future in trying to gain a solution from the interrogation. He put his hand inside his jacket and took out a small plastic bag of snuff, spat grossly on the floor next to Anke and rolled his bottom lip back to reveal a disgusting array of yellow teeth. He poured in a liberal amount of the brown powder and closed his mouth, deforming and distending his bottom lip. Realising Anke was watching the ritual, he looked through her with an opaque stare.

She looked away. It was a revolting sight. She couldn't stand those evil yellow eyes looking at her. They were small and heartless, hooded by screwed up lids, the pupils widely dilated. She felt a horror and contempt. The man was a slob who had no place in normal society. His grey unshaven face and gross belly made it difficult to equate him to an active unit of the security forces. The dirty and squalor of the hut reflected his attitudes; the single steel table with one drawer hanging out; wires from the radio handset hanging down the wall with several joins of twisted bare ends like half cooked spaghetti; the discarded torch batteries, cigarette packets and used razor blades that were thrown anyhow into the comers of the room all testified to his character. On the table, a shell case held down dog-eared log books and a number of worn out carbon papers. Littering the floor were many more discarded sheets and screwed up carbons along with bits of newspaper that had at some time contained food.

The building's concrete blocks had been painted white at some time or another. Now they were just grimy. On one wall hung a sun-faded picture of the president; opposite was a half goat-eaten calendar showing an Arabic text from the Koran under the ubiquitous picture of the prophet Mohamed's tomb in Mecca. Several Arabic words were scrawled on the wall in charcoal along with crudely drawn depictions of a rampant penis entering a pair of buttocks that could have been either male or female. In one corner and looking oddly incongruous with its garishly ornate red and blue velvet insulated coiled pipe and brass fittings, sat a water-pipe sat probably brought from Saudi Arabia some time or another. The ground around was littered with spent charcoal ashes and burnt tomato puree cans.

A dribble of brown saliva hung from the older man's mouth as he released a pool of brown spit on to the floor between his legs. He cast another furtive glance out of the little window in the direction of the tent at the other end of the site. Anke assumed he did not want his junior men to be involved with his new prisoners.

The man became increasingly agitated. He shuffled over to a rear internal door and unlocked the padlock with a key from a bunch in his pocket.

Fuel drums and bits of old oily engines were piled into what was a small store no more than a metre by three metres.

'*Ya-la!*' Get going! The fat man uttered the terse order and prodded Jack into the store with the butt of his pistol. He turned to Anke and kicked her to her feet. '*Ya-la,*' he repeated and pushed her in after Jack, causing him to crash down among the drums.

The door was pulled shut followed by the rattle and snap of the padlock.

'Fuck,' said Jack. 'These guys are not normal *Gesh*! They are not fucking *Gesh*, they're crooks! I tried everything with them; politeness, pleas, vagueness, warnings, threats. They are just ignorant bastards. They don't want to listen. All they have in their heads is that we are CIA or some other such agents tracking them down for their hashish.'

Anke hissed in disgust. 'They're both evil, that fat guy is half stoned and hates Westerners and particularly western women. I'm sure they mean to kill us.'

'Kill us?' Jack was dismissive. 'Don't be silly, they know they can't do that. It would create an international incident. They're only trying to scare the pants off us so that we leave the country and never come back.'

'No! Not so. I looked into the captain's eyes and they are evil. He has no sympathy for us. We are interfering with his dope and his power base. He will eliminate us.' She wanted to cry but was too overcome by anger. 'That tall guy is just a mouthpiece and a muscle man for the other one. Can't we trick him?'

Jack sighed. 'Be realistic, they have shot at us once and wounded you, and I have got gun barrel marks all over me where that bastard poked me for the last hour. These guys are crazy. If they suspect any sort of trickery, they *will* shoot us. We have to try diplomacy.'

'You're wasting your time,' she persisted. 'They'll never let us go. They have your passport and they know exactly where to find mine. Nobody knows we are here, not even those soldiers out there in that tent. We will just vanish. The bloody shepherd boy has already received a reward for alerting them that we were in the old mine. Remember when we saw the goats that afternoon, he must have been in the shade watching us from down in the *wadi*. You can be sure he will get another bunch of notes to keep his mouth shut. In any case he will imagine that we were returned to Cairo and that will be the end of it as far as he is concerned. We just don't exist and they know it. We will be assumed to have been lost in a diving accident or something, eaten by sharks. Who knows? There are so many ways we could just disappear round here. And by the way, I'm not wounded.'

'Not wounded?'

'No. I dug out a piece of granite that must have spat at me from the impact of a bullet on the rocks nearby. I repaired the damage and I'm okay.'

'Are you sure? That's good news. It puts a new light on things,' he said. Already he felt less depressed.

He groped in the dark for her shoulder and put his arm round her. He pulled her to him tightly. 'Sorry I was not able to convince them to let us go. But there is absolutely no reasoning with these guys.'

'I could see that. We have to think how we are going to fool the idiots.'

They remained silent and depressed for a long time until they heard shouts and the thud and of a ball being kicked around some distance off. The soldiers from the tent having their usual kick-around before sundown unaware that two foreigners were captive in their own compound. Jack and Anke considered shouting to attract their attention but Jack suggested it would only result in a twenty-four-hour guard being smacked on them immediately. And after that the captain and his crony would doubtless find a convenient time and place for an unaccountable accident to befall them. But with only two of them involved, with one of them three parts stoned, there was still a chance of escape.

After what seemed like an hour, they heard the monotone sound of the Koran being recited by the captain for his evening prayers.

'Fucking hypocrite,' said Jack. 'It must be about six o'clock. Wonder if they will feed us? I'm sure as hell thirsty. There is no air in here and I'm soaked in diesel. What a rat hole.'

'I want a pee,' said Anke.

'Have one. I doubt if you will spoil the Persian carpet.'

Anke had a pee while the chanting continued outside. Jack's depression deepened. He thought of the previous evening and how his beautiful radiant queen, that magnificent loin-clothed creature, had taken them to the most unbelievable heights and was now humiliated into squatting among diesel cans in a dark dungeon with all her kit gone and a hole in her leg.

The store was in total darkness and the stench of old engine oil and diesel added to their gloom.

The little air there was entered under the door. After two hours of confinement the feeling of suffocation, weariness and thirst was intense.

Jack thought he heard the rasping sound of bubbles being drawn through a water pipe and was sure he could smell the burnt heavy smoke of strong tobacco and hashish. He heard the squeak of the outside door and low voices in the room outside. It sounded as if the tall soldier was back.

'I'm going to ask for water,' Jack said, 'and maybe check the situation.'

'Perhaps we should wait 'til they are more stoned,' suggested Anke. And so they waited about half an hour before Jack banged on the door and shouted.

'*Moya! Moya! Owiz moya!*' Water, water, we need water.

The voices briefly stopped, then resumed with what sounded like a discussion. A few minutes later a key entered the lock and the door was pulled open. Fresh air rushed in and the tall man in dark green confronted them with a pistol in his hand. Jack and Anke were ordered out and given one of their own bottles of water.

The fat man sat where they had last seen him on his plastic wire covered chair. Now he was wearing a pair of dirty pyjamas typical of the evening wear worn in many parts of Egypt. On the table a smoky paraffin lamp gave the room long and fluttering shadows. Neither man showed any emotion although Anke felt they looked right through her. The fat man reached under his chair for his pistol and fixed his tiny eyes on her legs, now covered in long black smears of oil from the store. Both men stank of strong tobacco and the smell of hashish clung to their clothing. The atmosphere was electric with menace she thought.

The tall man took a torch from the table drawer and went into the store. He returned holding a greasy coil of six millimetre rope, still with its binding strings holding it together. Jack was stunned, it came from his own fisheries project and was one he had ordered from his own budget for the Dahab Fishermen's cooperative. Another example, he thought, of how aid frequently fell into the wrong hands. Some poor fishermen he was helping had probably been made to part with the rope to obtain some permit or whatever from this coastguard unit to allow him to fish in the area and go about his business.

The man took a penknife from his pocket and cut the bindings. He unwound a couple of fathoms of rope from the coil. Jack watched keenly. From a lifetime spent working with ropes he could tell exactly how much experience other people had with them simply by the way they handled the coils and the fibres. It was very evident this soldier had never had a new coil of rope at his disposal.

Immediately Jack handed the water bottle to Anke he was ordered to stand against the wall with his hands behind his back. He offered only token resistance, he knew what was coming and didn't relish any more barrel battering. He placed his hands obligingly side by side behind his back. Jack felt the grating of his wrist bones and the rope bound them, and he smelt the tang of diesel as it squeezed out of the rope when the knots were pulled tight and breathed a sigh of relief. His assailant searched his pockets but found nothing.

Anke protested loudly at Jack's treatment. This earned her a smack across the face from the tall man as soon as he had finished with Jack. She turned her head in contempt and saw a mocking smirk on the fat man's face, revealing his blackened yellow teeth. She shuddered. He was vile. Any doubts about him not having evil intentions faded, she knew they faced a battle for their lives.

Now tightly bound, Jack was kicked towards the store again and pushed roughly inside, the door bolted behind him.

Left on her own, Anke felt sick; she guessed what was coming. It wasn't fear that consumed her but a sense of being appalled at the task facing her, the amount of adrenalin her body demanded to handle the situation. Her captor bound her wrists behind her as he had done Jack's and swung her round to face him.

With one hand he yanked her T-shirt up, catching his fingers under her bra so that shirt and bra rested on top of one breast, exposing it fully.

'Fuck off you pig,' she yelled, trying to shake the shirt back down.

He understood all four words perfectly and hissed something she could not interpret into her ear. He put the pistol to her cheek. She was revolted by the stench from his body.

She tried to put space between them but he pushed her back against the desk. There was no way to retreat. His free hand moved up and mauled her breast, laughing as he twisted it painfully round and pointed the nipple at the fat man.

From the corner of her eye she watched horrified as the old man staggered to his feet and fumbled in his pyjamas as he approached her. His eyes were grey dilations of ice cold metal. The withered penis he held in his hand looked to Anke more like a dog's turd. Bile filled her throat as he squeezed her nipple and undid the zip of her shorts; she gagged and recoiled from the pistol, spitting phlegm over the man's face. She stamped on his bare feet with her boots and as he bellowed in pain and rage she managed to break free.

She charged round the room shrieking and spitting like a wild cat, kicking at everything in sight, sending the hubble-bubble crashing over to break in half and spill water over the floor. She kicked the chair at the tall man and as he swerved to avoid it she swept the paraffin lamp from the table to the ground. It smashed and its flame died, plunging the room into darkness.

Her back was against the door. She tried desperately to pull it open, digging the nails of her bound fingers into the leading edge and pulling as hard as she could. Suddenly the light of a torch beamed straight into her eyes and a fist was driven hard into her stomach. She fell to the floor with an agonised gasp of pain, doubled up and with all breath gone from her body. The worst would surely follow. She could only hope they got it over and done with as quickly as possible.

Anke heard the padlock slide out of its hasp as the store room door was opened, felt more agonising pain as a boot went in to her side. She was vaguely aware of being dragged and pushed through the door.

*

The sight of Anke's creased up and battered body being bundled in at his feet filled Jack with anger and hatred. He understood now the hunger a man could have to go to war and to kill.

He twisted his hands sideways and slipped them out of their bindings. He knelt down to Anke, sobbing in the oil and darkness and sat her up against a barrel. He cupped her chin in his hands and placed a gentle kiss on her cheek; he then felt for her bra and pulled it down over her breast then rearranged her T-shirt and zipped up her shorts so she felt somewhat more normal. As her sobbing eased he again kissed her cheek and slowly twirled his fingers in her hair until she seemed much more calm.

She remained huddled up. 'How did you free your hands?'

'That rope is six millimetre polyflake so the fibres are flat and greasy. Because they've been soaked in diesel, the strands run over each other like they have lubricant on them. Wriggle your hands a few times and all the knots slip. Try it.'

He felt Anke struggling for a while then a hand came round and groped for his neck and pulled him towards her. Her dry lips trailed across his cheek until they found his in a brief but affectionate kiss. Jack remained concerned.

'How badly damaged are you?'

She rubbed her ribs and stomach area and then got him to sooth her side by directing his hands in massaging circles. After a few minutes of this she said she thought everything was good enough and that they had better replace their bindings to fool their captors when they had the advantage.

From outside came the sounds of considerable activity. The outside door creaked open and shut several times. There seemed to be something happening with the jeep. They heard the clanking sound of steel sand mats and the scraping noises of a heavy object being dragged.

Jack speculated they were moving the box of dope. If their minds were engrossed in that there might be a chance to escape.

They heard more discussions from outside and then the thud of heavy stones being dropped on the floor.

'Maybe they are going to bury the box,' said Anke

'Or sink it.'

'Sink it?'

'Tie rocks to it and put it below the water for a day or two until their customer arrives.'

'Maybe.'

The sound of rocks grating on the steel table and the grunts of approval that seemed to come from the fat man fitted this idea. They heard the outside door squeak open and the men shuffle away.

'They can't be using the jeep,' said Anke. 'Do they have a boat?'

'Probably. Most coastal security units have rubber dinghies and outboards and there are outboard engine spares in this storeroom so I imagine they have one.'

They discussed possible tactics to obtain a weapon from their assailants and speculated about holding one man hostage and using him as a human shield, the much deplored method of Saddam Hussein.

Anke said she had never held a gun and wouldn't know how to use one. Jack confessed he was in much the same category, he deplored guns and violence in general. As they debated how they might overcome these reservations the door of the hut squeaked and the storeroom padlock rattled.

Their heart rate soared. What now? Were they to be executed, raped, tortured or what? Anke was sure the men would be seeking revenge for her outburst.

The tall man with the torch stuck the barrel of his pistol in Jack's face. He told them to stand up and not cause any trouble. Disobey and they would be shot. The meaning of his Arabic words were clear enough to need no translation for Anke. She drew her body up stiffly and painfully and staggered out to be confronted by the older man, looking grey and demonic yet still in his pyjamas. He waved a revolver at Anke, staring at her with obvious hatred and contempt. A replacement oil light sat on the table, the debris of its predecessor now pushed into the corner of the room.

Anke and Jack were ordered to stand against the wall, half expecting to be shot there and then. The tall man returned to the store and came back with a jerrycan of fuel. He gave the torch to the fat man who waved the pair outside.

The fresh evening air came as a huge relief after the squalor of the store and hut. Anke immediately felt her strength coming back. The night was black, with the moon yet to rise. There were no signs of the soldiers from the tent. Only the low growls of the mongrel bitch patrolling the compound disturbed the silence.

Jack and Anke were marched down the dry *wadi* to the sea. Anke noticed with satisfaction the old fat man was having trouble with his feet, shuffling along as if they pained him a great deal. As they drew near the inky water's edge it was just possible to make out the lines of an inflatable dingy, a Zodiac with a big outboard cocked up on the stern It floated motionlessly, tethered to a stake in the shallow water.

Devil crabs scurried away into their holes on the beach, mullets and milkfish plopped noisily as they dashed away from the shallows, disturbed by the light. This was followed by the swish-swish of the jumping garfish as they, too, responded to the torch and headed into deeper water. Wader birds made shrill cries as their flurry of wings hummed them off into the night. A white stork perched on the corner of the dingy languidly raised its long wings and lifted its draped body a few metres down the beach.

Jack found these peaceful sights and sounds hard to equate to their situation. His stomach churned. He thought of all the night fishing trips he had made in the Red Sea over a twenty-year period. Suddenly he felt overcome by a deadly determination that would allow him to coldly cope with any form of violence towards these men.

The Zodiac was about four metres long and Jack recognised it as the robust version used by the military. He judged the Japanese outboard painted army green to be about forty horsepower. In the middle of the wooden slats across the floor was the infamous ammunition box and beside it four loaf size granite stones each bound in a criss-cross fashion with the same six millimetre rope that tied their wrists.

Jack and Anke were ordered into the boat and sat on opposite sides near the bow. The fat man hitched up his pyjamas and sat on the port side near the stern. swung his legs inboard with great difficulty, gasping for air in great rasping breaths. When he recovered he took great delight in telling Jack they would go to meet the buyer of the merchandise and they would experience the man's displeasure when he was told these infidels had intended stealing his box. He gave a vile laugh as he added that the man was not used to infidels getting in his way. Anke cringed when Jack translated the conversation but got ready to release her hands.

The tall man lifted the drum of fuel into the dingy, untied the rope and pushed the boat into deeper water before climbing aboard allowing it to drift out into the night. Jack thought the two soldiers looked strangely incongruous in a boat. Their movements were unnatural and the jelly-like nature of a rubber dingy made it worse for them. The tall soldier manoeuvred himself very awkwardly to a sitting position on the ammunition box, but never failed to keep his revolver pointed menacingly at his captives.

Once they had drifted well away from shore, he put his gun into its holster and told his partner to keep him covered. To Anke's horror, started to lash a rock to one of her ankles. All was clear. It was she and Jack who were to be sunk, not the box.

'We wouldn't want you to fall over the side would we?' sneered the tall man in Arabic.

Jack translated and Anke spat over the side. He watched the knotting procedure carefully and studied the stones in the torchlight without saying anything. He glanced up at Anke; she looked terrified and bewildered.

Sluggishly the tall man returned to the engine and uncocked it so that it sat down in the water. *At least he knows what he's doing concerning outboards*, thought Jack.

The fuel pipe was stuffed into the drum of petrol and held in place with a rag. After three attempts, the engine fired up and jerked into gear. The boat quickly responded to the high powered engine and sped out into the night with the cool fresh air buffeting their faces. With no night vision while the torch was on, it was soon switched off. Almost total blackness prevailed.

Jack watched the vague outline of the rift valley mountains gradually getting smaller. He thought of the Garden of Eden and all it had meant to them. They could not, must not, let that slip from their hands. He leaned forward so that Anke could hear him.

'The rocks are round enough to slip out from their ropes if you jerk them and slide the bindings sideways.'

She nodded. He again leaned forward.

'Have your hands free and ready.'

She nodded again and the boat sped on for another ten minutes. As the mountains looked ever smaller on the horizon Jack's fears increased. *What should our next move be?*

Anke bent in towards him.

'Your hands free?'

'Yes.'

'Can you swim okay?'

He nodded.

Suddenly there was a sinister ripping noise followed by a high pitched whine screaming into the night. Anke leapt up as the boat veered off violently to one side. She was clutching her skin scraper like a dagger. Jack watched her raise her hand then bring it down with vicious force into the inflated hull. She stabbed again, drawing the blade back towards her to cause a second rip. Another piercing whine followed. The boat started to go dead in the water, and the whines of the engine began to fade. Jack's seat went soft beneath him as he struggled to release his stones. Totally unbalanced and panic stricken, the tall man lunged at Anke. She leaned backwards and slid off into the water, dragging one of her stones behind her.

Total pandemonium broke out as Jack grappled wildly with his second stone. The soldiers yelled plea for the reeking of the vengeance of Allah on the infidel and mercy for the faithful. The engine's earlier impetus continued to drive the boat forward but was also forcing the bow down. Jack felt a surge of water come inboard and swamp the vessel as he released the second stone off and dived clear over the side into the blackness.

When he surfaced he heard the engine about fifty metres away. It gurgled to a stop, released a final hiss, and died. Desperate incoherent cries came from the same direction. Jack closed off his ears and put his head down to start a crawl back to where Anke had gone over the side.

ELEVEN

Jack stopped and called her name. Nothing. He called again. Nothing .... Oh God no, he thought, not after all this. Everything flashed before him. He remembered the stone going over the side with her. The stones that he said would come free. She trusted him. She was the one who made the daring bid for their freedom. No, two bids for freedom. Back in the hut he was nothing but a bystander. Please don't take her now.

He heard a whooshing sound somewhere in front of him, followed by a frantic coughing, choking and thrashing of water. Jack crashed through the sea with all his power until he could see the white water. The struggling subsided and the choking ceased as Anke's head appeared before him. She was treading water and spitting.

'Jack?'

'Aye.'

'Thought you said those fucking stones were loose.'

He grinned and grasped her shoulders. He kissed her cheek, said, 'You're brilliant.'

'That's not what I was thinking when I was twenty metres down and still trying to free that rock,' she gasped.

'The boat sank and I think those bastards went with it.'

'*Sheise*. We won't lose sleep over them anyway. Where's home?'

Jack waved in the direction they had come. 'It's a long way. Can you swim that far?'

'I can. Can you?'

She said it full of confidence. Jack worried she might have underestimated the nine or ten kilometres back to the shore. 'Reckon there is not much choice, let's go.' He said set off towards the west, determined they would make it.

Jack knew he had stamina. There was that mile certificate he had won at school when he was twelve and the Red Sea was warm enough to prevent them dying of hypothermia, which could well happen if he attempted to swim such a distance at home. He had high hopes but after a minute or so Anke already lagged behind.

She told him to go on slowly while she removed her heavy boots. After that she caught up with him, her boots trailing behind on her binding rope, which was attached to her waist.

She ploughed dolphin-like through the calm water while Jack made do with five minutes of noisy over-arm alternating with five minutes of breaststroke while he got his breath back.

After an hour of relentless swimming Jack's pace slowed even further and Anke trod water from time to time, waiting for him to catch up.

'Christ!' he gasped, 'you're like a fish. Take it easy or you'll kill me!' He remembered seeing the little black and white swimmer logo on her T-shirt. 'Do you do much of this?'

'I belong to a club in Munchen but I've never taken part in any international events.'

'So you thought you would start now by beating the British contingent and almost drowning him.'

She laughed and they continued towards the distant shore. *You just can't win with this woman*, thought Jack. *If she was in a plane when the pilot suffered a coronary, she would produce a pilot's licence and take over the controls.*

'Must be over a third of the way,' said Jack. 'The mountains are looking much bigger now.'

During the next hour he had had to stop several times to rest, treading water a minute or two each time. He complained of cold and cramp in his fingers with each stroke. Anke offered encouragement. 'We are well over half way. It's getting lighter to the east. The moon will be up soon so it must be about midnight.'

Still they pressed on. Jack felt the cramp tensing in his forearms, forcing him to take slower less powerful strokes.

As the moon came up over the Gulf of Aqaba he saw in the distance the coastguard post they had left several hours earlier. Still a long way off but within striking distance. He rolled over on to his back and kicked for quarter of an hour, giving his arms a rest. He used the moon as a back sight to maintain direction. Anke cruised alongside in a languid slow crawl, looking as comfortable as any sea creature. Her boots floated a metre or so behind in her wake.

Jack turned over and did breaststroke for another fifteen minutes without daring to look up in case he got depressed. Every bone ached. The cramp had extended to his legs. *If only we can make the shore line anywhere and rest. Oh for rest.* Weariness engulfed his body. Exhaustion was near. He rolled on to his back and kicked. A breeze had sprung up, making matters worse. He tried kicking harder but quickly tired. As he resumed his breaststroke he allowed himself to look up. They had improved their position but only slightly. The shore was still about two kilometres away, perhaps a kilometre south of the hut.

'Rest,' he gasped. Anke stopped and waited while they trod water for a few minutes. She paddled over to him with her boots and a length of rope.

'Put the rope under your shoulders and lie on your back and kick. I'll tow you and you tow the boots.'

It seemed complicated but he was in no condition to disagree. He passed the noose over his head and under his arms and threw her the end. The boots he tied by the laces to the rope near his shoulder and rolled over on to his back. Anke had tied the rope to the belt of her shorts in the middle of her back and was separated from him by about three metres of slack rope. She set off unhampered by her trailing boots, dragging the kicking *Fischer* behind her.

She ploughed powerfully on, head down in a slow relentless crawl, for a solid forty-five minutes with Jack kicking in her wake as his brain told him this was probably how his world would end. He looked only at the moon while fighting the urge to submit to the cramp continually stiffening up the muscles of his thighs and forearms.

Anke's pace suddenly slackened. Jack stopped kicking and tried to float, succeeding only in wrapping the rope round her.

'Fisher,' she said softly, 'we've made it.'

She stood up, her shoulders out of the water. Jack lifted his eyes to the heavens and silently thanked her and his God alike while his feet slowly sunk to the soft sand below.

Anke gathered in the rope and pulled his head to her chest. She held it there for a long time while they regained some energy.

The moon was now high enough for them to see there were no soldiers between them and the hut, a good kilometre to the north. Anke ducked her shoulders back in the water to lessen the chances of being seen.

'What's the plan then?'

Jack felt renewed optimism. 'Head for the mountains, circumnavigate the hut and get back to where we left your bag.'

They breaststroked in to the shallows and lay there for a few moments. Jack crawled clear of the water on his hands and knees, unsure that his legs would support him. He emptied his shoes, wrung out his socks and replaced them on his feet. That felt much better. Anke did likewise.

Ten minutes later they moved away as silently as possible over the stones of the *wadi* keeping a low profile until they reached the flank of the Rift Valley. There they rested, feeling more secure now they were no longer out in the open. Up the coast on the shoreline north of the hut they could see torchlight and assumed it came from the army unit returning from its patrol or checking for its commanders and their Zodiac.

Jack felt stronger and a new sense of urgency. 'Okay, let's go. We have to reach your bag before dawn and get away from this *wadi* before those guys radio for a search party and the whole valley comes live with military.'

Anke was just as eager to find her pack and they headed for the gap in the hills without any further hesitation. It was five a.m. by Anke's watch, with a chink of dawn already behind them, when they scrambled up the same scree that he had helped her down from only eighteen hours earlier.

'How is your leg?' he asked, somewhat ashamed that it was only now remembering it for the first time in hours.

'Don't know,' she said wearily. 'I'll tell you tomorrow.'

It reminded him of Vivien Leigh's classic line in *Gone With the Wind*. 'I didn't mention it when we were swimming because I considered it might attract sharks.'

'Me too,' she replied with a shudder. 'But then I thought we were so coated in oil and stinking of diesel that no self-respecting shark would come within a kilometre of us.'

'I see most of it has washed off now.'

'A wash I could have done without,' she quipped. She gave him a tender smile. 'You, too, I imagine.'

He groaned.

They were relieved to find the packsack just as they had left it behind a rock. They fell upon the few bits of dry pita bread and cheese still sitting inside on top of the samples. As there was no water in her bag there was no option but to immediately head back to the road before it got hot.

They climbed to the higher ground again and took a straight line path to the minor ridge they had hung over on their first day. They resisted any temptation to revisit the old workings or glimpse again the Garden of Eden.

Jack insisted on carrying the pack as he had been neither wounded nor beaten. He knew he could never balance their account; Anke had twice saved his life with her daring actions to bring about their escape and then towing him through two kilometres of sea when his limbs had given up.

By ten o'clock they regained the high ground overlooking the cutting and waited until there was no traffic in sight before scrambling down on to the tar macadam and striding out towards Dahab as if nothing had happened.

A few minutes later a white Toyota pickup slowed down for them and they climbed up on to the tray and squatted among dozens of boxes of bottled water. They exchanged broad grins through the back window with the two young Bedouin men in the front who were surreptitiously sharing a bottle of beer before they got to Dahab and had to behave themselves. Anke joked that sitting among all those cartons of water and watching the men drinking beer was the greatest test of her sanity for the entire trip.

TWELVE

Brr. Brr ... Brr. Brr.

'Hello'

'There's an outside call for you, Jack.'

'Okay... Hey Leyla, can you talk to Rania for me and get her to tidy up my report? It is on disc. I've just this minute finished it and I've got a meeting straight after lunch with J.'

'Yes, all right Mr Polglaise I'll speak to Rania and, by the way, I checked in your airline ticket for you this morning.'

'Okay, thanks. How could we manage without you? Put him through now will you.'

'It's a 'her', Jack. Byeee.'

'Hello. Jack Polglaise here.'

'*Salem elay cum.*'

'Anke! Where are you?'

'Cairo.'

'I thought you were never going to call me. How did you get on?'

'I want to see you, Jack. Where can we meet?'

'I'm going to break for dinner in half an hour. What about the Alley Restaurant in Hoda Street? It's not far from Ramses. Ask any cab driver. It's an interesting old place. That's alley as of space between two buildings. Not Ali's restaurant. Got it?'

'Okay, Fisher. You still speak in riddles,' she laughed. 'See you in half an hour if the traffic will let me. Bye.'

'*Masalama.*'

Slowly he put the receiver down and stroked his beard. Stretching his arms, he rode his chair backwards so he could gaze distantly out over an ever moving Cairo.

A few minutes later, coming back down to four legs, he felt into his new replacement bag and wondered what the young soldiers made of his old one or whether those crooks had disposed of it and the contents that same fateful evening. He believed the latter. He took out a clean shirt, tie, pressed slacks and a bag with all its new scented Egyptian toiletries and strolled down to the male rest room.

'I told Rania to tidy up your report Mr Polglaise. Wow! You do look smart. Got a nice lunch appointment?'

'Yes,' he beamed.

'She must be very special,' Leyla teased.

Jack couldn't resist it, 'Worth her weight in gold.'

They both laughed for different reasons and he went down four flights to the street and headed towards Alley Restaurant. Twenty minutes later Anke walked through the door wearing a pale blue knee-length business suit with a plain white blouse and carrying a brief case. She was escorted by a tall fair-haired middle-aged man in a lightweight grey suit. He had a big smile. Jack was surprised to see such formality and was thankful he had dressed up for the occasion.

'Good morning, Jack.'

'Hello Anke. Err ... Katarina.'

'This is Mr Louis Van Smittand, head of Anglo-American Mining Company, Egypt Division. Louis this is Jack Polglaise. He is working with the US Government here in fisheries development.'

'Good morning Jack. Katarina told me she met you in Sinai and thought I would enjoy meeting you.' He spoke with a strong American twang. His smile was almost benevolent. 'We sure as hell don't get to meet anyone like Katarina every day. We have seen evidence of her work and could not help but make her head of our exploration programme for Sinai. But she sure is a tough dealer and don't sell herself cheap, at least her goddamn German lawyer didn't.' He laughed adding, 'We don't usually pay our geologists a percentage of profits when they work for us but when one comes from outside with just about a whole mine in her hand bag ... I guess we are on the weaker side of the bargaining table.'

Jack winked at Anke.

The American continued addressing Jack, 'Your friend here would not part with one scrap of information 'til we had contracted her. But I'll tell you one thing buddy, this is going to be big ... this is going to be the bonanza of bonanzas. Can't say more right now. You just watch the columns.'

Anke smiled. Jack thought she looked radiant. She caught his glance and her eyes filled with tears of happiness forcing her to look at the ground to hide them. Jack came to the rescue.

'That's really good news for you both. She is certainly tough, but I must tell you she is a terrible cook. She invited me to dinner one day and we could not even eat the food.' He caught her eye again; she smiled and blushed, 'But an absolutely dedicated geologist I agree.'

They chatted informally over lunch until the American rose and said he was due back at a meeting but would like to meet Jack socially when he was next in Cairo. He added that he would see Anke the next day in the office and not to worry about the bill, he would pick it up on the way out.

Alone together for the first time since they arrived back in Dahab, they looked at each other and gently touched hands under the table. Jack beamed at her and squeezed her hand.

'You've done it. Brilliant.'

She grinned back across the table. He felt inside his pocket and brought out a small a package which he handed her.

A little note fell out as she undid the red ribbon. She opened it out and read out the inscription; *To Eve from Adam. A gift from Bait min Dahab in the Garden of Eden.*

She smiled and fumbled with the package. She took out a natural gold nugget about two centimetres long in almost the exact shape of a fisherman's anchor mounted cleverly on a chain. She marvelled at it, at first speechless and then bursting into tears.

'I found it while Eve slept,' he whispered into her ear while he offered her a handkerchief, 'A nice man from Khan el Khalil engineered the clasp and chain for it. Put it on.'

He lowered it over her head and let it rest between her breasts. 'It's as I'll always remember you.'

His eyes brimmed; he kissed her forehead and dashed from the restaurant.
*

'Good evening, sir. You can undo your seat belt now if you wish. We are serving drinks. Would you care for champagne, burga...?'

'Champagne will be fine thanks. Do you have an English paper?'

'The *Egyptian Gazette* sir?'

'Thank you.'

Jack skimmed the front page. It dealt mainly with the worsening crisis in the Gulf and impending war but suddenly a headline focusing on a different topic caught his eye, *Government continues battle against drug traffickers*.' He sat up and read on with interest.

> *Two coast guard officers are to be posthumously awarded medals for their courage and bravery in combating drug traffickers. Yesterday government sources reported that the US warship Endeavour*

*picked up wreckage identified as coming
from the missing Zodiac patrol vessel of a
unit in the Gulf of Aqaba. In the same
area, cannabis with a street value of one
million pounds was picked up from the
water. Signs of a struggle indicated that
our gallant coast guards sunk the
smugglers' craft in the affray. No bodies
have so far been picked up.'*

Jack folded the newspaper, closed his eyes,
reclined his seat and let the champagne drift
around his tongue and trickle down his throat.

THIRTEEN

More than the one glass of champagne slid down Jack's throat during the uneventful club class flight to London.

He shut his eyes, closed out the comings and goings of the polite airline staff and allowed his mind to float back over the events of the previous week in Egypt and in particular to those three days in Sinai. It all now seemed a combination of wild fantasy and nightmare. None of it appeared possible sitting here in the civilised air conditioned sanctuary of the British Airways jet.

He had no souvenirs to take home and even the bruises had faded. There was nothing to hold on to except memories. He took up the *Egyptian Gazette* again and read the column on the front page. It left him staring into space.

'More champagne, Mr Polglaise,' came a distant and somehow understanding polite voice.

'Err ...yes please. Positively the last one. Thanks,' he grinned.

Jack sipped from the glass as if it were a chalice.

Yes, that's what this is and I am being wined and dined at Bait min Dahab by an Aryan goddess facing me across table of gold. Such ecstasy.

He jolted himself into consciousness. *Too much champagne. Pull yourself together. Where are we? How much further to London? What time is it?*

He looked at his watch. As he registered the time, five o'clock, he noticed the two bars of scabs on his wrist where ropes had burned.

No, it had not been a dream. But what now?

Home for a couple of weeks and then off to the Caribbean on a new contract; a new corner of the planet.

At least I'll be far enough away from that tall blonde German for her not to eat into my flesh anymore; driving me crazy. Too late. She's already under my skin. Taking my illusions of leadership with her. The most dynamic person ever to enter my life. Will I ever be able to forget the Aryan princess who took me so high that I held the earth in my palm, higher even than the nest of the osprey.

He sighed deeply and muttered quietly to himself, 'What's the price of your stubborn independence anyway?'

The question was unanswered and hung in his head as he drifted into sleep.

The voice of the captain over the intercom announced the temperature at London Heathrow as twelve degrees Celsius and that the day was rather wet and windy. They would be landing in ten minutes.

Jack groaned; twelve degrees and only the third of September. How harsh reality was. It had been in the mid-thirties when he had left Cairo. Two weeks would be plenty long enough in the UK.

A quarter of an hour later he made his way through the border control and customs very thankful for his British passport and the ease of the formalities. With only a shoulder bag and briefcase to worry about he was quickly through the green door and heading between the barriers leading out into the arrivals hall and the car hire section.

'Mr Polglaise?'

Jack swung sideways. A well-dressed young man held aloft a sign with his name written on it.

'Yes,' he said, somewhat surprised.

The man looked relieved.

Jack completed the walk from behind the barriers and met up with the young man at the end. A hundred and one questions buzzed through his head. The young man held out his hand. 'Mike Stephens,' he announced. 'You are Jack Polglaise from the USAID Egypt project?'

'Yes,' Jack frowned.

'I'm from the Anglo American London office and have an urgent message for you. Can we talk over there where it's a little more private?'

Jack was confounded. How did these guys know what flight he was on and what was their business? What had Anke cooked up for him now? Wasn't that entire episode over? He had never been part of any Anglo American deal. To his knowledge Anke had never mentioned him as a companion or anything else to do with her geological life and discoveries.

'I'm really sorry to bother you so soon on your return but our chief man in Egypt, Mr Smittand, I think you met him, is emphatic that you call him on your arrival in London.'

'Really, I'm surprised. I'm a fisherman, not a mining engineer.' He wondered about Smittand's motives. 'Did he say what he wanted?'

'No, but he said it was very urgent and that he had tracked down your flight through the USAID office in Cairo but unfortunately you had left before he could catch you. He is awaiting your call despite the fact it has gone eleven now in Cairo. I have a mobile phone so let's just find a quiet corner and get him now.'

'As you wish.'

What Smittand could want that could not wait another day? If he was trying to cheat Anke by buying favours off him he was out of luck. His lips were sealed. He was very much on the defensive when the call was connected and the phone handed over to him.

'Mr Polglaise?'

'Yes speaking - Mr Smittand?'

'Yes, I'm sure as hell sorry to catch you like this but you're the only person I know who might be able to help us.'

'Why?' replied Jack tersely

'As you're a good friend of our geologist, Katarina Hoffmann, it occurred to me that you may have an idea where she might be?'

'Where she is?'

'She didn't come into the office today as she said she would and when we got her hotel people to check her room they found it ransacked. The police are working on it and have taken away blood samples ...'

'You're joking!' spluttered Jack, 'blood samples?'

'Yes, it appears that there was a struggle. The police say her disappearance is probably the work of Moslem fundamentalist fanatics and there's a likelihood of a ransom demand being made soon. Personally, I have no faith in the police approach. I find it unlikely that fundamentalists would target her. I'm extremely concerned and believe whoever has taken her is after the secrets of her mineral finds.'

Jack choked back a rapidly rising sense of fear; the unbelievable had happened. Who could know of Anke's secrets; the German lawyer, the staff of Anglo American Egypt, maybe the waiter in Alley Restaurant overhearing their conversation ... who else could believe they could extract information from her without the knowledge that she held valuable information in the first place?

Smittand broke in on his thoughts.

'Are you still there Mr Polglaise?' I can understand you are upset as indeed we are but I can tell you frankly we will move heaven and earth to find her. Our man there with you, Mr Stephens, has made a provisional booking with Gulf Air for you, leaving at midnight and arriving here in Cairo at eight in the morning, if you would be kind enough to help us. Budget is no problem. We need Katarina safely back with us and we think your own knowledge is of paramount importance. We think ...'

Jack fought against the emotions welling up inside him. He needed to think clearly. 'We need Katarina back,' he echoed. Back for what? Her gold? He grimaced and interrupted Smittand.

'I'll be on the plane. Bye. Thanks for calling me.'

He cut the call and let out an agonised sigh. Stephens, at a loss to know what to say, held out the Gulf Air tickets like an olive branch. He took Jack's shoulder bag led him slowly in the direction of a sign saying Departures.

Stephens had no more information to offer and so he checked Jack's ticket in for him and bought him dinner. They had little in common and conversation was strained and it was with some relief that Jack shook his hand and passed through into the departure lounge. Here he could rest and take stock.

The more he thought about it, the less he liked it. Who else knew about their finds? He remembered the little gold nugget he had had made into a pendant. The goldsmith had given him a second look when he had told him that he had bought it in Upper Egypt. Surely he knew he was lying but there was no link at all with Anke and nothing to give away the huge extent of their find. Only Anglo American Egypt had the information and surely they would guard it well.

There must be someone from within the organisation, but why kidnap the geologist? She had not divulged the location. Then he remembered Smittand's loud mouth boasting in Alley Restaurant about the bonanza of all times. A very bad way to keep a secret.

Jack saw a fax machine in the corner of the lounge. He glanced at his watch, eleven thirty, and decided a fax to his home base was better than a call. He scribbled out a brief message: 'Had to return unexpectedly to Egypt for more work. Will make contact again soon with new ETA London. Jack.'

He boarded the plane aware he was breaching all his former self-imposed disciplines. These were uncharted waters he was sailing into.

What am I doing chasing three thousand miles into a web of trouble on account of a woman who entered my life for a mere three days? A woman I slept with; but never made love to.

He savoured the words 'Made love to', allowing them to roll around his head for some time. He had never entered her it was true, but 'made love to' was debatable. All the music came flooding back, the music of Bait min Dahab, the blue loincloth, the melting eyes, the transcending of spirits - higher even than the nest of the osprey. Jack's eyes clouded and he fought back tears. What was happening to his Anke?

The spirit of fight surged through his veins. He marched briskly to the first class seat provided by

Anglo American wishing the flight to Cairo to be quickly over so he could start pulling Egypt apart.
*

'I'm glad we understand each other, Jack. Katarina's disappearance is not for discussion here at the airport or for that matter in front of my driver. For now, we will keep the discussion limited to your forthcoming site visits in Egypt.'

Jack welcomed the this changed approach from Smittand and immediately had more respect for the brash American. Once alone in his office, a plush extravaganza of Western and Arabic opulence on the twelfth floor of a down town office complex, the mining boss ordered breakfast over the telephone and sat Jack down at a marble topped coffee table in a more informal area at the end of the room.

As soon as the meal had been delivered Smittand came straight to the point.

'Nobody, Jack, but nobody, in Egypt knows anything about Katarina. She travelled alone and apart from entry and exit dates to and from the country extracted from Immigration by the police, there is nothing to go by. She apparently entered the country through Israel on August the fifteenth and came to Cairo where her name was recorded on the registrations from the Hotel Victoria. Each time she moved hotel there should be a record of her place of stay but, as you know, the small hotels and campsites don't keep complete records and it will take the police weeks to sift through the scanty information. In any case, the police are not interested in history. They have an exit five days ago, presumably when she went back to Germany to engage her lawyer, and a new entry two days later. She and the lawyer guy booked into separate rooms at the Hotel Salem and the lawyer returned to Germany after one day, his business with us being completed. We met with you for lunch the day before yesterday after the lawyer had left and since then we have not seen her. We were curious why she did not show up yesterday and called her hotel to find out her plans ... you know the rest.'

Smittand looked shaken. Jack remained silent for a while, reviewing all he had been told before slowly uttering his thoughts,

'That makes me the last person to have seen her. Do the police know that?'

'No, and it not exactly true. The hotel people saw her when they handed her the room key at three p.m. After that she stayed inside.'

'But surely if she was removed from her room after what sounds like a noisy struggle the staff would know about it.'

'You would think so, but apparently not. The kidnappers used a rope out of the back balcony to get away and the management claims the downstairs coffee shop is a popular evening venue for local men and the presence of non-residents would be quite normal. It is rather less than a 'middle of the road' type of hotel, if you know what I mean.

Smittand said he went to the hotel as soon as he was told the room had been turned over. He called the police from there.

'What about her personal effects?'

'The police did not want anything touched so I came away. I am confounded, Jack, and very worried. Do you have any ideas?'

'Anke....er, Katarina ... is very resourceful and must be in a fairly poor state not to have outwitted her captors. What was that about blood samples?'

'There was blood smeared across the tiles on the balcony. Looked like she was dragged'

'My God! What are the police doing?'

'Until last night – nothing. They took finger prints, interviewed hotel staff and that sort of thing and said not to worry. To them, it was the work of fundamentalists who would soon approach the authorities with a ransom demand for the release of a political activist prisoner. They told me that in the case of a foreign tourist there would be no problem, a deal would be made and she would quickly be released. The country cannot afford to jeopardise its tourism industry any further and with the Saddam Hussein threat hanging over everybody, it was small fry anyway.'

Smittand's tone of voice told Jack he had doubts about the police theory. What did he really believe?

'How many people know about Anke's....er, Katarina's finds?'

He maintained eye contact, clearly anticipating the question. His response was emphatic, 'No one! That is, no one in Egypt from my company. Head office assay department obviously, but they only deal with figures that might be part of any task from the assay of raw materials to a concentrate. We don't specify which for obvious reasons. I handled this one personally. The results were faxed to me on that personal machine over there on my desk.'

He stressed that when a freelance geologist turned up with what appeared to be a fabulous discovery they treated it with utmost confidentiality. However, there were other companies that bid up prices on concessions even if they did not actually offer more money to the actual geologist.

'Katarina had told me you were her best friend here in Egypt and that she admired your professionalism, hence my frank manner when speaking with you at the Alley Restaurant. Forgive me if I was rather too open but I considered the matter safe with you; as I do now.'

Jack was satisfied with Smittand's explanation. He believed the man was genuinely worried about Anke's welfare as well as his possible financial losses. Smittand decided to be more divulge more.

'We have for some time been looking at the possibilities of the pre-Cambrian terrain of Sinai. We have had protracted negotiations with the government for the sole exploration rights but a foreign competitor has also been negotiating and the Egyptian authorities have been playing one off against the other. It was on the basis of Katarina's work that I made them an offer that they could not refuse. Since yesterday, we hold the sole exploration rights for a period of three months.'

Jack absorbed this news while continuing to consider Anke's plight. He heard the businessman droning on.

'It has cost us an arm and a leg,' said Smittand, 'and I've not yet told head office that we have lost our key player.'

'But you have the information from Anke?' said Jack. 'Sorry, Katarina,' he added. 'Anke's her nickname. Surely you have the location of her finds.'

Smittand shuffled his feet and looked pained.

'We know of a fabulously rich gold vein in Sinai; but Katarina never disclosed its location as that was part of the legal agreement we had drawn up to protect each other. The percentage clause was to be brought into effect on sighting the ore body.'

Jack nodded. All was clear now. Smittand had his head on the block if Anke was not back with the company in the very near future. This explained his desperate measures to summon Jack back from Heathrow despite knowing full well he may be of no help whatsoever.

So Anke had been even smarter than he had expected in keeping safe her secrets. But why had she been kidnapped? The rival mining company had a motive, but surely this did not happen in 1990 ... did it?

Smittand interrupted his thoughts, 'How well do you know Katarina, Jack?'

Jack treated the question with caution. 'I've not known her long but I think I know her pretty well. She's a wonderful woman and very straightforward.'

'Did you travel together?'

Jack's wariness increased. He was prepared to lie. 'No,' he said, which was basically true. 'I had dinner with her a few times.' The ringing of a telephone cut into their conversation.

Smittand took the call and turned to Jack with a grave look on his face. 'That was our man down with the police. The news is not good. They found a swab containing chloroform on the floor of her room and believe whoever did this drugged Katarina before hauling her away. We can collect her personal effects and the hotel is free to let out room again.'

'Chloroform ... ropes ... these guys came prepared,' said Jack.

Smittand nodded in agreement. 'Jack, you know what Katarina was like, what she wanted out of life, who she mixed with and such like. We don't. You are our main hope of finding her. Please can you check over the room and her things to see if there are any clues as to who might have taken her? I can make resources available to you.'

Jack looked at him. The big man was almost grovelling. Jack merely nodded. But what could he do that the police could not? Besides which he had to be somewhat careful not to make himself a prime suspect. After all, no one else had more to gain. It was far too dangerous for him to go snooping around. He would collect Anke's things and then bow out and wait for the police to turn something up.

*

What bothered Jack more than anything else as Smittand's driver eased the car through Cairo's mid-morning traffic was how Anke's captors discovered where she was staying so quickly in this city of fifteen million people when only the Anglo American boss knew it. Surely it had to be opportunist fundamentalists who had happened to single out a foreigner who was staying alone. On the other hand, an inside job from Anglo American was a distinct possibility, despite Smittand's claims of confidentiality. Either way, Jack failed to see how he could throw any light on it. No. He would pray for her and sit tight until the ransom demand was made. There was no other course.

A copy of the *Egyptian Gazette* poked out from the glove pocket, the same edition he had read on the plane the previous evening. It was too painful to read. Memories of Anke towing him in from the Red Sea, saving his life, and all their adventures together came flooding back. *Will I never, ever hold her again? That cannot be. I must keep hoping.*

His sleepless night of travel, the carbon monoxide fumes thick in the air, the constant stop-start of the traffic all combined to make him drowsy. He dozed briefly. When he next opened his eyes he realised they were in Heliopolis, the eastern section of the city where fine old colonial buildings mingled with modern high-rises and ornate green and white traditional mosques.

'*Allah Akbar,*' pealed out in an unsynchronised cacophony from several different mosques as the Imams called for midday prayers. Egyptian men in *jalibayas* scurried to make their ablutions and pray. It seemed so timeless and above the pain of kidnapping and violence that Jack found it difficult to balance the present with the immediate past.

'Hotel Salem,' announced the driver as he swung right off the main street.

The police presence was signified by the familiar black and white car parked near the main entrance and the half dozen well-dressed overweight Egyptians conferring in the foyer. So obviously CID men. Jack announced himself to the receptionist as a representative of Mr Smittand and was taken over to a plain clothes officer.

'I've been requested to take Miss Hoffmann's personal belongings, sir.'

The police officer raised his eyebrows.

'Mr Smittand advised me that you had phoned suggesting that we should take care of her things as the management want to let the room, *effendi.*' Bowing to courtesy, the police officer relaxed his eyebrows.

'*Taban,*' he agreed. Of course. He led Jack past an Out of Order sign to the stairs. One flight up, the officer stopped, panting heavily. He pointed upwards and told Jack to make his own way to the fourth floor where a policeman would show him Anke's room, number 406.

Two uniformed police stood outside 406. One clicked off the mobile telephone he was answering and indicated it was all right for Jack to enter. No attempt had been made to clear up the mess. Anke's toiletries were scattered around the entrance to the bathroom and her blue business suit lay in a crumpled heap on the floor, still with its hanger inside. The rest of her few possessions were cast here and there. A lightweight suitcase lay upturned and empty. In another corner the packsack that had become so familiar to him. Beside it was the clipboard she had used in Sinai with a clean sheet of blank notepaper on it – nothing else – newly sharpened pencils and a new notebook, also with blank pages. Anke had been thorough he thought, nothing in writing of her Sinai trip. She had cleaned it all out, probably while she was in Germany.

Jack began collecting her things; even her expensive walking boots were there. He felt as if she was already dead and he was clearing up after a dreadful accident. There was nothing to be found in the drawers, now upside down on the floor. He felt sick inside and stuffed the remainder of her things in the bag without bothering to fold them away.

He stepped across to the balcony, noting the chalk boxes and arrows scrawled on the floor to indicate where the body had been dragged. He saw a smear of dried blood running from where the French window slid across the doorway to the balcony edge. Jack winced and knelt down to look. It was as if it might be his last contact with her and he had to wipe his eyes with back of his hand before he stood up. The accompanying policeman had not helped by droning verses of the Koran the whole time.

As he cleared his vision, he went to the balcony edge for air and stared down into the mass of pipes, dustbins and filth. The only colour he noted in that back alley was the blue rope still hanging from its fixture on the balcony. Jack suddenly he went rigid.

Blue rope, his thoughts echoed. He swung round, staring incredulously at the dangling cord. *Pale blue polypropylene fibre flake six-millimetre.* The only rope in Egypt like that had been imported by his project. He smelt it and knew in an instant that he not only knew its origin but also the exact coil. Unless he was much mistaken his wrists still bore the scars from part of that same length.

Impossible. He drew the strands to his nose again and a cold shudder rocked his whole body. The rope had been trebled up for strength and the tell-tale triple groove in the balcony rim showed where the rope had run across it while Anke had been lowered. Back at the French window, Jack knelt and inspected the aluminium runner of the door slide. Against the leading edge was the crusty material of a scab. All was clear now.

Back outside in the car with Smittand's driver, he took the *Egyptian Gazette* from the glove pocket and read again the last line of the article, 'the bodies were never recovered'.

Jack took a deep breath and shook his head.

FOURTEEN

The last six hours had been a living hell. There were no parts of her body without pain. Ropes cut into her ankles and wrists, a gagging cloth pinned the corners of her mouth against her teeth and both hips were bruised and excruciatingly painful from where she had been rolling round the back of the jeep.

Anke had seen daylight come as the vehicle sped down well finished roads. She had been aware of it becoming dark then regain light within a few minutes; she had felt the swing of corners and noted the change of gear and pull of the engine – but had seen nothing. There had been the gruff Arab voices at a checkpoint and she had sensed the smell of the fuel tank being refilled some minutes after the vehicle had left the asphalt. Later it had returned to the surfaced road and sped on. In her weariness she remembered the heat of the day and the increasing fatigue in her body and the lingering nausea from the taste of chloroform in her mouth and nose.

She had wanted to vomit but knew she would probably have choked and managed to fight it off. Slowly her senses returned. She recalled her room in Cairo. Vaguely she remembered answering a knock on the door and two men rushing in on her. Then the stench of chloroform. The first man into the room was unmistakably the tall soldier of their nightmarish detention in Sinai; the same who had kicked and punched her. She could only assume that the other was his fat boss.

Disbelief and wretchedness overwhelmed her. Was there no end to their perversion? This time they would surely torture her to death. There would be no escape route put her way. Heaven only knew what her fate was to be considering the trouble they must have taken to find her and then drive far from Cairo.

How she wished Jack Fischer was on hand with his practical knowledge. He would be safely relaxing in England by now. If only she had been able to persuade him to have worked with her but then they might both be in this mess Jack was lucky but obviously not enough luck had rubbed off on her. He did not want to chase gold, did not want to chase fortunes, did not even want to chase her, she thought morbidly. Or did he? She remembered the look in his eyes when he had given her the anchor pendant from Bait min Dahab, she then thought of Bait min Dahab. Or did he? Tears burned in her eyes. She coughed and everything hurt more.

What seemed like hours later the jeep lurched off the asphalt and made a tortuous journey along a rough track for yet another hour. Many times she screamed out with pain as she rolled helplessly from side to side in the darkened jeep. She was unable to absorb many of the spine shattering jolts that rocked the vehicle as it lurched through the ruts. Finally, it rolled to a halt and the engine was turned off, the cab doors were opened and slammed shut. Gruff voices faded into the distance.

She lay still, bracing herself for the next onslaught. But nothing happened. Only the sound of the desert wind remained as it gently struck the jeep's side. She managed to draw herself up and prop her aching back against one of the wheel arches; it at least provided some degree of comfort. She listened for voices from her captors and eventually deciphered the distant roar that had been there in the background all the time – surely it was the sound of the sea.

She thought back over the journey. The five minutes of darkness earlier on must have been the Ahmed Hamdi tunnel under the Suez Canal, and she was now somewhere back on the Gulf of Aqaba coast; maybe even at that fateful army camp where they had been held captive a week ago.

That's what this is, a replay of the previous events but without the mistakes; a perverted revenge. She knew when she looked into the army man's eyes that he was beyond obscene and disgustingly fat. He was evil. His mind was warped and he lacked any measure of human forgiveness.

It slowly became dark; the day was gone. She had drunk nothing. She sensed her nostril and mouth membranes drying out. She had to get some water quickly. She banged her heels frantically on the jeep's steel floor and at long last the backdoor was opened. A flashlight shone in her face. All she could do was to make fierce sucking noises through her teeth. There was no chance of seeing who was there before the door clanked shut once more.

A few minutes later the footsteps returned. She recognised the tall man as he put a pistol to her head and roughly pulled down her gag.

'*Moya*,' he grunted, thrusting a plastic container of water to her lips.

She felt her lips cracking as she tried to relax the painful creases the gag had left around her mouth. The water soothed them somewhat as she gulped greedily from the offered jug. As soon as she stopped for air he yanked the gag back into place where it again cut into the corners of her mouth. The door slammed and he was gone.

So much for humane treatment, she thought; just enough to keep me alive until the time of execution. The nausea returned with the wetting of her throat. She drifted off and imagined she was dying.

How long she had dozed before the door opened she never knew but this time two men were there talking in low voices. All she remembered was the suffocating pressure of a rag in her face for the second time. Again, the stench of chloroform filled her nostrils.

*

Jack booted the accelerator pedal of Smittand's Land Cruiser down to the floor and watched the needle climb to 140 kmh as he surged up the road away from Dahab towards the mountains and southwards to Sharm el Sheik. He was exasperated by his inadequacies. Two days now since Anke's disappearance and all he had gained from his inquiries in Dahab and adjacent sites was confirmation from Anke's campsite that two military men had asked for her passport four days earlier. The owner had told them she had taken it with her and left for Cairo two days before. He told Jack the men were agitated and had stormed away without giving reasons.

As the Land Cruiser raced through the cutting at the summit of the hill Jack asked himself why he had ever suggested to that Aryan woman that they check out those copper stains. Life would have been much simpler had he forgotten about it. He then remembered the five thousand dollars in crisp hundred-dollar bills given to him by Smittand as working cash and now sitting against his chest. They reminded him how important those little copper stains had become and how urgent it was to find the geologist.

A million dollars would not have been enough so incensed was Jack with the events that had occurred. If his energy permitted, he would pursue the kidnappers to the ends of the Earth.

Ironically it was good that Smittand believed it to be the work of a rival mining company. Funds would pour his way all the time there was a chance he could track her down. Maybe he should tell the authorities all he knew and let them locate the army unit. However, he reasoned it wasn't as simple as that. There would be a cover-up to avoid a scandal, the men were presumed dead and had been posthumously awarded great honours, and the government would not admit such a mistake. Even if they did act, Anke's captors would panic and kill her, which at least didn't seem to be their immediate aim or they would have done so in her hotel room. They must have other plans.

Jack glanced at the radio clock. There was an hour to reach the airport at Sharm. He had earlier phoned for a seat reservation on the Hurghada plane. Frustrated with his efforts in Dahab, he had decided he needed help to infiltrate the local community as the most likely thing to have happened was that Anke had been taken back into Sinai to face trial with the 'big boss' their captors mentioned on their previous meeting. It was a wild guess but the fat man had already told her that was to be her fate when in the Zodiac a week ago. Wild shot as it may be, that was all he had to go on.

In Hurghada on the Egyptian coast of the Red Sea there were several skilful fishermen personally known to him. They knew most of the coast in detail. They also knew the water traffic and, more importantly, they knew the unofficial activities that went on. He hoped he could recruit one such man to work with him.

'Ahmed,' he called out to a greasy looking, boiler suited Egyptian bent over an outboard engine in a workshop doorway. The stocky man looked up and gave a big smile as he put down his spanner.

'Mr Jack. *Habibi*, by God what are you doing here?'

They came together and kissed each other on the cheeks and continued the Egyptian greetings another three times with several handshakes. Tea was ordered and a boy put in charge of the outboard repair.

Jack knew full well that Egyptian hospitality could not be rushed so tried to relax and camouflage the urgency of his mission. Ahmed had not worked with Jack for several years and now had his own business A decade ago they had worked together on a project. Jack had been almost one of their family at that time and knew he could take Ahmed into his confidence.

When the moment was right he spelt out the situation in slow precise Arabic; the discovery of the box of hashish, their capture, their escape and finally Anke's abduction from Cairo. No mention was made about finding gold. Ahmed listened with painful understanding. He knew only too well the role of the coastguard in the smuggling industry. There was little love lost between Hurghada's fishermen and the *Gesh* who often imposed unreasonable restrictions on their activities to give themselves freedom to conduct their own smuggling operations.

It was late afternoon when they moved back into the shade of Ahmed's house. The entire position had been reviewed and reviewed again. His old friend had become grave.

'You know, Jack, what I am thinking is that she will be taken to Saudi Arabia to be a plaything in a harem.'

'Don't be ridiculous,' exclaimed Jack.

'No, it's true. There are girls taken every year for that purpose. Some are taken on the promise of a good life, others by force, but they never come back.'

'You are joking. This is nineteen-ninety; she is a citizen of Germany and a very liberated woman. She will never accept that.'

'Then they will drug her or kill her. I'm not joking, Mr Jack.'

'I can't believe that,' Jack persisted.

'Wait a minute. I'll send for Ramadan Abrahim – remember him from the days of our fishing camps? He will tell you the same. Maybe he will agree to help us Wait.'

Ahmed got to his feet and called for his son and sent him running in the direction of the port. He fetched the hookah and began preparing the base of the smoking chamber.

'Mr Jack, Egyptian fishermen are the only good fishermen in the Red Sea and they can't bear to see their neighbour's fish dying of old age.' He paused and chuckled. 'They sail up and down the Red Sea fishing in places where they don't get caught for poaching, especially seeking *bouri*, mullets, which are valuable salted here. Our men go all the way to Eritrea these days and are often gone for three months. Some even go as far as Yemen, not many though because the Yemeni authorities are not kind to Egyptian fishermen and some stay in jail there a long time. But by making all these voyages and anchoring in some lonely places they know all that is going on along the coast. There are civil wars in Eritrea and the Sudan so they travel mostly down that side where there is not much coast guard anymore or the means to arrest them but sometimes they fish in Saudi waters because there are many Egyptians working for Saudi owners in the fishing business - you never find a Saudi at sea, Bedouin people. These expatriate Egyptians will never report one of our boats for poaching so they are quite safe there also.'

It was then that Ramadan arrived and they stood to welcome him; again performing the seemingly endless Egyptian pleasantries. Another round of sweet tea was ordered. Apart from a few white hairs Ramadan was still the same youthful alert seaman Jack remembered from ten years ago. He was tall and strong as a stallion and at the same time a courteous wistful gentleman whose manner told nothing of the daring rascal side of his character that came into play once he was aboard his boat.

Ahmed took up the conversation and spoke in quick Arabic with a lowered voice recounting the facts to Ramadan who only imposed with the occasional *'ti-ib'*, okay, or *'sa'*, exactly. After about fifteen minutes of continuous dissertation Ahmed finished and carefully refuelled the hookah.

He lit the hubbly-bubbly on its ornate stand, filling the room with dense clouds of heavy tobacco smoke. Finally, he passed the mouthpiece to Ramadan who rasped heavily on it, releasing more clouds of thick smoke. Jack felt his enthusiasm beginning to fade as he wondered if he might have placed too much hope on his trip to Hurghada.

At last, Ramadan addressed him with a slight raising of his eyebrows.

'*Mashekel*, Mr Jack'.

Jack's gloom increased, he did not want to know that it was a problem. That was already blatantly obvious.

Ahmed spoke with Ramadan again in hushed tones for a few minutes and they both took long inhalations from the water pipe. After that, Ramadan stood and bid Ahmed farewell then turned his six-foot frame to Jack and flashed him a grin, showing gold teeth and sparkling eyes.

'*Yala*, Sharm.'

Jack gave a sigh of relief, thanked Ahmed profusely for his help and apologised for the brevity and nature of his visit. As he and

Ramadan left for the airport, Jack noted nothing had been discussed; no money, no time, no plan. But Ramadan's abrupt attitude meant without a doubt Jack could count on him. He knew him of old. The best and toughest of all the fishermen he had worked with in Egypt. He was indeed lucky to have found him in Hurghada.

Later, as they drove up into the mountains leading away from Sharm el Sheik, the orange sun dipped towards the jagged rim in the west and the blue sea faded in his mirror. Jack pulled quietly to the side of the road at the same spot he had done the same two weeks earlier for his colleagues from Dahab. As the sun set Ramadan prayed, kneeling among the warm stones and facing Mecca in the same way millions of other believers were doing at that moment on that meridian.

Jack leaned on the side of the Land Cruiser and reflected on events during the last couple of weeks. He thought what a wonderful therapy it must be, for those few minutes every day, to bring one's self as Ramadan was doing, close to the Maker, or at least away from the rank disorder of life. He had noticed the air of calm that always followed the prayers of his Arab fishermen friends and wondered if perhaps the West had lost something.

After Ramadan said his formal prayers he remained on his knees and looked on into the sunset with an expression of serenity that reflected the total peace within him. Jack felt humbled to look on at that sun frazzled, muscular five-day bearded fisherman unashamedly communicating with his god.

He rose to his feet and slid his toes back into his sandals then sauntered back to their vehicle. He laid one hand on Jack's shoulder said, '*Nueba* captain. *Ala-tool.*' Directly to Nueba, thought Jack, as they raced back into the mountains. Nueba was past Dahab to the north, a sleepy village that seemingly had little reason to exist other than as the ferry port to Saudi Arabia. It consisted of a handful of grubby concrete structures associated with local administration and customs but little else.

From the south it was reached by a tortuous road through the ranges from Dahab. This finally descended in a series of switchbacks and escape roads before arriving at the port. Long before the ferry had come into existence a Bedouin village laid in the low oasis behind the beach strip to the south. Flanked by mountains and deep *wadis* at the rear and the exceptionally deep water of the Rift Valley close inshore, it was ideally situated for less official activities than the ferry business. It had for years been the smuggling capital of Sinai. Everything from hi-fi and televisions from Saudi to hashish from the east allegedly came ashore along this remote stretch of difficult coastline. The number of satellite dishes perched precariously on the roofs of shacks and the shiny new Toyota pick-ups parked among the camels was testimony enough to the success of the trade.

When Jack had done his survey there about three weeks earlier, he had seen an assortment of small boats. Some were sports boats left behind by the occupying Israeli forces; others were local *houris*, which were little more than canoes. Very few could have been classed as fishing boats and there had not been a trace of fishing gear anywhere. However, all those he interviewed swore blind that they were active fishermen and in pressing need of huge engines of great horse power. Jack had made them no offers of help.

He explained the results of his work mission to Ramadan and voiced his apprehension about speaking to the men himself. It would be better he thought for Ramadan to speak to them alone while Jack waited at the ferry port.

Once past the main Cairo turn on their approach down into Nueba, they were surprised to encounter a chaotic situation all the way to the port. The normally empty village was besieged by thousands of Egyptians surrounded by bundles, cases, small items of furniture and other personal effects. Lines of buses were packed with unshaven Egyptian workers, their possessions piled up like haystacks on the roof racks. Cairo taxis were there by the dozen. Hundreds of police and government officials stood around, the officials seemingly handling the hiring and loading of the vehicles or administering long food lines.

Ramadan stopped someone to ask the meaning of it all. After much gesticulation and quotations from the Koran it became apparent that the Egyptian workers had either been thrown out of Saudi Arabia or were scuttling out for their own good. The mass exodus had been brought about by a rumour that Saddam Hussein was to launch a full-scale attack on Saudi itself. The impression was that the Americans were taking over the defences of that country and the Egyptians were being made refugees from a war zone.

The Egyptian government regarded the situation as grave and was rescuing the displaced souls, feeding and transporting them back to Cairo where most of them had homes.

Jack thought the action somewhat draconian but it made him realise how serious recent developments were and wondered how much longer he would remain unaffected by them. Such a crazy part of the world he murmured to himself. Year after year he had dodged around the region's wars yet still managed to move from one job to another. It was ironic he had been chased out of Mogadishu and the Sudan and was now flirting with yet another conflict by his own choosing when he could so easily be in England safely out of the way.

He parked off the road and left Ramadan to his own investigations down at the oasis equipped with a hundred-dollar bill. He sauntered off towards the port mingling among the crowds and the mayhem to see if there was an English language newspaper available with information about the latest developments in the Gulf.

Shortly before ten o'clock Ramadan returned, his eyes dilated and his *jalibaya* smelling strongly of smoke. He got in the car and directed Jack to go south.

'The situation now is very complicated,' he said, 'all smuggling is now stopped in Nueba because of this refugee business; too much police and coastguard here. One boat came here yesterday and he took fright and returned back down the Gulf of Aqaba without making any trade. This was the boat of Sayeed Ria. He is a very daring smuggler. His family Yemeni. He is very clever and always finds a way but the Bedouin say he returned back without trading. They are very worried about so much activity in Nueba. They say that Saddam Hussein is a bad man because he is spoiling their business.'

'Quite despicable of him,' Jack agreed with a smile. 'Now what?'

'They say Sayeed Ria will probably go to Nabq because there it is only local coast guard and he has paid them well in the past to keep their mouths shut.'

'Nabq? That's right back near Sharm.'

'Before Sharm. It is five kilometres this side. It is a closed area because of the airport. Only military and police can go there. Sometimes fishermen go there by boat but they must first get a permission note from the coastguard. Plenty of lobsters there, Mr Jack. Very good place for fish also.'

Something about the twinkle in Ramadan's eyes told him that he was not in the habit of seeking these permissions himself.

'What about this man called Sayeed Ria?'

'He is Yemeni man, very tough man. You know what the meaning of 'ria 'is Mr Jack?'

'Yes. Tempest - storm. His name is Sayeed Tempest?'

'*Iowa*. He is tough man. He don't stop for no one. I know him all my life. Sometimes he stays on his boat one year and never goes on the land, Mr Jack. They say he is called Ria because he gets angry very quick. Everybody is afraid from him.'

'He smuggles hashish?'

'More; his grandfather was best Arab man who goes for slaves. He was plenty respected this man and plenty rich also. He used to get very strong man and woman from Africa for working in Arabia. Nowadays the trade is only for beautiful woman to live in harem.'

'Now? These days?' Jack could hard believe what he was hearing.

'Yes Mr Jack. Sayeed Ria cannot sail his boat anywhere empty. He must make trade. He picks up plenty nice black girl from Eritrea, young one from poor family and promises her nice job in Saudi Arabia. They go with him because war in their country and the life very difficult. He tells them they get papers in Gizan and get job with

Saudi prince. They go Mr Jack but never come back. He gets good price for them at special market.'

Jack shook his head in disbelief. He had never heard of such a thing. It was an impossible concept in 1990 and what of Anke... a plaything for a Saudi prince? He sneered at the idea. How much was she worth, he wondered, all six feet of her with a masters in geology, bet they didn't come like that in the market very often. Put her in a harem and she would have it rewired and feeding electrons into his Royal Highness's testicles within hours if he knew anything about her.

'When in Yemen he gets hashish from another trader in his family who brings it from the Hadhramaut on the south coast of Yemen. It arrives there by trading dhow from the East. This is very old trade, Mr Jack. It started before the prophet Mohamed. They bring the hashish up to Egypt because Egyptian men like it too much.'

He chuckled and patted a bulge coming from the inside pocket of his jalibaya. Jack smiled and understood where the first of Smittand's hundred dollar bills had gone but said nothing.

They wound their way back through the mountains and were well on their way towards the Nabq turn-off before there was any further conversation. Suddenly Ramadan sat up straight, straining his eyes and indicating to Jack to slow down. He watched the stony desert at his side and then quickly said, 'There. Fifty metres turn Mr Jack.'

Jack obediently slowed right down and dropped off the asphalt into the desert, engaging four-wheel drive as he did so.

'We cannot go by road; it is blocked by the police. But we can go in this back way through the mountains used by the Bedouin.'

They followed a small *wadi*, picking their way through the larger stones while trying to stay on the gravel. The alluvial fan soon ended and they found themselves snaking up a narrow gorge boxed in by high-sided mountains. Jack kept his lights dipped to see his way through the rocks but lost all sense of direction in the many turns of the dried stream bed. On the main road there was always a bright star to watch or the moon or something but in the *wadi* it was rarely possible to see the sky at all. The *wadi* came to an abrupt end with only scree running up before them.

'Low gear,' commanded Ramadan. The vehicle eased its way slowly up the scree for fifty metres to where it levelled on to a saddle with a similar scree running down the other side. The Land Cruiser slid down from the ancient watershed and picked up another small *wadi* leading seaward. After a further twenty minutes of difficult driving the gorge started to open out and the mountains abruptly ended.

'Off the lights, Mr Jack.'

They continued another hundred metres with only the side lights on.

'Off all. Stop the car,' Ramadan commanded, now fully alert. 'Stay here. I'll check.'

Jack sat tight while his old friend took off into the darkness. Ramadan had rejected the offer of a further hundred-dollar bill and Jack felt confident he knew what he was doing. The man's ways may not be conventional but neither was anything else about the whole mission. His thoughts turned to the overweight detectives in Cairo and he shrugged his shoulders. What other hope was there?

To Jack, Nabq was merely a name. As he remembered it, there were no physical structures to hang the name on. He had visited the place the day before he and Anke had set off on their eventful trip. He had been accompanied by a soldier who was at pains to point out that there was no settlement there despite Jack's protestations that it was a listed landing site.

Here the desert met the sea in an undefined line of salt pans, lagoons and shallow reef. Strategically it was important because of its close proximity to the airport and its command over the entrance of the Gulf of Aqaba. The only official access was from the south through the military camp near the airport. This had effectively barred development for many years and the rich fishing area had been neglected for about a generation.

With some difficulty a few Hurghada men had fished the region by approaching from the sea. They were frequently arrested by the small coast guard unit in the area who had to be bribed before releasing them. This unit had its own vested interest in keeping the shoreline quiet.

. The new moon had gone down shortly after sunset and the night was now very dark. By faint starlight Jack could make out the reef line about a kilometre away. He strolled a short distance from the car and wedged his body in front of a rock to shelter from the cool breeze funnelling down the valley.

Eventually he discerned three small yellow lights flickering and moving slowly along the reef edge. The lights grouped, spread out and regrouped as they progressed along the reef. He recognised them as the lights used by Egyptian fishermen for their unique and very successful method for catching lobsters. During low water spring-tides the creatures came up on to the surface of the reef at night to feed. The keen–eyed fishermen chased them through the shallows before pinning them down with a pronged stick. For light they used a specially soldered can with a long neck into which they put paraffin and hessian sacking. The hessian, which just protruded from the neck, was set ablaze to act as a light. Dashing across coral heads in fifty centimetres of water with a blazing flame just above one's head was not the easiest of jobs and only the very best fishermen ever attempted it. However, those who did succeed made fabulous wages by local standards.

Jack had seen Ramadan return to one of his fishing camps after only a night's fishing with three sacks full of creaking lobsters. But, like all the other lobster fishermen, he also bore plenty of scars round the ankles and lower legs where plastic sandals had slid off coral heads into crevices.

After what seemed like a couple of hours the fishing activity stopped and the lights disappeared from view. With nothing further to watch Jack stiffly drew himself up and wandered back to the car. In the comfort of the vehicle it was not long before he found his lids getting heavy and he dozed fitfully until the crunch of approaching feet on gravel woke him sharply. The big frame of Ramadan soon filled the passenger doorway and half a dozen creaking lobsters were released from a fold in his clothing on to the Land Cruiser's floor.

'Sharm. Let's go, Mr Jack.'

Creeping back up the *wadi* in the last of the night Ramadan recounted his visit to the reef. He had joined three Hurghada fishermen well known to him in the hunt for lobsters. Afterwards they had sat warming themselves round a single paraffin lamp drinking hot tea during which time Ramadan obtained all their news.

He said their previous night's lobster fishing had been curtailed because they had seen a coast guard jeep heading towards them in the distance. They had doused their lights in time and ducked down behind the rocks. The jeep had stopped close to the end of the *mersa* where the deep water came closest to the land. They left their vehicle lights on and within an hour a sambuk crept slowly up the *mersa* using the jeep's lights as a guide through the reef. The fishermen said they were so close that they could recognise the sambuk as the one belonging to Sayeed Ria.

After the sambuk had made contact with the men in the jeep some of the crew waded to the shore carrying a large wooden box. This was not an uncommon sight to the fishermen, but it was highly dangerous to be caught observing it, so they kept well down out of sight.

'What happened then?' enquired Jack.

Ramadan said that after the box had been put by the jeep a conversation took place. Finally, they took a big bundle from the jeep and carried it to the sambuk. They saw four men carrying it and they said it looked like a body.

Jack groaned and put his foot down harder on the accelerator causing the vehicle to lurch up the *wadi.*

'They left in the jeep, leaving one of the sambuk crew sitting on the box.' continued Ramadan,

'Why?'

'Because within half an hour the jeep returned back with diesel; two barrels of it from the army camp. They are all in this smuggling business, Mr

Jack. They took the diesel to the sambuk and the jeep left with the box. The sambuk also left.'

'What time was this?'

'The lobstermen could not go back to their fishing because the tide was already in so must have been about three o'clock. When daylight came the fishermen visited the place where the jeep was parked hoping by some miracle the coastguard had forgotten some of their hashish. But they found nothing, only a rag smelling like hospital, like when they put you to sleep.'

'Chloroform,' exclaimed Jack. 'That's it. That's them all right and the girl is now in the sambuk with Sayeed Ria on the way to God knows where. At least she is alive. They used chloroform to anaesthetise her when she was kidnapped in Cairo. Brilliant work Ramadan. All we have to do now is catch the sambuk. Where will he be by now?'

Ramadan thought out loud. 'Twenty-six hours ... after Safaga, maybe Quseir, Mr Jack.'

'We have to contact the coastguard or the air force and get him stopped.'

Ramadan laughed and let out a long sigh. 'He will be far from here by the time they think to do anything. He has been good at avoiding the authorities for fifty years. You can't stop him this way.'

'The military?'

'You saw the military in action yourself, Mr Jack. In any case, all the serious ones are busy now with the Saddam Hussein problem. No one is going to chase a *hawaja* down the middle of the Red Sea. In any case he will make Sudan by tomorrow and the Egyptians can do nothing there. There is a strong northerly wind and he has six pistons. He will make good time.'

'This is ridiculous,' Jack thought out loud. He felt so damned helpless.

'Don't worry, Mr Jack, we catch the seven o'clock plane to Hurghada and we will be only day and half behind him.'

Jack looked at Ramadan in the light of the dashboard and saw the fire of adventure in his eyes and thought, yes Polglaise, we are only going to be a day and a half behind him.

FIFTEEN

Ramadan phoned his brother in Hurghada from Sharm airport. He told him to have three barrels of diesel aboard his boat along with plenty of food and water and that he would be there in an hour or so.

Jack phoned Smittand's home number and got the mining boss out of bed. He told him he believed he had a lead on Anke but not to interfere with the police's own line of investigation in case he was wrong or to let the military know what he himself was doing in case they stopped him. He said he was pretty sure she was on board a boat in the Red Sea and was about to investigate. If Anglo American needed the Land Cruiser, it was at Sharm airport and the keys were with security.

He used the call for his flight as an excuse to sign off before Smittand could deluge him with awkward questions.

In Hurghada, Ahmed and Ramadan's brother had already loaded the diesel and were loading a barrel of water into the crowded little wooden boat when they arrived. The vessel's engine was running and water spluttering out of the exhaust. Ramadan sent a boy scurrying off for matches and tobacco and another for charcoal. He and Ahmed exchanged a few quiet words and then sauntered back to a fisherman's shack to gather up a hookah.

Jack was amazed that this tall tough man should only think it fit to gather up a water pipe as his sole possession when about to undertake a task that might take several days and involve considerable risk in other countries. In a similar situation he would have been going through a long check list, visas, foreign currency, forwarding addresses, bag of clothes, books and all the other trappings of his culture - but for Ramadan a water pipe, tobacco and matches were enough for sailing off to cross foreign boundaries and possibly encounter storms, hunger, pirates, smugglers and who knew what else. Jack marvelled at the simplicity as he tossed his kitbag into the stern and let go of the ropes.

Ramadan shouted some farewells and leapt into the stern, pushing the boat away from the quay as he did so. He threw the gear lever into astern and jacked up the throttle. With the helm hard over, the green vessel turned smoothly around and was soon surging full ahead clear of the moorings and off to the south.

Ramadan pointed out the channel to Jack while he busied himself with the yardarm and raising the lateen sail. Jack steered the boat past the Sheraton Hotel standing alone like an island of sanity in a crazed world and out into the Red Sea. Ramadan had his jalibaya gathered up round his loins as he leant all his weight on the rope hoisting the long wooden yard to its full height up the mast just like generations of Arabs had done since long before Christ or Mohammed. He returned to his position at the helm and tightened the sheet until the sail filled. *Mona*, officially Hurghada fishing vessel 297, creamed at the bow and, helped by its engine, made a healthy ten knots under full sail.

Ramadan perched besides Jack on the small afterdeck. He winked at Jack and flashed his teeth in a wicked smile that was a cocktail of courage and recklessness as he adjusted his headdress and fine-tuned the helm. Jack was exhilarated by the feel of salt and sun on his cheek and the thrill of the impending chase. He was free, at least for a while. Sayeed Ria probably would not stop until he was past the Egyptian border, so for the next two days all they had to do was move southwards as fast as they could.

*

Anke felt the hell of consciousness arriving; she was no longer transferring from one nightmare to another. Instead, reality was etching a focus that did not drift anymore.

Her first sensation was one of nausea. It stemmed from her head and went in spasms down to her stomach. The pounding at her temples and the saliva welling in her throat made her swallow in great gulps. She realised she was no longer gagged and that her mouth had relaxed into a more comfortable position while she was unconscious.

She conceded vomiting might alleviate her feeling of wretchedness. She gave up fighting it and rolled her torso to one side to be sick into the blackness that surrounded her.

She could vomit only bile. She had eaten nothing for at least twenty-four hours and there was nothing for her to release. Her stomach hurt and her head throbbed and reeled. She grew aware of sharp spasms of pain in one of her ankles.

She sunk back into her original position with her eyes closed. Maybe sleep would take her away, she would die and go to the other side. The Golden Covenant, she mused, the ram's horns covered in gold and the precious stones ... surely she was on the way to the other side ... all the treasures of Moses' people flashed before her ...she started ... her head jerked and she sat up.

Now she was aware of the reality around her: the motion, the surge of water, the smell – she shuddered – the engine noise, the rush matting that scratched her legs and arms. Now there was no doubt; Anke knew she was on board a boat; a nasty, horrible, smelly, rolling boat. The noise of water and the lurch of her surroundings could have no other meaning.

She blinked. It made no difference whether her eyes were open or shut, all was darkness. Something else started to nag at her through her wretchedness, the pressure from her aching bladder. She had not peed for at least twenty-four hours and it had to happen now.

As she squirmed in agony she received more stabs of pain in her right ankle. She couldn't move.

It seemed to be fixed with metal yet her left ankle was free. She remembered having being tied up and realised her hands were now at her sides and mercifully free. Only the right ankle was tethered.

Painfully she manoeuvred her stiff body, pivoting on the shackled ankle and sliding down the matting towards the sloshing bilge water. It had to do. Prisoners of war must have had to endure worse. She slackened off her shorts and eased her pants down. She let out a curse as the boat lurched and she lay awkwardly on one hip. The sound of water hitting water assured her she had at least made it to the prisoners' latrine.

She wriggled back to her former more comfortable position but the splitting headache refused to go away. She concluded that her wretched state was compounded by weariness and she should try to sleep and hope daylight might bring some order back into her life.

Her thoughts wandered to Jack and how they had helped each other during their previous ordeal. Now she was alone. Nobody would have any idea where she was. She had been able only to glance of her captors but that was enough to confirm one was the tall, mean looking military man who, ten days ago, had punched her in the stomach. He had not drowned as they had supposed but was now in charge of her daily dose of anaesthetic.

She felt another rush of nausea and realised she was truly frightened. Until now, she had been able to think her way through fearful moments; often anger had protected her or she had gained courage by diverting her attention to helping others less able to cope than herself. This was different. She felt utterly alone.

The helplessness and hopelessness appalled her. She shivered. She thought of her mother and father and how they had muddled through life in their quiet unassuming way, how they had made sacrifices to put their only child through university. Probably she would never see them again. There were so many ways she could have been a better daughter. Her tears flowed freely as she recalled how she had not even paid them a visit on the eve of her departure from Germany more than eight months ago. Just a casual telephone call. 'See you sometime next year. I've had enough of those pigs in the office. I'll write later.' She sung out her goodbyes and hung up, not even wait for the customary farewells.

'But Katarina ...' she remembered her mother saying.

Her selfishness appalled her now. What a mess. If only she had phoned during the two days when she was back hiring her lawyer. She remembered thinking about it and putting it off, telling herself that she would inform them later about her company and all her finds when it was all tied up. Now they would never know. She would forever be the wayward daughter that went off to the east and never came back. The thought depressed her deeply, which in turn sparked anger that generated adrenaline. Suddenly, she was wide awake and alert. She tried thinking of Cairo but nothing would come back to her, only the stench of chloroform and the rough handling from of the tall soldier. What would be happening there? How did she leave her room? Surely she would be noted as missing sooner or later. Smittand would want to know why she had not turned up at his office. Surely by now the police would be looking for her.

She turned her attention to the possibilities of escape. A long swim? That never bothered her. The Gulf of Aqaba was only thirty kilometres wide at its widest. She could reach one side or the other.

She leaned forward and groped around the ankle that was paining her. As she suspected, it was bound by two circles of a chain that was wrapped around a stout wooden spar that she guessed was the base of the mast because she felt a slight movement each time the boat lurched. She felt a heavy padlock gripping the two ends of chain together. There was no slack. Her ankle was raw and painful where the links ran close to the bones. She found that if she pushed her foot forward slightly to change the pressure points she could move her ankle about an inch, but no more. She was well and truly chained to the mast and there looked to be little likelihood of escape.

Her depression returned and her fears increased. Whatever did they intend doing with her? She slunk back on the rush matting, growing more and more weary. The motion was agonising and she vomited again, although only saliva came up. She imagined a merciful death must soon overtake her.

When she jerked into consciousness some indeterminable time later, Anke found she had lost most of her headache. Gone, too, were much of the confusion and horror of her previous awakening. Instead, she felt a mounting revulsion against those who were perpetrating crimes against her. The lurching movement of the boat was much greater and the longer gap between successive rolls suggested they were further out into the Red Sea than before.

She could discern the faintest outline of the vessel's wooden timbers high up across the void in front. She reasoned there must be a small gap between the boat's deck and the hull provided by the spaces between the ribs. However, it only allowed enough diffused light through for her to make out the murky shape of the hull. She thought it was the most appalling place imaginable.

*

The breeze freshened throughout the morning and by midday a heavy swell accompanied the tailwind on Ramadan's boat. It surged bravely southwards, keeping the Red Sea coast to starboard side where Safaga, the sleepy little phosphate port with its overhead load-out system for cargo boats, slid by in the heat of the day.

With his two nights of little or no sleep, Jack was to fall into fitful jerks of drowsiness. At one point he nearly fell over the side. Ramadan nudged him to indicate a comfortable shade area below and so he turned in and left the skipper to himself at the helm.

Jack did not even remember settling down among the fishing lines and blankets before he was dead to the world. The incessant throb of the diesel engine lulled his weary body. He woke feeling refreshed and relaxed to long shadows and fading light. The big sail struggled to remain full as the engine speed overtook the dropping breeze. There was a dampness in the air as the evening humidity approached dew point.

Jack allowed himself a minute of quiet reflection before joining his companion on the aft deck. How was his poor Anke enduring her captivity with Sayeed Ria? He twice repeated the thought. Had he really said 'his Anke'? Had he somehow admitted for the first time to his inner self that she was not one more person he was going to allow slip out of his life? She had somehow lodged inside him and refused to dissolve. He realised his only way forward was to come to terms with it, even if it meant compromising his independence. With that bitter pill swallowed he felt body and soul straining to bridge the gap between them so that he could pour out these admissions to her. A sense of reckless romanticism surged through his veins, thoughts that expanded and developed as the night went on.

He eventually snapped out of his daydreams and returned to the aft deck to join his companion, taking the helm from him as he sat down. Ramadan had been sitting comfortably on the rough planking with his back to the setting sun and one arm draped over the tiller. He was busy tying new hooks on to a hank of nylon line. Around one of his big toes was a loop in the line that he pulled against to tighten the hooks. Around the other big toe was a second line that trailed back over the stern into the boat's wake.

Glancing up at the fading sky, he tidied up his new gear and wound in the trolling line. Catching Jack's eye, he lifted up the corner of a wet sack and showed off a glistening kingfish of about eight kilos, and two bonito. He shrugged nonchalantly and without saying a word replaced the sack and went forward to wash himself in preparation for his evening prayers.

Jack loved it. Ramadan was one of those ever resourceful, ever energetic men who made up the vibrant core of the fishing community the world over. How thankful he was to be part of that community himself.

As Ramadan prayed Jack silently offered up his own pathetic little request for the safety of Anke. He embarrassed himself. He felt clumsy and inadequate in the unaccustomed use of prayer. He reconciled himself with the thought that Ramadan would do a better job and that surely the Maker would listen to a more faithful servant.

Ramadan rose from his prayers smiling widely and, as if to acknowledge Jack's thoughts, told him in no uncertain terms that everything was all right, Jack nodded his appreciation, not daring to ask for more.

In the evening cool Ramadan scraped and cleaned the fish, cutting off just enough flesh for their supper while opening the rest into butterfly fillets and lightly salting them. He fanned the charcoal embers and put the kettle on for tea and then set about supper. Egyptian fishermen were among the best cooks Jack had come across in a work environment and Ramadan was no exception.

He pounded garlic cloves, ginger and fresh chillies with a pestle and mortar and rubbed the mix into the flesh of the fish. Then he prepared a tomato puree based sauce using onions, okra and basil. Ramadan's brother had stocked them well. Before any cooking began a couple of beakers of rice taken from a sack were carefully cleaned. Using an old battered aluminium saucepan stored in a locker supper was eventually cooked. To Jack, the smell of cumin, and then of lime juice, being squeezed on the fish grilling on the charcoal with its rich basting of marinades was as good as any in the world. His mouth watered long before Ramadan laid it all out in a communal tray on the afterdeck. They ate ravenously, squatting around the food and eating with their right hands in the age-old traditional way that put life in perspective for Jack. Above them the great lateen sail flapped gently beneath a sky lit by thousands of stars and the crescent of the new moon sitting close to Venus. An orange glow in the western sky created a stark silhouette of the Red Sea hills.

The two men talked quietly about events that had occurred in the years since they had first worked together. Jack was saddened to hear how Ramadan had lost his wife and young daughter in a tragic bus accident while he was at sea some years earlier. *Allah Karim*, God is merciful, he had said and 'It was God's will.'

Jack could not imagine why it should be the will of God to pluck innocent lives from their humble existence, but there was nothing to do other than agree with Ramadan and echo it was indeed so.

After a respectful pause the conversation changed to more comfortable topics. The spiralling cost of fishing and the squeezing Mafiosi tactics of fish buyers were discussed at length. It was the same banter that could be heard from Mo's Fish Bar in Oregon to the Cadgwith pub in Cornwall; fishermen's talk the world over.

Ramadan cleaned up the supper things with a bucket of sea water and went forward and brought out the hookah. Jack saw the glow from the charcoals followed by the gurgling sound as the smoke was pulled through the water chamber to cool it.

The heavy scent of locally grown tobacco hung in the air as the boat moved along at the same speed as the following tailwind. It felt as if their whole world was moving along with them as the pipe was passed between them and the stars took over from the setting moon. The *Mona* pushed relentlessly southwards, always with the white ribbon of fringing reef on her starboard beam. The little lacing provided by Smittand's hundred-dollar bill topped up the perfect nature of the evening. Even before Ramadan turned in, Jack was recounting to himself the most ecstatic moments of his desert experiences with Anke. His mind was made up as he steered the *Mona* past the twinkling lights of the sleepy old phosphate town of Quseir and on towards Mersa Alam.

Twelve kilometres of desert and reef passed by each hour. The gap between himself and Anke was no longer widening and Jack reasoned that Sayeed Ria could not sail on for ever nor, like the albatross, he would not shake off the *Mona* so easily.

His Anke, he paused in reflection again caught off guard by the possessive pronoun, his Anke, oh yes, he certainly wanted the bonding. It was a strange sensation. He glanced upwards as a puff of wind ruffled the great sail and the boat gained another knot of speed. He would buy Anke nice presents, he would spoil her with pretty dresses and the things women love, he would no longer be on the defensive, he would take her by the hand

and allow her to feel his affection. He would court her in the traditional old-fashioned way, buy her flowers, invite her to concerts, take her for picnics by the river and walks in the mountains. He would write her love letters and do everything step by step so as not to miss out on any aspect of the development of their relationship. He would savour it all.

After processing these thoughts several times, the chill of the midnight air forced him to stand and stretch his legs. He temporarily lashed the helm and leaned against the water drum and watched the phosphorescent flare swirl away in the wake of the propeller.

He remained like that for several minutes with his back to the cabin listening to Ramadan's deep restful snores like an orchestral accompaniment to the throb of the diesel engine. The *Mona*'s course remained constant and he had no need to readjust the helm lashing. Instead he gazed astern at the array of stars in the northern sky and the ribbon of white reef lying behind them. Only the company of Anke could have made it more perfect.

He recalled their supper in Bait min Dahab. He rested his eyes on the white foaming phosphorescence then slowly released the button on the top of his shorts and ran the zip down. He gently unfurled his manly treasures and allowed them to bask in the starlight. Taking up the water can they used during ablutions he delicately washed every part. The cool water did nothing to halt the expanding, tightening muscle. By then he was thinking only of Anke's thighs, her beautiful full breasts, her rounded bottom and tawny pubic curls. His eyes lost their focus on the foaming wake. His pulse quickened, the washing water beginning to feel like honey; Anke's breath was all coming back to him. He could feel her long racking inhalations and the tightening of his own spine. He clenched his toes and gasped and the white foam filled his closed eyes. After ten long hugs, Anke disappeared from his view.

It was around two in the morning before the snoring stopped and a harsh cough indicated Ramadan's awakening. He gave a satisfied glance up at the sail and briefly studied the dim profile of the land, mentally noting their position. There could be no mountain or indentation of the coastline that was not familiar to him. When he joined Jack on the afterdeck he conveyed his pleasure at their progress.

Using a short length of hose, he siphoned off the second half of their first barrel of diesel and filled the vessel's tank to the brim then fanned up the charcoal and scurried round making tea. The sleep had completely revitalised him. His quick actions told Jack that he shared his enthusiasm about catching up with Sayeed Ria.

The two men sat together on the afterdeck for the next couple of hours drinking strong sweet tea and talking quietly about their past lives. Jack found himself frequently straying back to the subject of Anke as if she had been part of his life for much of the decade rather than for a handful of days.

Mile upon mile of deserted coastline rolled by in the starlit night. They each speculated as to the vast number of virgin fishing grounds they passed over and the huge red snappers lurking in the depths just dying of old age in the absence of good fishermen like themselves to catch them. Jack enjoyed these speculations and expressions of bravado; the same that inspired fishermen the world over to be eternal optimists. He liked Ramadan and although his Arabic was far from good there was never any need to repeat any part of their conversation. It was as if they could each anticipate the other's next sentence. Jack revelled in the beautiful sense of brotherhood existing between them as true professionals; it made complete nonsense of racism and fundamentalism.

An hour before dawn, Jack turned in and entered a deep and overdue sleep.

SIXTEEN

Anke had counted four periods of daylight and was dozing in a period of darkness when she was suddenly woken by a change in motion. The craft's violent roll set items careering about the deck overhead. Fetid bilge water swept up beside her, raising the edge of the rush matting. She was seized with terror, fearing she was about to sink with the boat while still chained to the mast.

Four days of hell. An ankle bleeding from the chaffing of steel links, a stomach that could retch no longer from seasickness, and buttocks and elbows so sore from the endless rolling of the boat. No relief to be had in any position. Was this the end? Her newfound agony overrode all her previous discomforts as she hung on for grim death, the boat heaving over nearly on to her beam ends. Anke clung on to save herself from being flung across the abyss of the bilge as far as her restraining shackle would allow. Minutes later, all motion ceased as suddenly as it had begun and the boat regained an even keel. There was not even the sound of water rushing past the hull; only the throb of the engine remained. Above deck activity intensified. Anke heard quite clearly for the first time the familiar harsh commands from the stern and the patter of feet running to and fro.

Within minutes the engine speed dropped to only ticking over. This was followed by a new command from the stern and the splash of an anchor and chain going over the side. She assumed the boat had arrived at some sort of anchorage.

Shortly after, the engine stopped and complete silence prevailed. Anke shifted herself into the most comfortable position and waited. Was this to be the moment of truth? Was this where she would suffer whatever was being planned her, the administration of the final punishment for crossing swords with drug barons? Regardless of what her captors intended, she decided to attempt whatever opportunity for escape occurred. This would be her last chance.

She had hoped that as traders the men up on the deck would have some respect for their merchandise and soon start to consider whether it was in good enough condition to deliver. She reasoned that having her dead on arrival would probably do them no good at all. Maybe the time to launch an escape bid was rapidly approaching. The skipper and the crew had probably had little rest during their exodus from Egypt and may not be very alert. Her thoughts were interrupted by a shout from above.

'*Allah Akbar.*' The cry to prayer broke the silence.

Anke groaned. 'Fucking hypocrites,' she muttered. How her assailants could reverently go down on their knees and pray while treating her worse than a caged animal was beyond imagination. She recalled the hostile look of the crew member who handed down her daily ration of hobs and unleavened bread, and refilled her grubby water container that reeked of detergent. She remembered his uncompromising expression of intolerance towards the infidel.

The cultural gap between herself and this old sailor, bound by staunch fundamentalism, was as wide as it could possibly be. In his view there was no place in this life for her as a liberated woman, not to mention a non-Muslim. She represented a group of lesser humans completely alien to him; a group that demanded of him less compassion than that given to the donkeys and camels of his home village. He could treat her the way he did without compunction because she was outside of what his narrow vision considered as good.

These thoughts did little for her overall morale yet strengthened her resolve to escape however slim the chances of success.

As she listened to their uttered responses and verses from the Koran she despised their religion all the more. When the prayers ended all became quiet apart from the occasional patter of feet on the deck.

Anke took stock of the situation. Four days and nights of travel. Where was she? She had no idea of the speed of the boat but estimated it to be two or three times that of walking, so perhaps they had travelled three or four hundred kilometres a day, which meant that they could be as much as fifteen hundred kilometres from Sinai. She shuddered. They must be at least in Sudan or maybe Saudi Arabia or Yemen if they were on that side of the Red Sea. The thought was chilling.

The journey had been hellish at best and the violent rolling of the final few minutes had been absolutely dreadful. She reconsidered those frightening moments. That sudden pitching had surely rolled her towards the port side, which meant they had definitely turned right to approach the anchorage. The wind and the waves always came from the north in that part of the Red Sea and had been following them all the way. In that case she must be in Sudan, a country riddled by abject poverty and civil war. In all probability she was outside the jurisdiction of Egypt and, as far as the world at large was concerned, had simply disappeared. No one had the slightest knowledge of her whereabouts. It was her against the rest of the undeveloped world.

It was a daunting and depressing thought. What chance did she stand with her travel experiences limited to a few weeks in Israel and Egypt? She knew little of the language and even less of the culture. Even her knowledge of the geography of the area was superficial. Always with maps to refer to she had never memorised the details. She could only think of three towns in the whole of Sudan, the biggest country in Africa. She recalled Khartoum, the capital, on the Nile and Juba in the south, where the fighting was going on, and the Red Sea town of Port Sudan. That was all she could picture and she felt disgusted with herself for being so ignorant. She felt an urgent need to get ashore and discover the rest of its geography, even if it meant walking the length and breadth of that vast land to regain her freedom.

Her enthusiasm quickly waned with the realisation that she was in no state to walk anywhere after almost a week of near starvation and continual vomiting. She doubted she had the strength to stand, never mind trudge across Africa.

She stroked a hand across her breasts and then her buttocks and groaned in despair. If things continued this way for much longer in she would be able to slide into a size twelve dress – unimaginable ever since she was about thirteen years old.

From above deck came the sudden sizzling sound of food being dropped into hot cooking oil. Soon after the aroma of frying fish assailed her nostrils. Sharp stabs of hunger shot through her stomach for the first time since her abduction. She felt absolutely ravenous.

After ten minutes of listening to the sizzling Anke could stand it no longer. She struggled into a squatting position and banged on the underside side of the deck with her palms and shouted all the Arabic words she could muster relating to food and eating.

A brief silence followed, then an outbreak of chuckling from the crew before they renewed their conversation. She heard no movement towards the hatchway.

Anke yelled again in German and English until she was hoarse. She let loose the longest string of abuse that her English vernacular vocabulary would allow and slumped back into a lying position, exhausted. Peals of coarse laughter came from the crew; clearly words depicting the sexual act and lengthy curses insinuating births out of wedlock were internationally understood.

Shortly afterwards the hatch was lifted. A halo of stars met her gaze, providing a backdrop to the outlined frame of a crewman who passed down a giant wad of hobs wrapping up several pieces of fried fish and a handful of sticky dates.

She grabbed them quickly and offered a curt 'thank-you' more from habit than desire. She passed up her empty water can and the hatch cover was left open briefly while it was re-filled. A short blast of fresh cool night air rushed in to replace the rising hot foul stench of her prison. All too soon, down came the water and out went the stars and she was left again in total darkness.

Anke clutched the food in her lap she groped for every last morsel, eating savagely, spitting date stones and fish bones carelessly in the direction of the bilge. Even the foul water tasted better after a solid meal. The supply of fresh air further eased her nausea. She could only pray that the food would stay down and renew her strength. She soon slumped back to the lying position and she fell deep asleep.

*

The *Mona*'s second day of pursuit went without event. The northerly wind blew at a constant force four all day and the sun shone relentlessly from six till six. Ramadan pulled out a small tarpaulin which he jury rigged on extension poles to provide shade over the helm position. They caught half a dozen fish by trolling in the early morning and then stopped in the hope of gaining another tenth of a knot on their speed.

By nightfall the island near Wadi Gimal was on the horizon in front of them. Ramadan elected to take the inside passage and save a kilometre or so. The new moon shone in the western sky for the first two hours after dusk and the *Mona* was safely through the tricky passage between the north of the island and the mainland before it set. They recalculated the positions of the two boats and concluded that Sayeed Ria was now probably no more than twelve hours ahead and they would catch up with him soon after the Sudanese border. Quite what their plan would be then they were not sure. It didn't bear speculating about, Ramadan conceded. After all, it was possible that Sayeed Ria had chosen to take the route down the Saudi coast.

About nine o'clock Jack decided to turn in but and was about to make himself comfortable when there was an almighty bang. The boat plunged down low in the bow while the stem nearly lifted out of the water. This was followed by the racing of the engine under no load and the jangling of metal. Jack was hurled forward into the fuel drums. In the night gloom he saw Ramadan leap to the controls and heard the engine die away to a ghostly silence followed by a click as he released the stop button.

'*Allah Karim*', God is merciful, uttered Ramadan.

The *Mona* slowed to an amble with just a slight hissing sound round the bow as she parted the waves with aid of the big sail. From below the boards came the occasional slosh of bilge water.

Jack's first reaction was that they had hit a coral head and slid over the top, losing the propeller in the process. But they were still under way and after a few seconds spent watching the long wave patterns he knew they were in deep water and could not have possibly hit a reef.

Ramadan bent low over the stern and by the time Jack made it back to the helm had straightened up, dragging with him a handful of loose ends of plastic pallet straps that trailed back down under the stern of the boat.

'*Allah Karim*,' he muttered again as he went forward to his kitbag and rummaged around briefly before producing new torch batteries that he quickly loaded into the flashlight before returning to the stern.

Jack took charge of the helm and tightened in the sail, resetting the vessel on course. The two men stared down into the water to examine what the propeller had struck.

Part of the bundle of plastic pallet straps and heavy sheeting that had been buoyed up by strands of thick polypropylene mooring rope was all round the stern. It was a lethal raft of man-made garbage that had probably been washing round in the sea for weeks and could have tangled with a boat's propeller at any time. Had it not been dark they would probably have seen it in time even though due to the amount of green algae it would have been barely afloat. Encountering such hazards was nothing new for either of them and an experience that they sadly conceded was on the increase.

Ramadan took the flashlight and lifted up the floorboards aft of the gearbox. His fears were realised. All the bolts connecting the propeller shaft with the back of the gearbox had been sheared off. There was nothing to connect the power from the engine to the propeller.

He studied the shoreline for a few seconds then directed Jack to alter course towards the land, indicating a silhouetted mountain peak as a heading. The north-west evening breeze off the land gave them a good reach towards the nearest place they could beach the boat and they sailed on at about three knots. Ramadan searched among his tools and returned to the coupling some minutes later with a pathetic assortment of old rusty nuts and bolts but after some consideration tossed them all back in the toolbox.

It took nearly two hours sailing under a light wind to gain the coastline and creep down the outside of the reef. The two men were in low spirits and spoke little of their misfortune. True to his normal ambivalent manner, Ramadan praised Allah for not making life more difficult than it already was. He cast his eyes up at the big sail that barely filled in the light breeze and commented to Jack that they had no need to rush so long as they made the anchorage of Wadi Gimal by daylight. He made no mention of the fact that they had no choice in the matter.

Around midnight Jack thought he could discern a break in the white ribbon of surf marking the reef. Ramadan came aft and took the helm, easing the *Mona* closer in towards the breakers. Tightening in the sail, he steered the boat as close as he dared to the shallow water. Jack could feel the sucking in the wave trough that precedes the first crest to crack into curling white water. Skilfully Ramadan took his vessel along the front of the reef until he came to the entrance of the *mersa*, which was little more than a narrow cleft in the steep faced reef. Jack knew Ramadan would need the full width of the entrance to push their craft deep enough inside against the offshore wind to gain a safe anchorage.

Jack saw the coral heads awash just inside them. He anxiously watched Ramadan clip the northern shoreline at the entrance to allow enough room to reach well into the sheltered haven before the southern side of the *mersa* became a threat. The *Mona* coasted noiselessly further and further away from the open sea into the tranquillity of Wadi Gimal and they were safe once more.

When only a whisper of wind remained and the big sail slackened completely, they dropped the anchor over the side. Jack marvelled at the depth of these *mersas*, more than twenty metres in this case. He always allowed himself the pleasure of surprise when he anchored or cast a fishing line in such places. They were close enough to toss a stone to the shore on either side and yet deep enough to float an oil tanker.

They brought down the sail and after debating the likelihood of sharks, Ramadan stripped to his briefs and plunged in. Each knew the dangers of night swims in *mersas* and Ramadan didn't hang around. He swam rapidly to the northern shore, dragging a line behind him. A few moments later he called for the line to be fastened to the bow. Soon the boat was beached.

With the Mona resting on the sand and soft corals the two men worked in waist-deep water to clear the propeller of the plastic strapping and old rope and pile it up on the beach. A closer examination of the stern gear would have to wait until daylight. In the meantime, Ramadan used his flashlight to check the engine mountings for damage. He soon shrugged his glistening shoulders and turned to the fire box where he quickly fanned up the charcoal and got fresh tea under way.

The broken coupling was not the end of the world, thought Jack, but it would cost them at least a day while they found appropriate bolts and reconnected the two flanges. Ramadan said he would hitchhike the thirty kilometres south in the morning to a small phosphate mine where he thought he would be able to get spares.

As they both looked blankly at the calm waters of the *mersa,* reflecting on the times they had spent there ten years earlier during a long fishing camp. Jack suddenly leapt to his feet and clambered forward and snatched up an old net anchor made from ten millimetre reinforcing rods.

Helped by the torchlight he guided one of the anchor flukes through two adjacent holes of the coupling's two opposing flanges. He pushed the anchor abruptly downwards to snap the fluke off from its welding at the boss. Using a hammer and a wrench he bent the protruding ends of the bar back over the edges of the flanges to create a crude bolt. Ramadan looked on sceptically without saying anything.

Jack repeated the exercise with another fluke from the anchor. The coupling of power to the propeller now looked possible with two of the five positions secured. Ramadan got up and quickly hacksawed off the remaining two flukes of the anchor. Within an hour the coupling was lashed together by four anchor flukes. Hardly the equivalent of five high tensile steel bolts, thought Jack, but beggars couldn't be choosers. With a bit of luck his lash-up would stand up to half of the full engine power.

They pulled the boat back into deep water by heaving on the stern line. They raised the anchor and Ramadan gingerly put the engine in gear. The coupling jerked and accepted the power and the *Mona* chugged out towards the open sea. Once more they headed south and, with the sail back up, made a surprising five or six knots at half throttle.

At first light, the spindly outline of the overhead load-out system of the phosphate mine lay ahead and by seven o'clock they had berthed on its lea side.

As it was a Friday Ramadan donned a white jalibaya and went ashore. Most of the small mining community were at the mosque at that early hour but he had assured Jack that after prayers he would find a helping friend.

During his absence Jack dismantling the jury-rigged coupling and secured the main engine down on its beds. He also tightened the bolts on the stern tube to prevent water coming in. That done he sat on the stern, basking in the sun to await Ramadan's return. By mid-morning and the heat drove him into the shade. With still no sign of

Ramadan he began to doubt the availability of spare bolts and wished he had not so hastily dismantled their faithful lash-up.

Partly to escape the heat and partly from the frustration of waiting he decided to put on his mask and snorkel and make an underwater inspection of the propeller area.

He cut a remaining tight ring of plastic off the shaft and looked at the rest of the hull. There were no worrying marks to be seen and the soft green of her paint was clean and without marine growth. This indicated she had been recently hauled out and freshly painted, a fortunate fact that surely accounted for her good speed.

Satisfied with the state of the propeller and the hull he turned his attention to the pale blue expanse of deep water behind him to see if there were any interesting corals or shoals of fish. Suddenly he froze. He felt his pulse racing. Only three metres away were the piercing black eyes of a barracuda that was probably as long as he was.

It hovered in a stationary position as if summing him up. The skin covering its foot-long jaw did not quite hide the mass of menacing spike-like teeth lined up inside. Jack was instantly terrified. There was no shallow water to back paddle into; and the predator could tear into any one of his limbs at any time it chose. He felt his back touch the hull but kept his eyes fixed on the menace in front of him. If he turned and hauled himself into the boat there was a chance that his trailing legs would present a target the barracuda could not resist.

Terror gripped him. He felt his limbs shaking. He doubted his ability to climb the rudder in such a state. The giant fish's gaze was unrelenting. No sooner had Jack gained the corner of the stern than the barracuda manoeuvred a metre closer. Jack slackened his grip on his snorkel's mouthpiece and blew frantically into the water to unsettle his aggressor. It had no effect.

Suddenly there was a violent cascade of bubbles and a shock wave as the big fish turned in a flash of silver. Jack registered it as the rush that preceded an attack. As he fought for vision in the air-filled water he suddenly saw a concrete block hurtle past him into the gloomy depths. The barracuda had gone.

Jack lost no time in hauling himself up the rudder. Ramadan grinned down at him from the load-out jetty.

'*Agam! Mish quieese*, Mr Jack'.

'You're not joking,' responded Jack. He ripped off his mask and snorkel still shaken by the encounter. 'Barracuda no good' was an understatement he would remember for a long time.

'Thanks.'

Ramadan held up a plastic bag with half a dozen nuts and bolts inside and scrambled down to the boat. Jack congratulated him and thought it best not to question the delays in the light of recent events. He drew his own conclusions from the aroma of Ramadan's jalibaya and hoped some of Smittand's hundred-dollar purchase still remained.

By noon they were away with a nine-hour delay to their chase of Sayeed Ria. They reckoned this put them an even day behind him. The wind freshened during the afternoon to force six as they followed the long low coastline towards the notoriously windy Ras Banas, a hooked peninsular extending well out into the Red Sea. The fine dust collected by the hot desert air and swept out to sea made landmarks difficult to distinguish. The Mona took full advantage of the wind and sped along well away from the coast, surging down the hissing seas, her stern being lifted high above the crests from time to time.

Ramadan talked seriously about their tactics. He said that the *Mona* should no longer hug the coast after Ras Banas but head directly for the Sudan border. This was because it would soon be dark and Foul Bay, the next stretch of water, was so called due to the mass of small reefs. Also, if Sayeed Ria was on that coast, he would not stop now until he was in Sudan, especially as the Berinice navy base was close by. He suggested they should make for Mohamed Qol, the first safe anchorage on the Sudanese side of the ill-defined border with Egypt.

Between Ras Banas and Mohamed Qol lay two to three hundred kilometres of no man's land. The coast was poorly charted and on maps had two borders, one political and one administrative. The mountainous land had a coastal plain of extreme desert. Drifting sand, shallow lagoons and uncharted reefs made coasting hazardous even in daylight. As for the night, Ramadan, who knew well all the inside passages, was not prepared to weave in and out in the dark. In any case, here was a good opportunity to gain ground on Sayeed Ria. Jack liked the idea but hoped they would not overtake the Yemeni *sambuk* lurking somewhere inside of them.

The stiff breeze slackened off before sunset and once they were clear of Ras Banas it dropped to a light air. With no more help than this they continued on during night and all next day. As the wind became lighter so the air got hotter and stickier and more humid.

Ramadan siphoned more diesel into the engine's tank and tapped the barrel. They were well into their second one and would need to refuel somewhere in Sudan if they were to make the return journey to Hurghada without stopping. Jack wondered about that.

They again discussed tactics. Supposing they overhauled Sayeed Ria on the high seas. Were they to throw grappling hooks and board him like the pirates of old? Not possible they agreed. For certain Sayeed Ria's men had weapons. No self-respecting Yemeni was without at least a handgun and more than likely they would have an automatic weapon on board.

Jack said it was crucial the Yemeni remained unaware of their pursuit otherwise they would be sure to dispose of their cargo and that would be the end of Anke. Ramadan did not want to talk about options until he knew of the whereabouts of the sambuk. 'It depends on the place,' he kept repeating.

They sighted land for the first time since leaving Ras Banas on the evening of the following day. Ramadan said they were abreast of the Sudanese border, although he never made clear which one, nor did it matter. They had not sighted any other vessel and the only life form they had noticed had been the occasional seabird.

They sailed on all night, at first with Jack at the helm under instructions to keep the coastal profile far off to starboard, ensuring the vessel stayed well outside the reef. They changed watches at about one in the morning and Jack turned in, glad to sleep in the first cool period for many hours. He slept deeply and only awoke due to an abrupt change of motion as the vessel altered course across the swells. Lifting his head and shoulders up above the level of the gunwale he could see nothing and looking astern he could make out the vague outline of Ramadan standing astride the tiller on the afterdeck, peering into the gloom ahead. He went and joined his companion.

Ramadan pointed to a single tiny light on a distant shoreline. 'Mohamed Qol,' he said.

Jack picked out white fringes of surf quite close to them and wondered where the passage might be through the reef. It amazed him that such a seemingly sheltered and localised individual as Ramadan from the small fishing community of Hurghada should have such profound knowledge of areas far from his home.

They skirted the north-south running reef until a gap appeared in the water. Ramadan pulled the helm hard over and the *Mona* rolled her way through the passage. She skimmed over lightly coloured water that must have been very shallow having the bottom sand stirred up. Eventually they were free of the heave of the big swells and entered the tranquillity of a large lagoon.

Ramadan pointed the boat towards the flickering yellow light and gave the helm over to Jack. He set about bringing the big sail down and stowing it around its yard.

With the sail furled away, Ramadan prepared the anchor and ropes while making long and searching stares into the depths of the bay. Soon they could make out a line of small *houris*, wooden canoes, moored close to the shore, and then sighted the small shanty village. A few more flickering lights came into view as life started a new day in Mohamed Qol.

The skipper motioned to Jack to cut the engine back and knock it out of gear. He dropped the anchor over the side. Suddenly the long awaited quiet prevailed. The dawn was gaining strength and both men strained their eyes into the depth of the lagoon searching for a sambuk. They could see none.

EIGHTEEN

Ramadan looked furtively round the bay all the while he fanned the charcoal into life for fresh tea. By the time daylight arrived it was obvious there was no vessel within the seven or eight miles other than the small *houris* lying off the beach by the village.

Mohamed Qol was no more than a cluster of cardboard and wooden shacks. The only concrete structure was an ice plant and raised water tank provided by some earlier aid programme. Whether it was operational was doubtful. Certainly no noise of a generator came across the water.

Some of the local fishermen were already in the water with their cast nets long before the sun cracked the eastern horizon, catching their bait for the day and possibly their breakfast too. Ramadan beckoned the first mobilised *houri* to come over as it set off for the fishing grounds.

The primitive wooden canoe paddled up alongside. The reek of shark liver oil used as a preservative on the naked wood filled the morning air. A basket of shining silvery sardine lay in between the Sudanese fishermen. Still flapping, they would shortly be used as live bait to catch jackfish that formed the mainstay of their diet and subsistence living.

The two young men with their traditional white head wraps were strikingly black in comparison to their Egyptian counterparts to the north. Somewhere along their journey southwards they had crossed the division between Arab and African. Although they shared the same language and same religion as the Egyptians, their African features of big wide smiles and perfect white teeth immediately set them aside as a different race. Jack felt as if he had entered another continent. Whatever understanding he thought he had concerning Anke's abduction now faded into oblivion and a sense of overwhelming hopelessness came upon him.

The two fishermen were keen to chat to their visitors. Ramadan offered them snuff, which they took with great pleasure. He declined to join them later for hospitality ashore, explaining they were in a hurry to go to Port Sudan. When he inquired about other sambuqs passing by the lads told him that six Egyptian mullet fishing boats were working about twelve kilometres south and that was all they had seen lately.

'No,' the other interposed, 'a Yemeni sambuk stopped here yesterday night.'

Despite the lilting dialect Jack understood and leapt to attention. Ramadan questioned the youth in earnest. It appeared that the Yemeni sambuk left very early in the morning as they were cast-netting the previous day. The lad said he would not have noticed but for a whiff of fish being cooked that had drifted across the water causing him to look seaward as the silhouette left the *mersa*.

'Who was it?' demanded Ramadan.

'One of the smugglers.' The fisherman shrugged. 'There are many.' Clearly such sightings were commonplace.

'Sayeed Ria?'

He did not know and was not interested. He had only glanced up at the time.

Ramadan thanked them and wished them God's luck with their day's fishing. They doused their basket of sardines briefly back in the water to revive them and paddled off into the sunrise.

Jack anxiously asked for an Egyptian translation of the conversation in case he had missed any of the details.

Ramadan said he believed Sayeed Ria had been in the *mersa* twenty-four hours ago. It was enough to go on for the time being. They would head for Suakin.

Jack cast his eyes towards the *houri* paddling into the distance. How paradoxical, he thought, that circumstances allowed those two primitive young men and the complex whiz kid Anke to come so close to each other and yet not interact. How would they react if they knew a white woman was held captive aboard the dhow that left yesterday?

Perhaps he and Ramadan should engage the help of the authorities in Port Sudan. Then he remembered the rundown state of the Sudanese navy, the lack of coastal policing and the bludgeoning bureaucracy and decided they had few prospects of gaining any help from that quarter.

Ramadan confirmed his views. No Egyptians or Yemenis called into Port Sudan because it was a nightmare. They preferred to shelter and take stores from the little ancient port of Suakin, sixty kilometres to the south, where the authorities were more lax and tradition made it commonplace for strangers to call.

Ramadan raised the anchor and the *Mona* again sprung into life, heading south between the islands and reefs in a calm and perfect September morning.

*

Anke could barely able to believe the improvement in her physical and mental state. She knew that they were back on the open sea from the boat's slow rhythmical roll and the slosh of the ever present bilge water. But now the motion was gentler than before. Most likely the wind had dropped for the passage was definitely more comfortable. Sleep had refreshed her and the latest meal had so far stayed down. Altogether she felt an upturn in her fortunes.

Later she heard the sizzle of fish frying on deck. It had to be calm for this was the first time she had detected cooking occurring at sea. She waited until it finished and banged again on the underside of the deck with her palms.

It was met by grunts and chuckles followed by a gruff directive from one in command. Sometime later a flood of brilliant sunlight streamed in and another meal of fish and dates wrapped in hot hobs was passed down.

She grabbed it with relish, determined to rebuild her strength. When she handed up the empty plastic water she can gave a genuine expression of thanks to the familiar blank unshaven face that had served her several times before. He managed a begrudging '*Afwan*', welcome.

She regarded her shackled ankle. It was tired and stiff. She sank back against the hull and ate thoughtfully. That brief '*Afwan*' had been her first communication with the enemy. If only she could nurture the relationship and persuade him to get her unshackled, that would be a start. '*Muftah*', yes *muftah*, that was the word for key, remembered it from her days in hotels. She noted the motion of the boat and realised there was no sensation of seasickness. Maybe she was getting her sea legs, or rather sea bottom; she corrected herself with a wry smile.

There was no more food that day, no chance to try out her prepared speech about a *muftah*. Darkness descended and she dozed well into the night until she realised the monotonous note of the engine had dulled to a mere ticking over. The boat 's rhythm was almost still and only the hissing of water round the bow indicated it was moving forward.

She pulled herself upright and listened for signals from on deck. But there were none. The engine cut and finally stopped. All motion ceased and only harsh whispers came from aloft followed by what sounded like rush matting being dragged around and laid over the deck and hatch cover. She heard a quiet call to prayer followed by harsh low key responses.

Anke felt a surge of adrenaline. Maybe this was the end of her journey and her delivery to the drug baron was imminent. The adrenaline abated as the prayers were followed by loud snores and periods of absolute quietness. Finally, she also slept.

She was awakened at first light by the hatch being uncovered and lifted. More fish and hobs were passed to her. Struggling to the sitting position she spluttered, '*Muftah, muftah.*'

Her pleading look was met at first by surprise then a look full of contempt. Her spirits fell. She had been unprepared and made a mess of it. But why breakfast so early? She had seen a few fading stars still in the sky behind her guard and the crew were already busy. Empty oil drums were being trundled around the deck. Perhaps they were going to refuel. The journey was not yet over; at least not for the vessel, she added as an afterthought.

The day grew hotter and more humid. Activity above deck ceased. The bilge needed pumping out and the fetid smell of diesel, oil and her discarded products became extremely unpleasant. She prayed for fresh air. At least during the windy days the constant need to pump the boat out kept the stench at a less nauseous level. She perspired profusely. Her shorts and T-shirt were soaked by the middle of the day and felt clammy and disgusting. She shouted for water but there was no answer, no acknowledgement, no refusal, nothing.

The crew were either asleep or ashore. She drank the last drop of water to soothe her drying mouth. She shouted several times more and banged the underside of the deck. Silence. She despaired. But as the chink of light gradually faded and evening approached, the temperature mercifully dropped. Anke marvelled at the strength that was allowing her to survive.

With nightfall came the sound of distant voices and the shouts and heaves of men struggling with full fuel drums. Heavy baskets thudded down on to the deck and among other mysterious sounds Anke heard the bleating of a goat destined for some future dinner.

Her renewed shouts again for water were shortly answered by an unfamiliar crewman who was plainly in a hurry and with no mind to leave the hatch cover open more than a few seconds. Soon afterwards the small engine for the bilge pump sprang into life; evidently the stench from below was too much even for the seamen's nostrils.

The bilge was pumped dry and the small engine stopped. By then most of the activity on deck had quietened down. Only muted conversation and the occasional rasping suck on a hookah broke the stillness. Anke wondered if they would set sail that night or stay and rest for another day.

Her thoughts were interrupted by the distant buzz of an approaching outboard engine. Her nerves jangled. This was it; her final delivery to her drug lord. What fate was to befall her? She began to tremble and sat straight up to gain control of herself. The outboard stopped and a small boat bumped against the hull. She heard the familiar gruff bark of their commander come from the newly-arrived craft followed by more footsteps on deck as people climbed aboard.

Anke heard the rush matting being removed from above the hatch. She held her breath, her time had come. She bit her teeth hard together.

*

With his mind no longer preoccupied by the weather – it was a perfect September morning – or by the problems of the coupling or navigational challenges, Jack was restless. He fell silent and moody as they chugged along in a calm sea just outside the fringe of the reef. He felt depressed and out of his depth, dropped from a James Bond world into the real world of logistics, regulations, time frameworks and the Sudan.

He knew full well he was no international investigator so what the hell was he doing blundering off into the Third World without papers, without visa, and without a shred of evidence for the purpose of his mission. He recalled the clashing smells of chloroform and of breakfast cooking – hardly enough risking prison for. He must be crazy to imagine he could find and free Anke himself. He had to be realistic. He had to summon the help of the authorities.

His depression was affecting his judgement. He had almost quarrelled with his companion when Ramadan wanted to look for a passage through the reef and converse with the locals and Jack had insisted they waste no more time and go to Port Sudan. Fortunately, Ramadan said nothing and they continued on in silence.

In late afternoon they sighted the tall white stick of the Sanganeb lighthouse at the end of the Wingate Reefs, made famous by Jacque Cousteau doing so much of his work there. Ramadan said his prayers and cooked up a wonderful fish supper in the hope that Jack would come to his senses and not involve the Sudanese, but to no avail.

They cleared the lighthouse soon after nine o'clock with Jack, at the helm. He pulled the tiller over and pointed the *Mona* at the lights of Port Sudan. It must have been gone midnight when they entered the harbour as the half moon was well up. A light beam flashed at them when they passed under the Port Authority watch tower at the entrance of the *mersa*. Ramadan acknowledged it with a couple of flashes from his torch, the normal procedure for the small fishing boats.

Ramadan steered a dwarfed *Mona* close under the enormous stern of a bulk grain carrier moored alongside the harbour wall to deliver flour to the beleaguered country. He proceeded along the branch channel to where the local fishing boats moored. It was obviously not the first time he had done this and Jack marvelled again at the range of the man's experience.

He suddenly felt heavy and depressed, wishing he had heeded his friend's apprehension at coming to Port Sudan. Never mind they were here he would show the courage of his convictions and waste no time in confronting the authorities. Despite Ramadan's protestations, he summoned the help of an old man fishing in his houri nearby to take him ashore.

As he walked up the main street towards the city police station he congratulated himself on how easy it had been to enter the country without papers.

Almost the only sounds were a dog baying in the distance and the ever-present background hum from the port of ships' generators. The occasional strip light flickered above tattered posters of the president, surrounding his image in a haze of mosquitoes and night flying insects. The smell of camel dung and goats hung in the still air. Jack knew Port Sudan of old and chose to walk in the street and avoid the pot holes and broken culverts over open sewers that turned the footpaths into obstacle courses even in daylight.

The only signs of life in the *suq* area were the deep snores of merchants sleeping among their merchandise at their market stalls. He passed a couple of fighting cats and four dozing camels before he saw the illuminated radio mast of the police station, in itself something of an advance when he recalled the six-week long black-outs of his previous visits.

A young soldier was asleep in the sentry box at the entrance to the police station yard. His short machinegun rested peacefully across his lap. Jack thought better than to pass him and gently imposed,

'*Salem alay kum Offendi,*' Peace be with you officer. The youngster jolted upright position and looked confused.

Jack spoke slowly in Arabic. 'I want to speak to the senior police officer.'

The guard looked both puzzled and annoyed and kept his hand securely on the Kalashnikov as he escorted Jack to the into the police station, passing another sleeping soldier stretched out on the walkway under the veranda.

The young guard tapped nervously on a steel door. There was no answer. He tapped again with greater conviction.

A muffled '*Iowa*' came from within and the soldier opened the door. He spewed off an explanation in rapid Arabic to the portly man who confronted them as he laboriously removed his body from the table top where he had obviously been asleep.

The senior man desperately tried to pull himself together on hearing the word '*Hawaja,*' the foreigner, the non-believer, but clearly an important visitor. He groped about the floor behind the desk of the dimly lit office for his official cap to cover his bald head and regain some semblance of importance. He straightened his uniform and repeated, '*Iowa?*' He followed his pained expression with the hint of a smile for the foreigner.

'*Iowa.* Yes.'

Jack realised he was about to be swallowed up by the enormous chasm of Sudanese bureaucracy and he experienced a terrible sinking feeling. 'I need help ...'

The officer cut Jack off and ordered the guard to get tea for them.

He invited Jack to sit on a tubular steel chair with a shaky back leg. Its original green colour had long been worn off to reveal the shine of the underlying metal. The seat had also seen better days with its interlaced multi-coloured plastic strips hanging down in several places leaving only the fore and aft sections safe to sit on. He accepted it cautiously. The officer left the room and could be heard passing water nearby. When he returned he pulled another chair out from behind the desk and slumped into it heavily. He asked Jack his nationality.

'British.'

That seemed to please him immensely and he beamed back.

'Liverpool?'

Jack shook his head and was about to come to the purpose of his visit.

'Ah, London then,' stated the officer in the clear belief that British men hailed only from one or the other of these ports.

Jack thought better than to pursue the geography lesson any further.

'Passerport.'

He handed the document across the desk and was about to start off the explanation of his mission when the young soldier returned with the tea. He loitered round the door before being curtly dismissed and sent back to his post. The officer pushed the tea over to Jack. He then folded his arms across his great chest and flashed another broad smile at his visitor.

'Liverpool. Me I know,' he said in broken English. 'Me seaman before policeman. English man good, very good English man. Good Liverpool.'

Jack was delighted the policeman had such a high opinion of his countrymen and birthplace but soon found he had exhausted his knowledge of the language and for that matter most other worldly things. They struggled on in Arabic.

After they drunk their tea the officer turned his attention to the passport. He held it at arm's length, trying to bring the official stamps into focus but without success. He turned over page after page, scanning the cluttered stamps and signatures before giving up and asking to be shown the Sudanese entry.

Had Jack had his wits about him he could have pointed to any of the poorly defined stamps and they would most likely have been accepted. Instead he chose the route of honesty and said there wasn't one because he had come from a boat and would get a stamp in the morning.

The policeman interrupted him before he could explain any further. What business had made it necessary for Jack to come to the police station during curfew?

Jack looked shocked. 'Curfew?'

'Midnight until five o'clock.'

'Sorry. I didn't know.' He apologised.

'Your boat name?' The officer scrabbled in the drawer hanging out of the desk for an exercise book and writing instrument.

'*Mona*,' sighed Jack.

'Ah. You came by yacht?'

'No sir. It is an Egyptian fishing boat. We are looking for a missing person, a woman kidnapped by a Yemeni *sambuk*, gassed in Cairo, tied up ... 'Jack paused to see if the officer had grasped the essence of what he was saying before he carrying on.

'Wait.'

Jack hesitated, not sure if he had got the message through. The officer pushed his cap back and scratched his head. Jack took that to be a bad sign and repeated what he had just said in slower more deliberate phrases.

'Big problem.' the reply came at last.

Jack was relieved. He seemed to have taken it on board.

The portly officer scooped up a telephone sitting on the floor behind the desk, grunting loudly from his efforts. He dialled a number three or four times without response and tossed the apparatus back on to the floor with an *'Allah Karim'* for good measure. He rose to his feet, straightened his uniform and directed Jack to wait a minute as he shuffled out through the door.

He heard him disturb the sleeping soldier and gruffly issue an order. The soldier appeared through the door, rubbing his eyes and adjusting the machinegun slung over his shoulder. He took the officer's chair from behind the desk and positioned it by the door, plonking into it and making himself comfortable.

Jack took this as another bad sign. He heard a jeep start up and drive away, another sign perhaps of impending action. The soldier went back to sleep and Jack also made himself comfortable. He could have a long wait; a minute was not a minute in Sudan.

After about an hour in which he had studied the lopsided picture of the president for the fourth time, memorised the writings from the Koran, and assessed the heaps of dead files tied up in bundles with string, Jack followed the soldier's example: he slumped back against the wall and slept heavily.

Loud footsteps and voices outside eventually disturbed him. Then the call to prayer from a nearby mosque burst into the morning air and jolted him into action. He stepped round the still sleeping soldier and located the open latrine outside. Over his shoulder he glimpsed in the early morning light the bottoms of three officers praying in a secluded part of the yard.

A new police officer entered the office and directed Jack to follow him. They walked the length of the building under a low veranda and up a few steps to a door where a guard opened the wooden door and made an announcement before bidding them go inside.

Jack was led through a reception area to a doorway clad in heavy red curtains. Gilt edged portraits of the president hung on two walls and an expensive presentation of a verse from the Koran on another. A large framed photograph of a dignitary shaking hands with the president had a prominent position behind the big red leather topped desk. The desk displayed a leather padded pen holder with gold pens sticking out of it and leather-bound ornate calendar showing last month's dates.

The soldier opened one of the window's shutters and drew the Venetian blind to keep the room private and impressive. Behind the desk sat an educated looking man in a lightweight civilian suit. Jack recognised him as the dignitary shown shaking hands with the president in the photograph.

The man signalled Jack to sit down. He took out a brand of European cigarettes and offered them to Jack before taking one for himself. He placed it in a cigarette holder and accepted a light from the officer standing nearby. He briskly commanded the attendant soldier in terse Arabic to bring tea before turning to Jack with a smile that revealed finely crafted gold capped teeth. Using a gentle soft colonial tone of English, he announced himself as head of security for the Red Sea province and assured Jack he was at his service. At the same time, he took Jack's passport from his jacket's inner pocket and turned the pages.

Jack was not so naive as to imagine that head of Red Sea security was at his service nor was he deceived by the seemingly relaxed nature of the interview. Men of this fundamentalist regime did not rise to their positions without trampling on a few bodies on the way and it was obvious that he had already studied the details of his passport several times beforehand.

'You travel a lot Mr Polglaise?'

'Yes, sir,' Jack responded. He moved quickly on to avert further discussion of his passport. 'I came to you for assistance, as I told your officer earlier,' he nodded to the portly man standing at the side, 'I am pursuing a kidnapped woman.'

The head of security listened as Jack told his story. A couple of times he shuffled his feet under the table, impatient for him to finish. As he spoke Jack realised his story might easily be regarded as fantasy, his own credibility at stake. A further sinking feeling clouded over him.

'Did you bring any alcohol, whisky or such like into the country, Mr Polglaise?'

'Alcohol,' exclaimed Jack, his irritation apparent. 'No none.' Why would he bother to bring alcohol when he was seeking help to find a kidnapper? He felt testy.

'You know the Sudan, Mr Polglaise. You have been here in May 1985. You stayed here three months. It says so in your passport. You know the regulations. You must know also about the war in the south of the country and about the curfew and the conditions for foreigners. You have no visa, no entry stamp. Which ministry are you working with?'

It was getting worse. Jack felt the interview had turned into an interrogation. He started to protest. 'I said I came by boat ....'

He was brought to sudden halt by the curtains over the door being swept aside. An officer in white uniform entered. He had an armband bearing the word Coastguard. He spoke rapidly to the security chief and seemed relieved to find Jack sitting at the desk. After a rapid and, to Jack, unintelligible exchange, the coast guard took instructions and departed.

The security chief beckoned to the portly policeman and spoke quietly in his ear for some time. The man clicked his heels, saluted and also left smartly. The head of security regarded Jack. 'The coastguard tells me you entered the harbour at one o'clock this morning, contravening the security regulations, and that your boat has been taken to the coastguard post until the matter is settled.'

Jack slumped back in his chair thoroughly depressed and dejected. He thought of Anke being taken further away; if only he had heeded Ramadan's warnings. Was there no compassion in these people? He became aware the security boss was speaking to him, again using his softer voice. Maybe he sensed something of his predicament,

'Don't worry, Mr Polglaise, I will give this matter top priority and settle everything. Take your tea. You must tell me more about this woman.'

Although what followed was a formal question and statement format Jack felt the tension had eased although he still had to go over the same points several times. At the end of the hour-long interview he had little idea whether the security chief believed him or not. The Achilles heel of his story was clearly that he had said nothing to the Egyptian authorities.

Jack was told to go with one of the officers to get his papers in order while other necessary steps were being taken. Reluctantly, Jack stood up and thanked his interrogator as they went out through the curtains together and to where the portly officer was waiting to take Jack to the jeep.

They drove in the rickety vehicle down the dusty and now busy streets of Port Sudan to an old colonial building in the port area. Hundreds of Sudanese labourers covered in flour dust waited to be paid or to receive further work for the day. Jack climbed the stone steps into what must have been a fine building in its time. Ahead of him, the policeman thrust his way through a crowd of bureaucrats and bookkeepers who loitered everywhere with apparently no work to do. Jack glanced into several offices piled high with what looked like generations of dusty accounts tied up in haphazard bundles. Cigarette butts and sheets of used carbon paper littered the floor. It was so familiar to him and the inevitable time-wasting factor hung heavily on his shoulders.

They stopped by a battered metal door. Its paint had largely disappeared long ago and the frame was covered in brown stalagmites formed from generations of spewed snuff reaching up from the floor. Painted in the middle of the door in English block capitals with an Arabic translation scribbled underneath was one word: IMMIGRATION.

*

Anke was totally unprepared for what followed.

When the hatch cover was pulled off and she looked up into the starry night she immediately detected the sweet smell of a woman's perfume. Her astonishment rapidly turned to dismay as a girlish giggle and Arab curses made in a deep crackling female voice came from above.

Two baskets rained down beside her followed by a pair of feet in flip-flops. The new arrival gave a shriek invoking Allah's mercifulness and came to rest on the rush matting beside her. Before Anke could take a close look the hatch cover banged tightly shut and the boat's engine leapt into life, followed soon by the hiss of water beneath the bow indicating they were again on their way to sea.

Anke gently prodded the new passenger to alert her of her presence, not caring whether she was friend or foe. '*Salem alay kum.*'

The woman let out another shriek and bobbed up in surprise only to bang her head on the underside of the deck. She cursed loudly in a deep broken voice.

Anke could only smell her. The crack on her head failed to silence her. She bombarded Anke with a stream of questions in a language Anke had never heard. The husky voice rose up and down and occasionally broke into falsetto without ever waiting for an answer. At last she gave an overdue groan and furiously rubbed an area Anke took to be her head and continued to curse in Arabic. 'God is merciful.'

She stepped on Anke several times without apology while she grappled with her baskets. No sooner than had she made herself comfortable she became upset again by the boat's change of motion as it reached the open sea. Each time the boat surged on a wave she let out a shriek like an excited child.

Anke had so far remained silent. Her companion had taken up all the space, filled it with her perfume, continuously chattered, cursed and bustled. She showed no resentment for being cooped up or any surprise at going to sea. It left Anke totally bewildered. Finally, she broke her silence. 'Hi. What's going on round here?'

The scrabbling stopped. The hustle and the bustle stopped. A worrying silence followed. Perhaps the newcomer was surprised to find she was in the company of a European woman. It maybe overawed her temporarily.

Anke grew impatient for an answer. 'Where are we? Where are we going? Where are you from?'

There was another pause. The boat rolled but no shrieks came this time. The voice spoke nervously with a slight croakiness. 'Who?'

'Who?' echoed Anke. She was expecting an answer not a question. At least there was a sign of some sort of communication. 'Who? Me? I'm Anke. What's your name?'

'What is your name?' repeated the deep throaty voice that somehow incorporated 'r's into words that did not contain the letter. 'Your name is

Miriam,' she said. Then giggled and corrected herself, 'My name Miriam'.

She gave a laugh that ended in a falsetto squeak. It was contagious and brought tears to Anke's eyes. She laughed, too, the first time for a week. An alliance was struck and she breathed a sigh of relief.

'Where are we?' repeated Anke very slowly.

'We are Suakin,' came the crackly voice sounding slightly surprised.

'You live Suakin?' replied Anke remembering Suakin as the old port of the Sudan.

'No, no, no. Me Eritrean. My home Eritrea.'

'Ah,' said Anke, thankful to have solved the problem of the language that spewed forth when Miriam first arrived.

'You?'

'I'm from Germany.'

'Ah.' She paused thoughtfully, 'Parlo Italiano?'

'Nein. No La La.' It was Anke's turn to giggle at the confusion. Miriam grunted and sounded disappointed at Anke's lack of lingual skills.

'You no speak Italiano. Too much Italiano in Eritrea. Plenty speak Italiano in Asmara, in Mistaya.'

'Are we are going to Eritrea? Anke asked.

'Eritrea? Eritrea?' repeated Miriam, still puzzled at Anke's ignorance. 'No, we go to Saudia, going to Jidah.' For the first time her voice showed a hint of anxiety.

'Jeddah?' repeated Anke.

'Aye, Jidah. Me Miriam maid. Make plenty money in Saudia. Work for big man. Work for sheikh; clean house, good for me, get plenty money. Send to my mother in Asmara. Mother poor woman; need money for clothes. Me good girl, work hard in house. My father mort. War. My brother mort also.'

'Ah,' said Anke sympathetically. 'This is your first time to Jeddah?'

'Aye. First time.'

There was silence. Anke considered all this latest information. She understood Saudia Arabia to be a well-developed country, although on the brink of war with Iraq. Why was she being taken there? The authorities would surely release her straight away, wouldn't they? The question hovered in the air and wouldn't go away. She did not understand why the newcomer was catching the boat as if it were a ferry or a *suq* truck. Nothing made sense.

Anke put her hand out until it touched Miriam. She jumped but allowed the hand to find hers. She told the young Eritrean she was her friend and there was something she must know about her. She squeezed the hand and guided it through the darkness to her shackled ankle. Miriam felt the chain and the bare foot and gasped. Quickly she drew her hand back into the darkness and shrunk away. She began to wail. 'You *magnoona*! You crazy woman,' she shrieked.

'No, no, no,' pleaded Anke. 'Me prisoner. They bad men.' She banged the underside of the deck in a mix of anger and frustration.

The sobbing stopped. There was another silence until Miriam quietly voiced her disbelief. 'You prisoner?'

'Yes.'

'Why?'

'They are bad men. They bring me from Egypt.' Anke stopped there. There was no point in frightening a possible ally with a complicated account of the events that had brought her here.

'Egypt,' echoed Miriam incredulously. Another prolonged silence followed.

Anke realised she must give her companion time to adjust and say nothing to arouse thoughts of her being mad. She detected sharp regular clicking noises from Miriam's direction and she got a whiff of spearmint. She grinned; Miriam was popping bubble gum. She tried to picture what her companion looked like. It was like trying to imagine a disc jockey whose photo you have never seen. The girl's arm felt very slender and the hand she had squeezed was slim with several rings on it. She wore flip-flops, but so did everybody else, and she popped bubble gum. Her giggle was girlish but her deep husky voice could have been from an Arab or African woman of any age. It would be a long time until the daylight gave any clues.

Anke tried to resume their conversation. 'How is your head?'

'Aah,' she groaned, '*mish tamam*'. She used the Arabic, her head was not good.

Anke sensed a lack of conviction and that Miriam wanted sympathy more than treatment. She heard her rubbing her head furiously like a child to make it better. Anke asked her how old she was.

Miriam turned the question back on Anke without answering it. 'How old are you?'

'Twenty-eight.'

'Twenty ... one, two, three, four, five, six, seven, eight,' Miriam counted. Twenty-eight,' she repeated. 'Me same same. Twenty-eight.'

Anke thought she was lying but at least they were getting on well again. The bubble gum was cracked loudly.

'No children?' asked Anke.

'Three.' She paused, 'Killed in the war.'

They both knew she was lying. She popped a bubble and retracted the statement with an infectious laugh.

'No. No children.' She shifted towards Anke but made no concession on her age.

'You. What you doing here? Where your children?'

Anke eased her stiff ankle round for a couple of links and winced at the pain.

'No children. Not married.'

'Oh.'

Anke waited for the inevitable.

'Why?'

There was no easy answer to that. At least, not one that would satisfy the fact hungry Miriam.

'I'll tell you tomorrow.'

'Okay. Tomorrow. Why you prisoner?' It was as if Miriam felt safer by asking the questions rather than answering them and was prepared to keep up the pressure. Anke thought carefully about her response.

'Because I upset their boat. Sunk their boat; sunk, down, sunk, you know sunk?'

'Sunk ...you mean ...in the sea ... down?' She stamped her foot on the hull.

'Yes.'

'Oh. Why you sunk their boat?'

Anke pressed on; perhaps eventually her tale would make sense.

'Because they tried to kill me.'

'Kill you?' gasped Miriam followed by the inevitable 'Why?'

We're getting somewhere at last, thought Anke. 'Because I know where they hide big box of hashish.'

'Aah,' sighed the Eritrean, the long drawn out breath suggesting she at last understood Anke's story. She shifted round until she was stretched out and apparently more relaxed.

'I understand.' She whistled again and fell silent. A quarter of an hour went by punctuated only by more popping of gum. All part of the thinking process, Anke decided.

'Why they take you to Saudia?'

'Don't know. Do you have any idea?'

'No, you no work as maid.'

There was nothing more to say and they receded into their private thoughts. It was a while before Miriam spoke again. 'Tomorrow, me, you, in Saudia. Me your friend. I speak for you.'

'Thank you, Miriam.' Anke felt moved by the girl's conviction and courage.

The boat carried on at full speed and with a monotonous slow roll that eventually lulled Anke into dozing off. Miriam was far too excited to sleep. She shuffled about endlessly and finally woke Anke up.

'Where *muftah*?'

'Where is the key?' repeated Anke drowsily, 'Where is the key for the chain?'

'Yes. Where *muftah*?'

'Up.' She tapped the underside of the deck though really having no idea. There was a silence apart from more popping of gum.

Suddenly Miriam burst into action and began rummaging furiously in one of her baskets. She elbowed Anke a couple of times during her mad scrabble, but without any apology. Eventually there was a pause followed by a tiny click and their whole world changed. Anke saw a pale yellow light shining beneath the breast of the young Eritrean. She gasped in amazement. By clasping the torch against her stomach Miriam had beamed the light up through her scantily clothed breasts and on to her downturned face.

Miriam was revealed as probably no more than eighteen, wild and beautiful. Long wavy black hair fell loosely out of her headscarf, the big eyes twinkled and blinked from behind long curling lashes. The silk wrap over the top of her body was almost transparent, clinging to the sharp contours of Venus-like breasts, pyramids with hard nipples provocatively piercing the folds of the material. Her body moved gracefully as she turned to face Anke.

She directed the beam quickly round the hold allowing Anke to see much of it for the first time. Then it shone on her, very briefly full in the face and then down and over her body coming to rest on her shackled ankle.

Miriam pulled in a deep breath, 'Allah! My God!'

Anke was shocked to see the ankle was worse than she had imagined. It looked raw and swollen. There were bruises and patches of dried and fresh blood where the chain had rubbed for nearly a week.

Miriam climbed over Anke's outstretched leg to investigate more closely. She raised the lock and looked at it. With the sweeping gesture of a magician she pulled a hair grip out from under her head scarf and tried to poke it into the keyhole.

It was too big and she tossed it into the bilge with an air of disgust. She let out a big sigh and squatted back on her haunches to turn her attention to the rest of Anke. As she moved, the light caught Miriam's thin shapely legs and shining knees poking out from beneath a white under-skirt. Her very dark skin reflected the light like it was polished ebony.

The light followed Anke's long bare legs – so very pale in contrast and a good deal thinner than she remembered them. It flowed over her filthy cut-off denim shorts, unzipped down to the crotch for convenience, and on to the once blue T-shirt now covered in oily stains. Judging by the grimy state of her arms Anke assumed her face and hair must have looked a similar mess. She shuddered and felt a deal of sympathy for Miriam beholding such a sight for the first time.

The illumination cast by the torch showed Miriam's face as vibrant and indicated a sparkle of intelligence with eyes that darted about taking in everything they saw. The cheek bones were high, the nose straight, the neck long and slender matching the fine bones of the arm and hand that Anke had touched earlier. Despite the cramped and unfamiliar nature of her surroundings she moved about quickly and accurately, bouncing down on her haunches and up again with total ease and at great speed. Despite her wretched condition, Anke felt inspired by this precocious and vibrant new companion. Miriam offered hope.

'Tomorrow I am washing your broken leg,' said Miriam as she shut off the light leaving Anke with a final frame image of eyes fired with determination and a flash of white teeth all were surrounded by a mass of wavy black hair. Miriam was like no woman she had ever seen.

They slept as night gradually overtook them and the boat steamed on through what must have been a calm sea. Miriam occasionally stirred and turned full circle like a cat and instantly settling back into a deep sleep. leaving Anke who had no reason to be so tired, to fitfully doze for the next hour. During these wakeful periods she continuously considered her destiny in Saudi Arabia. At least this hell pit of captivity would be over by morning. Or would it? Doubts still lurked.

Anke had long been awake and aware of the dim light of morning when the sound of footsteps on the deck eventually disturbed Miriam. She woke with a start, rubbing her eyes furiously and coming almost instantly awake. She bid Anke good morning and enquired about their position. Had they reached Jeddah? She dived into a basket and produced some sort of comb, which she stabbed aggressively into her wild hair. Contented shortly that most of the tangles were dealt with, she tied everything back with her headscarf and deftly manoeuvred herself over the bilge and peed loudly into the water. Anke decided she possessed no inhibitions whatsoever.

Miriam asked Anke if there was any food or water to be had. Under Anke's instructions she banged hard on the underside of the hatch, shouting harshly in Arabic at the same time. Nothing happened.

'*Allah Karim,*' she cursed quietly, amusing Anke who had seen it all before.

She banged again and shouted louder. Heavy footsteps came across the deck followed by the sound of the rush matting being removed and the hatch cover opening. Cool, fresh early morning air surged in and Miriam stood up, just able to see over the hatch combing.

She demanded to know if they were near 'Jidah'. The crewman cursed at her in a rough and uncompromising voice. When she complained there was no air, no food and no water he barked back at her and threw the hatch cover down into place so violently that it would have cracked her on the head had she not rapidly ducked. Again they were plunged into darkness.

Miriam was angry. It had not occurred to her that she could be a victim of their hostility as well. She cursed Arab men for behaving so disgustingly towards women. Eritrean men were not like that she claimed. They respected their womenfolk. She brightened up, 'I see Saudia. Not far. I see the land but no houses.'

Anke was pensive. 'Where's the land? Which side?'

Miriam tapped the hull behind her. Too quickly she sprung up and hit her head on the underside of the deck.

'*Allah Karim,*' she wailed, but the concern was not for the painful bump on her head, 'The sun, Anke, the sun ... it's on the other side. It cannot be

Jidah. It is Sudan or Eritrea. It cannot be Saudia. We cannot find Jidah today. They are bad mans.'

The words were taken out of Anke's mouth. They were indeed a night's travel south of Suakin and had not crossed the Red Sea. What was going on, whatever possessed these pirates to go to Eritrea and into an active war zone? There seemed no end to her misery.

Miriam contained her fear with anger. Her courage concealed a horror she fought to subdue. She may be precocious, thought Anke, but she was also very brave. Anke felt the young Eritrean touch her cheek with the back of her hand. A gesture she interpreted as a sign of comradeship against a common aggressor.

Little by little Miriam adjusted to the new situation and stopped muttering in her own language and cursing Arab men. Every so often she bounced up from her haunches to bang on the hatch cover with her fists.

Eventually footsteps came overhead and the matting was pulled back. Miriam was poised, waiting. The moment the cover was open her hands grabbed the combing and she heaved herself up on to the deck.

Several men immediately rushed forward and ordered her to get back down. Miriam responded with a volley of shrill demands.

Anke saw the back of her red and black floral dress trailing into the hatchway and the shadows cast by her flaying arms as she raged on at the *sambuk* crew. During a brief lull in the crew's shouts she delivered an uninterrupted speech that went unchallenged by any of them. When she at last stopped to draw breath an authoritative voice boomed across the deck from the stern.

'*Bas*!' Enough!

Reluctantly, her mutiny ended, Miriam climbed back down and squatted next to Anke The hatch cover rattled violently and slammed shut behind her. They were again plunged into darkness. Miriam was silent.

Barely able to contain her admiration, Anke nudged her and giggled, 'Well, what happened?'

Miriam slowly related the events above deck. She had told them they had tricked her. They had countered that they would still be going to Saudi but later. First, there was business to be done. None of which was hers. They had threatened that if she did not remain below deck and keep her voice under control they would chain her up like the white woman.

She had complained about the lack of air, food and water and that they kept their animals under better conditions. The goat running round freely on deck was proof of that. They had finally listened to her but she had no idea if they would do anything. Except maybe chain her up as well. She gave a derisive snort.

A few minutes later the hatch cover was pulled back and water, hobs and fish were passed down. Two crewmen attended this time. Miriam handed up the empty water container and asked for an extra one. A full gallon can duly arrived. She argued at length over the lack of air with the crewman Anke had found more tolerant than the others. Eventually he relented and returned with a small block of wood, which he set on the hatch combing before replacing the cover. This left an inch gap along one side and allowed an appreciable amount of light and air to enter the hold.

Anke was impressed with what Miriam had achieved and they settled down to eat in better mood. Miriam was still sufficiently agitated to complain that Arabs overcooked fish and that there was not enough salt. It was beyond Anke's comprehension how she could be concerned over such trivia while her whole future was at stake. She suggested that she should offer her services as chief cook and they both chuckled. The Eritrean stared at Anke open mouthed when she saw her laughing.

'How can you laugh so much with your leg broken? After eat I clean all for you.'

Anke thanked her and watched her nimble fingers adeptly sort fish from bones, tossing the latter into the bilge behind her. She spat any scales in the same direction with little finesse. Anke noticed that although her friend ate at twice her speed, all but the tips of her fingers remained unsoiled. Her own hands were a mess and she had to lick almost every part to clean them. She thought there was much they could learn from each other.

Among Miriam's treasures was a small sachet of Omo washing powder, the universal cleaning agent of the developing world. She proceeded to remove it from inside its protective plastic bag. She also took out several items of carefully folded clothing. One piece she was particularly proud of she held up for Anke's attention. To Anke the metallic blue top with spangles trimming the collar, cuffs and lapels resembled a Quality Street chocolate wrapper but she conceded that Miriam. with her dark skin and slender body, probably looked electrically beautiful in it. She said as much.

Miriam told her that she had bought it for Saudi and that it was very expensive ... nearly twenty dollars. Anke whistled, that was like two hundred in her world. Miriam refolded the garment with exaggerated loving gestures and replaced it in her basket. Before putting back other items she looked carefully through her possessions and cast her eyes furtively round the hold. Not finding what she wanted, she pulled the scarf off her head and let her hair tumble down on to her shoulders.

Anke watched her with interest, fascinated by her beauty as she used both hands to pull her hair to the top of her head and arrange it in a knot so that it was out of the way. The light coming in through the gap under the hatch fell on to her shoulders and down across her chest. Anke noted the fine bone structure, her long thin arms and small wrists. Her shoulders were narrow yet her chest was well developed with high well-separated breasts. The girl's skin was smooth, unblemished and the colour of dark coffee. She had jet-black hair with strong curly eyebrows and extravagantly long eyelashes. Her beauty held Anke's attention as if by magnetism. Rarely had she seen such perfection in a woman nor, come to that; such self-confidence in a young person.

With her hair under control, Miriam sprang into action. She poured washing powder and water on to her headscarf and manoeuvred herself to be able to stretch across Anke. Her silky wrap trailed down and caught in the bilge water. She dragged it back but when she saw the oily smears it now carried, she pealed the whole thing off and dumped it in one of her baskets, adding a sharp curse at boats in general.

To Anke her beauty had been apparent enough through the hazy material of her wrap but seeing her now naked to the waist, her gleaming mobile body unhampered by clothing, made that beauty even more entrancing.

Anke wriggled up the matting to give Miriam more room. This unsettled the chain and snagged an old scab, causing fresh bleeding. She winced with the pain and threw her head back, shutting her eyes and biting her teeth hard together.

When she reopened them Miriam had her back towards her and was crouching over the bad leg.

She could feel the cool soothing water bathing her ankle. Long fingers tenderly lifted the metal off the skin while the soft material of the scarf patted and cleaned the sores below. She went meticulously around the whole limb, removing dried blood and grease. She squeezed fresh water on to the raw spots to take the heat out of them. Satisfied that the ankle was clean, she ripped the scarf into two pieces, folding one half and carefully passing it round the metal several times so that none of the chain links rested directly on the skin.

Only when Miriam had finished wrapping the scarf around the chain did Anke relax and lie back against the hull. She let out a big sigh, hardly believing her ankle felt so much more comfortable.

Miriam swivelled round, half facing Anke and displaying her Venus like-profile. She cocked an eyebrow as if to ask about the improvement. Anke let out another sigh of relief and added a smile of deep gratitude.

Miriam set about cleaning the rest of the foot with the remaining piece of cloth, running her palm down over the top while supporting the instep with the other hand. She separated the toes and stretched them out one after another, delicately squeezing fresh water in between them. She squeezed the ball of Anke's heel and massaged her instep for several minutes.

Anke watched the lithe wasp-like waist and glistening shoulder blades busily putting back a week of strength and circulation into her foot. How beautiful it was, how beautiful she was. In Germany she could have gone to a hi-tech rehabilitation clinic and paid a fortune and still not have received more effective treatment. Miriam used a natural talent and expertise to instinctively do what was needed. An animal instinct surrounded in perfume and clad in Quality Street wrappers, Anke smiled to herself. She thanked God for Miriam – the fantasy maidservant come true.

Miriam considered her treatment had only just begun. She wedged herself across the bilge and turned to face Anke with the abused foot on her lap. She continued the massage by stretching out the toes and squeezing them in an endless rhythm that matched with the throb of the engine. They spoke together for a long time; simple phrases that needed no explanation, a child-like dialogue in an ever apparent adult situation.

When the younger woman spoke she held Anke's gaze with an entrancing glint, hoping to uncover the secrets that the blonde European surely had hidden beneath those soft blue eyes and tangles of golden watch-spring ringlets. There was so much to learn and discover about what really went on in the mind and body of her fair-skinned sister of the north.

Anke's mind was following another track. She felt the blood pulsing round her isolated foot for the first time in ages. She felt, too, Miriam's thigh under her Achilles tendon and the hard edges of her strong fingernails as she massaged her sole and instep. She savoured the girl's crackling deep voice and husky laugh that ended in a squeak. It was impossible, but it brought tears to her eyes.

An hour later Miriam declared the foot therapy was finished and climbed back over the outstretched leg to proceed with the wash. She took the free foot into her lap, delicately washing and massaging that as well as the injured limb. Anke protested that she could do that herself. Miriam ignored her, saying that the prisoner had suffered enough and must allow her to spoil her this first day.

As the long brown fingers sponged away the oil and grease Anke noticed how Miriam's nails had been dyed. The remains of a henna pattern marked the backs of her hands. She thought of asking her about it and the curious cross tattoo on her wrist when Miriam raised her leg slightly and began the washing process of the soft area behind the knee.

Anke flexed slightly and gave a little giggle, somewhere between embarrassment and sublime pleasure. Miriam paused and grinned. She looked at her straight in the eyes and mischievously rubbed the silky cloth slowly and delicately several more times over the same tender skin behind the knee. She watched Anke's eyes close and her face soften into a deep glow. It was with a knowing smile that she confidently continued on up her thigh without stopping and completed that part of the wash.

Turning to the shackled limb, she gently spread Anke's legs so she could kneel between them to wash the areas not covered in the original foot therapy. By raising her knee off the matting she caused Anke to slide down. Their bodies briefly collided and they both laughed. Anke hauled herself back up the mat wondering at the unanticipated surge of reckless enjoyment felt from her contact with Miriam's goddess-like bosoms.

Without hardly a pause, Miriam stroked the silky cloth gently over the back of the raised knee, deliberately lingering in the softest most delicate dimples. Anke no longer made any effort to conceal her enjoyment. Washing was taking on a whole new dimension.

Miriam bunched up the bottom of Anke's T-shirt and held it up to her nose, already wrinkled in anticipation. Anke needed no more prompting and peeled it off, freeing her hair with a shake of her head as she did so.

Miriam squatted on her haunches and studied every aspect of the Aryan woman. Anke sensed her nipples tightening and was on the point of looking for a way out when Miriam spoke in a new quiet and intense voice, 'You are a beautiful woman, Anka.'

Anke looked down at herself and her erecting nipples and gave a self-conscious grin.

'No, it is you that is the beautiful woman. I am the smelly woman.' She laughed, raised an arm and made an exaggerated sniff.

Miriam handed her the wet cloth and sprinkled it with Omo. She remained crouched as she followed Anke's hands as she washed her forearms and raised an elbow to scrub an armpit.

'First time I see a white woman with no clothesez,' she said, 'You are so white and I am so black. How can that be? Also you have hairs that are yellow on your head and now I see you have plenty hairs under your arms that is brown. How can that be? I have black hair here and here.' She pointed and giggled, setting the mood with her infectious laugh.

'The sun,' said Anke. She worked up a good lather while enjoying Miriam's attention. She accepted a fresh slosh of water from Miriam. 'My first wash for a week.'

The young Eritrean continued watching every movement, her bottom lip gradually slipping to allow a gleam of white teeth to sparkle through. Anke cupped first one of her heavy breasts and then the other, lathering them thoroughly. Blissful. She shook her head, tossing her hair back and briefly shutting her eyes. Miriam's gaze didn't falter. With her mouth still partly open she tongued her drying lips. She watched Anke's hands massage off the grime in circling upward movements that raised the soft lobes and allowed the nipples to poke up between her fingers.

For the first time since leaving Cairo Anke felt wonderful, totally absorbed in the escapism surrounding her. She filled her lungs and thrust out her chest in celebration of her improved welfare. She let out a big sigh and emotionally thanked her friend for restoring her morale.

Miriam's eyes were mostly locked on the parts of a white woman she had never seen. Anke matched her gaze briefly and noticed how the dark ebony tips of Miriam's breasts were changing shape and puckering up, perhaps explaining the intensity of her silence.

Miriam took the cloth from Anke and moved behind her to begin washing her back. She sung quietly in a soft chant that was pleasant and hypnotic. It was Anke's turn to be silent as the lithe fingers tended the muscles in her back removing the fatigue.

Miriam indicated for Anke to hold her hair up and then delicately cleaned the soft skin behind her ears and around her brow. Anke felt the young Eritrea's breasts rubbing against her lower back.

A wild and new uncontrolled wave of hormonal pleasure surged through her lower body. That was the moment she gave up questioning the roots of the pleasure that grew inside her in every direction. Recklessly, she decided to let it take her wherever it was going.

A rivulet of water escaped down her neck and ran down over her chest towards her stomach. Miriam stretched over her shoulder and arrested it, scooping her hand up under the soft tissue of her breasts, brushing one nipple with her fingers and the other with the sensitive underside of her wrist. Her singing faltered and she caught her breath. Anke could feel a flood of perspiration escape from Miriam as she slid away from her shoulders.

There was a charged feeling in the air while Miriam recovered a hand towel from her basket. She patted Anke's face dry, then her back and chest before she wiped the gleaming perspiration off her own body. She teased Anke about her red cheeks and nose and splashed some of her scent on to Anke's pale neck then rubbed it behind her ears.

Her courage and ego now boosted to new heights, Anke slid her pants and shorts down to her knees in a single smooth motion. She next withdrew her free leg completely out and pushed the two garments down towards the chain leaving them stranded like washing on a line.

Miriam giggled at these antics and studied Anke from her squatting position across the bilge. Her friend, now totally without clothes save those hanging from her left ankle, showed no sign of embarrassment. She looked in awe at the area of tawny curls that stretched from one side of her lower stomach to the other, a patch as big as both her stretched hands. The curls encroached slightly down her thighs but ended against creamy white skin at every frontier. The patch was high and rounded like a baby's head set between wide hips.

To Miriam she represented the ultimate woman; the splendid golden Goddess of the North whose mystery and sexual prowess had long been her fascination. She moved closer to Anke, making no effort to conceal her intrigue and in no mind to give her the water she was anticipating. Anke expected the Eritrean's inspection, and savoured it. She was not ashamed of her body and now was flying high on exhibiting it.

Gently lying back against the hull she allowed her stomach to flatten. Realising that Miriam had not resumed her singing, she wondered if she had embarrassed her. She suddenly remembered the custom of female circumcision in Africa and sat up quickly. What if Miriam was circumcised, would she not be shocked at her own lack of it? The question taunted her and she became impatient to find out.

She questioned Miriam about the custom in a respectful and gentle way. But her friend was confused and failed to understand what she meant. Not wanting to dampen her excitement, she rolled her tongue round her lips and reassured Anke that she was beautiful.

Anke was determined to overcome the language impasse and make Miriam understand her question. She graphically explained her question by touching parts of her body. As she did so, a cobweb of her juices hung from her fingers and a musky heat floated up to her nostrils.

Miriam's confused expression suddenly
vanished. She threw her head back and laughed
with a great sigh of relief.

'Closed? No, no, no. Not *habishee*, not Eritrean.
This is for Sudani only.'

Anke leant back against the side of the hull,
much relieved, pleased to have cleared that up.
Miriam hopped about from one leg to another,
hauling her pants off from under her petticoat.

'Look, I same like you,' she cried, her eyes
ablaze. 'No closed. Not Sudani. Look!'

Anke sat up excited.

'All is working very good,' Miriam grinned,
offering the surprised Anke a fall inspection. She
was so pleased to prove that she rose above the
barbaric customs of Africa. She hoisted up her
skirts so that they rested on her waist, sat on her
haunches and faced Anke. The light from the
hatchway fell on her so that Anke could see every
detail.

'My God,' breathed Anke as hot surges pulsed
through her. How can a woman produce so much
wetness? She must be going out of her head. It was
as if Miriam was an animal on heat. Anke felt her
pulse thumping inside her and her breathing
becoming shorter and more deliberate. Hotness
spread throughout her body.

Anke had never looked intimately at woman's
anatomy other than her own. She was fascinated
and somewhat overwhelmed by the exaggerated
female features she saw in front of her.

'Working good, no cut,' Miriam repeated with another infectious laugh.

Anke moaned in appreciation, completely lost for words, wondering if she was going to explode in some way. Never had she experienced such a powerful arousal. She watched Miriam squirm involuntarily and tried to come to terms with the throbbing in her lower body and the uncontrollable contractions. She was getting a whole new lesson in her own sensuality.

Miriam's face said it all. She was on cloud nine, cruising, charged with her own vitality and virility. Miriam rose from her squatting position, letting her skirts fall back in place. Her eyes were half closed as she climbed over Anke's outstretched leg with the water jug. Her back to Anke she knelt by the chained ankle and started to wash the clothes that hung there. Anke, her eyes blurred and locked on the slender waist in front of her, let waves of unchallenged erotic pleasure ripple through her abdomen. She sucked hard on the knuckle of her index finger, feeling the pulse in her vagina surge with the rhythm in her stomach. She laid her hand, hidden from Miriam's view, on top of her pubic hairs and entwined them with the same rhythm.

The shorts and pants were lathering well. Anke saw Miriam slowly slip a hand beneath her skirt. Miriam squeezed the suds with the other hand slowly and methodically never once turning around.

Anke's fingers move down through her own curls to the soaking heat below. Hidden from Miriam's view she held her fingers there under pressure daring not to move lest she lost control. She breathed heavily and waited. Miriam swayed ever so slightly, her head bowed and hidden from Anke. The fingers slowed in the suds, then stretched out straight. She momentarily stopped swaying; the fingers quivered and then clenched the soggy denim with all their might until the knuckles showed white. There was a massive shudder and guttural moan, then Miriam's head crashed in spasm several times against the wood of the mast before she crumpled into a heap.

Anke's heart raced. She bit her finger, feeling her body boiling over. She brought her fingers slowly and decisively up and across the top of her womanhood, arching her back as she did so to absorb the full power of the disintegration that followed.

She let out a wild sobbing groan that was sweet and long; taking her out into blue cool space; taking her out past a smiling Miriam; out past the nest of the osprey and into the arms of the man from Bait Al Dahab.

*

'*Malesh*! Tomorrow we go and catch Sayeed Ria in Suakin.'

Jack heard the words as hollow encouragement as Ramadan went forward to wash in preparation for his prayers, leaving Jack to his own thoughts.

What a mess he had made of it. He had no faith in the security head's promise to follow everything up for it transpired he had dismissed his story as an ill-conceived fantasy. Ramadan had established from talking with the local boatmen that the only Sudanese naval patrol vessel had been lying idle at its berth for nearly a year awaiting spare parts.

Anke? What of Anke? She was nearly two days ahead of them if she had not been dumped somewhere. The Sudanese would do nothing other than make a big fuss detaining him. They had to stay another day to satisfy the immigration authorities and have endorsements made on his passport. It was another day wasted in getting photos for signing and all the time an armed guard had been placed near the vessel in case they attempted to move the boat.

During the two endless days tied up to the coast guard jetty Jack made frequent visits to the immigration office and the police station but never again succeeded in seeing the chief of security.

Having been delayed for so long in Port Sudan, Jack was not prepared to commit the mission to any further escapades into the unknown. Suddenly, everything changed. As they steamed back out of the *mersa* on the afternoon of the third wasted day Ramadan heaved the tiller over at the point where Jack expected them to be pointing northwards and back to Hurghada.

There was no hiding the broad grin on his face as he thrust it into Jack's hand. '*Yala habibi*.' Let's go my friend. With that he went forward to hoist up the mainsail with the boat pointed in a south easterly direction.

He laughed over his shoulder at Jack's hesitant expression. He tied his jalibaya up past the waist and lent his weight into heaving up the heavy spar. The double blocks creaked and the big lateen sail filled out, blocking out the setting sun. At last, they were away from that festering hole of Port Sudan. Jack felt his excitement returning.

During the night they changed watch a couple of times and by daylight they were coasting into the quite waters of the Suakin *mersa*.

*

In stark contrast to Port Sudan, Suakin had an air of magic about it. One of the oldest ports on the east coast of Africa it had become an almost forgotten backwater; its original coral city now a crumbled ruin. It stood on a small island at the landward end of a creek that penetrated deep into the desert. Its remaining once regal cream and white coral buildings glistened in the early morning sun. It exuded a sense of peace and timelessness. Built by wealthy traders and merchants of Arab and Turkish origins it finally passed into colonial administration as an outpost of the British Empire. The island in the end of the creek was no bigger than two football pitches yet was surrounded by a safe deep water anchorage

Today, all that remained intact of this city that once rivalled Venice for the elegance of its quays, courtyards and places of great importance were the minarets and elegant facades of the mosque. In earlier times the entire site was occupied by grand two and three-storey homes, palaces and warehoused all constructed of coral rock skilfully cut into quoins by the best masons of the day. Teak from Goa and Burma used for lintels and rafters still remained, protruding at odd angles from half decayed buildings.

During its long history Suakin had served as the major trading point between Africa and Arabia. The market area, now based on the mainland. continued to be the nucleus for nomadic traders heading off inland with their camel caravans. Every known item of camel tackle and other necessities used in desert life was to be found in its suq.

Although now little more than a shanty town Suakin still attracted the most diversified groups of people anywhere on the African coast; a place where strangers continued to make up the majority of the population. Among those gathered in one of its coffee shops were likely to be tall Africans from Mali and thin giants of the Dinka tribe of southern Sudan, Eritreans, Bedouin Rahshrida tribesmen and fair-skinned Arabs from the north all mingling in their individual national dress. Often pilgrims from West Africa on their once-in-life-time journey to Mecca became stranded in Suakin perhaps through lack of a visa or, more often than not, a lack of funds, and remained there for a generation never earning enough to go forward or back.

Suakin had over the centuries held a key position in the slave trade, in the spice trade, in cotton and leather, shells and fish exports. Major commerce and the big money transactions all came to an end on a single day in the early years of the century when it was decreed that the province's administration be moved to Port Sudan, the modern deep water port.

Suakin was never dismantled but left as a ghost city totally intact. Its strong Moslem culture meant that there was no theft, no vandalising or plundering to deface the glorious nature of the place. Only time and the elements were allowed to destroy it. Once the protective plaster coatings were no longer maintained the coral rock decayed as it became exposed to sunlight and block by block the city collapsed so that very few buildings remained intact. Whole fronts or backs of houses had fallen down allowing today's visitors to gaze in awe back into history and wonder what events had taken place in those half rooms now hanging precariously in the air.

Jack was enchanted as the early morning sun caught the white walls and the minarets of the tall buildings crammed along the water's edge and gave them the aspect of an ancient Manhattan in Africa.

With the sail stowed away, they had motored quietly into the narrow passageway close under the coast guard look out. A black figure stood outside and gave them a welcoming wave rather than apprehend them. They passed on deep into the *mersa* and along the creek on the north side of the decaying city where many abandoned *sambuqs* had been hauled out on to the salt flats, their ancient timber ribs sticking out from them like so many chops from a belly of lamb.

Further up the *mersa* piles of fresh wood lying on the ground hinted at some boat restoration work in progress. There were also heaps of gnarled branches of locally grown wood that would serve as future natural knees and round frames. Alongside was a half planked felucca. They got a wave from a carpenter tending a smoky fire, a black kettle sitting on the embers. It was all so different from Port Sudan.

They passed a small flotilla of sail powered canoes and rowing boats as they cruised up the mersa but saw no active or other large vessels. The intensely black fishermen in their contrasting white turbans were cast-netting sardines as their forefathers might have done a thousand years ago. To the south, where the coral platform ran into an expanse of shallows, three fishermen with girded up jalibayas, herded fish into their set nets.

The overall air was one of timeless tranquillity, a sense that Suakin had been bypassed by the twentieth century and that it didn't really matter.

Ramadan steered the *Mona* into a berthing area on the north side of the *mersa* where there was a cluster of small local boats, some afloat, others hauled out for repairs. They cast a stern anchor out and coasted in until the keel nudged the sandy mud.

Ramadan spoke briefly with the local boys that gathered to greet them as he waded ashore with the bow line and sent one of them running off on a mission. Another was directed to the boat and scrambled aboard enthusiastically. He squatted in his bedraggled state on the afterdeck with one arm over the tiller in much the same way Ramadan did as captain of the vessel.

Jack laughed as the dripping urchin took up his position as watchman with such authority. His eyes sparkled and a wide grin displayed a magnificent set of white teeth, each one separate from its neighbour. He was filling the same role as had been played by his ancestors over thousands of years of visiting traders. Merchantmen had called here over millennia, sailors weary from long voyages, anxious to stretch their legs and savour the delights of freshly cooked meats, new tobaccos and, in less strict times, the indulgences of the flesh provided by the harems of the town's businessmen.

Ramadan sauntered over to a group of fishermen who were overhauling a net. They invited him to share tea and he beckoned Jack to join them. Jack recognised a couple of the older men from times he had spent in the area several years earlier. What they lacked in sophistication they certainly made up for with their warmth and open friendliness. Four other fishermen drifted over and joined their group and the conversation turned to the new felucca being built close by.

Jack waited patiently for Ramadan to steer the conversation around to the Yemeni *sambuk*. He achieved this quite cleverly when, after forty minutes, the topic led to trade in Suakin. But when Jack searched the faces of the fishermen for some encouragement he found none.

One of the older fishermen said Egyptian and Yemeni *sambuqs* often stopped at the entrance of the mersa and left after taking supplies. Nobody took any particular notice. In any case, none of the fishermen had been out of the mersa in the past few days. If Ramadan needed to know about *sambuqs* it was better to talk with the traders.

Ramadan thanked them and he and Jack walked off over the salt flats to the sprawling market area. They agreed it might be better if Ramadan talked to the merchants on his own in case they became suspicious of Jack's presence and held back information. They agreed to meet at the charcoal market after midday prayers and Jack drifted off in the direction of the causeway and the old city.

He met up with old friends at the fishermen's co-op and took his breakfast with them. They also had nothing to offer about recent visiting *sambuqs*. Hassan, a gentle old mechanic whose education went right back to the British period, explained to

Jack in a soft broken English that it was normal
for more than half the faces in the village street to
be those of strangers and so no one could say
exactly if crews of a visiting boat were there or not.
No one took any notice.

Jack felt convinced he and Ramadan were
wasting their time and might as well turn back,
although he clung on to the hope that his friend
would uncover something. He felt he was clutching
at straws as he wandered through the archway
into the ancient deserted city and sought the
shade of a narrow street between half intact
buildings.

The solitude revived his spirits. As he picked his
way through the fallen coral blocks he sensed a
renewal of spiritual contact with Anke. Her being
kidnapped and whisked away in a sambuk was
something he frequently considered unrealistic,
and yet here he was among what was until
recently a beautiful and functioning city. Now it
was an abandoned ruin. Was that in itself not a
testimony to the inconceivable happening?
Wouldn't the carvers of those fine elaborate teak
doors consider it unimaginable that someday the
whole city's inhabitants would walk out and never
come back?

Jack gained strength from this reverse logic.
Images of Anke floated in and out of his thoughts
and finally dominated everything else. He needed
to provide a balance to such imaginings and so
pulled out his notebook and let his mood move the

pen. Between phrases he stared vacantly into the waters of the *mersa* allowing his inspiration to organise itself into lines. He sat there until he heard the noon day prayer call come chanting out of the mosque by the market.

Ramadan was excited. He said he had at first drawn a blank but at the last minute located the man who might be able to supply them with diesel for the homeward journey. He had questioned the merchant about providing fuel for other visiting *sambuqs*. At first the man was reluctant to discuss the subject because of the black market nature of his trade. When Ramadan asked directly if he had recently supplied Sayeed Ria the Yemeni the merchant had become nervous and tried to divert the conversation. He said because he risked imprisonment he never asked customers their business nor did they ask his. However, after going to the mosque together to pray the merchant had softened and agreed to bring three barrels after dark for the *Mona*. He had added with a wry smile that if he could supply the Yemeni he could certainly help an Egyptian.

'He suggested that we ask the donkey cart driver tonight if he delivered to Sayeed Ria,' reported Ramadan.

With nothing else to do until the evening, they went to one of Jack's old haunts on the outskirts of the town where many Eritrean refugees had set up small stalls and temporary homes and where Jack proclaimed the best coffee in Africa could be found.

Numerous Eritreans had settled in this southern sprawl of Suakin, some of them women escaping the protracted war across the border. Many had been there several years and had built shacks used as homes and small subsistence-level businesses.

Jack stooped low to lead Ramadan into one such wooden shack. They were greeted by the pungent and aromatic scent of roasted coffee and frankincense. The room was dim but homely. Shafts of sunlight coming through half opened shutters picked out blue smoke rising from the embers in the firebox. A small portable cassette player balanced on a suitcase in the corner issued soft Eritrean music. In another corner two men sat talking together on a low bench. One was a young Eritrean, a leg stretched out in front of him and a shining new crutch resting against his shoulder. The other they guessed was the Sudanese driver of the Bedford truck parked outside.

As the four of them exchanged greetings the elegant Eritrean woman who had been fanning the charcoal with her back to Jack and Ramadan rose to her feet and turned to welcome them. She was stunningly beautiful, in her late twenties perhaps, her jet black hair tied loosely behind with a pale blue silk scarf that showed off her high cheek bones, long fine nose, twinkling eyes and large gold hooped earrings. Her coffee coloured skin shone from the effort of reviving the fire. She dabbed the beads of perspiration from her nose and, with a gentle smile, gestured for them to sit down

The woman turned towards Jack and shot him a glance that hinted at faint recognition. He now remembered her, too, and returned a big smile, holding her gaze,

'Eighty-six?' he prompted

Her face broke into a glowing smile, 'Ah Habibi, 'He had got the right year. 'You come back to Suakin.'

'Only to see you,' he jested, 'And for the best coffee in Africa.'

'Fatimah,' she called over her shoulder as she gave Jack a firm handshake.

Another tall, slim, dark-skinned beauty dressed in a flowing yellow tobe appeared in the rear doorway tying her hair back as she came forward. She hesitated for a split second before bounding over to Jack, shaking his hand furiously and kissing him on both cheeks.

Greatly warmed by the moment, Jack introduced Ramadan and they were soon engaged in chatting with both sisters in the shade of their coffee shop. They sat back and relaxed while the two women set about the elaborate and ritualistic preparations of the coffee.

They took white beans from a flour sack, dusted them off and placed them on a small round tray made from a powdered milk tin top with a long handle brazed on to it. Fatimah squatted by the fire box and fanned the charcoal with an aluminium plate until sparks were flying. She chatted with the men in Arabic and broken English as she worked, her voice seductive and full of charm. Her well-spaced teeth gleamed as she spoke and her big eyes flashed and twinkled in the dim light. The folds of her dress clung to the curves of her upper body as she worked.

Jack reflected on the numerous hot dusty afternoons he had spent with these two refugees in their coffee shop feeling the zap from the caffeine shots and enjoying the sensual thrill of watching their slender bodies pound coffee beans and fan charcoal.

Occasionally one moved so that the light was behind her silhouetting her body in a silky haze. Afternoons passed so easily in this enchanting atmosphere and soon merged into the cool of the evening.

Today was no exception. The sister in the pale blue dress shook the tray so the beans rolled over and over until they were uniformly brown and the irresistible aroma of roasting coffee filled the air. She put the roasted beans into a mortar and pounded them with a shiny wooden pestle. The shape of her breasts slid up and down under the fabric of her dress, her dark hard nipples clearly defined. Jack and Ramadan exchanged contented glances; no man could fail to be swept up by such an alluring sight.

The woman tipped the ground coffee on to a folded newspaper and slid it into the slender neck of an earthenware globe-shaped pot with long phallic spout. Before returning it to the charcoal Fatimah pushed a piece of cinnamon bark down the neck and introduced a plug of loose weave polypropylene sacking to act as the filter.

The brew simmered for a few minutes before being carefully poured into two tiny china cups no bigger than egg cups, each previously laced with a generous teaspoon of local raw cane sugar. Fatimah served the concentrated coffee on a tin tray. Jack found the rich aroma combined with the gold earrings and her white flashing teeth almost intoxicating. The pendulous bosoms and their hostesses' delicate Eritrean perfume was enough to send even the most indifferent head reeling: even before the caffeine shots.

As tradition dictated, the coffee was drunk in a single shot in the way a tot of whiskey would be, as were the refills. Only the third and final shot was sipped and savoured. By this time the recipients were well hyped up and were content to await sunset and the delivery of their diesel.

Before they left, Jack drew Fatimah to one side and asked her discretely if they had a Yemeni boat crew pass by in the last few days. To his surprise she nodded in the affirmative. She turned to consult her sister before adding that although they had not had any customers from a Yemeni *sambuk* they knew one had called there three or four days ago. One of their Eritrean friends, Miriam by name, had arranged an unofficial ride to Saudi with the boat with the idea of seeking work there.

Fatimah said Miriam was a wild and energetic girl who was a law unto herself. She had been trying to get an illegal entry into Saudi for some time to earn big money to send home to her mother. They had told her to be careful but the headstrong girl had paid no attention. There was no dissuading her. She had made a deal with the man who supplied the black market diesel to arrange a passage with the Yemeni boat that was in port a few days ago to take her to Saudi Arabia. She was nowhere to be seen now and they assumed she had gone to Jeddah.

Fatimah told Jack that Miriam had been luckier than most in that she had escaped into Sudan. She had helped the EPLF there and earned some money but not enough to send home to her mother. The girl believed Saudi Arabia was rich and could make as much there in one month as a maid as she could make in the Sudan in a whole year.

Jack's news puzzled Ramadan. 'Not Jidah, Mr Jack ... not Jidah ... not possible ... too much police; too much coast guard. Sayeed Ria will never go to Jidah. He will go to Midi in Yemen by Saudi border and move his cargo to Al Muwassamo a few kilometres away close to Jizzan on the Saudi side. This is the way they work. This is the way for hundreds of years.'

Jack was stunned. This put a completely new slant on all their plans.

'Let us try to find out for sure that it is Sayeed Ria,' said Ramadan, 'The donkey cart driver – he will know tonight.'

Ramadan bought a few fresh supplies and the two ate hungrily after evening prayers. It was their first meal of the day and they were also still on a high from the strong coffee of the afternoon.

About eight o'clock they heard a shout from the shore and could just make out a donkey cart in the gloom. Ramadan put away the hookah, rolled up his jalibaya and slid over the side into the shallow water and waded into the beach.

Jack watched the donkey being led into the water until the cart was up to its axles and heard the rumble and splash of heavy drums as they were rolled off into the water. The youth and Ramadan pushed the just-floating barrels out until they reached the side of the sambuk. Ramadan scrambled aboard and grabbed two specially prepared ropes, each with one end attached to the boat. The free ends he passed under the first of the floating barrels and within seconds he and Jack had lifted it on deck. The other two quickly followed and soon all three were safely stowed. The empty barrels they tossed over the side in the direction of the beach for returning to the merchant.

Ramadan carefully counted out the money to the boy who repeated the count in a very business-like manner. It seemed of little concern that the currency was Egyptian pounds rather than

Sudanese ones. Ramadan added ten pounds as an exceptionally generous tip and encouraged the lad to share tea with them.

The youth gratefully accepted and climbed aboard. Ramadan soon steered the conversation round to the lad's other recent customers.

'Sayeed Ria?' echoed the youth. 'You know him?'

'Not so much, but everybody who sails in the Red Sea knows him somewhat. He is an exceptional captain and a very tough man. It happens we were sailing close to him for several days coming down from Egypt but then we got delayed in Port Sudan and he went ahead of us.'

'You won't catch him now,' the lad laughed. 'Sayeed Ria left here three days ago.'

Ramadan was hardly able to contain himself. He raised his eyebrows and winked at Jack to restrain him, "That's true,' he laughed 'especially as he is going south and us north.'

Shortly afterwards the Sudanese slipped away in the dark to round up his empty barrels that had drifted away up the *mersa*. Within ten minutes Ramadan had the anchors on board and the *Mona* was steaming quietly down the *mersa* towards the open sea. Curfew or no, he was wasting no time.

There was a reasonable breeze from the north, a silvery light from the moon and a trail of phosphorescence from the propeller as they stole out under the coast guard lookout without a sign of recognition. They soon felt the heave of the swells of the open sea as Ramadan leant his weight behind the halyard to hoist the big sail. It unfurled majestically in the cool night air and the boat bounded forwards, picking up another couple of knots.

Ramadan returned to the afterdeck and heaved the sheet in tighter than ever and hauled the helm over towards himself. Almost afraid to ask, Jack cocked an inquisitive eyebrow when Ramadan looked in his direction.

'Yemen. *Alla toole*. Mr Jack,' he yelled with a big grin. At last he was in control of the mission certain that they were not on a wild goose chase. He was brimmed with enthusiasm; every action had a sense of urgency. He pulled the sheet in even tighter and the boat heeled over a degree or two as she bounded south eastwards on a fast reach.

*

'What about papers?' Anke inquired.

'The captain of the sambuk will arrange it,' Miriam replied. But her voice lacked conviction.

Anke decided on a change of topic, keen to stir Miriam out of her nervous depression.

'What about boyfriends? Do you have a boyfriend?'

Miriam rolled out one of her best husky laughs ending in an impossible squeak. 'Boyfriends? Ah, too much boyfriends.' She laughed again and paused for thought. 'When you live a life that is sometimes near to dying and sometimes your boyfriends never come back from fighting ... or when they come back from the fighting they have one foot blown off by mine or have bullet in arm ... you must love a lot because, who knows?'

She left the question hanging in the air and popped a bubble of gum. 'When I was young, fifteen, fourteen, I can't remember, we spent too much time in the dark. When the sun was up we were hiding in shelter under the ground and when it was night we tended the crops and moved the animals from place to place. Always plenty of young fighters will want to be loving with me. When we are hiding under the ground during the day and we hear the jets going overhead looking for something to shoot at, often then we would make love just to say "to hell with Mengisto!" Even if it was not possible to make love properly ... I mean put it inside ... I would make his milk come by playing.'

She giggled. 'This was the life as I grew up. It is good for all young fighters. They give me gun when I was sixteen. I think I was grown up by then. But boys ...' Another husky laugh, 'I like boys too much. Sometimes I am nursing the wounded fighter back to health in Suakin. Sometimes maybe he has one foot gone and he is afraid for himself and must prove he is still man. He is so happy if I make him get big. He will cry to the God that he can still make love. When he sees that white stuff fly on to my skin he is so very very happy and quickly he gets better and starts new life again.'

She sucked in a great big gulp of air and sighed
as she released. She chuckled, 'All people should
be loving like this and then all is happy, no
fighting and no wars.'

Anke was amazed. What a philosophy. What an
incredible character Miriam was turning out to be.
She had little idea of the events the girl spoke of
and felt huge admiration for her. Indeed, she was
somewhat overawed by her openness, she had
become the junior partner in their relationship.
Miriam clearly had never considered feminism an
issue of any importance. It was a disease of the
west.

Wrapped in a blue chiffon robe, Anke
contemplated the events of the day. Miriam had
remained quiet for only a few minutes following
the dramas of the early morning. She had finished
washing Anke's clothes and then fitted each of
them out with fresh attire from her treasure
chests. The day became a steaming hot and airless
calm. Despite the small gap under the hatch cover,
the hold turned into a sauna and each
intermittently dozed hoping the cool of the evening
would soon come.

As the light faded and a merciful breeze came
through the gap they caught the smell of fish
cooking and suddenly felt hungry. Anke asked
Miriam how far she thought they had come in time
since leaving Suakin.

'One day and a half by *sambuk* takes us to
Mitsiwa,' she said. 'Some refugees used to come to

Suakin by this way before the planes stopped them. This *sambuk* cannot go to Mitsiwa. It is very dangerous. We will stop somewhere after dark I think, before we come near to that place.'

Anke considered the options and motives facing her. She would surely not be taken off the *sambuk* here. Before she could expand that logic, the boat's engine slowed down and idled as it glided to a halt. She heard the rush of the anchor rope being released – then silence. It was about an hour after dark when their supper was pushed through the gap under the hatch cover. Shortly afterwards all activity on deck ceased.

After they had eaten Anke and Miriam sat up beside each other and talked. Their conversation had become more fluent as each gained familiarity with the other's peculiarities of speech and accent.

Miriam was clearly frightened by their close proximity to areas patrolled by the air force planes hostile to the Eritrean People's Liberation Front. She feared once daylight came they might be considered targets by the planes. Miriam told Anke of the Eritrean freedom fighters' struggles – many things she had never heard before.

Miriam described the underground hospitals in Eritrea, the farming that was done only at night, the risk to life and limb of being seen during the day as jets and helicopter gunships patrolled the sky. She said that they would win their independence only if the supply of guns and weapons was stopped from reaching the government in Addis Ababa. Miriam talked about the young freedom fighters she cared for in a makeshift hospital in Suakin. Some had lost their legs or feet from stepping on mines and were learning to walk again with artificial legs provided by Anke's own country. She said German people were very clever to make new legs.

Anke was stunned by the experiences Miriam had undergone by in her short life and also by the matter of fact manner in which she spoke about these things. She made light of her struggles to survive as a child in the village where her mother still lived and where she had lost several family members to the war. All her generation had endured such a life.

'Most mens do not stay in one place with the woman,' she said. 'They have job to do. They must fight with EPLF to make country free. Even when this war is finished, God willing it is finished, each man will travel where he finds work, it is the nature of men, and although he may love his children he will always sleep with another woman when he is in faraway place until he returns to his village. This is the way of most mens. Women must also take care for themselves. It is not so wrong, Anka. It is life. We are here only for short time and if we spend half that time waiting for the perfect man it is waste. Body will burn up and become useless. When we are old it is time to live with family, we can make house, make small shop maybe, but not when young. Before long time it was not like that. Before Italian people come to Eritrea, before EPLF, Then, we must do what our father told us. But not now. Now is different. If we must take up gun, if we must make training in camp with soldiers we also must know who owns who?'

She broke off and laughed.

Anke had always believed woman's emancipation had its home in the West. She was taken aback by Miriam's calculated sense of reasoning. She no longer saw her as a peasant girl from the patriarchal society she had first imagined. What Miriam didn't know in scientific terms she certainly made up for in worldly knowledge. She also had a far better idea of how to deploy her sexuality than most of her so-called liberated sisters in the West who were caught up in the twin spirals of class and consumerism.

Miriam's next words seemed like a deliberate challenge, tossed right into the sensitive area Anke had hoped she would avoid. 'What about you, Anka? You have boyfriends? 'Don't white womens have lots of boyfriends?'

Anke felt for Miriam's hand and gave it a squeeze. She needed to dissolve her own logic and align a new Anke with the philosophy expressed so vividly by Miriam. She spoke softly and slowly, carefully choosing every word. 'At the moment, Miriam, I think I am in love with a man for the first time in my life.

Her listener was excited, attentive. At last she was beginning to draw Anke out of herself. 'Who? Where is he?'

'I met him in Egypt. He is an Englishman, a fisherman; we went together into the mountains and into the desert. He was very kind to me' Anke felt tears welling up and tried to fight them. 'He is slim and very strong but Miriam ...' She swallowed hard there was a lump in her throat. In an instant the whole world went before her eyes. Egypt and all her experiences with Jack, the fabulous gold find, his love and encouragement. It was all there, vivid and crowding her vision. Her lips trembled. The pain in her heart was as real as the one in her ankle, 'But Miriam, he was considerate he could write poetry and ....'

Miriam grabbed her as she collapsed into helpless sobbing convulsions. No consoling was possible. Miriam knew all she could do was to hold her tightly and let her cry it out.

Anke eventually became aware of the arm gripping her round the shoulder and preventing her sliding down into the bilge. She dragged herself up into the sitting position and cleared her eyes with the palms of her hands. She sniffed quietly, offered an apology. Miriam felt for her hair and pulled the locks back from her face, touching her cheeks delicately as she did so. She left one hand resting on her shoulder and put the other round her waist and gave her a sharp hug.

'Will you show him to me one day?'

Anke tried to turn tears to laughter. 'If you promise not to steal him.'

Miriam hugged her even tighter before easing her hold, 'Would I do that?'

If ever a friendship was sealed, it was then.

They continued talking well into the night. They mapped out each other's future in fantasy terms, riches from Saudi sheiks, weddings and children. They teased each other about what they could and could not do with men. The lurid details of some of Miriam's tales held Anke's attention so well that she could have retold them word for word without missing a single detail. Their physical therapy of the morning was matched by the mental therapy of the night. Anke had not engaged in such open and intriguing conversation about sexual relationships since she was a teenager, nor had she enjoyed a discourse so much in a long time. Miriam was able to hint at the most erotic and basic behaviour without giving explicit details.

By the time she would normally have been asleep, Anke felt a longing within her to have one final story that would blend fantasy into reality; an anecdote that would wing them back to where they had been in the early morning. Cautiously she said, 'After hearing about you I guess I am very shy about boys.'

'Shy?'

'I mean I don't have boyfriends very much. I wish I was more like you. I always take men too seriously and am afraid to give them too much in case they try to own me.'

'Never,' cried Miriam. 'They can never own you.' She laughed. 'We have so much to give them they will always do as you want in the end. They can never own you. Don't worry about that.'

Anke wondered if she been living under a false illusion for half her life. Did this precocious eighteen-year-old creature of the desert have a better understanding of men than she at ten years her senior? It seemed to be so. Miriam was puzzled, almost worried. 'You never had a boyfriend, Anka? You girl?' the Eritrean said in a worried soft voice.

What the hell, thought Anke. She would settle doubts about her virginity straight away; it was time to speak openly about herself. 'Yes, of course. Several.' She heard Miriam sigh with relief. 'But I think badly sometimes about men and am afraid they will take me over.'

'You have no children. Is that why? Is that because you are afraid to be owned by a man?'

'No. Many white women these days have their children without marriage, without living with a man full time. There is plenty enough money for that in Germany. But I want to have my children with a man who will be a good father and a good partner for me also. It is not easy to find a man like this ... and I have met plenty of bad ones while looking!'

Miriam remained puzzled, curious. 'But what about you Anka? What about your life? What about relax? What about good times? You are very beautiful: you have beautiful body. All is working very good.' She gave a mischievous chuckle that provoked both of them into reflections on the early morning. 'You cannot live for long time without love can you?'

Anke thought about it. 'No. Not usually.'

'Not usually?' repeated Miriam, turning it into a question that demanded an explanation.

She was good at that, thought Anke. She paused before answering. 'I mean I like to think I can love freely whenever I want. Then I get this warning light flashing in me that tells me not to get owned. It takes over and I turn away.'

Two gum bubbles popped. 'No man can own you Anka unless you want it to be like that. Maybe you are afraid that you might want it and prefer not to take the risk. I take care not to give them baby. I like to make man feel good and happy but if he tries to own me then, like you, I ask myself if he is the one to be the father of my children. Is he the one to take home to my mother? Can he love me more than his friends? When I find the answer is no I am never unkind to him but I let him know that he shares me with his friends. This way there is a balance. This way we all give, we all take.'

Anke sighed and pushed her hand deeper into her lap, craving to touch or to be touched. She wasn't sure which or how.

On impulse, she turned slightly towards Miriam, and lay with her side against the hull and her lower breast resting on what she deduced to be Miriam's outstretched arm. Her friend made no attempt to move it nor did Anke pull back. She enjoyed a wave of pleasure as the heat of her friend's inner arm melted into her bosom. She retracted slightly as if in some sort of game until only her nipple touched the softness of Miriam's skin. The nerve endings quivered in ecstasy firming it into a tight thimble-like protrusion.

Miriam's inner elbow never moved. Anke thought she was asleep and lay still herself except for ensuring the movement of her breathing kept the erect nipple caressing the softness of Miriam's skin. Eventually she had to turn on to her back to give relief to her ankle.

Miriam stirred immediately, unwilling to allow the contact to be broken. She settled back with her elbow touching Anke's stomach. They lay still for a while. Anke's inner thoughts raced round her head, her skin was sensitised to the limit. The theme of the morning returned. Its topsy-turvy cascades of reality and fantasy raised the heat levels in her lower abdomen.

She briefly tried to rationalise her out-of-character behaviour but soon gave up. She tried to pin the responsibility for her desires on to the seductive actions of her friend and then she wanted to acknowledge that perhaps she had latent lesbian tendencies of her own. She rationalised everything was due to extenuating circumstances. Finally, she admitted that the expression of her own sensuality was all that was left to her in the hell hole of her captivity; she could suffer its suppression no longer. Her body craved for touch and orgasm and it mattered only that the person with her cared and was equally sensitive. She had a screaming desire to state her claim to womanhood regardless of the oppression she was under. She could and she would state that claim.

She let out a large sigh and thrust her hand deeper into the folds of her *tobe* until it was over her pulsing pubic mound. There she let it rest but idly plied her fingers over the curls. She thought about Miriam's slender shoulders and remembered how fine the bones were in her arms and how she could spring about with such agility. She remembered too the great mound of black hair that disappeared up under her skirts when she had demonstrated her lack of circumcision. Anke's whole body trembled at the thought. She had imagined nothing like it before. The contours and wetness of the girl's genitalia created the most erotic sight she had ever seen or heard of. She lay there visualising it for a long time, all the while becoming hotter and stickier.

The night was still hot and, lacking any motion from the boat, the hold was very humid. The *tobe* Miriam had lent her stuck to her skin. She was restless and uncomfortable. Her companion must have been similarly affected as she frequently shuffled about and muttered to herself in Eritrean. She frequently brushed against Anke in the pitch dark of the hold Always there was some minute part of them still in contact. It was as if in the total blackness they each needed some sort of reference point in the otherwise indeterminable expanse.

To Anke it was more than a physical link, it was a bond of understanding. Sometimes it was a shoulder against an arm, sometimes a heel against a calf and another time it was Miriam's elbow against her side. Each contact lasted ten or fifteen minutes and occasionally she could feel the Eritrean's perspiration mingling with her own. On one brief occasion she felt her pulse quietly pushing the blood around her slender body.

Anke gained a tremendous sense of wellbeing from their contact. It accentuated the intimacy of Miriam's presence and brought fresh memories of the electrifying youthful beauty she had seen that morning. And with it came vivid flashbacks of those glistening high ebony breasts and slender thighs.

Anke's index finger probed further into the material of the *tobe* until her dampness oozed through. Beads of perspiration were building along the line of contact between Miriam's arm and the softness of her side.

They remained like that for some minutes. This time Anke believed her friend really was asleep.

She felt a longing deep inside. She did not know how to deal with the momentum that had built up. She did not want Miriam to sleep.

She felt butterflies in her stomach. Perhaps she had reached a new level of sensual awareness and happily shut her eyes to allow the effect to ripple through the rest of her body.

Slowly it dawned that the ripple was coming from a muscle in Miriam's forearm where it lay in contact with her stomach. A flood of juices suddenly surged through Anke's groin and she swallowed hard, causing her to cough slightly. She realised the rippling effect in her arm was being caused by the steady movement of the Eritrean's index finger somewhere in the dark.

When she coughed the rippling movement stopped. Anke waited breathlessly and silently. The rippling movement resumed. Anke inwardly groaned. Nothing could stop her now. Turning slightly, she located Miriam's forearm and gently caressed the skin with the backs of her nails, gradually working down until she felt Miriam's wrist. The movement of the girl's forefinger had stopped but she had not moved anymore and pretended to be asleep.

Anke was delirious with anticipation. It was so difficult to control the slowness of her soft tantalising circular strokes her fingertips were making on Miriam's arm. The strokes gradually traced the back of Miriam's fine boned hand. This was new territory. Anke had never before done anything like this, and she was determined not to fail now. Her heart pounded and sweat poured off, soaking the *tobe* wherever it touched her skin.

She had reached the point on Miriam's hand where the fingers divided. She felt the wetness on her index finger and at the same time she touched a patch of that black pubic hair.

The game was up. Miriam uttered a long sigh of ecstatic pleasure and grabbed Anke's fingers and guided them into the depth of her heat and wetness. Anke moaned in sympathy and allowed her fingers to touch those parts that had haunted her thoughts ever since the morning. It yielded to her touch and she gently encircled it with the inside of her fingers Miriam drew her breath in long rasps.

The wild Eritrean wasted no time. She thrust her pelvis out and in a mad frenzy clawed at Anke's *tobe*, pulling it free from her legs until she could run the palm of her hand steadily and determinedly up her thigh.

There was too little time. Anke knew it. She prayed for the ultimate pleasure to last longer but realised she was already losing control. Miriam's hand explored her mound while her long fingers divided and probed the soft, sticky skin below. The pleasure was unimaginable. She had no time to evaluate it. Her body was pumping juices on to Miriam's hand in a delirium of ecstasy like in a male orgasm. Never had she experienced anything like it. She felt as if the bottom was falling out of her stomach.

Miriam's treasure house squirmed beneath her own fingers. Her moans and her breath had quickened. She also had no way out. There was a sudden contraction deep inside and she shuddered incessantly. Anke held on tightly and gasped as her own orgasm reached a crescendo, thrusting her pelvis upwards and racking her body from end to end.

She only remembered the pumping that took over her groin, the ecstatic pleasure that allowed the pulsing to merge into full orgasm and with it a merciful release, its relief and its peace.

They both slept, their shoulders touching and the *tobe* hanging partly on and partly off Anke's outstretched frame.

NINETEEN

A sudden burst of activity on the deck late in the night brought the women sharply awake. Anke nudged her friend. Miriam immediately sat up and shuffled around readjusting her clothing. Anke did likewise; tugging at her *tobe* to give herself some semblance of decency should the hatch be opened. Subdued voices came from nearby above deck.

Two crewmen barked out instructions and numerous footsteps passed overhead towards the bow. Several dull thuds were followed by a clatter that sounded like their own hatch cover being removed, yet it came from further down the boat.

The crewmen yelled more instructions. Suddenly there was a shriek that could only have been that of a young woman. A series of girlish yelps followed.

Anke froze, imagining the worst. Miriam grabbed her firmly by the arm. 'They bring many Eritrean girls to the boat,' she whispered. 'I don't know what they do.'

Her words were drowned by the roar of the engine leaping into life. They heard several more excited squeals from the new contingent of girls and a final command from the stern as the gear was engaged. The *sambuk* was under way once again.

Within five minutes the motion of the boat indicated they had regained the open sea. It soon became very apparent that they were in for rough ride. The calm weather of the past few days was over. Miriam secured her baskets by wedging them behind her while Anke wriggled into the pants and shorts that had been hung on her ankle for the last twenty-four hours and donned her T-shirt. She jammed herself firmly between two longitudinal timbers. Pain again reminded her of her damaged ankle, which had been relatively comfortable since the chain had been bound up.

The mast creaked and they heard shrieking and whining from the new arrivals who were housed in the forward hold behind the bulkhead. The *sambuk* developed a strong roll and that kept making Anke slide down towards the bilge. She tried sitting more upright and dug her free heel deep into the matting, tight against the timber.

Miriam was less fortunate. Being shorter than Anke, she did not occupy the full distance between the timbers and so the boat's movement made her slither down to the bilge, each time protesting noisily. The women in the next hold were faring even worse, judging by the steady flow of sobs and wails coming from that direction.

Anke tried to talk to Miriam about the arrival of the Eritrean girls but she was sullen and untalkative, clearly worried about the rough sea. The waves hissed past the bow and the bilge water sloshed round their feet. When Miriam clutched at her arm Anke felt a tremble in her hand.

Conditions rapidly worsened. They heard materials and crew sliding around the deck The *sambuk* frequently leapt clear of a wave and crashed down into a trough, its whole structure shuddering. With the propeller clear of the water, the engine would momentarily race. The bilge stank horribly, the filthy water sloshing from side to side, often lifting the rush matting and soaking their feet. The small petrol driven engine used to pump out the boat laboured under the load, screaming as a severe roll left the suction point dry. Its rasping whine sounded like some sea monster's dying breath.

Anke's personal nightmare worsened as the mast developed a slight swivel with each roll or forward pitch and gave a sharp tug on the chain round her ankle. Miriam whimpered and lurched forward, vomiting uncontrollably. She continued retching for a long time afterwards.

The *sambuk* had become a hell hole. Endless cries of pain or terror came from the women in the next hold. Some chanted prayers. Somewhere up on deck a barrel had worked loose from its lashings and trundled to and fro with each roll of the boat.

Eventually the relentless slamming of the vessel as it fell and shuddered into a trough persuaded the skipper to cut back the engine and they continued at a reduced speed without falling off any more waves.

Anke was surprised to find she had overcome her seasickness. She reasoned this was due to attending to the frightened Miriam, still clinging to her with a frantic arm lock. She dismissed all thoughts of seasickness and concentrated on digging her heel tight into the matting to secure her position.

The journey through the rest of the night and well into the next day was the longest twelve hours of Anke's life. She constantly feared being dislodged from her position between the mast and hull and being flung about the hold while tethered by the ankle. Surely that would break every bone in her foot. The thought was horrifying. The added weight of Miriam made the task of anchoring herself down even more difficult. Occasionally the foul bilge water surged so far up the side of the hull that they almost floated off the rush matting.

For hours Miriam made no sound other than the spasmodic dry retching that racked her body. By contrast, a non-stop wailing came from behind the bulkhead where some poor demented soul sought to alleviate the suffering of her kinsfolk by incessantly crying to her God.

With the hatch cover tightly secured there was no indicator of time and the hours dragged by endlessly. Anke managed to relieve herself only by pushing her shorts and pants a fraction down her thighs and urinating down the matting. It was a dreadful experience. She felt wretched.

They were brought no food or water and Anke doubted the seamen above deck fared any better. Miriam was reduced to a subdued and pathetic little bundle at her side. Her body smelt of vomit and her clothes were soaked in the stinking mess of the bilge. Anke's heart went out to her. It was all so different from the joyful moments of the previous day.

Anke wondered how much longer she could endure the strain of continuously bracing herself against the hull. What little light there was on the other side of the hold had faded. She dreaded the night ahead. Briefly, she dozed but then woke with a jolt.

She was suddenly more awake than before. Slowly it dawned on her that the motion was far less violent than it had been for most of the journey. She prayed their voyage might be coming to an end as she could not last much longer.

Slowly but surely the *sambuk* adopted a more even keel and the violent rolling movement ceased. The bilge water subsided to their feet. She whispered into Miriam's ear that things were getting better. Miriam gave no response.

Anke sat up straight and eased her aching back. She no longer had to brace herself, the motion was almost gone. She nudged Miriam and again spoke softly in her ear. There was a little recognition but no movement. Anke cuddled her head. What more could she do?

Suddenly a pandemonium of activity broke out above deck. Numerous orders were shouted. Men ran to and fro to obey them. Anke heard the familiar sound of the anchor being heaved over the side and the rush of rope followed by the cut of the engine.

Miriam clawed herself back to life and stretched her tense limbs. She showed no interest in asking about Saudi or anything else. Like a child she waited for Anke to hand out information as it came to her.

The pump engine wailed and clattered for another quarter of an hour to clear the remaining bilge water. Above the noise of the overworked machine a few miserable sounds still emerged from the next hold. The prayer master resumed in an exhausted but grateful tone. Anke wondered if all the women had survived the journey as some of the sounds that had reached her ears early on had been quite pitiful. At least Miriam was showing signs of perking up. She had sat up and was wiping her face with the cast-off *tobe*. She had even muttered profanities, which Anke took as another good sign.

Activity continued on deck. Fish sizzled in the pan but was never brought to them, although it was not particularly wanted by Miriam who had groaned when Anke had suggested it might be on the way.

Shortly after the men settled down to eat there was the sound of an outboard motor boat. Anke never heard it leave and assumed it stayed with them. As the evening wore on it became apparent nothing more would happen that night. The rasping sounds from the hookah soon died away. Even the Yemeni had had a tough day.

When the next day dawned they had no need to bang the underside of the deck to attract attention. Before it was properly light the crew were busy cooking and soon the hatch cover was taken off completely. A bearded crewman stuck his head well down into the hold and looked quickly at the two women. He grunted something in Arabic.

Miriam responded by demanding water enough to wash and inquired irritably if they had reached Jidah. She stood up stiffly and unsteadily as she spoke and peered over the combing.

'Where is this?'

From his gruff reply Anke picked up the words 'later' and 'after eating.'. Miriam stood on tip toe, staring into the gloom of the lightening dawn. She watched other crewmen proceed along the deck to open the other hatch.

They removed the other cover and one man stuck his head down inside for several minutes. Miriam heard flurry of weak protestations from the girls down below and an exchange of questions followed by volleys of abuse from the Eritreans. A second crewman stuck his head down the hatch and there was another exchange of enquiries.

Miriam turned and spoke to Anke in a hushed voice. 'There is something wrong with the others. Maybe some is dead.'

She poked her head back out and strained on tip toe. A crewman walked briskly back past her.

'Down,' he shouted. She cowered back and popped up again when he was past. She watched him go to the stern and talk to the man she recognised as the captain who had brought her on board.

'The non-believer – *Hawaja*?' she heard him ask in an alarmed voice. The crewman reported no. 'Thanks God,' came the captain's reply. After a few more brief exchanges a third man was commandeered from the cooking area and sent to the Eritreans' hold.

Miriam ducked back into the hold to report all this to Anke then took another look. She saw two men descend into the hold while a hush fell over the occupants. The men emerged, dragging with them the thin body of a black girl. The girl she was wet all over. The hair that covered her face was streaked with oil, as were her bedraggled clothes. Her arms and legs hung out all angles from under her *tobe*.

Miriam dug her nails into the wood of the hatch and gasped. She swallowed hard as she watched a crewman pulled the hair away from the girl's face and bent low, listening for breathing. He shook his head and muttered in Arabic. He tugged on the mooring rope tethering the fibreglass dory alongside and pulling it abreast of the dead woman. There was a sickening thud as the girl's body was bundled unceremoniously over the side and dropped into the dory.

Miriam sat beside Anke, shaking in disbelief as she related what she had seen. They heard the outboard start and the dingy pull away.

Shortly afterwards the other two crewmen appeared in the open hatchway with two jerrycans of water and passed them down without saying a word. The death of the Eritrean had a sobering effect on the ship's company. Anke was not surprised and wondered how many more of the girls had come perilously close to death during their nightmare trip. The girl must have been drowned in the bilge while too weak from seasickness to save herself; or maybe she had a malarial attack and died as the result of foetid air and weakness. There might yet be others who would not recover. She shuddered, it was devastating to think that any of them could have suffered the same fate.

They washed in silence cleaning vomit, urine and oil off their lower legs and then drank from the jerrycan to refresh parched lips and throats. There was little to remind them of when washing had taken on such a different dimension. That now appeared almost as a figment of imagination, Anke conceded to herself.

A few minutes later the sun poured its first rays into the boat and an aluminium dish of hot hobs and fish was lowered down to them. They ate silently. The food gave them both strength but Miriam was the first to loosen up. Anke decided death was something the Eritrean had come to accept and understand more readily than herself, who was still stricken with horror.

Miriam was strangely dismissive about her compatriots in the next hold. She complained to Anke that they should never have been there in the first place. She could tell by their dialect that they were simple village folk who had never moved off their farmland. She said they were naive and young. She found it strange that so many of them were there on the boat together. It seemed unlikely they were all looking for jobs as maids.

In the full light of day Anke saw her friend's expression had become grave and dark; she looked burdened with more than just fear. Something menacing was brewing inside the eighteen-year-old that made even Anke wary.

The gloomy mood continued to hang over them. Miriam no longer sprang about but prowled like a cat in uncertain territory. A blanket of suspicion and anger descended on her. She realised now that she had been tricked. She had to draw on her reserves, waiting like a cornered animal for a chance to unleash its vengeful energies on its aggressor. She ignored the chance to climb out of the open hatch and challenge the crewmen and sat quietly on the mat next to Anke. She spoke slowly and carefully in a low voice.

She told her that when she was working in Suakin the freedom fighters had mentioned that pirates from Yemen had taken boatloads of young girls to a place called Midi where there was a specially convened market at which these innocent girls, many still virgins, were sold. The merchants who bought them represented rich princes and businessmen in Saudi. The girls were taken in secret to harems and were never heard of again. They were sold as playthings - never let out and probably killed when their owner tired of them.

Miriam said she had not believed it at the time. Communications were bad and country people often confused or mixed legend with reality. It was part of their culture. She had no way to verify the story but remembered one fighter said he believed it to be true because he had heard it from a Yemeni who had been shipwrecked in Eritrea when his engine had failed, drifting for many days before ending up on a reef in the north of the country. The man was angry because a Yemeni *sambuk* involved in this evil trading of young girls had passed him by without offering assistance, an unforgivable act.

'The fighter warned me not to go with a Yemeni,' Miriam said. 'But because I was in Suakin and there were no others, I thought I had found a genuine trader. Now I know different. This is not Jidah.

She waved a hand over her shoulder, 'This is a tiny island with only two small sun shelters and millions of birds. I can see the sea in all directions and there are big waves everywhere except where we are in the quiet place on the down side.'

Anke groaned. There seemed to be no end to their misery. 'Surely they don't think they can take a freedom fighter like you and a white German woman into harems and not have problems?'

'Arab men very stupid, especially in the ways of women,' Miriam said. 'They treat their own women like slaves in many cases and think they can do more than that with foreigners. In Saudi, women have nowhere to run to. A woman on her own will be taken by the police and put in the prison and forgotten about. They call her prostitute. It is very dangerous for us now. These bastard men think they have us trapped and will not stop until they collect their money.'

The anger in her voice hinted there could well be some surprises in store for those above deck if she had anything to do with it. Anke felt slightly reassured and oddly curious, 'How much will they get for me?'

'High price likely,' said Miriam. 'They seemed interested to keep you alive.'

'Maybe I'll be taken to another place to meet the hashish baron.'

'All the same anyway when they have had what they want.' Miriam ran the edges of her forefinger symbolically across her throat.

Anke's sense of anger started to stir.

They heard the boat with the outboard return and the man climb on board. As he spoke to the captain they caught the words, '*alla tool*'– straight away.

Miriam stood cautiously under the hatchway to better catch the conversation and report back to Anke. 'He talk of "another boat" and to "finish everything that night". They mentioned "the big island" and the boatman say they "ready to receive them" and that "God willing, many sheiks will be happy".'

Anke wanted to believe it was all a fantasy but a twinge of pain in her ankle reminded her it was far from that. There was a strong possibility her fate would not be confinement in some harem but at the disposal of some deranged drug trafficker at some medieval Arab fortress. She was beyond being terrified and accepted Miriam's stance that she had nothing to lose and a break-out was the only solution. But how, especially with a chain holding her to the mast of a *sambuk* on some desert island off an Arabian shore. The odds were stacked frighteningly high against her.

Revived by having breakfast, she felt her former strength and reason returning. She checked the chain around Anke's leg and readjusted the cloth wrapping where metal had again come into direct contact with the skin. She assured Anke ankle looked much better than when she had come aboard in Suakin. As she gave the toes a quick massage heavy footsteps came across the deck and the sunlight was blocked by two Yemeni crewmen lowering themselves into the hold. They moved away from the hatchway to let more light inside.

Anke recognised the one who regularly passed them food. The other thick set and heavily bearded and short with oily hands and feet. He carried a large spanner, gripping it by one end as if it were a weapon. Miriam looked up from where she squatted over Anke's foot. She registered the spanner and made no move. She decided to keep her mouth shut.

The familiar food man spoke gruffly and slowly in the direction of Miriam. He said that they were soon to move. The white woman was dangerous on a boat and had to be controlled. Anke was about to launch a violent protest when she saw the man with the spanner take a key from his belt. Miriam nodded.

The man continued to give instructions to Miriam that Anke found difficult to follow. He signalled to the other man who tapped the spanner sharply against the hull as a warning. Miriam gave another sullen nod and moved out of his way. The greasy man with the key moved towards Anke. She pulled her face back and turned away from the stench of diesel and garlic coming off him. She bit her lip as he bent over her and an appalling pain ripped through her ankle as he roughly pulled the links over her damaged flesh to reach the lock.

Suddenly all tension left the ankle and the chain fell away under her leg and round the mast.

Her foot was free at last and she rested it stiffly against the hull for the first time of the voyage. Anke drew it gingerly up towards her before setting it down flat on the matting. Her knee joint seemed to have no strength and she gasped at the effort.

The men turned to Miriam and shoved her roughly down on the mat alongside Anke. They dipped the chain under Anke leg – this time the right one – and then securely around Miriam's left leg. As Anke opened her mouth to shout at them Miriam intervened. 'They tie us together for transport in small boat; don't fight now or they will hit you with spanner.'

Anke reluctantly submitted to the new shackling; she should have expected as much. The chain looked even more cruel wrapped over Miriam's fine bones. Their ankles rubbed tightly together and the lock was only clicked shut after five turns had been made round both legs each one tighter than the one before. Miriam flinched, her face etched with agony, as the pressure increased on her ankle bone.

The men climbed out of the hatch. Miriam grated through her teeth, struggling frantically with the chain, yelping, tugging and hissing all at the same time. 'Bastard men!'

Anke tensed, half expecting her ankle bone to crack. Being chained to a tigress was no picnic.

Miriam turned to one side and, with her face screwed up with the effort, gave a final jerk on her leg. Both felt a sudden merciful release from pain as their ankle bones were freed from point to point contact. Miriam gasped; the chain had slackened off. She grinned at Anke as beads of perspiration bubbled out of the flanks of her nose. Anke could hardly believe it.

'Can you get your foot free?'

'Maybe,' said Miriam. She fiddled with the links now hanging slightly looser round their ankles. Anke noticed the spread of Miriam's feet, shaped by many years of barefoot walking and running. They were generous flat pads, quite different from a European's.

Despite all the wriggling and tensing to release her foot Miriam succeeded in doing little more than tenderising all the flesh in the region. At one point it did look vaguely possible but they needed to stand on one leg to put it to the test and Anke didn't think she could stand on two for the moment let alone her weak one. They sat and assessed the problem.

'Move your toes, bend your knee many times,' Miriam urged.

Anke struggled to get her left leg to do what she wanted it to. It felt heavy and removed from her body, not wanting to respond to messages from the brain.

Miriam pointed to the old scarf she had used to wrap the links before. Anke passed it to her and she threaded it under the links and pulled it up to form a cushion between their bones. Hardly had she finished than they heard grunts above deck. Seconds later the two crewmen peered down into the hold and told Miriam they were to come up. They lowered a thick rope but Miriam refused to cooperate until her bags had been gathered and passed up on deck. She and Anke then held on to the rope to be hauled up the hatchway until they could balance themselves on the combing. There they were left to their own devices.

The glare and heat of the mid-morning sun were overwhelming. Anke squinted and almost wished she was back in the hold except that the air in the breeze tasted so much better. They wriggled together out on to the deck. Anke wondered what the men must have thought of them; how this brace of scarecrows could be considered such good merchandise that they would lure a lot of money from the sheiks was beyond her imagination.

She caught the eyes of the men sitting back in the stern and assailed them with a far from complementary verbal volley in clear German followed by another in even more articulate English. She demanded an audience with the captain and their immediate release. She knew the words were a complete waste of time, even if they had been understood, but she couldn't stop herself from saying them.

The response was complete indifference. Without a word, a wiry man with a grey chinstrap beard stood and spat over the side. He took up the mouthpiece of the hookah and sat down to enjoy a long inhalation. He blew out a cloud of smoke then signalled his fellow crewmen to order Anke and Miriam into the long flat-bottomed boat that had formerly carried the corpse.

The oily crewman with the spanner sat some distance away lovingly fondling his weapon while the other waved for them to get in the boat. There were to be given no help.

The women made a brave attempt to stand. Anke remembered the three legged races of her schooldays and grabbed Miriam round the waist. She was a good half metre taller than her friend. Swaying slightly, they stumbled towards the side of the vessel in a crab like shuffle.

After only a couple of faltering steps their co-ordination broke down and they sat down awkwardly on the deck. Miriam suspected the men were smirking and completely lost her temper. She shrieked at them for more than a minute; in Arabic, Eritrean and a dreadful vernacular English. She ended up by spitting violently in the direction of the group in the stern. Anke felt her shaking and feared what might come next.

The man with the spanner got to his feet but made no move forward. His companion placed a restraining hand on his arm and he sat back down again grumbling.

Eventually Anke and Miriam worked out how to get down into the dory by lowering themselves backwards while holding on with their hands. It would have been good fun, Anke commented to

Miriam later, if it had not been so serious. The more sympathetic of the crewmen passed down Miriam's bags. He told them to wait quietly and not make any more trouble.

Anke took heart in the continued improvement and mobility of her now freed left leg. She was also convinced that the chain had more movement in it when they had briefly stood up. She wriggled her ankle to reaffirm her conviction. This time it was Miriam's turn to wince. She realised there was no way her own foot was going to slide through. When the crew went to attend to the rest of their passengers Miriam tried to rearrange the slack links around their ankles. It was something to do to calm herself after the outburst with the crew. Anke encouraged her: 'If we take the slack out of each turn and bring all the slack to the last turn perhaps you could you get your heel out then.'

Miriam tightened the links on the top three turns and gained a good two links of slack. She still had a turn and a half to go. They heard voices above and stopped immediately.

While they waited for the next break Anke viewed their surroundings. Ahead of the boat lay a low coral island with two semi-derelict huts made from blocks of coral rock. There was no vegetation whatsoever. Noisy seabirds were everywhere, showing little regard for man's presence. Thick layers of guano covered all but the shoreline. It was no place for man whatsoever. The sea could be heard crashing on the windward side of the island

and occasionally she saw spray and spume lifting high into the air in that direction. She thought it possible that the sea flowed right over the island top during storms. Over it all hung the stench of recent bird droppings and disgorged fish rotting in the sun.

She studied their *sambuk*. It was a traditional small Arab dhow with white tallow outside and bare grey hardwood on the topside. The only painted area was the raised stem with its sun shaded area back by the helm. She had seen pictures of such boats sitting so innocently together on quiet beaches in brochures advertising holidays in Arabia Felix. The thought was abhorrent.

Anke had seen only five crew members in all plus a young man in a clean white *futah* who she took to be the owner of the fibreglass dory. Two big newish looking Yamaha outboards cocked up on the stem displayed the number forty, which she took to be the horse power. They were separately fuelled by large fifty-litre plastic jerrycans lashed on to opposite sides of the boat. She judged the dory to be about eight metres long with three thwarts and a small foredeck. She and Miriam sat facing aft in the middle of the central thwart, not having much faith in the stability of small boats.

The activity up on deck had increased. They heard more Eritrean voices and suddenly a line of shrew-like dark faces with gold earrings and white teeth peered down at them like so many birds on a fence. Anke saw them as immature versions of Miriam, younger and somehow more timid. They were clearly scared stiff and huddled together like starlings. When one moved so did the others.

Miriam would have nothing to do with them. They were clearly well down the pecking order as far as she was concerned. Anyway, as she put it to Anke; she had enough to worry about without having to respond to their incessant jabber of questions. The only answer she gave them was that the white woman had to be chained up to prevent her jumping over the side. That seemed reasonable enough so the Eritreans went on to concern themselves with how much further they had to go by boat before they could make their fortunes in the land of riches. When they were all assembled on deck the greasy crewman ordered them to get down into the dory. Anke couldn't believe what she was seeing. 'What all of them?'

Nobody took any notice and one by one the braver ones clambered down; the more timid were pushed aboard. Anke counted eighteen of them. Had they been of European build the dory would surely have gone straight to the bottom. But as there was not one among them weighing more than a hundred pounds, the dory stayed afloat and remained surprisingly stable.

The girls resumed their uneasy jabbering. They nervously clutched their bags and the slightest motion of the dory caused the prayer-master to pipe up again from somewhere up near the bow.

Miriam groaned. 'I hope we are not going far,' she said, dreading the next stage of the voyage.

Anke could discern no other land nearby. The sea looked decidedly unfriendly beyond the shelter of their little anchorage. White tops defined the waves on an endless expanse of sea in all directions. A cloud of wheeling birds was the only other sign of life. Anke saw the young man from the dory in deep discussion with the wiry man she assumed was the captain. They looked far out to sea and then up at the sun, followed by furtive glances at the laden dory. Finally, with a sweeping gesture, the youth seemed to convince the older man and they shook hands ceremoniously.

The youth gathered up his *futah* and tucked it up under his belt and climbed down into the stern of the dory. Anke noticed the shiny butt of a hand gun protruding from under the folds of the material. It horrified her that such a young man should be armed.

The first outboard was uncocked and lowered into the water and then the second. The youth squeezed the bubble and after two short tugs the engine leapt into life. Anke felt her pulse racing and adrenaline flowing as she recalled her last trip with an outboard. She sensed there would be nothing simple about the next stage of their trip to Saudi Arabia. She braced herself, clasping the thwart tightly with both hands. Miriam again fiddled with the chain links biting painfully into her ankle bone.

Without any further delays the dory was untied and they were on their way, reversing until clear of the *sambuk* before accelerating forward into a wide arc leaving a fine white crescent of wake behind them as they set a southerly course clear of the island. Some of the Eritreans whimpered as the second engine fired up. Its surge of power surprised them after the plodding thud of the big diesel engine of the *sambuk*. They sped along at the speed of a car. Miriam shrieked, grabbing Anke by the knees with one hand and the edge of the seat with the other.

Their hair swept out behind them and the rush of air dried their perspiration. The youth squatted down between the huge engines as his dory skimmed the waves creating a continuous crackling noise as the water slapped the underside of the hull.

They continued down-wind of the island for some time before they left the cone of protection it provided and they encountered the full force of the open sea.

Looking back over the shoulder of the helmsman Anke was amazed to see how quickly their *sambuk* and its little anchorage had faded into the distance and disappeared from view. She had never travelled in a boat going so fast and she was surprised how little water came on board apart from the occasional spray. The dory was overtaking the big swells of the following sea and briefly dragging off its plane, causing it to squat as it went through the crests. The white foam hissed close to the gunwales on either side before the hull dipped and raced down the front of the next wave at a hideous speed. This caused ever more shrieks from those of the Eritrean girls brave enough to be looking.

Miriam hung on, presumably feeling sick. Anke didn't ask; she was more worried by the white crests. At times, there was no freeboard so those who had their hands clutching the gunwale found their fingers dragging through the waves. She searched the face of the helmsman for signs of alarm but saw only an air of machismo. And when he caught her looking he responded with a big grin that did little to lessen her vehement distrust of all the men she had dealt with on this voyage.

There only sign of land was a long breaking reef, a froth of white and green, off to the left. They cruised parallel with this reef for about a quarter of an hour or at least ten kilometres, Anke estimated

Looking away ahead she saw on the opposite side and a number of tiny low islands peeping out of the sea maybe a metre or so high. They were so far away she could only see them at the top of each wave. There was, however, no sighting of the 'big island' referred to back on the *sambuk*.

As they cleared the southern end of the long reef, the youth adjusted the helm slightly so that the boat raced obliquely across the waves. The change in the motion made it more difficult to stay firmly on their seat and they had to brace their feet and cling on even tighter. Spray continually lashed the backs of their heads as the youth shifted to adopt a less casual position.

Quite unexpectedly the waves developed an erratic pattern and the boat slammed into them, taking on a few buckets of water that rushed past their feet and back into the stern. Again the youth showed no concern and made no attempt to slow down; instead he leaned forward and released a self-drainer plug under the stem thwart.

In the few seconds that the youth's eyes were turned down and distracted with the drain plug, the dory plunged into an unexpected trough. It reared up at an ungodly angle as it climbed the next crest then flew into the air before crashing into the next trough. The erratic movement hurled the women crouched in the bow area and back down the boat to collide with those in the stern.

The impact of moving bodies swept Miriam and Anke back towards the outboards. There were shrieks and pandemonium everywhere. Water poured in over the stern where everyone had been flung. The tillers were pushed to one side as one of the girls landed heavily them. The half swamped boat took an uncontrolled arc to port, dipping all of one side below the water and immersing the stern completely. Several girls were thrown into the sea.

Anke was half in and half out of the crazed boat with Miriam screaming and thrashing her arms in all directions. She struggled free from the tangle of fuel pipes and heaved herself clear of the boat. She dragged the distraught Miriam in after her by her shackled leg. Mayhem surrounded them. The dory had travelled on for only a few more seconds before the second outboard gave up the struggle. Shrieks and cries for help came from all directions over a wide area.

From Miriam, there was nothing to be heard; somehow she had got under Anke and was now beneath the water.

TWENTY

The wind was fresh north-easterly once they were clear of Suakin Mersa. Ramadan pushed the *Mona* to the limit and her lower bulwarks frequently creamed along just above the sea. Jack busied himself with securing all loose items for what promised to be a lively trip. He tried to imagine a chart of the Red Sea with all the various reefs and country's boundaries and realised that at the best he could only guess the course and distance. Yet Ramadan, who had probably never seen a chart of the Red Sea, was confidently tuning the course to a heading relying only on a backsight of the coast guard lookout and a particular mountain. Having set the vessel on that heading he checked an old compass he had stored in a locker and took note of the direction. They maintained that course for their entire journey.

An hour later he kept glancing off to the southward and eventually picked out a dull whiteness in the gloom. He said it was the last coral reef before coming near to Yemen and eighteen to twenty hours would get them there – God willing.

The *Mona* pitched and rolled all night. The wind gradually shifted more easterly and angrier, catching them more on the bow than before. By dawn the wind direction veered another point and the sail no longer helped them. Ramadan stretched and rose stiffly from the position at the helm that he had not left all night. He instructed Jack to run down wind briefly while he brought down the big sail and stowed it.

The rest of the day they battled on through pitching seas often two or three metres high with creaming tops. Jack remembered painfully how rough the Red Sea could become. Had he not had the company of Ramadan Ibrahim he would have been thinking as much about his own safety as he was that of Anke.

They spoke little to each other all day, each preoccupied with his own thoughts. Cooking was impossible in such conditions so for the whole trip they ate only a handful of dried dates with sips of unboiled water tasting of rust from the drum. They were crusted in salt and baked by the sun. Most efforts to keep out of the direct sun were thwarted by the wind and continuous roll of the vessel. Ramadan wrapped his head in his traditional red and white scarf while Jack yanked his baseball cap down tightly over his ears.

That evening Ramadan commented on the increasing number of birds flying past and said he hoped to see areas of reef soon.

'The Farsan Islands?' Jack enquired hopefully. He knew of them from having seen them from the air, spread out like a string of many beads laid on an opalescent green cloth. They looked idyllic from thirty thousand feet but that was not the word he would use to describe anything in that pitching cantankerous sea. With only an hour to go before sunset they stood a good chance of being shipwrecked on them.

'*Iowa, sharb kateer*,' replied Ramadan cautiously. Yes, and plenty of coral.

With every new flight of birds he stood up and scanned the eastern horizon. Eventually he was convinced he could see something and adjusted the helm a point to southward. As the sun set the wind dropped slightly but the sea decreased considerably. They were clearly getting the benefit of shelter from land somewhere ahead. When it was almost dark Ramadan moved round the boat and filled a bucket full of flying fish unfortunate enough to land on board during the day. He grinned at Jack and they both smacked their lips at the thought of supper.

Jack was the first to see the surf line in the almost total darkness. He called to Ramadan who leapt up and dropped the throttle speed. Moving in cautiously closer until the line of the reef became clearer they followed it southwards to find an indentation that allowed a bit of shelter and a cut in the waves. They gingerly moved into the quieter water until the wave motion was lost completely.

Jack went up on to the bow and watched the water get paler as they crept nearer and nearer to the shore. When he could see the bottom he signalled to Ramadan and threw the anchor overboard. By the time he had made the rope fast and got back aft his friend had shut off the engine and washed in preparation for his long overdue evening prayers.

Jack pondered their next move. *God only knows where we are. Perhaps in the morning we will pick up landmarks one of us recognises. Then what? Will we be able to trace the footsteps of Sayeed Ria?*

There was no hope of fanning up charcoal. The fire box was soaked. While Ramadan prayed, Jack cleaned out the ashes and gathered fresh charcoal from a reasonably dry locker.

'They must keep her on an off island some days,' Ramadan said sometime later as they picked their way through the remains of a heap of barbecued flying fish. 'He must arrange for the transfer of the two womens before they are brought to the coast otherwise people will know about his business too much. There are many small islands close to Midi with such places they can hide them. In the old days many slaves were kept there and markets organised.'

Two women? Jack suddenly remembered the Eritrean that had possibly been picked up in Suakin. Ramadan suggested that next day they moved through the reefs until they came to the high islands to see what they could find found out. 'But we have to be careful for the Yemeni respect only their own clan and not any government.'

Jack needed little reminding of that from his past experiences in that country, he only wished he understood the geography better. At first he had believed their best hope would be to confirm that Anke was held in captivity and then somehow negotiate with her captors. He now realised negotiating with pirates, kidnappers and drug barons was a woeful idea. Ramadan eased his depression slightly by reminding him of the first rule of combat: the element of surprise. And they had that advantage. Neither Sayeed Ria, nor anybody else, had any idea of their mission. If challenged they could just be any other Egyptian boat come to poach the locals' useless mullet from the lagoons.

Ramadan suggested that they passed by the high islands with shacks on them to see if there was any human presence. If there was, he would call back during darkness to check them out. This seemed to be highly dangerous to Jack but he retained an inborn faith in Ramadan's ability to judge the situation correctly. It was not much longer before extreme fatigue overcame them and they fell asleep.

The stars were still bright over Arabia Felix when they awoke and fanned up the charcoal to make sweet hot tea and cook the flying fish left from supper. They refilled the fuel tank from one of the barrels and Ramadan pumped the bilge dry. He said his prayers as soon as there was the faintest glow in the eastern sky and afterwards started the engine. Jack noted with some satisfaction that he prayed longer than usual and assumed that the day ahead would require more than its normal amount of support from the powers that controlled them.

'*Yala.*' Ramadan nodded to Jack and they were off again, backing quietly out of their shelter and then making good speed following the reef to the south. Ramadan looked all around the seascape for familiar sightings before shrugging his big shoulders. There was a glint of gold teeth as he grinned nonchalantly at Jack. He had no idea where they were. Jack hardly expected him to.

*

After three quarters of an hour Ramadan nodded to the distance on the starboard side at a series of low tiny islands just showing above the sea.

'We are past the Farsan Islands,' he said. 'We are nearer to Yemen than I expected. We are more south by about ten kilometres than I planned. Strong currents and wind, Mr Jack.'

He sounded quite disgusted with his error in navigation. Jack thought it miraculous that he had any idea at all of where they were.

Two or three specks of rock and a bit of breaking water hardly represented convincing landmarks in the Red Sea where there must be thousands of similar features.

The breeze was still stiff but less than the day before. It had shifted round another point so that now the long reef they followed offered a little shelter but the big seas were still cracking well on the far side of the reef. Ramadan said it was about twenty miles to the high islands and then another twenty to Midi on the Yemen-Saudi border. He wasn't sure which country the particular reef they followed belonged to but the only boats that ever came that way were mostly Yemeni; Saudis seemed uninterested in fishing, he added with disdain.

When they reached the southern tip of the broken water Ramadan said they should head off to the port side towards the high islands. Ideally, they should approach them in the evening when the sun was in the west so no one would notice them; no self-respecting Arab ever looked into the sun. That was the plan.

TWENTY-ONE

Anke briefly panicked. She squirmed and thrashed around in the water, looking desperately for Miriam. Suddenly there she was right beneath her. She hauled her to the surface and pulled her head up out of the water. Although stiff with terror the young woman managed to exhale water. She coughed frantically then launched into an almighty struggle that dragged both of them under a second time. Anke grimaced with the merciless pain being inflicted on her ankle. She tried treading water but her foot remained strapped to Miriam's. Due to the weight of the chain pulling their feet down the Eritrean was submerged even deeper because of the great difference in their height.

Anke gulped in a lot of water while trying to keep her friend's head out of the sea. Miriam made it worse by gripping her round the throat and thrashing her legs about. Anke was convinced the furious struggle would drown them both. She yelled at Miriam to let go of her and take it easy. Then the horror dawned that the girl was a non-swimmer.

Prising Miriam's arm away from her throat she got a gulp of air before she went down once more. When she surfaced Miriam's agonised face was right by hers coughing for all she was worth. Anke yelled angrily in German. 'Stop!'

Miriam shifted her grip to her shoulders and continued coughing but lessened her struggle. Anke grabbed the chance to fan out her hands and keep them afloat long enough to get some breathe back. 'Don't struggle or we have no chance,' she wheezed, her mouth half under the water. Miriam still kept an iron grip round the shoulders and her legs thrashed and jerked in spasms of panic. There was a sudden lull in her movements. For a second or two Anke thought her mate had drowned and kicked hard to bring her face higher out of the water. Her foot crashed into metal and for that instant she imagined she had kicked the bottom. Then she realised: it was the falling away of the chain running over her foot. Both here legs were free. Anke bobbed higher in the water. 'Fucking chain's gone,' she spluttered. 'We have a chance.'

'No swim! Foot small but no swim!' wailed Miriam

Anke was regaining her strength. Her willpower was back. 'Just do what I say. You are brilliant. No more struggle. I'm going to hold your head from behind so your mouth is out of the water. Don't worry, Miriam. Try to relax. We have a chance now.'

Anke saw Miriam was terrified but clung on to the all–important instinct for survival. Hadn't she just forced the chain off her foot? *We have to make it somehow. We just have to.* She swivelled on to her back and supported Miriam's head from behind with her hands. The reef was some three hundred metres away and her first reaction was to head that way. The water would be shallow enough to stand and they could get rest.

She took a look to see what had happened to the others. The heavy seas obscured most of her vision but in the distance she glimpsed a glassy patch of fuel on the surface of the water and a jerrycan bobbing nearby. That was all.

Kicking her legs and swimming on her back, they gathered enough speed for their legs to float up but with Miriam kicking in a wild and uncoordinated manner progress was very slow.

Anke looked once more towards the shallows. She was alarmed to see no progress had been made, if anything they were drifting further away. She thought she saw a dark figure crashing its way towards the reef. From atop the next swell she looked again and was sure the figure furiously swimming towards the white water was the youth who had steered the boat. She realised a strong current had pushed him sideways. She noted, too, the size of the surf ahead of him and knew there was no way she could beat that current in a lifesaving mode of swimming. Nor was she prepared to ditch her friend and strike out on her own. There had to be another option. Perhaps the low islands downwind and with less of a current? Those she had seen before the accident happened.

She took a backsight on the reef and made a guess at the islands' direction as best as she could remember them from a few minutes earlier.

She kicked slowly and methodically, the water hissing green and white all round them. She told Miriam they were going to the islands, to believe in her and not exhaust herself by struggling. Anke found it easier to say those things than to believe it herself.

Looking again towards the site of the disaster she found it incomprehensible that a few minutes earlier there were a dozen people alive out there. The thought revived her determination to overcome the odds as she paddled them away from the sickening location.

Now that her mission was set and her course determined Anke disciplined herself in the rate at which she expended energy. She begged the frightened Miriam to let herself go limp so that she could kick her legs unimpeded and move them along. Slowly Miriam gained confidence in this manner but she remained afraid. 'What about sharks?' It was her first question of many and Anke sighed with relief that she was at least showing signs of recovery from a near drowning.

'Don't even think about it. They only feed at night and there is plenty for them to eat back there.' She broke off, appalled at what she had said. The cruel reality made her feel very vulnerable and she kicked more intensely.

'Farm girls no swim,' said Miriam. She took in a mouthful of water and clamped Anke round the waist in terror.

'Just shut up until we are out of it,' ordered Anke. She struggled free and set them back on course.

Ten minutes later, with the shallow reef fading into the distance, she cast another furtive glance over her shoulder. She saw nothing but an endless open expanse of sea. She realised they must be several kilometres off so told herself not to be depressed and to refrain from looking for half an hour. She kicked and prayed and thought of her mother and father. She tried to imagine how she and Miriam could possibly be saved from a seemingly inevitable fate.

A shoal of flying fish surfaced right by them and glided gracefully downwind, skimming the wave tops before plopping not so gracefully back in the water. Miriam shrieked. Sea birds expressed minimal interest and circled briefly overhead and moved on. Anke thought of the man from Bait min Dahab.

When the estimated half hour was up she turned them sideways to the swells and looked for the islands. Again she saw none. She waited for a big wave to lift them and she looked again. They both looked. Nothing.

'Where we going?' Miriam spluttered in a pathetic little voice.

'I thought I saw islands this way before we sunk.' Anke replied without conviction.

'Yes, there was islands ... but far away. I want to kick also.'

'OK. But like me. Do it slowly.'

Miriam was certainly a tough character, Anke decided. However, what better time to learn to swim than when you are faced with drowning as the alternative?

Anke continued swimming on her back with Miriam's head cupped in her hands, the girl's wild black hair floating forwards over her shoulders. Her friend copied her leg kicks and they moved on with a distinct wake behind them for another half hour. Anke felt herself tiring and was glad of this new cooperation. How much longer they could keep going was very much on her mind. Her ankle had completely loosened up but remained very sore and she still felt weak from captivity and insufficient food. Sitting in the same posture in the *sambuck* for so many days together with the seasickness had sapped a lot of her normal strength. Now, with the glare of the midday sun in her face, her head was starting to ache and she felt weary.

It was her plucky companion, now kicking like an outboard, who gave her the encouragement to carry on. She looked at Miriam's wild hair again trailing over her dark face and her floral *tobe* floating up in their wake and she knew she had to make the supreme effort to save her. She steered them broadside to the next big wave so when it lifted them they could view the horizon downwind.

And there it was. They both saw it briefly as the crest raised them. A mile or so away was a low sandy key with a fringe of white in front. A flock of seabirds wheeled over it marking the position well. They both cried out to whatever god there might have been out there before turning to kick with renewed determination.

It took them another half hour to reach the island and swim down its side just outside the breakers. They crabbed their way into the lee side where coming ashore was safe. The cries of thousands of seabirds were a welcome in itself.

Anke's feet touched first after she had navigated them carefully through the sharp coral heads to an area of fine sand in the lee of the beach. She steadied herself and gave Miriam time to gain her feet also. Their two-hour ordeal was over. With tears in her eyes the little Eritrean looked up at the tall Aryan and hugged her emotionally.

They slowly waded to the sandy shallows and flopped down in a few centimetres of water to rest. Miriam peeled off her *tobe* and rung it out before tossing it on to a bed of shells by the water's edge to dry. Anke did likewise with her T-shirt and they wallowed bare-topped just submerged beneath the water out of the sun's heat for a long time

Eventually Anke rolled over on to her stomach and propped herself up on her elbows so that she could survey her wasted body. She was certain now she could get into a size twelve and commented such to her friend. She tossed her head back and tucked the wet ringlets behind her ears so that she looked like a seventeen-year-old and grinned down at Miriam who was peeping up at her from under an elbow.

'Well this is wonderful. We have the sun, the sand, the beach and the coral reefs – all we need now are the dry martinis and the boys.'

Miriam laughed and stood up provocatively pointing her shining breasts at the island and kicking water over her friend. 'Only the boys will do just fine.'

They laughed as they rounded their clothes up and dressed, setting the birds off into another frenzy of wheeling, squawking mayhem. Miriam located an old piece of cloth that at one time might have been a fisherman's *futah*. She recovered it from among a pile of flotsam containing many plastic mineral water bottles and bits of drift wood. Shaking it out she took it down to the water's edge and gave it a thorough rinse. After wringing it out she ripped it down the middle and tossed one piece to Anke.

'Your head,' she ordered and fashioned her half into a scarf that covered all her head except her face.

'*Shamps*! – Sun!'

The last word was more a warning than a suggestion and Anke took heed silently. She was well aware of their desperate situation and was happy to let Miriam's survival instincts guide her.

They explored the island – a mere hundred metres by fifty and composed mostly of sand with coral fringes at sea level. The windward side was a raised coral platform deeply dissected by the ravages of weather and almost impossible to walk on bare footed. The rest was a sandy crescent rising a metre and a half above the sea and home to thousands of seabirds mostly of a species not unlike the gulls Anke was familiar with from the North Sea. There were some wading birds and a few herons. Close to where the pair of them had landed was a group of four pelicans, their huge beaks hanging heavily just above the water. There was no vegetation to be seen anywhere.

Many of the birds had nests with eggs or chicks in them, the nests so closely clustered that it was difficult to walk between them. Anke thought this amazing as it was nearly October and she assumed they must either nest all year round or have two breeding seasons. The parent birds protested violently at their wandering through the nesting sites and made frequent low level attacks and dive bombings. The whole island stank of bird excreta and rotting disgorged fish. Only the area where they had come ashore was easy underfoot, for Anke at least. Miriam seemed oblivious to any difference in the various substrates.

At the highest point of the island they found a collection of pallets and driftwood, coral rocks and tin cans. It had seemingly been fashioned into a shelter by visiting fishermen who had chosen to camp there. Miriam cleared a small floor area and then began rebuilding the two walls. Anke copied her and soon they had the semblance of a shelter. They heaved a couple of pallets on top of the walls and Miriam gathered up the remaining trash and tossed it on top of the pallets to stop the sun coming through.

The two women crawled underneath thankful for the shade and the stiff cooling breeze that funnelled through. The birds settled down and stopped their incessant shrieks. Anke wondered how long they could survive without food and water. She was already gasping for a drink. Food might not be a problem for a few days at least. They must surely be able to catch crabs and fish from the shallow pools by the sea – or eat seagulls? The thought of eating raw fish or bird was dreadful but it was an inevitability they must face. But water?

They could not drink sea water so the only alternative she could think of was distilled water. Could they find enough plastic bottles and plastic sheet to make fresh water by condensation – a solar still? She recalled the plastic mineral water bottles lying round the shore in their scores when Miriam was preparing their head scarves. Some had droplets of water inside them – maybe this was a chance. She would check it out when it was not so hot. The odds were stacked against them.

They would rapidly weaken without water. They must attract attention to themselves quickly. How far were they from shipping lanes? They had not seen a vessel all day.

Miriam meanwhile reached the worrying conclusion that the first vessel they were likely to encounter would be one from the people seeking for the missing dory and who would probably be even more hostile towards them than before. How would they know if a vessel would rescue them or simply return them into captivity?

'Fishermen use the island judging by the camp fire sites and fragments of netting lying round,' said Anke, 'They would not be involved in drug running and slaves. We must signal to fishermen.,'

The idea seemed sound enough until they wondered how distinguish the difference between friendly and unfriendly boats. Miriam suggested that as any search for the missing dory would be carried out that day or the following one they should resist attracting a boat for at least a day and hope they didn't perish in the days that might follow with no boats. Anke agreed and they rested and dozed until late in the afternoon.

Anke woke with dry lips and a raging thirst and decided she must try the condensed water theory while there was still some sun. She wandered down the beach where she discovered that the plastic bottles that were open topped and exposed to the wind were dry but others that had tops on or that had their opening buried under the sand had steamy droplets of water inside them.

Inverting the first one she picked up she released a tiny crab and a stream of wet sand. She tossed it down in disgust and studied others more carefully before picking them up. She found one lying flat with the bottom half full of water and the top surface covered in steamy drops. This simple fresh water still excited her until she realised that it would be impossible to get to the fresh water without first mixing it with the salty water. She searched for a sharp shell to puncture the bottle in situ from underneath and drain the salt water away before inverting it.

This she managed after a fashion and frantically shook the fresh water beads on to the palm of her hand, lapping them up with her tongue like a cat. There was less than a teaspoonful and although it tasted more of contaminants than salt she was encouraged and so set herself the task of preparing as may bottles as she could for the coming days.

When Miriam arrived an hour later to see what was going on Anke had about thirty bottles set out in orderly rows, each with its own top or improvised stopper made from polystyrene and partly filled with sea water. She was bent over in the shallow water washing out plastic bottles with a dozen or so empty ones beside her on the beach.

Miriam watched without saying anything, wondering what sort of white woman magic she was about to perform. After watching her lay out a new batch and plugging their necks she demanded an explanation. Anke led her over to an undisturbed steamy bottle that she had purposely left to show her and pointed to the beads of fresh water. She studied it for a long time before flashing a generous smile. 'You good.'

She stalked off over the top of the island engulfed in a swarm of protesting birds. Five minutes later she returned with her *tobe* bunched up in front of her. She sat down next to Anke and gently placed a couple of dozen brightly speckled eggs on the sand beside her. Anke inwardly groaned and hoped Miriam knew what she was doing.

The Eritrean cleaned a plastic bottle and cut it in half with the edge of a shell. She cracked open an egg as if about to put it in a frying pan. Keeping the shell's edges close together she attempted to separate the white from the rest. Only a few drops fell into her container so she opened the shell to see what the problem was. Facing her was an almost fully developed chick. She tossed it into the sea in disgust and proceeded to the second one. Anke felt a spasm of nausea but said nothing.

Miriam fared better with the second egg and separated out a reasonable amount of liquid before tossing the rest away. The third egg must have been freshly laid for it produced a lot of clear liquid. Miriam raised the container to her lips and sucked in a mouthful of egg white and rolled it round her lips before swallowing. She licked her lips and wiped away the long strand of egg white running from her chin to the container. She passed it over to Anke saying, 'Good, we have sweet water.'

Anke tried desperately not to think about it and looked hard at her solar stills and then up at the setting sun. The gulls circled in their thousands overhead and she wondered how often they laid their eggs.

A few eggs and discarded embryonic chicks later, Miriam had a full container of clear liquid which she presented to Anke. Gingerly she offered it to her lips. Almost before the liquid touched them she gagged. Miriam took it from her and studied her miserable face. There was another way, she said.

She took an egg and gently tapped a tiny hole in each end with the point of a conical shell. She put one hole to her lips and sucked hard. The liquid part of the egg entered her mouth and she swallowed with an expression of delight. She prepared another one and handed it to Anke.

Her friend found this recipe more acceptable as the contents arrived so far back on her tongue it was impossible not to swallow them. Once the ordeal of the first one was over she managed half a dozen more before declaring she was no longer thirsty. Miriam finished off the contents of the container and looked rather pleased with herself. Something then distracted her at the water line near to where she had dumped the half developed chicks and broken egg shells.

The water's edge was fizzing with a frenzy of activity as small fish gorged themselves on the discarded material. The backs of the fish were out of the water it was so shallow. Miriam caught Anke's eye and indicated that they should spread out and enter the sea. They crept up on the feeding fish from the seaward side before suddenly rushing towards them, scooping wildly with hands and feet. A dozen or so fish struggled in the shallows while others darted clean out of the water on to the sand. They ended up with about twenty small sardine-like fish flapping helplessly halfway up the beach.

They looked at each other in total amazement at their success and could hardly believe fishing was so easy. One minute there was nothing and the next there was more than they could eat. But how to eat? Anke half expected Miriam to open her mouth and pop one in head first like a seagull would, and was quite relieved when she didn't.

Instead she gathered them on to a piece of plywood and sawed off their heads with a shell and cleaned out their guts, some of them still wriggling throughout the process. After de-scaling she washed them and left them with Anke while she went off along the beach. A number of greedy looking gulls hung around after she had gone and polished off the fish heads, remaining close by in the hope that Anke's attention might wander.

Miriam soon returned with salt scraped from a dried out rock pool. She salted the fish and placed them securely inside a water bottle. She told Anke that they could be washed and dried tomorrow and by midday they would be quite edible without cooking. It was Anke's turn to be sceptical but at least the idea was infinitely more acceptable than gulping them down live.

They took a last walk round the island as the sun set and located some long sticks among the drift wood. Lashed together they would serve as a flagpole when they needed it. Anke thought again about the dried fish they would eat tomorrow and remembered the last time she ate dried fish on a mountain ridge in Sinai with the man from Bait min Dahab. She wondered if he ever thought any more about her. She clasped the little gold anchor that still hung round her neck after all she had been through and let the thought hang in her mind.

TWENTY-TWO

They came close in to the southern tip of the long reef in order to turn to port once clear of the coral. As they were about to round the cape Ramadan suddenly stood up and fixed his eyes on the reef. Leaping forward he dropped the engine speed and turned the vessel abruptly towards the breakers. 'What's that?'

His question needed no answer. Jack followed his gaze and saw only too clearly the raw flesh and mutilated body of a dark skinned male jammed between two coral heads in the surf line. Between the surges of the long seas there were moments when the corpse was almost fully exposed and others when it was engulfed by white water. Ramadan pushed the *Mona* in as far as he dared to get a closer look.

The horrific sight immediately made them both feel sick. The middle section of the body was worn down to white bone where the surges lifted it up and down between the two coral heads. Various parts of the corpse's innards trailed away through the water to become wrapped across nearby corals that held them like Velcro. A host of carnivorous small reef fish swarmed in the area. Ramadan muttered something in Arabic and knocked the boat out of gear so that it fell away from the reef on the wind. He turned to Jack. There was nothing they could do, he said.

How the man came to be in such a situation was beyond their comprehension. It was clear he could not have been there very long. They let the boat drift away from the ghastly scene while they mulled over the possibilities. As they idled Jack, who was standing near the bow, noticed something on the water. 'Look, oil. A boat must have gone down.' He pointed excitedly to a shiny patch on the water up ahead.

Ramadan studied the sea to the east and engaged the gear to move their craft into the rough water off the cape. In the middle of the tidal race a shiny patch of water trailed off towards the south. He knocked the engine out of gear again and stared down into the water. Although too deep to discern anything it was apparent that a light fuel was finding its way to the surface drop by drop and spreading out in iridescent rings and drifting away on the current. Ramadan sniffed. 'Benzene. Outboard fuel.' He again put the engine in gear. 'Accident; no good place here, big waves and strong current.' He pointed to the cape as if to say they should have known better, '*Ras*, Mr Jack.'

They moved the *Mona* slowly to the south, following the slick. When they were a few minutes clear of the cape they found the fuel had broken up and spread out over a large area. They scanned the horizon for signs of survivors. It was obvious that the poor fellow who had made it to the reef had done so at his peril but others might have drifted with the current.

Ramadan said that it was not uncommon for the light dories used by the Yemeni fishermen to be swamped because they put too much power on them. They obtained smuggled benzene from Saudi for next to nothing and didn't consider other factors when piling power on the stern. It looked as if that was what happened here and they should spend at least this day looking for survivors. God willing there would be some. Jack agreed wholeheartedly and climbed up on the after-deck and to scan the surrounding waters.

They searched hard further away where the oil trail had largely broken up and evaporated. After a while, Ramadan pointed to a distant seagull that appeared to be standing on the water. The bird flew off as they approached what were several bits of flotsam. They each scooped up various items from both sides of the boat and tossed them on to the deck. A lump came into Jack's throat as his hand clasped what only could have been a local woman's purse – gold spangles over a cheap synthetic inner bag.

He turned to see Ramadan had fished out a half empty perfume bottle, a plastic bag of coloured hair rollers, a plastic bag of women's clothing and numerous other similar items that left no room for doubt. Jack tossed his gold spangle purse on top of the pile and went forward for the water jug. He took a long deep drink before passing it to his friend.

'Poor bastards,' he eventually choked out.

Ramadan put the engine in gear and opened the throttle before anything else was said. He gave the helm to Jack and pointed south before going forward and climbing part way up the mast until he was able to stand on the stowed spar of the lateen sail and give himself the highest viewpoint.

He indicated they should head a touch to the west where a number of small islands lay dotted on the horizon. For the better part of half an hour he remained with one mighty arm clamped around the mast straining to hang on while he shaded his eyes with his free hand and scanned the endless expanse of water. When a rapidly strengthening breeze made it too difficult to see regular distances he climbed down and joined a very subdued Jack on the afterdeck.

'I don't like it, Mr Jack. One small boat has sunk with women on board. Maybe not your friend but it is possible. There cannot be so many womens travelling in this place.'

Jack refused to accept such a conclusion. he pointing to the pathetic pile of belongings decking. 'These things are not belonging to Anke.'.

Ramadan agreed. 'More likely to Eritreans. I think we can check around these sandy islands and then return to the big island this evening. If we are questioned, we say we came to report the body on the reef.'

He was felt distraught. *Have we come all this way to find such a terrible truth? I don't believe it.* He thought of Anke's swimming ability but then remembered the chloroform and doubted she would have been able to act so decisively this time.

The first of the tiny islands they approached was a mere sandbar with a dozen or so seabirds standing on its crest that watched the boat steam past. No signs of human disturbance. Ramadan pulled the tiller slightly towards himself and pushed the *Mona* on in a more westerly direction towards the next tiny island. They rolled uncomfortably on that tack for the next twenty minutes.

As they approached they saw the derelict remains of a fisherman's campsite. Nothing stood more than a foot high on the sandy key except the sea birds and there were hundreds of those. The shoreline was littered with flotsam especially the mineral water bottles that were the scourge of the Middle East beaches. Some lay so thickly there that they were lined up like soldiers. They passed it by silently without saying a word and continued on to the west.

TWENTY-THREE

Anke scooped out a shallow depression for her bottom and lay on her back, quietly watching the million stars above before she felt the need for sleep. Miriam had already crawled in under the makeshift shelter and was curled up sound asleep. It felt beautifully cool for the first time since she left Egypt. The earlier breeze had subsided to a light air and even the seabirds were quiet. She drew up her knees and placed her elbows on them as she studied the sea. If only she knew where they were. *Are we off Saudi Arabia, Yemen or where? I'm sure we crossed the Red Sea, so where could we be? How far is it to the mainland? Maybe I could swim there? Where is the big island the others had spoken of?*

So many questions and not a single answer. As Miriam had suggested, if a boat came along soon the chances were that it would be from the same clan. *I don't want to throw away the chance we've now got to escape from them and their evil intentions. Even living on birds' eggs and raw sardines is better than surrendering.* At least for the time being.

As the night cooled Anke crept in besides Miriam behind the low walls and out of the breeze and was glad for the warmth of her back. As she drifted off into sleep she promised herself that during the long hours of the next day she would experiment with making fire. She dreaded the thought of those raw sardines.

There was no risk of sleeping in. Miriam and Anke were rudely awoken early by the screech of circling sea birds and the scrabbling of webbed feet on their pallet roof. The whole colony commenced work at dawn it seemed.

The adults squealed and cried with anger as they fought each other for captured fish to drop down the gullets of incessantly squawking chicks. There was bedlam all around their shelter. There was nothing for it but to get up and go down to the shore in order to avoid the continual rain of wet sand and excrement that filtered down through the pallets.

They washed and examined the rows of plastic water bottles. Miriam was disappointed that there was no fresh water until Anke explained that the process depended on the sun. She looked up at their shelter on the top of the island and agreed they must flatten it during the day because searching vessels would recognise the new construction.

They lifted the pallets down and left them more or less as they had found them and they also knocked down the walls until they stood only one rock high. They were careful to leave a clear space in the middle that they could lie down in without being seen.

Miriam went to gather eggs. Anke lacked enthusiasm but conceded that she was very thirsty – a thirst that never seemed to leave her. She went back down to the shore and looked hard at her solar stills and desperately hoped they would come up with something before midday. Picking her way along the beach she found odd bits of string and discarded netting that could be used to tie the sticks of their flagpole together. She tied them up in a bundle.

Miriam soon returned and joined her with a clutch of eggs in a fold of her *tobe*. She spaced them out in the shallow water. Anke was curious to know why and raised her eyebrows.

'Fresh eggs today, still warm. Cool them off first.'

Anke laughed. 'Better if they were completely cooked.'

'No. Just lay. No chicks today.'

Anke scrutinising the new cluster of eggs. 'How do you know?'

'Yesterday I took all eggs out of twenty nests and threw them away and put stone by empty nest.'

The wanton destruction disturbed Anke until she considered the million other birds circling overhead and the shit that fell down on them and didn't feel so bad anymore.

'So today all eggs in these nests freshly lay,' said Miriam 'No chicks.'

She was right. The egg sucking was less of an ordeal this time, especially as they were cooled. The next hurdle was the sardines. Miriam had already shaken them out of the plastic bottle and was washing the salt off them. Anke declared that rather than eating dried sardines she would devote all her energies to creating fire, even if it meant rubbing two sticks together until midday.

She recalled again Jack's salted shark meat and confirmed without enthusiasm that she was looking forward to the salted sardines. Miriam cocked an eyebrow and looked at her curiously.

One slight problem Miriam had overlooked was that they were not far from the throngs of seabirds circling overhead which were also interested in a tasty meal. After laying the sardines out on a nearby rock Miriam turned her back for an instant and lost the first fish in a flurry of wings and screeches.

Miriam shouted at them, hurling a handful of shells at the nearest ones to little effect. They would surely lose them all before long so she gathered up the fish once more and retreated to their shelter where she laid the fish out on a piece of plywood in the middle of the floor. With Miriam sitting as guard nearby the gulls soon lost interest.

Picking up two of the long sticks they had collected the night before, Anke set about lashing them together with the assorted bits of twine and netting she had found. When finished she held the pole upright to test its height. Miriam stood back and nodded approvingly. She cast her eyes out to sea and said it could probably be seen for miles if they had a decent flag on it. All they had found so far for that purpose was a sheet of white plastic. Miriam prevented Anke from using that because she said a white flag represented a burial site in that part of the world and it would bring them bad luck.

Anke was still holding her flagless flagpole when Miriam shouted, 'Get down! Boat!'

Anke flung the pole aside and crouched down following her friend's gaze to the south-east. The sun sparkling on the wave tops made it hard to see but by shading her eyes she caught distant glimpses of a boat with traditional short mast and stowed boom. It was four or five kilometres away and heading in their direction. They ducked into the low remains of their shelter. Anke felt her heart pounding.

'Do you think they saw the pole?'

'I shouldn't think so. It is too far.'

'Looks like a *sambuk*. Will it be the same bastards?'

'My God,' murmured Miriam, 'maybe it is. They are coming straight for us'

They spread themselves low either side of the fish and lay watching for the white spray that showed every so often from the bow. At first the boat only appeared from time to time, hidden in the waves, but gradually it took shape – a black object against the sunlight.

The bow rose and fell into the swell as it drew nearer. Anke spied on it through a chink between two stones, her pulse thumping. It was obviously intent on coming to the island. Only when it was so close that she could clearly see an Arab man standing in the stern, did it veer off and skirt the island at some distance.

'It's them,' hissed Anke 'I don't think it is the same *sambuk* we were on. It's not big enough but they do seem to be searching.'

She and Miriam lowered their heads down on the sand making it impossible to see anything. The vessel came so close that they could hear its engine. They waited for it to come into the beach but after a few minutes the engine noise faded and Anke risked a tiny peep.

'Phew, I think they have passed us. I was sure they would notice the bottles lined up on the beach.'

Miriam took a quick look and threw herself down flat again. 'Keep down, they are looking this way.'

With their faces against the sand they listened as the sound of the vessel's engine faded into the distance. Anke remained fearful. 'Who do you think it was? Was it one of the kidnappers? The Yemeni?'

Miriam thought about what she had managed to see. 'It wasn't a *sambuk*,' she said after a while. 'It was painted green. They never paint the *sambuks*. They cover the outside with lime and camel fat which makes them look white and inside they put shark liver oil which is stinky but always looks brown; 1 have seen them doing it in Eritrea. Same like the one we were on. I have never seen one with green paint. To me it looked like the mullet boats that used to call into Suakin for supplies. The Egyptians are poaching mullets to make *faseerh* all along Red Sea.'

'Can it be? So far from Egypt?'

'Don't know. The Egyptians are crazy for their salted mullets. They stay six weeks, sometimes catching them from the lagoons in Eritrea when the planes are not busy. Could be they come this far. There are too many planes in Eritrea these days; it is too dangerous for them.'

'They are heading north towards Egypt,' said Anke. She propped herself up on her elbows for a better look. The green boat was a long way off, its only indication the wispy smoke from its exhaust and white wake.

'Something else,' said Miriam. 'Did you see the size of that guy standing in the stern? He was tall and heavy. I never saw a Yemeni like that. They are all tiny people.' She leapt up. 'They were Egyptians,' she exclaimed.

Anke caught her excitement. 'Come on, you're right, they're not Yemeni. Come on, come on.' She was waving her arms round like a windmill, sweat running down her face.

Miriam grabbing the flagpole and waved it about frantically. They both shouted until they were hoarse but the speck of a boat never altered its course

'Too far away,' wailed Anke.

She scrabbled round for strings to tie the plastic to the flagpole. That was not good enough for Miriam. She peeled off her *tobe* and hitched it to the top of the stick and ran a slither of wood through it a metre further down before quickly hoisting it aloft again. It billowed out, a voluminous dark flag that nearly carried her off her feet. Her body glistened with perspiration as she waved it round like someone possessed. With both arms locked round the pole she still managed to jam two fingers in her mouth and whistle at a terrifying pitch.

The boat was now very distant and continuing without change of direction. Anke was exhausted from waving her arms about. She turned to her companion suddenly aware of the ridiculous spectacle that they had created. Affected by the sun, lack of water and exhaustion she sat on a pallet and rocked in delirious laughter until tears ran down her face. Every time she tried to explain she burst into another fit of giggles.

Miriam stared at her, stony faced with one hand on the flagpole and the other on her hip. Rivulets of sweat ran down her bare chest. She demanded to know what was so funny.

Anke wiped the tears away 'So funny? Can you imagine what we look like to a would-be rescuer ... you like Girl Friday and me like a discarded

Barbie doll, both with our heads tied up in rags. Any normal sailor would think he was hallucinating and be afraid to come ashore in case he found we had fish tails. He would run a mile'

Miriam looked at herself and wiped a new stream of sea gull excrement off her shoulder as a fresh one arrived on the top of her head and made its uninterrupted way down her cheek.

She grimaced for a second and she too started to giggle. The sun beat harder than ever and she began to rock with laughter until she was shaking so much that she had to cling on to the pole for support.

The thousands of birds that spiralled overhead pelted them with a blizzard of seagull shit as if to confirm their departure from sanity. They laughed and laughed until they were too weak to bother to wipe the streams of white and green slime running like rivers down their faces, chests and legs. Surely they had reached the first stage of madness. The air was a bedlam of whirling, screeching birds that had taken an unprecedented dislike to the flag waving and wolf whistling. The cloud rose into the air like the mushroom from a nuclear blast while the lower members maintained a continuous dive bombing campaign. So aggressive did it become that they had to cover their faces with their hands. One dive bomber caught its webbed feet in Anke's straying ringlets. She thrashed her hands round to free it before grabbing a stone in self-defence.

For the second time in her life, a stone froze in her hand. She stared hard into the northwest where surely she had just seen the tiny speck turning and presenting a side profile. Miriam grew concerned at her friend's sudden quietness and stared at her. Then she followed Anke's gaze until she saw it as well. They looked up at the birds making a white column high into the sky and suddenly became soberly aware of what they had done. The tobe fluttered bravely at the top of the flagpole. They looked seaward again and saw the boat's bow was heading straight back in the direction of the island.

Recaptured or rescued? What would it be? The die was cast. Anke moved close to Miriam and put her arm round her tiny waist. They stood stiff as sentries until they could see the green of the hull and hear the engine.

They dropped the pole and Miriam recovered her *tobe*. They bounded down to the beach and waded out into deeper water waiting anxiously for the boat to swing round into the lee of the island. Anke ducked beneath the water to wash away the seagull slime. Her heart as raced as her mind prayed for a friendly boat.

She waved again incessantly as it drew nearer. They heard the engine drop to a tick over as it crept in to avoid the coral heads. Miriam was nearly up to her neck before she shouted to Anke to wait. She did wait. It seemed like a long time. How were they going to tell the crew what had happened? She was counting on Miriam. She turned back towards her to make sure she was all right. Her friend was right behind her. Suddenly Miriam grabbed her wrist.

'No Yemeni. Look, white man on boat.'

Anke swung round sharply. 'What?' It was surely an apparition. A bearded man wearing a baseball hat was climbing on to the foredeck.

'It can't be,' she cried.

He threw off his baseball cap and tossed it over his shoulder as he stood, feet together, on the edge of the deck. He flew forward into the water, a splash and he was ploughing towards her with a fast overarm crawl, his face submerged and his feet kicking furiously.

She responded with an Olympic freestyle. The water foamed in both directions. There was less than five metres between them. She surfaced. He surfaced. They locked together, they sunk and kicked, they came up and gulped air and locked their lips together a second time, they sunk and kicked, gulped air and tried to speak at the same time. They spluttered and sunk a third time. They kicked and came up, gulped air and kissed again before they broke free.

'How? Why?' she yelled.

The boat brushed alongside and passed them without their noticing and drifted in towards the sandy shore.

Jack never noticed Ramadan's face beaming down at them nor did he see him reach down and drag a bewildered Miriam aboard. The first time they were aware of their presence was when they happened to look round and saw two smiling faces from inside the boat patiently watching and waiting for them.

TWENTY-FOUR

'*Clamsa yum*, Mr Jack.' It would be five days of strong wind, Ramadan told Jack. He knew from experience that to put the *Mona* into the teeth of the wind for a thousand kilometres back to Egypt was more than any sailor would do out of choice, especially as there was characteristically a southerly wind to follow. Jack cocked an eyebrow in a mischievous grin. '*Zuarba*?'.

'Yes, Zuarba – *ya-la*!' Let's go!

Ramadan pulled the helm hard over and the *Mona* crossed the swells and bounded before them like a greyhound. Ramadan went forward and hoisted the great sail high and proud above the deck, giving them shade as well as and speed. He hauled in the sheet and cut off the engine to conserve their precious fuel supplies.

It was the first time Jack had travelled under just sail in the Red Sea and it felt marvellous. The water creamed away from the bow with the force six wind pushing them on from behind.

Anke beamed at Jack from behind the water jug, knowing full well from his grin that there were still surprises in store. '*Zuarba*?' she questioned.

'We cannot go back to Egypt yet because of the wind. After three days it will change direction and there will be a fair wind to travel back up the Red

Sea. Zuarba is a cluster of high volcanic islands, uninhabited and beautiful. They are about half a day from here and we can shelter there and rest. The islands are rugged and mystical as if they are the home of the gods, quaternary extinct volcanoes amazingly beautiful; you'll love them. Most have vertical sides with craters but there is one tiny bay that provides perfect shelter at the base of an ancient lava flow. It has a small beach of white shells. The waters are full of red snapper that are just dying of old age.'

'The photo you showed me? I don't believe this.'

'Yes, that's right. We'll shelter there. It's far from the border. No smugglers, only the odd fishing boat sheltering. Maybe nobody. It is a perfect place to rest and talk. There is so much to talk about. I ...'

A lump came in his throat. Prepared speeches log-jammed and refused to spill out. He felt his eyes brimming and turned away.

Anke scrutinised him. 'Let's talk about that in Zuarba.' She squeezed his arm and dug Miriam in the ribs with her outstretched toe to distract her from the water bottle.

'By the way, this is the one I spoke to you about. You remember your promise?'

Miriam flashed her big eyes at both of them over the top of the bottle. She gave a wicked smile that broke into a husky laugh and ended in the inevitable squeak that got everybody else laughing. 'I don't remember any promises.'

It was a conversation that mattered little to the men. They laughed at Miriam who was back to herself again - an impossible person.

Jack decided the nice thing about being under sail was that they could talk with only the sound of the sea for accompaniment. He knew he was falling hopelessly in love and the lingering glances he was getting from Anke told him she knew it as well. He felt himself sliding into a hopeless spiral of romantic carefree abandonment and this time he was not going to resist it.

They sailed on through the day until the crater topped mountains of Zuarba appeared on the horizon. The late afternoon sun made them more magnificent than Jack remembered them. They soared stark and royal out of the oceanic depths of the Red Sea on all sides. The alternate black lava flows and white ash layers gave them a lunar appearance. Their crater rims were tinted with lilac edges by the setting sun.

The ravages of sea storms had removed the lower skirts of the volcanic cones so that passing fishermen were confronted by vertical walls of rock, often hundreds of metres high. Anke, fascinated by the geology, pointed out a single perfect cone and was delighted to hear that it was the one beneath which they were to spend the night.

Ramadan started the engine to manoeuvre the boat into the lee of the majestic cone and glide in towards the white beach. Jack was right thought

Anke. This, if ever, was the home of the gods. High volcanoes surrounded them, cutting out what remained of the sunlight. None were active but recent tongues of lava flows wound down into the sea like frozen rivers of black clinker. Columns of hexagonal pillars made palace steps into the temples of the mountains.

It was breath-taking in its beauty and even Miriam, a bit subdued in trying to avoid seasickness, was as chirpy as a sparrow and asking questions in all directions.

They made their anchorage at dusk in the calm water in front of the sand. The place was deserted. There they carried blankets, a tarpaulin, a Tilly lamp and stores ashore and set up camp.

'Welcome to Zuarba,' Jack shouted to Anke, his hands in the air like an excited childhood explorer.

Tiny ghost crabs scurried to the water's edge and the occasional seabird swooped in to its night perch high up in the rocks. A single tamarisk tree at the back of the beach hosted a couple of crickets that serenaded the night, tropical style. Great warmth issued from the black volcanic rocks as they gave up the energy they had absorbed from the sun's rays during the day.

Miriam, Anke and Jack explored the small beach in the brief period of remaining daylight picking up pieces of driftwood for a fire and enjoying the scents and fragrances rising from the salt-loving plants that had forged an existence where the sand met the lava rocks.

Turning back towards the camp they saw Ramadan silhouetted against the western sky amid a shower of sparks as he brought hot coals from the boat's firebox to the campsite. Jack smiled. Ramadan was beyond using Boy Scout techniques to start a fire. Like the rest of them he was starving hungry. There were to be no delays in starting the cooking process. They had caught two superb kingfish while under sail and one was promised for supper.

The women bathed and washed in the shallows, anointing themselves with the luxury of a jerrycan of fresh water from the *Mona*'s supply. The men soon had a good fire going and the smell of grilled fish drifted down the beach.

Their stories gradually unfolded as they sat round the fire until late in the night. The fate of the girls from Eritrea was unknown but it was assumed all had drowned as Miriam doubted if any of them could swim. She decided that she would learn without delay; lessons could start next morning. They laughed at her and pulled themselves out of the sombre mood.

Anke wanted to know what caused them to turn back to the island after you had passed by. Was it their flag? She tugged jokingly at Miriam's *tobe*.

Ramadan grinned across the fire, showing the best of his gold teeth. He pointed to the sky.

'The gulls? I thought so,' said Miriam. 'It is the first time shit falling on my head has ever done me any good.' She pointed at Anke 'She went crazy about that. She fell over laughing; I thought she had gone mad.'

'I think we were both going that way,' said Anke. She pulled Jack into her arms and rested her head on his shoulder.

Ramadan excused himself to return to the boat; to make sure it was secure, he said. But soon he was back, bringing the hookah with him. It passed among them several times and Jack suspected that Ramadan had spiced it up somewhat with some of Smittand's special for he felt more wonderful than ever.

Miriam opted to sleep on the boat after doing a dance on the beach and singing to the night sky, much to everybody's entertainment. She said she didn't think the island big enough to sleep three and skipped off towards the anchorage with Ramadan following in her wake.

TWENTY-FIVE

That is the way it was. Jack was left on the blanket by the fireside under a million tropical stars with the person he had vowed never to let slip through his hands again. She gave a wistful sigh.

'So you've balanced the books, Mr Polglaise?'

'I never thought of it like that.'

'We would have perished in a few days with only seagulls' eggs and sardines.'

'I would have been eaten by sharks.'

'The sun would have dried us out.'

'I would have drowned.'

'What about the Caribbean?'

'What about the gold mine?'

There was a long silence before she swung round and positioned herself in front of his face. She slowly removed his shirt and pulled him down on to the blanket.

'I'll think about that tomorrow,' she said softly.

'Tomorrow? Promise?'

'Promise.'

He slid his hand round her waist and up under her T-shirt. Her bare ribs felt like gold bars to his fingertips. The eternal flame she had kindled in Bait min Dahab overhauled him as he drew her close and slipped off her garment.

It began like a replay of Sinai but this time they both knew the fantasy was for real, each movement was an irrevocable endorsement of their bonding; each caress a release of bottled up longing. They pulled the blanket over them and escaped their remaining clothes.

This time there was no symbolic reverence for the Garden of Eden. This time there was an earthiness hand in hand with a burning long desire. Before he pulled her hips to his she was awash with rivers.

There was no need to guide Jack to where his heart and soul wanted to rest. He could have approached her from any angle he ever dreamed of and nature would have allowed him to enter deep within her body. Her desire was such that she recklessly offered herself as an unashamed, deep and welcoming sanctuary that swallowed him and refused to let him go.

Rippling spasms engulfed them. They gasped and moaned at the ease with which their orgasms unexpectedly overtook them, swamping them, drowning them in mutual and uncontrollable passion that caressed them until dawn.

*

In the early morning they swam and lolled about in the shallows watching a nearby host of small coral fish. A yacht had sought refuge there during the night and lay at anchor some distance off. They saw a figure leaning over the side collecting water in a bucket. They donned some clothes for decency and lazily swam out to say hello.

They caught the smell of coffee on a stove. An elderly man sitting under a limp Danish flag beckoned them aboard to share it. They readily accepted his enticing offer. He introduced himself as Ernest and proudly showed off his modern cabin, his radio, fax machine, auto pilot and numerous other electronics of a modern trans-global yachtsman. He sombrely told them it was to be his last trip. His female companion for many years had suddenly passed away from a brain tumour while they were in Polynesia.

They had married at her request during the last days of her life in a wonderful ceremony organised by the islanders and a local missionary. It had somehow made her passing more acceptable, he said. He smiled and poured them another cup of good percolated coffee.

Jack and Anke returned to the *Mona* keen to share their new found happiness with Ramadan and Miriam. Their sudden arrival was greeted by two heads appearing rather sheepishly from under the same blanket.

Anke needed no explanation for the look Miriam's eyes flashed in her direction. She understood, too, the reason for the satisfied look on Ramadan's face. Anke returned a broad smile that told much of her own night's activities.

They visited Ernest several times over the next two days, swimming out and sharing coffee. On the last occasion Jack lingered for a second coffee following Ernest's invitation to look at his latest navigational equipment while Anke went to give Miriam her swimming lesson.

It was a blissful couple of days. Jack and Anke, now mercifully fitted out with a pair of Ramadan's sandals, went for long walks among the volcanic rocks looking for zeolites in the cavities. They even scrambled up to the top of the cinder cone of the nearby volcano and peered down into its collapsed crater.

Miriam spent much of the on the *sambuk* with Ramadan. He had made her a fishing line and she spent hours dangling a line over the stern. He had even anchored the boat so that her line could reach down the steep drop-off to catch sizeable fish. Several times Jack and Anke looked up from the beach on hearing a yelp from Miriam and watched her excitedly haul in a nice snapper. She kept them in food for their supper on both days and with some to spare for Ernest.

By the time the wind dropped on the third day Miriam was confident enough with her swimming to make it alone from the boat to the shore and continually entertained her companions with repeated squeals of pleasure at mastering the art.

During day three Ramadan announced that by the following morning the northerly wind would have blown itself out enough for them to proceed back up the Red Sea.

As Anke and Jack lay on the beach that evening with their backs against the tarpaulin he put an arm tightly round her shoulder and spoke softly in the direction of Orion.

'I sent a telex to Smittand today.'

'What! How did you do that?'

'From Ernest's yacht.'

'What did you say?'

'I said you were safe and rescued from an island off Yemen and would be back at the office in about two weeks' time.'

She sat bolt upright. 'Will he believe you?'

'The navigation equipment gives the lat. and long. position of the transmission.'

Anke remained puzzled. 'Two weeks?' She detected a tremor in Jack's reply. 'I said you had to travel back up the Red Sea and when you arrived in Egypt you had an important wedding to attend'

'Wedding?' Anke whispered with quivering lips.

Jack pulled her down on top of him and before their lips could meet he spluttered out the formal question.

Later that evening they all discussed their plans and concerns about the trip back to Egypt. Ramadan made light of having to stop at Suakin to refuel and moved on to other matters: 'You know how it is, Mr Jack; a man needs a wife and children. God has found one of these for me and we are working on the other.' He raised his hand for the almighty Egyptian handshake with Jack.

Miriam grinned: 'I go to Egypt with Ramadan. He is important captain, Anke, and clever fisherman too. Not to mention ...' she burst out laughing and buried her head under the blanket to avoid a playful clip behind the ear from Ramadan.

Jack slipped an envelope into his friend's hand and said, 'Don't open it now. Keep it for the baby and think of Anglo American ....'

They hugged each other tightly and shortly after hauled up the anchor to make their way out from the islands and back up the Red Sea.